THE BOUND MAGE

BECCA CALDER

THE NEW DOMINION
THE SHADOWED SEA
AETHERIS
THE SHADOWED VEIL
ELUNETH
LUMARIA
ITHRALIS
THE TEMPLE

ORINFAEL
ELVANFAL
TIRNAVEL
THE ALDERWILD
FAERWYN
THE SILVERFANGS
STORMPORT
SINDERFAL
N
W
E
S

CONTENTS

CONTENT WARNINGS

The Bound Mage is a dark fantasy novel that continues to explore themes of captivity, trauma, and survival in a world marked by systemic violence and control. It contains depictions of psychological manipulation, gaslighting, and coercive control, as well as scenes involving torture, magical experimentation, and the abuse of power. The story portrays the aftermath of an emotionally and physically abusive romantic relationship, with a focus on recovery. Throughout the narrative, characters grapple with PTSD, panic attacks, and the struggle to reclaim autonomy. There are also instances of forced drugging, reproductive control, and the threat of sexual violence, along with moments of blood magic, warfare, and brief mentions of self-harm and suicidal ideation. Reader discretion is advised.

PROLOGUE

Garrick Shaw stepped over the broken threshold of the fae palace, scorched runes crumbling under his boots. They had taken the palace days ago, but the air still stank of blood and magic. Soldiers sifted through the wreckage, glass crunching under their boots as they searched for anything of value. It had cost the Arcanum a great deal to take the seat of the fae monarchy—and even more to hold it.

"We've secured most of the lower levels." The Commander escorting him scrubbed a hand over his face, smearing soot and blood across his skin. "Our forces are sweeping the western groves for stragglers. Any fae we can subdue, we bring in alive—most have stopped fighting."

Garrick nodded. It had been the same in Aetheris—where they'd taken the fae so completely by surprise that their governors had been killed or clapped in iron before they even knew they were at war. Even Prince Loren hadn't realized he'd been betrayed by the man he'd called a friend until the chains closed around his wrists.

But here, there was only one fae the Arcanum cared about.

"Where is she?"

"She's taken refuge in the grove, sir." The Commander shifted on his feet, tugging at the black sash that crossed his chest. "We've surrounded it...but our forces haven't been able to get past the first line of trees."

"Of course you can't," Garrick snapped. The Eldergreen wasn't just another stand of trees. It was the soul of the fae, a snarled web of ancient power far older than anything that stood around it. It would protect her—or try to. "Let me try to speak to her."

The commander shifted his weight, his eyes flicking to the trees. "With respect, sir—I'm not certain that's a good idea."

"We have to act now." Garrick shook his head, already turning away. "The king is still trapped on Eluneth. Take his queen, and Corwin Shadowbane will kneel. Fail, and this war drags on for generations."

He crossed the ruined hall with long strides. He'd bowed here once, falling to his knees before the King and Queen who had deigned to *allow* him to study the power flowing through this land. They'd welcomed him as their son's friend—and now, he walked through their ruined home with a ring carved from the bones of their dead on his hand, the power they coveted so desperately burning through his veins.

The fae had brought this on themselves. For years, they'd refused to share their power—banning humans from their institutions and outlawing the use of amplifiers. If they had bent just a little—if he'd held even a fraction of this power when Selene fought to bring his son into the world, his wife would not have died in her birthing bed, one of thousands of humans lost to the fae monarchy's blind insistence that magic belonged to them alone.

So now it would be taken from them—by force.

The air changed as cracked marble gave way to living earth, growing wetter and warmer with every step he took into their sacred grove. Even the light was different, slanting through the twisted canopy like moonlight through stained glass. His ring buzzed against his skin, its hum deepening to a low warning as the grove's power swept over him—and found him wanting.

Vines wrapped around his boots, forcing him to stop as the trees leaned in around him, thorny branches blocking his path. Magic lived here, but not the kind he knew. There were no structured runes like the ones his human peers used with studied precision, no trace of the channeled intentions the fae wielded as easily as they breathed. This was older—wilder.

"I just want to talk to her," Garrick said into the crushing silence, as if the trees themselves might hear him. "No harm will come to her by my hand."

For a long, tense moment nothing happened. The vines held fast around his boots, the air heavy in his lungs as that presence weighed his words. Then, at last, the vines loosened, the trees drawing back just far enough to let him pass.

"Thank you," Garrick murmured. He pushed forward, branches scraping across his neck and shoulders in silent warning as he pressed deeper into the trees.

He found her at the center of the grove. Uncrowned, her pale hair hung loose, surrounding her like a silver cloud. She wore only a simple shift, her feet bare on the soft green moss that blanketed the clearing. But a sword hung loose in her hand, its blade dark and wet with blood and its edge still humming with magic.

She hadn't run. Hadn't begged.

She'd waited.

Garrick drew to a halt just short of the clearing, roots rising in front of him in silent threat. Their message was clear—the grove had allowed him to come this far, but he wouldn't take another step without a fight.

"Your Majesty," he said. "Lysa."

She looked up at the sound of her name, and for a moment, he saw the queen who had stood at her king's side. That female had smiled at him, welcomed him into her home. But this one—this one only looked at him, her fae-green eyes as cold as they were bright and wild.

"Your son is alive," Garrick said when she didn't speak. "Loren was captured without injury. He'll remain that way–"

"If I surrender," the queen finished for him. She lifted her chin, her hands tightening around the hilt of her sword. "Is that your offer? My son's survival in exchange for me?"

Garrick held her gaze. "His safety. Your daughter's safety–she's still just a child, by your standards. What will happen to her if this becomes a war? This doesn't have to be–"

"You think this isn't already a war?" Her voice didn't rise. It didn't have to. "You broke your word to us the moment you slipped that ring onto your finger. How dare you wield our dead as a weapon and speak of peace to me?"

"This ring only levels the field," Garrick snapped, the protest spilling out before he could bite it back. "The fae have hoarded magic for centuries—"

"Hoarded?" She laughed, the sound ringing out bright and hard like bells through the trees. "We *protected* it. But we failed to protect it from *you*."

Her gaze pierced him, pinning him to the spot.

"*We* do not lie," she said. "We are bound to the truth–even when it breaks us. But you? You smiled at me, at my children. You studied our texts, shared our food, called my son *friend*. But every word you spoke was with a blade hidden behind your back."

"I tried to work with your people—"

"No." The queen shook her head, her voice like steel. "You tried to use us. And when we did not bend, you decided to take what you wanted by force."

The magic surrounding them stirred with her anger—roots coiling tighter, leaves rustling in a wind that didn't touch Garrick's coat. Deep in the grove, stone cracked and groaned, the air coming alive as something vast and ancient roused from its slumber.

"This is your last chance, Lysa." Garrick took a step closer, pushing forward despite the roots that clawed at his ankles. "Come with me peacefully. Or I'll break this grove to take you."

She stared at him, and for a moment Garrick thought she was going to fight–but then the sword fell from her fingers, landing soundlessly at her feet. He held out his hand, relief flooding him as she raised her gaze to his. But instead of taking it, she stepped back, her chin lifting.

"You'll try," she said.

Garrick lunged, but vines tangled around his boots, thorns whipping across his neck and shoulders. He staggered, nearly falling into the clearing as she tipped her head back, a low, shuddering moan rolling through the trees.

"Lysa!" Garrick cursed, fighting his way forward. "Stop! There's still a way—"

She opened her eyes.

They glowed, bright with power as aether rose around them, pulled directly from the marrow of the land. Light poured from the moss under her feet, threading through the roots and racing up the trunks before bursting from the canopy like a storm of stars spilling into the sky.

"You were never meant to touch this power," she said.

The ground heaved under his boots, roots tearing free like serpents. The glow illuminating the clearing turned white-hot, searing his vision and filling his nose with the reek of scorched bark and the tang of molten magic. Every hair on his body rose, the breath crushed from his lungs by the terrible certainty that he had made a fatal mistake.

But it wasn't lightning that struck.

It was magic.

Garrick clawed for his power, smearing his fingers through his own blood to sketch the first strokes of a warding rune. Desperation sharpened the lines, his voice breaking as he tried to give them shape—

"*Thyra,*" he rasped, hope surging as the rune flared once, power humming through the bone around his finger. But then the hum became a scream, a hairline fracture splitting the bone an instant before it shattered. Pain lanced through his hand, racing up his arm as his grip on his magic tore loose with a crack that drove him to his knees.

He crashed into the moss, that ancient power grinding him into the ground. Dirt filled his mouth, choking off his voice. His vision swam with black spots, blurring. But he could still hear it—his entire world narrowing to the low, thunderous heartbeat of the Eldergreen surrounding him.

It wasn't trying to push him out any more. It was consuming him.

Garrick clawed at the earth, scrabbling for purchase as more roots lashed around him, binding him fast. Thorns pierced deep, blood slicking his hands as he dragged himself forward against their hold. But he didn't stop. If he didn't move—if he didn't get out—he would die here.

He tore free, scrambling through twisted roots and thorns—

But then the world went still.

And Garrick Shaw knew nothing more.

———

THE FIRST THING GARRICK REGISTERED WAS THE LIGHT—BRIGHT AND sterile.

The second was pain.

A low, radiating ache throbbed deep in his bones, humming beneath the skin like an old wound newly cracked. He tried to move, but something tugged at his arm. A restraint? No—a bandage. He ripped at the gauze, suddenly desperate to see what remained—

"Easy," a voice said. "You've been under for three days."

Garrick turned his head. Slowly.

Darian Hale sat beside his bed, as immaculate as ever. His dark uniform was spotless, his hair tied back with not a strand out of place. He held a folio in one gloved hand, his sharp blue eyes raking over Garrick with surgical precision.

"How many casualties?" Garrick croaked.

"Twenty-three dead. Fifty-seven wounded—most from the pulse of power when the grove collapsed. You were the only one inside. If you hadn't managed to crawl to the edge they wouldn't have been able to pull you out." Hale paused. "You're lucky to be alive."

Garrick wasn't sure he agreed. He turned his hand, flexing his fingers despite the pain. Deep lines of charred flesh crawled up his forearm, and the skin where the amplifier ring had sat was nothing but a blackened ruin. Treating a wound like this would have been impossible for a human Healer before, but with fae magic at their disposal he might use his hand again.

"The queen?"

Hale didn't even blink. "Dead."

Dead. Garrick closed his eyes. He should have been relieved. Or angry. But he just felt...empty.

"Did they retrieve her remains?" He'd craft his next amplifier from *her* bones.

"No." Hale sighed, closing his folio with a snap. "You lost the Eldergreen, Garrick. Our forces were driven from the palace–from the forest entirely. Anyone who tries to enter now..." He shrugged. "It will have to be retaken in pieces, at great cost."

Garrick stared at the ceiling. "I failed."

"Yes," Hale said pleasantly. "And they voted you High Magister anyway."

Garrick's head turned sharply. "What?"

"The Arcanum convened while you were unconscious. Unanimous decision." Hale shrugged. "You're a hero now. The man who walked into the Eldergreen and lived. They're saying the grove spat you back out because it feared you."

Garrick's throat worked, but his tongue stuck to the roof of his mouth. How would they have voted if they'd known the truth?

"Oh, and I've been appointed High Inquisitor." Hale rose, smoothing his coat. "Which means I'll be the one cleaning up your mess. Try to pull your weight, Garrick." He paused, his shadow falling across the bed. "After all, you didn't crawl out of that grove just to quit now, did you?"

CHAPTER
ONE

Araya screamed into the gag, her desperate cries for mercy garbled by the filthy wad of fabric. Rough hands shoved her down. Someone else forced her sleeve up, exposing her forearm. Araya thrashed, kicking wildly until a knee slammed into her ribs, driving the breath from her lungs.

"I heard she had everything." The thickset runesmith loomed over her, his ink and blood-stained fingers pawing at the *ly'ithra* rune inked at the base of her thumb. "Bonded to Jaxon Shaw—she even worked with him, didn't she?"

"And she still ran." The woman holding her down scoffed, digging her knee into Araya's ribs until black spots danced across her vision. "Ungrateful little halfblood."

Araya cried out against the gag, desperate to make them understand. She hadn't run—she'd been *taken*.

"It's in their nature," the other woman sneered. "I just can't believe he wants her back—"

Araya bucked, frantic, but they crushed her into the table. The gag choked her, thick with the stale taste of sweat and dirt. Her magic flared, desperately trying to protect her—but her power was nothing more than a flicker under her skin. She had nothing left.

Jaxon—he would fix this. He always did. If she could just get to him—if she could just explain…he would believe her. He had to. He knew she couldn't lie.

"Bloody hells," the runesmith snarled. He caught her wrist, twisting viciously. "Strap her down properly before she knocks over my tray. Get her legs, too. Don't need her kicking me in the gods damned teeth."

Leather bit into her skin as they bound her to the table, pinning her arms and legs. Araya sobbed into her gag, tears cutting through the dirt and sweat crusted to her skin.

"That's better," the runesmith said. He rolled his shoulders, his sour breath licking over her skin as he leaned forward. "Now, be a good girl and hold still. We wouldn't want to slip, would we?"

The first needle plunged into her arm.

Fire. Pure, blinding agony. It seared through her veins, scorching muscle, bone, and marrow. Her back arched, the rough leather biting deep into her skin. But there was no escape.

"Pathetic, Starling." Jaxon's voice coiled in her ear, slithering into her mind the same way it had when he whispered those soft promises—all those lies. Before he reminded her that she was nothing but a possession—*his* to use as he saw fit.

"I warned you," he whispered. "Your place is on the floor at my feet."

Araya choked on the dirty gag, twisting in her restraints. The straps cut into her wrists, harsh leather abrading her skin—

No. Not leather. Silk.

Her eyes flew open. Her tongue stuck to the roof of her mouth, bile sour at the back of her throat. No rancid gag. No cold iron. Just a bed and dim sunlight shining in the window, illuminating the unfamiliar room.

This wasn't Kaldrath, but it wasn't Jaxon's bedroom or even her small room at Serafina's house either. She wasn't even in the New

Dominion. She was on Eluneth, where she had spent the last week as the honored *guest* of Prince Loren of Valendral, heir to the fae throne and the miserable bastard who had *rescued* her from her carefully curated life against her will.

Whoever was at the door knocked again, hard enough to rattle the chair jammed against the doorknob.

"Coming," Araya croaked.

She freed herself from the tangled sheets, dragging a robe over her sweat-soaked nightgown. She moved the chair away from the door, cracking it open just enough to peer out at the fae Healer who stood on the other side.

"You were screaming," Ilyana said, her delicate face creased with concern.

"I had a nightmare," Araya said, her hand still tight on the door-frame. Ilyana had been here every day—checking on her injuries, asking questions. All on Loren's orders, no doubt.

"Ah—" Ilyana's expression softened with understanding. "That's not unusual. Many refugees have nightmares—"

"I'm not a refugee." Araya interrupted. "And I don't need daily check-ins with a Healer. I'm sure your skills could be put to better use somewhere else."

"Of course." Ilyana inclined her head, making no move to step away. "But I'm here now—so I may as well have a look."

Araya sighed, letting the door swing open as she stepped back. They'd had a variation of this argument every morning for the past three days. The Healer wouldn't leave until Araya finally gave up and acquiesced to the exam.

Araya flinched, hissing a breath in through her teeth as Ilyana pressed two fingers to the edge of the fading bruise at her temple. The Healer didn't comment, simply adjusting the angle of her touch as she mapped the bruise with practiced care.

"Still a bit tender," she murmured. "Any dizziness when you stand?"

Araya shook her head.

"Good." Ilyana took Araya's hand, moving it carefully to manipulate the joint. "This has healed nicely as well." She turned Araya's hand, studying the rune inked at the base of her thumb. "And how old were you when they bound your power?"

"Seven." Araya tugged her hand out of the Healer's grip, tucking it back inside her robe. "Why?"

"So young." Ilyana sighed, a frown creasing her forehead. "It could explain the nightmares. You never got the chance to grow into your full magic—much less develop the stamina to wield it. Since your runes don't work here you're replenishing power more quickly than you're accustomed to—"

"What?" Araya straightened, her heart racing. "What do you mean they don't work?"

"Human runes don't hold power themselves, they borrow it. When you crossed the Veil you cut them off from their source—" Ilyana blinked, her voice faltering as Araya stared at her. "Didn't Prince Loren explain this?"

"His Royal Highness hasn't taken the time to explain anything," Araya snapped. "I haven't even seen him since he dragged me here against my will."

"Oh. Well—" The Healer cleared her throat. "You were in much better condition than most fae who arrive here. Your magic was depleted, but you weren't malnourished or gravely injured. It's already recovering—it will keep growing to what should have been your natural limit here. Far past what the humans ever allowed."

"No—" Araya's stomach twisted. "I don't want that. Undo it." Her voice broke, catching in her throat. "Please."

"It's not something that can be undone," Ilyana said gently. "Or something that can be stopped. Some refugees—especially if their power was bound young—say it feels like too much, too fast. But I have exercises that will help you build your magical endurance. And if you're worried about the *ta'nara* rune, you don't have to be. Fae don't conceive unless both partners are willing. If you want either of them removed, we have runesmiths who can assist—"

"*Removed?*" Araya barked out a short laugh, pressing a fist to her mouth when it caught in her throat, too close to a sob. "I—no. I don't want that."

"No one will force you to remove them," Ilyana said quickly. "Many females choose to leave them intact—even bonded females. As long as you stay on this side of the Shadowed Veil, you don't have anything to fear here."

"Until he crosses." Araya gave a brittle laugh. "What happens then?"

"No human has ever crossed the Shadowed Veil," Ilyana said gently. "He can't hurt you here, Araya. You're safe."

Araya turned her back on the Healer, staring out the window at the churning wall of shadows that stood between her and everything she'd ever known. Crossing it once had almost killed her—but if any human could figure it out, it would be Jaxon Shaw.

"—my only goal here is to support your recovery," Ilyana was still speaking, her voice steady, too earnest. "Physically, magically, and emotionally. Others have found it helpful to speak with fae who have been through the same things. If you ever wanted to talk to someone else who grew up in the camps—"

"I don't."

"Healing takes many forms." Ilyana sighed, glass clinking and leather creaking as she packed up her bag. "If you ever change your mind, I'd be happy to put you in contact with them."

Araya didn't respond, staring out the window long after the door clicked shut. She had no interest in sitting in a room full of so-called survivors and sifting through the wreckage of her past, pretending to find comfort in rehashing the horrors they had all endured. Maybe they had fooled themselves into believing they were safe here— beyond the Arcanum's reach.

But Araya knew better.

She stepped away from the window and crossed the room to the wardrobe, her fingers closing over the handle with sudden purpose. She was done waiting for Loren to come to her. If he wanted to keep her a prisoner here, he needed to understand the consequences.

The fae might be confident in their safety, but Araya *knew* Jaxon. He wasn't *just* a commander. He was the son of the High Magister, heir to the most powerful man in the New Dominion. And she was his bonded fae ward—they would never just *let her go*.

He had Loren's blood—and hers. All of her notes. It was only a matter of time before he followed her through the Veil. And when he did, there would be no sanctuary left for anyone.

Despite Loren's promise that she wasn't a prisoner here, Araya expected *something* to remind her that her freedom was nothing but an illusion. But the door opened easily at her touch. There was no flare of magic, no guard waiting to stop her. Only an empty hallway.

Someone had thrown back the curtains, but the pale, mist-thinned sunlight that shone weakly through the glass only illuminated the thick dust that still covered most surfaces. No one had bothered to light the aetherlamps, casting everything in an eerie half-light.

Araya hesitated, toying with the Arcanum's Eye resting against her throat. She hadn't been able to bring herself to take the amulet off, clinging to the sense of safety it offered even if it was useless here. This had to be some sort of trick—a play for her trust. These were the same people who had drugged her and stolen her across the Shadowed Sea, ripping her from everything she'd ever known.

At least if they were trying to make her believe she had choices, she had some sort of chance. There was a city here—somewhere. If Loren wouldn't see reason, surely someone there would help her. If she just found the right person and appealed to their conscience—

But she'd never accomplish any of that from inside this room.

With a deep breath, Araya stepped into the hall, closing her door softly behind her. She hesitated, half-expecting Loren's shadows to flicker at the edge of her vision—but the only shadows she saw were the ones she would have expected to see in an abandoned castle.

She moved slowly at first, part of her still waiting for the invisible leash to snap tight and guards to burst into the corridor, dragging her back to her room. But the only sound she heard as she passed door after closed door was the scuff of her own boots against the stone floor.

Loren had to be here somewhere—along with Thorne and Nyra and whoever else attended a fae prince—but Araya couldn't shake the creeping sense that she was completely and utterly alone.

She tried to retrace the path Loren's shadow had led her along that first night, but it all felt different in the strange half-light. Corridors stretched too long, the threadbare tapestries blurring together until she wondered if she was circling the same wing over and over again. Still, something tugged her forward, urging her deeper into the heart of the castle.

She knew she was getting close when the furniture was no longer shrouded beneath dusty sheets. It gleamed as if freshly polished, all of it boasting the curling, fluid lines of fae craftsmanship. Finally, a hallway opened into what must have once been a personal sitting room. A book lay facedown on the low table, its spine cracked and pages slightly curled. The cushions on the settee had been pushed askew, like someone had only just left. But the hearth was dark, and the cup of tea on the side table had long since gone cold.

Stepping cautiously into the room, Araya breathed in the somehow familiar scent of cold rain and granite. But it was only a fading trace. Loren had been here recently, but he wasn't now.

Emboldened by his absence, Araya drifted into the room, skimming her fingers over the soft fabric of the settee cushions and the cool, polished wood. She paused at the book, studying the looping script on the cover. Valenya—of course. She squinted at the letters, trying to pick out the familiar shapes of the runes she knew, but it was like trying to put together a puzzle with no reference.

With a sigh, she moved on, exploring the room slowly until she found herself standing before a painting shrouded in white linen. Unable to help herself, Araya reached out. She only meant to lift the corner—but the entire sheet slid free, engulfing her in a cloud of dust. She coughed, choking as she stared at the painting it had shrouded.

Loren was so young—no more than twelve or thirteen—but his face was already a near-perfect echo of the male she knew. The crowned male beside him could only be his father. They shared the same sharp cheekbones and raven-dark hair. But Loren's eyes— those were his mother's, dancing with a joy she had never seen in person.

His mother—*the queen*—stood beside them, her silver hair spilling like moonlight over her bare shoulders. The child in her arms couldn't have been older than three or four, those same green eyes beaming at the artist with open delight through a curtain of wild dark waves.

Araya blinked, her eyes burning for reasons that had nothing to do with the dust in the air. It was a moment suspended in time—a memory from a world long ago turned to ash.

Both of Loren's parents were long dead, slain in the first years of the New Dominion. And his sister—Loren had refused when Araya offered to try and find out what had happened to her. He'd been terrified to draw the Arcanum's attention to her, clinging to the desperate hope she might still be alive somewhere.

"If you're looking for Loren, he's not here."

Araya jerked back, whirling to find Thorne Emberwood leaning in the doorway, arms crossed over his chest. The weak sunlight caught the red-gold threads in his auburn hair, brightening it until Araya could hardly believe he ever passed as human.

"Loren is in Lumaria." Thorne's amber eyes flicked from her to the portrait, seeing far too much. "He left this morning. He won't be back until tomorrow."

"How do you know I was looking for him?" Araya lifted her chin, refusing to back down. "Maybe I'm just lost."

"You're a long way from the guest wing." Thorne's lips twitched, his serious expression slipping. "You were so enthralled by that portrait you didn't even hear me come in. Another minute, and you'd have been rifling through his drawers."

Heat rushed to her cheeks, but Araya held her ground. "I wasn't snooping. I need to talk to him. He can't keep me here. Jaxon...he's going to come for me. And when he does, people will get hurt."

"You're not the only one worried about that." Thorne's voice lost its humor, the weight of his words pulling it flat. "But people are going to get hurt no matter what. Loren just doesn't want you to be one of them."

"If Loren doesn't want me to get hurt, he made a grave mistake stealing me out from under Jaxon's nose." Araya looked away, nails biting into her palms as she fought to steady her voice. "Are you here to escort me back to my cell?"

"I thought you might prefer a tour." Thorne smiled, but his eyes stayed sharp. "So you don't get lost the next time you sneak into Loren's rooms."

Her pride begged her to refuse. The words hovered on the tip of her tongue—but the truth locked them behind her teeth. Thorne was offering her something she couldn't afford to turn down. If she wanted to escape, she needed to know where the doors were.

"Fine," she said stiffly. "Lead the way."

CHAPTER

TWO

He shouldn't have left her alone.

Loren shifted in his seat, barely listening to the advisor as he droned on about rations and supply lines. This meeting was important—a dozen small fires ready to become infernos. But his mind was fixated on the stubborn, silver-eyed female back at Ithralis.

He'd spent every day since she'd stumbled into his room avoiding her. Eloria hadn't said anything yet, but Thorne hadn't bothered to hide his disapproval. Even Veria had finally snapped, chasing him out of the kitchens when he tried to inspect Araya's breakfast tray to make sure she'd eaten enough.

The truth was, he didn't dare go to her himself. Not when she hadn't called for him. Not after he'd taken her against her will. Drugged her. Dragged her through the Veil and nearly killed them both. But when her nightmare hit just as they reached the cliffs it had taken everything he had not to turn and race back to her. Even now, he could feel the lingering echo of her terror pulsing in his chest like a second heartbeat.

If he had gone to her...would she even have looked at him? Or would she have turned away?

Eloria stepped on his foot—hard.

Loren hissed, jerking his foot away. He straightened in his chair, meeting the expectant stares of the advisors who had helped his sister run the fae government for the past twenty years—all of them waiting for him to respond to a question he hadn't even heard.

"Apologies," he said, clearing his throat. "I was...distracted."

A chair creaked, a rustle moving through the room as several council members shifted in their seats, exchanging sidelong glances. Loren recognized many of them—veterans from his father's council or peers from his own youth—but the prince they remembered had been a diplomat and a warrior, raised from birth to rule. Loren couldn't help but wonder what they made of the broken prince that had returned to them?

The High Arbiter leaned back in his chair, studying Loren with sharp eyes. "I asked how long we'll be keeping your return a secret?"

Loren frowned at the older fae—Maelor, maybe? He'd been part of his father's Small Council too. Surely he'd known his name once? "As long as necessary."

"That is not a real answer," the High Luminary cut in, her voice cool. "Surely the people deserve to know their prince is free."

Loren pressed his lips together. He didn't feel free.

"His return could bring hope," someone else argued. "With rations tightening and so many going hungry, it could be what we all need to brighten our spirits—"

"Or spark chaos." Eloria's Commander at Arms said, his expression hard. "Unless we make it absolutely clear who holds the crown now."

Silence stretched, thick with expectation as every member of the Small Council turned their attention to the head of the table—where Eloria and Loren sat side by side.

"That's a fair question—" Eloria started.

"And an easy one to answer." Loren cut her off, ignoring how she stiffened beside him. "Eloria is making the decisions."

Not the answer she might have given. And not the one they had expected, judging from the startled glances exchanged around the table. But Loren wouldn't have taken back, even if he could. Eloria had led them for more than twenty years now. Years he'd spent locked in a cell, with only the shadows for company. They were better off with her.

"We're still working out the details, Cormac," Eloria said after a beat, smoothing over the uneasy silence. "I will continue to act as the voice of the fae monarchy—for now."

"Very well then." The High Arbiter cleared his throat, his glance flicking down to the stack of papers in front of him. "I suppose we should hear from Eryn next then."

Loren's gaze slid to the male near the center of the table. Eloria's spymaster looked like a clerk or a scribe—unassuming, forgettable by design. But every face at the table turned toward him expectantly, their silent deference speaking volumes.

"The situation in the New Dominion has worsened," he said. "My sources say the Arcanum's so-called High Inquisitor is personally leading a new crackdown in the fae districts—searching for someone."

His gaze drifted toward Loren, flicking away again the second their eyes met.

"Travel restrictions have been implemented across the fae districts. Any fae found outside designated areas without documentation are being detained on sight—many have not resurfaced."

"Interrogations?" Eloria asked.

"They've become standard procedure," Eryn confirmed. "Anyone suspected of harboring fugitives is being questioned—some publicly, some...less so." He turned the page in front of him without looking up. "There are unconfirmed reports that Garrick Shaw's son is personally involved."

Of course he was. Loren clenched his jaw, tightening his grip on the shadows as they hissed and churned around his feet. Jaxon didn't just want his toys back—he wanted to make an example out of anyone who might have even considered helping them.

"Operative Finn Greenvale has gone to ground," Eryn continued, flipping another page. "His identification papers are holding—for now—but extractions have stalled. We'll need to reroute."

"What about Serafina Hart?" Loren demanded.

Eryn blinked at him. "Who?"

"The Healer," Loren said tightly. "She's the one who got me out."

"Ah, yes—the turncoat." Eryn flipped through his notes without looking up. "Intelligence indicates she was intercepted shortly after your extraction. We've seen no evidence that she's been executed, but without contact we have to assume—"

"She risked everything to get us out." Loren stared around at the gathered advisors, hardly able to believe what he was hearing. "She stayed behind to give us the best chance at escaping—and we're not even *trying* to find her? How many others has she saved?"

"The sympathizers who remain in the New Dominion know the risks." Eryn frowned, closing his ledger with a snap. "It's not that we aren't grateful, Your Majesty. If the Arcanum took her...well, there's just not much we can do."

"Serafina Hart isn't just a sympathizer," Eloria said, her voice cooling. "She's the reason my brother is even sitting at this table. We can spare something to find out what happened to her."

Eryn stiffened, his jaw tightening. "Of course, Your Majesty," he said after a beat. "I'll issue a quiet inquiry. But like I said, if she's already been captured it's likely too late—"

"Do it anyway," Eloria said. "Quietly."

The High Arbiter leaned forward again, his chair creaking. "Given Jaxon Shaw's involvement, it seems prudent to speak to the female that came here with you. Our reports indicate that she's his bond—"

"Don't call her that," Loren growled. "She was as much his prisoner as I was. And you *won't* be speaking with her."

The shadows curled around his boots, hissing their agreement. Araya had been through enough already—she didn't need to be interrogated on top of it.

"Regardless of what you call her, Eryn's reports indicate she worked closely with the younger Shaw and his father." The Keeper of the Coin pursed her lips. "Her insight could be invaluable—"

"Assuming she even intends to share it," Eryn murmured without looking up from his documents. "His Majesty calls her a prisoner, but she didn't leave the Shaws willingly. We cannot be certain she will work against them at all, even if she is the prince's mate."

Loren's head snapped up, shadows shivering around him. They shouldn't have known that. No one knew the details of their escape —or his relationship with Araya. No one but him, Thorne, Nyra, and—

Eloria.

"You briefed them on her?" he demanded.

"They need to know, Loren," Eloria said, her voice carefully even. "There are a lot of factors at play here."

Loren's hands curled into fists under the table, his nails biting into his palms. He forced himself to look away from his sister, not trusting himself as the shadows writhed around his boots. They hissed and spat, muttered demands clawing at the edges his control.

No one here had seen the marks Jaxon had left on her—body and soul. None of them woke from her nightmares, their hearts racing with her terror. She hadn't even admitted the full truth to herself. The last thing she needed was to have every choice she made picked over by the Small Council like vultures.

"Regardless of the details," said the High Arbiter, eyeing the restless shadows warily, "Araya Starwind's role in your escape cannot be ignored. At the very least, we need to confirm her loyalties. If you won't bring her from Ithralis, perhaps one of us could go there—"

"Absolutely not."

The shadows hissed their agreement, the temperature in the room plummeting.

"We've all been through a great deal, Your Majesty." The Keeper of the Archives folded her hands calmly, giving him a sympathetic look. "But the information she holds could matter to many. I understand the instinct to protect your mate, but I've heard she's something of a scholar herself—"

"She's a resource," Cormac cut her off, his voice hard as steel. "A tool. We've all had to set aside sentiment for the good of our people. That includes you, Your Majesty."

The shadows surged from the corners of the room, joining the darkness coiled at his feet. It rose around him, bristling with rage as Loren fixed his temper on Eloria's commander at arms.

"Speak of using her again," Loren snarled, his voice low and lethal, "and Jaxon Shaw will be the least of your concerns."

Cormac paled, but held his ground, his jaw clenched tight as the shadows closed in around him. The advisor next to him leapt to her feet, her chair crashing to the floor as she scrambled away.

"We're still assessing the best approach, Cormac," Eloria said, her calm voice cutting through the tension like a knife. "Until a decision is reached, Araya will remain safely at Ithralis under Loren's watchful eye. That should be enough to satisfy everyone for now."

Cormac dipped his head, sinking slowly back into his chair. But the shadows hissed, wood splintering as frost crept across the table. Because Eloria hadn't outright rejected his demand—she'd told him *not yet*.

"Loren," Eloria murmured. "Please."

He gritted his teeth, digging his will into the darkness. But it fought, twisting against his command.

She is ours, they snarled, dark voices rising around him like a tide. *Ours*. Protect *her*.

"Enough." His breath fogged the air in front of him, his hands clenched white-knuckled around the edge of the table. "There's no fight here. Not right now."

The shadows shivered, reluctantly curling back across the table. Loren dropped heavily into his chair, releasing the breath he'd been holding as they settled at his feet. But their threat lingered, clear in the brittle silence they left in their wake.

"And will you be remaining at Ithralis as well?" the Steward of the Hall asked finally, his voice polite but pointed. "The people need to see you, Princess. The mood in Lumaria—"

Eloria inclined her head, as calm as ever.

"Now that my brother is settled and recovering I'll be spending the majority of my time in Lumaria," she said, "Now please, let's continue."

The discussion turned to rations—hoarding, dwindling stores, the latest supply failure—it all blurred together, painting a grim picture of their chances for survival here. Loren forced himself to listen. These were his people. Their survival was his duty—but a flash of silver by the door caught his eye.

He stood, shoving his chair back so hard it screeched across the stone. The bond was a blade between his ribs, stealing his breath as he caught Ilyana's eye. He'd asked the Healer to look in on Araya—if she was here now, something was wrong.

"Loren?" Eloria asked.

"Continue without me," he said, already moving. He didn't look back to see the disapproving looks he was sure were aimed at his back. He didn't care. Let them judge him. It didn't matter what they thought. Not when Araya needed him.

***

"How is she?"

"Physically? She's recovered wonderfully." Ilyana crossed her arms. "No lingering side effects from the concussion. She has full mobility in her wrist. Magically, her power reserves are recovering nicely. She's having some growing pains, but nothing unexpected."

Loren braced his hands on the back of the chair. "And mentally?"

"That's a harder question to answer." Ilyana let out a slow, measured breath. "Mental healing isn't a straight path—"

"Try," Loren growled, barely curbing the urge to bare his teeth at the Healer. The shadows at his heels stirred, as restless and unsettled as he was.

Ilyana's head jerked up, her bright blue eyes sparking with anger.

"Spending all of her time alone in her room isn't helping," she snapped. "I'm a Healer, not a spy, Your Majesty. If you want to know how she's doing you should try asking her yourself."

"She doesn't want to see me," Loren snapped. "Maybe after her runes are removed—"

"She refused." Ilyana crossed her arms, glaring at him. "She seemed...panicked by the idea. I told you it wasn't a good idea to bring it up this soon—"

"She has to have them removed." The bond twisted under Loren's skin, digging its claws into him as the shadows hissed at his feet. "I don't care if it's dormant. I want it gone."

"And *she* doesn't," Ilyana snapped back. "It's not your decision, Your Majesty. It's her body. We do *not* force *anyone* to have their runes removed before they are ready."

Loren clenched his jaw. "The *ly'ithra* rune suppresses her magic. It was designed to keep her in submission—"

"And like I explained to her, it doesn't work here," Ilyana said. "As long as she stays on this side of the Shadowed Veil, it's nothing but a scar. Unless the human mage that claimed her manages to cross the Veil and find her, she's perfectly safe whether the rune is there or not."

Loren exhaled sharply, raking a hand through his hair. His shadows curled around him, echoing the frustration clawing at his ribs. Ilyana had come highly recommended by Thorne. She'd spent years treating fae brutalized by the Arcanum, earning her place as a Healer trusted by refugees and warriors alike. But she didn't know Jaxon Shaw. Not like he did. She had no idea how far Shaw would go to reclaim what he thought was his—or to break what he couldn't control.

"What about the other fae who survived the camps?" he asked.

"She refused to speak with them."

Loren's grip tightened on the back of the chair until the wood groaned beneath his fingers. The sharp creak echoed in the quiet room, but he barely heard it over the pulse pounding in his ears. He had dragged her from one prison and placed her in another. She was surrounded by strangers, in a world she had no ties to, and now…she was choosing to stay cut off.

"I don't want her to be alone here," he said. "She's been having nightmares. Even if she wants nothing to do with me, I want her to have *someone*."

"And who have *you* talked to?" Ilyana asked gently. "She's not the only one at Ithralis who suffered at the New Dominion's hands, Your Majesty."

Loren flushed, suddenly all too aware of the vivid scars that still branded his throat and wrists. "We're not talking about me," he snapped.

Ilyana frowned, but whatever answer she might have made was silenced when the door burst open, slamming into the wall with enough force to rattle the lamp hanging from the low ceiling.

"Loren!" Eloria stormed into the room, her green eyes blazing with a fury that could have melted stone. "You cannot just *walk out* on the Small Council. You are the *prince*!"

"And *you* are the regent," Loren retorted. "I had something I needed to do."

Eloria's expression darkened, her gaze flicking to Ilyana. "And how *is* Araya?"

"Why do you want to know? So you can brief your advisors on her?" Loren turned his back on her, glancing back at the Healer. "Thank you, Ilyana. You can go."

"Stay," Eloria said. "Just for a moment, please. I think my brother needs a reminder of the intricacies of the mate bond. Can you give us an overview?"

On some level, Loren was aware of the Healer staring at him, her mouth hanging open in disbelief—but his immediate attention narrowed on his sister. His reckless, impudent sister. Who had just carelessly handed over yet another secret that wasn't hers to share.

"This isn't necessary," he said, fighting to keep his voice even.

But his heart thundered in his chest, the shadows at his feet pulsing and coiling up his legs like restless serpents. He gritted his teeth, trying to force them back down. They weren't in any danger here—Araya wasn't in danger. But they fought him, hissing words he couldn't quite understand as they fed on his shame, reflecting it back into the world with every flicker of darkened aether.

"Go ahead, Ilyana." Eloria turned her back on him, apparently unconcerned by the murderous darkness churning around him. "I'm especially interested in revisiting the consequences of an unreciprocated mate bond—say if one half of the pair took the other's blood and name in order to escape the New Dominion."

Ilyana blanched, her wide eyes flying to Loren. "Tell me you didn't."

But he had. He'd taken her blood without her consent, binding her name to his. It had been the only way to save her life, but that didn't change the horror of what he'd done, turning a sacred gift into just another cage.

And no matter how much he despised himself for it, he couldn't take it back.

"Does she—" Ilyana asked.

"No," Loren forced the word through clenched teeth, his voice rough. "She doesn't know."

"Goddess," Ilyana whispered, her face pale. "You have to tell her. If you've claimed her...the bond isn't going to stop trying to drag you together. She'll think she's going mad." Her eyes flicked to the shadows that had risen around his boots. "It will tear you both apart. Emotionally—magically. The longer it drags out, the worse it will get."

"Father only made it two years after Mother died," Eloria said quietly. "And look what *dara'el* has become. Is that what you want your legacy to be?"

Loren could only look away, shame burning like rot under his skin.

"Thank you, Ilyana," Eloria said finally. "You can go."

The Healer turned so quickly she nearly stumbled, yanking open the door with shaking hands and disappearing into the hall. Loren didn't watch her leave. His jaw clenched, the shadows curling restlessly around him, whispering as they fed off the storm inside him.

"You had no right to do that," he spat.

"I have every right." Eloria folded her arms across her chest. "You should be here—in Lumaria, where your people are. This is where you belong. Both of you. Not hiding in that crumbling castle ignoring each other."

Loren opened his mouth, but she raised her voice, cutting him off.

"You walk out on the Small Council whenever it suits you. You refuse to step into your role as prince." Her voice sliced through the air like a blade. "Our people are refugees in our own kingdom, crammed together like rats on a sinking ship, clinging to the last dry planks. And the children—"

She stopped, taking a deep breath.

"I know you think keeping Araya in the dark protects her," she said more quietly. "But parents are already making impossible choices. If this continues...they'll beg the New Dominion to take their children. Just so they'll have food in their bellies. She grew up in one of those camps. Do you think she could live with that?"

"I already stole her choice once," Loren snapped. The shadows slipped his grip, spiderwebbing across the walls in dark veins that pulsed in time with his ragged breaths. "I'm not going to use starving children to manipulate her into accepting another chain."

Eloria sighed, her expression shuttering as she stared at the writhing shadows.

"You should still tell her the truth," she said softly. "Just...tell me you'll consider it, Loren. Please. I hate seeing you like this."

"Just go, Eloria," Loren ground out. The shadows bucked at the edges of his control, their hissing voices drowning out the pounding of his own heart. "Leave me alone."

Eloria just shook her head, staring at him like she didn't recognize the male he'd become. "I'll see you tonight, Lorendrael," she said softly. "It's your homecoming. Try and show up for it."

CHAPTER

THREE

The castle was a relic of another world. Moss and creeping lichen clung to pale stone walls crowned by brittle, long-dead vines. The wide, unbarred windows yawned open to the mist-heavy air, their frames streaked with water stains.

It wasn't a fortress. Even in good repair, these walls would never have withstood the Arcanum's forces. But now? The gate didn't even close. When Jaxon came for her, he'd be able to walk right in.

"It's smaller than I expected," Araya said, staring down at the pier far below. Nyra's boat was still tied there, the female's silver hair catching the weak sunlight as she scurried across the deck. The only path down was the staircase they'd climbed—narrow and slick from constant moisture. A fall from this height—Araya wasn't sure if it would be better to smash into the rocks or hit the water and drown.

"This was never a primary residence," Thorne said. "It was a retreat for the royal family and their closest friends. A place to honor the Goddess and learn from her acolytes."

"But there's a city?" Araya asked.

"Lumaria," Thorne replied, glancing at her. "Eloria moved the court there about twenty years ago—to be closer to her people after her father died."

"Is it far?" Araya stared down at the waves, keeping her voice carefully neutral.

"It's about a half day's walk, if you take the coast road." Thorne's lips twitched, but he didn't call her on her thinly veiled attempt to get more information. "The temple road is much shorter, but it runs through the forest."

Araya frowned, glancing at the dark line of trees. "Why is that a problem?"

"Because not all of the shadows here are as tame as Loren's." Thorne gave her a faint, humorless smile. "Trust me. If you're thinking of trying to run, do it during the day. And take the cliff road."

There wasn't much else to see. Thorne didn't press her, just nodding in approval when she navigated them through the halls back to the guest wing without guidance.

Alone again, Araya rifled through the desk drawers. To her surprise, she found a neat stack of parchment, along with a quill and a small pot of ink. It wasn't much—but it was something.

She sat down at the desk, smoothing the first sheet with a steadying breath. Then she uncapped the inkwell, dipped the quill, and began to write—carefully noting everything Thorne had told her. The coast road. The forest. Lumaria.

Finally, she sat back, staring down at the page and willing an answer to take shape.

None did.

The knock at the door made her jump, startling her so badly that she left a crooked slash of ink across the page. Araya set it aside, blowing on it hurriedly before crossing the room. She pulled open the door, expecting Thorne or Ilyana. Or—gods forbid—Loren.

But instead a strange fae female stood there. She tilted her head, her blue-black hair cascading over her shoulders and her green eyes dancing with good humor.

"Well," she said, her common accented with the lilting cadence of Valenya. "Look at you."

"Can I help you?" Araya asked warily.

"I'm actually here to help you." The female lifted a shimmering swath of amethyst fabric. "I brought you a dress for dinner."

"Dinner?" Araya echoed. All of her meals so far had come on trays left outside her door—somehow always still piping hot no matter when she discovered it.

"Yes, dinner." The female swept by her without waiting for an invitation, moving to hang the gown on the door of the wardrobe. "Someone brings you food. You eat it. Sometimes you even talk to your friends."

"I don't have any friends here," Araya said warily.

"Not yet," the female replied, hanging the dress with practiced ease. "But I thought you might want something nicer to wear. And maybe a little help getting ready."

Araya's gaze narrowed. "Did Ilyana send you? Or Loren?"

"Oh, no." The strange female laughed, tossing her head back. "They'll both be terribly cross when they find out I dropped in on you. I'm sure you've noticed, but they both seem to think they know what's best for everyone."

Despite herself, Araya smiled.

The other female grinned. "You can call me El," she said, throwing herself down into one of the chairs by the fire. "Come on —sit. We don't have to get ready yet, and I want to know *everything*."

It was impossible not to like El.

Despite Araya's resolve to keep her guard up, she found herself reluctantly drawn in by the fae female's easy charm. El had immediately made herself comfortable in one of the padded armchairs, draping herself over it as if they had known each other for years. She chattered nonstop and laughed easily, filling the quiet room with a warmth Araya hadn't realized she was missing.

And somehow, without even meaning to, Araya found herself *enjoying* it.

"And you worked?" El asked. "*In* the Aetherium? I've never heard of a fae female being allowed to do that before."

"Well, it does require special permission...but I wasn't the only one," Araya said. "There was a whole workshop full of us to imbue amplifiers—but I stopped when I was bonded."

"To a human mage," El said, sitting up a little straighter and eyeing Araya with unabashed curiosity.

Araya tensed, twisting her fingers into her skirts. "It wasn't like you're thinking."

"No?" El's green eyes widened. "Then what *was* it like?"

"We were...friends first," Araya said slowly. "Of a sort. He sponsored my apprenticeship—kept me out of the slums. Bonding is an arrangement that benefits us both—one I could have refused if I wanted to."

"And yet you're here—a world away from him." El studied her, her expression unreadable. "Did you love him?"

Araya's throat tightened as a flicker of memory surfaced. Jaxon's grip, the press of wood under her cheek as she begged him to stop. But he hadn't. He'd—

"Araya?" El asked softly.

"I don't want to talk about this any more." Araya stared at the fire, fixing her gaze on the flames.

"Alright." El studied her a moment longer, the warmth in her green eyes dimming. "You must have questions of your own. This is your chance—ask me anything."

Araya opened her mouth—then closed it. She had a thousand questions, most of them too revealing to ask outright. But if El was willing to answer them...

"People keep saying it's dangerous outside the castle," she said, choosing her words carefully. "Why? What's out there?"

"Oh, the *zal'vorr*." El shuddered dramatically. "They're animals—or they were, before they were twisted by the shadows. They're most active at night, but you could run into one at any time if you stray too close to where the shadows thicken."

Araya only barely managed not to roll her eyes. Fae might not be able to lie, but it didn't make them immune from superstition. Maybe the Veil itself was dangerous...but the mists that rolled off of it? The fae in the New Dominion blamed them for everything from illnesses and disappearances to bad luck. As if poverty, starvation, and the strict rationing of magic weren't the obvious culprits.

It was just easier to fear the dark than to face reality.

Still, she nodded, schooling her expression into something neutral. "Good to know," she murmured. "Does anyone else live here?"

"At Ithralis?" El raised her eyebrows. "No one really *lives* here anymore—except for you, Loren and Thorne now I guess. Everyone else is in Lumaria—"

To Araya's surprise, El chattered on without hesitation. "Finn's still in the New Dominion, of course, but he's always the mediator," she said, grinning. "If there's any conflict, you can bet he'll be the one smoothing things over. But Nyra was probably the root of the problem in the first place."

El rolled her eyes, shaking her head with a small smile. "She goes back and forth the most. She'll set sail for the New Dominion with tonight's tide now that her boat is repaired. I don't envy her. It's bad enough to sail through the Veil, but to do it at midnight?" El shuddered dramatically.

Midnight tonight. Araya couldn't help how her heart skipped a beat in her chest, but she kept her breathing even, willing her body not to give her away. That was it—her chance. She just had to find a way to take it.

"Will Thorne go back with her?" Araya asked, struggling to keep her voice even.

"Not this time," El said. "He's staying—for Loren. They grew up together, you know. They're practically brothers. Thorne has never forgiven himself for not being there when the Arcanum took the Aetherium."

"He was at the Aetherium?" Araya frowned. "But...he's part-human."

"Oh, he's half and half," El said, waving a hand like it made no difference at all. "His father was King Corwin's commander at arms and his mother was a human Healer. She was close friends with the queen, actually. Thorne was raised alongside Loren, taught by the same masters." She leaned back, her expression softening. "I doubt there's anyone Loren trusts more."

Araya stared at her, trying to reconcile the words with the history she'd grown up with. The Arcanum had only overthrown the fae monarchy because they hoarded magic, refusing to share it with humans. The idea that a half-human could have walked the halls of the Aetherium and trained alongside fae royalty—it just couldn't be possible.

"Could one half-fae really have changed anything?" she asked quietly.

"There's no way to know, is there?" El's eyes turned distant, her gaze fixed on the crackling flames. "But should haves and could haves haunt us all."

For a moment, neither of them spoke. But then El leaned forward, resting her hand lightly on top of Araya's. "We're all very grateful to you for bringing Loren back to us, you know."

"Oh—" Araya coughed, pulling her hand back. "I didn't really do anything..."

"You were the one who got Serafina in to see him. And you removed the collar." El cocked her head, frowning. "Without that, none of this could have happened."

Araya had no argument for that. She twisted her hands in her lap, rubbing her thumb absently over the rune inked on her skin. "I didn't know Serafina was involved in smuggling fae out of the New

Dominion," she admitted. "I just...didn't think anyone should be in that much pain."

Not even rude, inconsiderate fae princes.

El studied her for a long moment. "You're angry at him, aren't you? For bringing you here?"

Araya's breath hitched, her fingers tightening slightly.

"It's hard not to be when he tore me away from everything I knew. I had a life there—a life I worked hard for." She had to force the next words out past the lump in her throat. "He took that away from me without even asking what I wanted."

"That must be terrifying," El murmured. "I'm sure he felt like he didn't have a choice. He was a good male—before. I think he still is, underneath it all, even if he's struggling."

"You knew him before?"

"He's older than me, but yes—I did." El's smile turned wistful, almost sad. "He was kind. The sort of male who would have made a good king." Her gaze lingered on the fire, shadows dancing across her face. "Maybe he still will—if the right people stand beside him."

Araya swallowed, something unsteady twisting in her stomach. "Do you think he'll let me leave?"

El glanced away, for the first time seeming to lack an easy answer. "I think if it were up to him, he'd let you do whatever you wanted," she said finally. "But a crown isn't just a piece of metal. It's a promise—and sometimes we're forced to keep that promise, even when it hurts the people we love."

"Loren doesn't love me." Araya almost laughed.

"Maybe, maybe not." El shrugged. "I just hope you can find a way to forgive him. I know he didn't handle things well. But he isn't heartless. He'd redeem himself—if you gave him the chance."

"I don't know if I care about his redemption," Araya admitted. "I just want to go home."

El smiled sadly. "I can understand that."

They sat in silence for a moment, until El stood, shaking out her skirts like she could shake off the dark mood that had settled over the room. She lifted the dress from its hanger, holding it out.

"We should get you ready for dinner now," she said, her voice forcedly light. "My reputation couldn't bear it if you looked anything less than stunning."

Araya hesitated, her fingers brushing the edge of the gossamer fabric. "I'm not trying to impress anyone."

"Please—" El snorted, giving the dress a little shake. "You deserve to wear something that makes you feel powerful. Like a queen."

Araya scoffed. She was no queen. But she let El help her into the dress anyway, the fabric hugging her torso before it flared out at the waist in a waterfall of deep purple and shimmering silver. And she couldn't help but return El's smile when the other female stepped back, clapping her hands in delight.

"What did you want to do with your hair?"

"I usually just braid it back—" Araya stopped at the look of abject horror on El's face. "Did you have another idea?"

El ushered Araya to the vanity, weaving the front sections of her hair into a delicate crown with practiced ease, leaving the rest to flow over her shoulders in loose, cascading waves. The dress really did bring out the shift from deep red to violet, emphasizing how the purple entwined with deep burgundy.

"I love your hair," El said as she stepped back to admire her work. "It's beautiful."

Araya swallowed hard, staring at her reflection. Her hair was one of the most fae things about her—something she'd spent her entire life hiding. To see it highlighted and celebrated instead…her chest ached with a feeling she couldn't quite name as El gave her a final satisfied nod.

"Perfect," the other female said. "Now for me—"

She flicked her fingers, a ripple of magic brushing away the dust and smoothing the creases that had settled in the layers of her own dress.

Araya caught her breath, her heart racing in her chest at such a casual use of power. But El just looped their arms together, half-dragging Araya toward the door.

"Come on," she said, her grin bright and full of mischief. "I have a feeling you're going to make quite an impression at dinner."

Araya laughed, letting herself be pulled along. She slipped and slid in the ridiculous silk slippers El had dug out from the back of the wardrobe, but the other female only clutched her arm tighter, both of them giggling like children as they stumbled through the halls.

"Alright," El whispered when they finally approached the carved double doors to the dining room. "Brace yourself."

Araya laughed, but the sound died on her lips the moment they stepped inside. El hadn't been joking—silence crashing over the room like a wave.

Thorne sat beside Nyra across the table, his expression tight as he looked from El to Araya. Nyra had gone rigid, her grip on her goblet white-knuckled. Her gaze flicked toward the head of the table, where a golden-haired male gaped at them with what could only be described as abject horror.

And then there was Loren.

Araya's breath hitched in her throat. Loren had bathed—thoroughly. His hair, once matted and unkempt, now sheared to his chin. The filthy, ragged prisoner who had haunted her dreams for so many months was gone, his prison rags and borrowed clothing replaced by a finely embroidered black tunic and pants, paired with shining leather boots.

But it was his eyes that froze her where she stood. Those sharp, vivid green eyes burned with a fury that set her heart racing in her chest.

Araya swallowed hard. She was almost certain his anger wasn't directed at her, but it still struck her like a physical force, stealing the air from her lungs, making her legs feel weak. The air in the room changed, crackling with something charged and dangerous.

"El…" The golden-haired male beside Loren gripped the prince's arm like he expected him to erupt. "Are you mad?"

"Mad?" El said, sweeping the room with a stare that could have made kings falter. She stopped at Loren, meeting his anger without a drop of fear. "Did you honestly think I'd let you send her a tray to eat in her room again? Our parents would be horrified by how you're treating her."

"Eloria," Loren snarled through gritted teeth, his voice dangerously low. He ripped his arm free of the other male's grip and barked something in Valenya, his words quick and harsh.

Eloria. The realization hit Araya like a punch to the gut, stealing her breath. El—the female who had laughed with her, dressed her, and done her hair—wasn't just some kind stranger. She was Princess Eloria of Valendral. The fae regent.

Loren's sister.

CHAPTER
FOUR

Eloria.

The name sat like a stone in Araya's chest, heavy and cold. Only a lifetime of schooling her reactions kept her expression neutral as Eloria grinned at her, those green eyes—so clearly the same as Loren's now that she saw them side by side—still sparkling with mischief.

"I told you they'd be cross," the princess said in a loud whisper. Then, with effortless grace, she swept across the room and claimed the empty seat beside the golden-haired male at the head of the table—leaving only one unoccupied chair.

Right beside the glowering prince.

"I don't want to impose." Araya took a half-step back, not daring to meet Loren's scowl. "I can eat in my room—"

"Nonsense," Eloria said, slicing through her protest with a wave of her hand. "That would be a very poor way to thank you for returning my brother to us. Please—stay."

Araya hesitated, her mouth watering as the scent of roasted fish and fragrant herbs filled her nose. The meals here hadn't been *bad*, but after spending an afternoon talking and laughing with *El*—no matter how much of a deception it had been—the idea of going back to her room to eat alone by the fire made her chest ache.

Araya eased into the empty seat beside Loren, careful not to brush against him. Fury radiated off him in waves, mirrored in the shadows that pooled at his feet, shifting restlessly. One reached for her—a single tendril brushing against the hem of her dress before it whipped back, torn away.

The golden-haired male was already filling another plate, piling it high with roasted fish and vegetables steeped in a fragrant sauce. He held it out to her, but before Araya could reach for it, Loren snatched it from his hands and set it in front of her himself.

The other male sighed, shaking his head, but his blue eyes sparkled as he caught Araya's gaze. "Here I was, trying to make a good impression, and I've already made an enemy." He laughed, holding up his hands in mock surrender. "Should've known better than to get between a male and his...plate."

Loren's head snapped up, the shadows hissing at his feet—but across the table, Thorne choked on a laugh, failing to muffle it with his fist. Nyra nudged him sharply with her elbow, but it was too late —the tension had cracked.

The strange male leaned forward, bracing his forearms on the polished wood. "I'm Galen," he said. "Eloria's mate—husband, as the humans would say. You know Loren, obviously—and Nyra and Thorne. And I suppose you know Eloria now, too."

"*El* and I had a lovely afternoon," Araya said, her smile brittle. "Until I found out about the title she conveniently forgot to mention."

Galen shot Eloria a look, his brows lifting as he leaned slightly toward her, lips quirking in a crooked, indulgent smile. "El always means well," he said dryly. "She just—"

"She just sticks her nose where it doesn't belong," Loren cut in, setting his wineglass down a little too hard.

"Don't take it out on Galen, Loren," Eloria said. "Just eat."

Loren bared his teeth, but no one seemed interested in fighting him. Around them, conversation resumed. The bright, lilting tones of common spoken with fae accents flowed through the air like a swift, glittering river, sweeping Araya along without ever truly including her.

With everyone's attention elsewhere, she dared a tentative bite of the fish. The delicate flesh flaked easily against her tongue, a burst of briny citrus easing the tight knot in her chest. Araya let out a long breath, some of the tension she hadn't realized she was holding finally draining from her limbs.

But beside her, Loren hadn't moved. He didn't join in the chatter, didn't reach for his fork. The shadows pooled beneath the table, muttering darkly amongst themselves as if they shared his foul mood.

No one spoke to either of them until an elderly fae female stepped into the room, her silver hair braided into a crown and coiled neatly at the nape of her neck. She set a covered tray down in front of Loren, lifting the lid to reveal a dark, honey-glazed cake. A dish of stewed fruit in a fragrant syrup sat beside it, the scent of cinnamon and clove curling through the air.

"Welcome home, Your Highness," the female said warmly. Then, to Araya's surprise, she bent down and kissed Loren on the cheek, as if he were her own child. "I made your favorite."

Nyra made an exaggerated noise of protest, setting down her fork with a theatrical clatter. "Excuse me! I'm the one leaving, Veria. Shouldn't the cake be for me?"

Veria straightened, her bright eyes crinkling at the corners as she fixed Nyra with a mock-stern look. "I would never forget you, girl," she said, tapping Nyra lightly on the shoulder as she passed. "Your cakes are already on the ship, where you can't eat them all before you go."

Laughter rippled around the table, and even Loren snorted into his wine.

"Thank you, Veria," he said, the tension draining from his shoulders as he smiled warmly at the older female—a startling transformation from a male who had been so full of anger just moments ago. Then, without another word, he picked up a serving spoon and passed a portion of the cake and fruit to Araya as though it were the most natural thing in the world.

"Thank you." Araya stared down at the plate, the warm, spiced scent of the honey-glazed cake curling up to meet her.

Loren didn't answer, but the tension between them seemed to ease slightly as he picked up his own fork, and for the first time since she had woken up here, Araya let herself believe she was just...eating dinner. She took a bite of the cake, and for a moment, she wasn't a prisoner or a problem to be solved. She was just a guest at the table.

"You should ask Loren to show you Lumaria," Eloria said suddenly, her bright voice cutting through the fragile peace Araya had found.

"Oh—" Araya laughed nervously, resisting the urge to glance over at Loren. She wanted to get to Lumaria, but not with him looming over her. "I'm sure Loren has better things to do—"

"You'd think so, wouldn't you?" Eloria laughed, ignoring the way the shadows at the edges of the room darkened. "Of course, Lumaria's nothing like it was before—it was just never meant to hold this many people."

Araya opened her mouth, not quite sure what to say in response, but Eloria breezed on.

"We do the best we can, of course," she said. "Food is rationed, and we build everywhere we can—but every year more of us are lost. Now, with the New Dominion blockading the few shipping routes we had left..." She trailed off, lifting her glass. "Time is running out. That's why you coming here means so much to us."

A chill crept down Araya's spine. She set her goblet down carefully, her fingers tightening around the stem. "Excuse me?"

"Most humans see the fae as little more than a resource to bleed dry," Eloria went on, still smiling. "But all of our reports suggest you lived rather comfortably, didn't you? Especially compared to the other fae females in Aetheris. Is that because of the work you did for Jaxon Shaw?"

Araya flushed, shrinking back from the pointed words. But Eloria didn't give her a chance to answer.

"You must have been very valuable to him." Eloria leaned forward, resting her chin on her hand. "And imagine, he didn't even realize who you were."

"I—" Araya glanced around the table, desperate for an ally. But no one met her eyes. Nyra studied her wine. Thorne's expression had gone unreadable. Galen looked suddenly very interested in the stitching of the tablecloth. Only Loren looked up—but not at her. His glare was fixed on his sister, fury etched into every line of his face.

"That's enough, Eloria," he snapped. "Leave her alone. She's not your game piece."

Eloria ignored him. "We could make it worth your while," she said, her gaze never wavering from Araya's face. "What did Jaxon Shaw offer you? Safety? Comforts? We can do all of that. Goddess, if you can help Loren take control of the shadows—" she laughed, shaking her head. "I'd happily crown *you* queen."

"I don't want to be a queen—" Araya glanced warily around the table, lingering on Loren's dark fury. "I just want to go home."

"Ah," Eloria's expression softened. "That's something I cannot give you, Araya. But I can give you freedom. Here, with us. Where you're more than a source of power for some human."

Freedom. Araya stared at the fae female, the word scraping across something raw inside her. There was no such thing as freedom—not for someone like her. Not with Jaxon still searching for her.

Whatever Eloria was asking her to do...she couldn't. Not even Jaxon would be able to save her from the consequences of betraying the Arcanum so openly. And Eloria? She'd already lied to Araya once, all without ever speaking a false word.

Araya swallowed hard, her hands curling into fists in her lap. The fae were playing as much of a game with her as the Arcanum. Neither of them cared about her—only what she could do for them.

She opened her mouth, ready to refuse—but Loren stood so suddenly his chair fell backward, shadows swirling around them both.

"You will do nothing of the sort," he hissed, his sharp glare cutting across the table like a blade before settling on her. "I won't allow it."

"You won't *allow* it?" Araya shoved to her feet, heat flaring in her neck and ears. He had no right—not after everything he'd done. Not after tearing her life apart. "And who are *you* to command me? You aren't *my* prince."

"You don't understand the game she's playing," Loren growled. Shadows peeled away from him like smoke, dark tendrils brushing over her skin in a cool caress totally at odds with the fury blazing in his eyes. "Just because she can't lie doesn't mean she's telling the truth. She wants you to do the same thing for her that you were doing for Jaxon Shaw."

Araya bristled, the judgement in Loren's voice slicing deeper than it should have. As if she didn't already know exactly what they all thought of her.

"You're going to have to be more specific," she said coolly, holding his stare without flinching. "I did a *lot* of things for Jaxon Shaw."

Gasps rose from around the table. A chair scraped back, Galen moving to put himself between Eloria and her brother.

But Loren paid no attention to his sister.

"You're very ungrateful for someone who was rescued from a nightmare of her own making." He stepped forward—so close that his shadows engulfed her, hissing words in a language she didn't understand. They reached for her, wrapping around her ankles and crawling up her arms to loop around her throat.

"You think I should be *grateful*?" Araya laughed in his face. "You didn't *save* me, Loren. I know what it feels like when someone takes my power. You *used* me." She rubbed her lip, the phantom taste of his lips and her blood coating her tongue. "Was the kiss really necessary, or was that just for fun?"

The room was utterly silent. Galen stood frozen in front of Eloria, whose calm mask had cracked, unease flickering over her face. Even Thorne had tensed in his seat, his amber gaze locked on the shadows like he would throw himself across the table and rip them from her throat.

"You have no idea what you're talking about," Loren said. His voice shook, not with rage now but something more fragile and broken.

"Don't I?" Araya demanded. She stared up at him, meeting his blazing gaze with unwavering defiance. "I've spent my entire life making the best choice I can. I understand what you did and why. But it was no different than what Jaxon did to me."

Something in Loren's expression shattered, his shadows sliding from her skin like water. "Araya—" he started, her name strangled on his lips.

"I'm not afraid of you," she cut him off. "So unless you plan to compel me again, I'll be making my own choices. And you'll just have to deal with it."

Loren recoiled like she'd struck him. His mouth opened—then closed, twisting in a snarl. He turned on his heel, his shadows lashing out in a violent wave that sent dishes clattering to the floor and shattered goblets. He stormed out of the room without another word, the door slamming behind him with a deafening crash.

For a moment, no one spoke. The only sound in the room was the slow drip of red wine, spreading across the white tablecloth like blood. Araya's heart pounded, her hands shaking. But she held her head high, refusing to cower in front of them.

"Thank you for the dress, *El*," she said, dropping her napkin beside her ruined dessert. "But I'm not feeling very sociable right now. If you'll excuse me."

She didn't wait to be dismissed, shoving through the same doors

Loren had slammed. Nothing had changed. These people weren't her rulers. She couldn't trust any of them. Just like in the New Dominion, the only person here who cared about her safety and happiness was her.

She wouldn't sit here, waiting to be played like a piece in their game. Nyra's boat was leaving tonight—and she intended to be on it.

CHAPTER

FIVE

LOREN STOOD ON THE BALCONY OF HIS BEDROOM, STARING OUT AT THE MIST. It rose over the walls, wrapping the entire castle in its oppressive embrace. It clung to his skin, cold and damp. But the chill did nothing to soothe the anger that still burned in his veins. Not at Araya. Not even at Eloria—but at himself.

"Well that was an absolute disaster." The air beside him rippled as Eloria shed the illusion she'd cloaked herself in. "Storming off— very mature."

"As mature as you going behind my back after I explicitly told you to leave her alone?" Loren glared at her. "You were going to tell her about the bond! She isn't some doll for you to play dress-up with—I don't want her involved in any of this. Just leave her *alone.*"

"As regent, I can't do that." Eloria leaned against the railing beside him, her voice as cold as the wind that stirred the shifting mist. "Until you're ready to step up and start acting like the king you were meant to be, it's on *me* to make sure our people survive. If she needs to accept the mate bond for you to gain control over your magic, then that's what she has to do. I won't let them suffer just because you're too paralyzed with guilt to even share a meal with your own mate."

Loren clenched his jaw, the words he longed to throw back at her souring on his tongue. She was right. She was the one who had been here, leading their people. All he'd ever done for them was bleed.

"I don't want to force her," he said finally. "Don't you think she's suffered enough?"

Eloria sighed, the accusation draining from her face. She leaned against the railing beside him, looking down at the skeletal remains of their mother's once lush garden.

"I object to your characterization of being mated to you as *suffering*." She knocked her shoulder against his. "Any fool can see you care about her, Loren. Why are you making this so difficult?"

"It's not that easy."

Of course he cared about her. But that didn't change the simple truth that she deserved a chance at freedom—*true* freedom. The chance to make a choice, to live the life she wanted. But instead, she was cursed with him—the mate bond between them nothing but another chain.

"It *is* that easy," Eloria insisted. "You aren't in that cell anymore. Your mate is here. She's safe—because of you. If you'd just stop pushing her away—"

"And what do you think I should say to her, El?" Loren asked bitterly. "That I tied her to me without her consent? That if she goes back to the only home she's ever known they'll torture her—because of me? The last thing she needs is another male controlling her— acting like he is entitled to her power and her body. Being bonded to me is no better than being chained to Jaxon Shaw."

"I don't understand how you can possibly believe that." Eloria scowled at him, her shoulder bumping his. "You're *nothing* like him, Loren. Do you think he ever felt a fraction of the guilt you're drowning in?"

Loren didn't answer.

Eloria shook her head, straightening as she tugged the threads of her illusion back into place, aether twisting and bending around her. But her voice lingered, drifting through the darkness long after her form had dissolved.

"There's too much at stake here to just let her go without trying, Loren," she warned. "You've already claimed her—now talk to her. And if I were you, I'd start with an apology."

Loren stood there a long time after she'd vanished, his hands aching where they clenched around cold, unyielding stone. Far below, brittle, bone-white branches twisted in the wind, cutting the mist into strange shapes—like bits and pieces of nightmares brought to life.

But Eloria's words churned in his mind, a splinter he couldn't dislodge. She acted like she hadn't been standing in the same room when his shadows ripped free of his control. Loren would never forget the way Galen had thrown himself between them, ready to die to protect his mate. Any other time, Loren was certain the shadows would have obliged him. After all, they had already tried to kill Eloria once, and he'd been powerless to stop them.

But tonight, nothing could have shaken their focus from the infuriating female he'd bound them both to. Loren could still feel the warmth of her skin beneath his fingers, the bright flare of her defiance as she'd stared him down.

She should have run screaming from the room. Any sane female would have. He could have hurt her. He could have *killed* her. But Araya hadn't flinched. Not even when the shadows wrapped themselves around her throat, licking over her skin like flames.

Never hurt, the shadows hissed, their whispers curling around him like smoke. *She is yours. Ours. Ours to protect. To keep.*

"You wrapped around her neck like a noose," Loren hissed. "You're starving our people, twisting the animals here into monsters —if that's how you protect *us* how can I trust you to protect her?"

Not us, the shadows whispered, their voices splitting and overlapping in a chaotic chorus of confused echoes. *Not us. Not us.*

They crawled up his legs, wrapping around his arms and twisting threads of dark silk around his heart. The bond stirred in answer, an aching, primal pull that anchored itself behind his breastbone, digging in like claws.

It didn't matter that she was perfectly safe inside these walls. It didn't matter that he could feel her at the other end of it—angry, but unafraid. The bond still howled, demanding that he see her safe with his own eyes.

Loren snarled, slamming his hands into the railing. Stone cracked beneath his palms, pain lancing through his hands. But it did nothing to muffle the agony as the bond tore at his sanity, digging sharp claws into his heart.

Ours, the shadows whispered, their voices rising. *Ours. Ours. Ours. Ours—*

Loren's head pounded, their words beating against the inside of his skull as the shadows pressed in around him on all sides. Coiling around his ribs, his throat, his legs—winding tighter with every ragged breath as they screamed at him to go to her.

"You can't make her accept us," he ground out, his breath short. "Even if we tell her, she could still reject us."

Tell her, the shadows chanted, their voices rising to a fever pitch. *Tell her. Tell her. Tell her—*

Loren groaned, gripping the railing hard enough that the rough cracks bit into his palms. The mist churned below, a mirror of the storm that raged in his chest.

"Fine," he snarled.

The shadows leapt, writhing with hungry anticipation, but Loren held up a hand, halting them.

"But if she rejects us—if she doesn't want the bond—you will stand down. You won't speak to her. You won't touch her. You will leave her alone. Completely. No matter what Eloria says, we will not force or manipulate her into reciprocating."

The shadows recoiled as if he'd struck them. The air thickened, sharp with their outrage, their voices rising in a thousand overlapping snarls. *Never. Ours. We are hers. She is ours. You cannot—*

Loren gritted his teeth, holding firm even as they clawed at him, desperate to break free.

"That's the deal," he growled. "Take it, or stay here trapped with me until this kills us both."

The darkness faltered, rippling with reluctant submission. *Ours,* they whispered at last, low and sullen. *But hers to choose.*

"Very well," Loren muttered, turning toward the door. The shadows trailed him, heeling like eager hounds despite his censure.

Maybe once she rejected them they would finally understand that the best way for them to protect her was for Loren to stay far, far away.

And if they didn't...well. That was his problem, not hers.

CHAPTER
SIX

Araya changed quickly, trading the amethyst dress for the soft leggings and tunic she'd found shoved in one of the drawers. Thick socks and sturdy boots replaced the delicate slippers, and she shoved the knife she'd palmed from dinner into her belt, its weight a surprising comfort against her hip. She wasn't a soldier. Not like Jaxon—or Loren. But at least she wouldn't be walking into the unknown unarmed. And of course, she had her magic.

Araya closed her eyes, reaching inward to brush the well of power inside her. It hummed under her skin, far past the level where she would have begged Jaxon to siphon from her. The Arcanum had always warned that untrained fae were dangerous—that their own magic would consume them if it wasn't leashed. But now...Araya shivered. How much more could it rise before she drowned in her own power?

She took a slow breath, steadying herself. Once she made it back, Jaxon would help her. He'd siphon off the excess magic, calm the chaos under her skin, and shield her from whatever punishment the Arcanum had waiting. He always had. She just had to reach him—

prove to him that she hadn't run from him. Not willingly. That she could still be exactly what he needed.

It didn't matter that he had drained her dry and left her broken on the floor. Loren and Eloria might dress it up in prettier words, but they wanted to use her too. At least with Jaxon, she understood the rules.

Yes, he'd hurt her—but he'd also protected her. No one else had been willing to take a chance on a desperate halfblood fae. Everything she had, she owed to him. And the sooner she made it back to the New Dominion, the sooner she could make this right.

She slipped into the corridor like a shadow, her footfalls nearly silent as she crept through the dark halls. Thanks to Thorne's tour she found her way back to the main hall easily. The double doors to the dining room stood partially open, the wreckage of Loren's temper little more than another shadow in the dark.

Araya sidled into the courtyard, freezing as the door fell shut behind her, louder than it had any right to be. She held her breath, half-expecting one of Loren's living shadows to unfurl from the dark corners of the courtyard. But nothing moved.

Araya laid her hand against the wall, her skin prickling as strange magic washed over her. But she couldn't make any sense of whatever spellwork the fae had woven into the stones. Bracing herself, she stepped through the ruined gate. But no wards flared to life. No alarms rang out. The only sound was the wind, moaning through the stones as it swirled the mist into strange shapes.

She was clear.

Araya crept toward the narrow stairs carved into the cliff, her heart racing with every step she took closer to freedom. She couldn't see far with the mist pressing in around her, but she could hear the waves crashing against the cliffs. Nyra's boat was down there, waiting for her. All she had to do was get on board, and by this time tomorrow she'd be home—

Something moved in the mist.

Araya froze, clutching her stolen knife until her knuckles ached.

She held her breath, squinting into the darkness—but the only thing that moved was the dense, churning fog.

Araya exhaled sharply, shaking her head. She was being ridiculous. The creatures in the mist were just stories. Whispered tales meant to frighten children. She edged forward, taking another step toward the stairs—

And the mist blinked.

Araya stumbled back, a scream catching in her throat as the *thing* peeled itself from the mist. It dragged itself forward, too-long limbs folding and stretching at unnatural angles as its head swiveled from side to side, searching for her with milky, sightless eyes.

Move—she had to move. Araya spun, skidding on the wet stone —only for another one to materialize from the mist in front of her.

The stairs. She could still get to the stairs—

She turned again, her breath tearing from her lungs as she sprinted for the edge of the cliff.

But the *things* moved with her.

Another one rose from the mist—so close she nearly slammed into it. It shrieked, slashing at her with a twisted claw. Araya stumbled back, a sob catching in her throat as every instinct screamed at her to *run*, even as her mind whispered the truth.

She wasn't fast enough.

Araya threw up a shaking hand, her power sputtering at her fingertips as she desperately tried to remember *anything* that could help her—but the runes she'd learned had never been intended for combat. They were crafting, amplifying, sustaining—not fighting.

The nearest creature hissed, letting out a sputtering rasp that sounded too much like a laugh to be anything else, taking a slow, deliberate step forward.

Araya turned and ran.

She sprinted as fast as she could for the trees, her boots sliding in the slick mud. Movement flickered in the mist, a hollow snarl sending a fresh surge of terror clawing up her spine. Branches lashed her face, clawing at her clothes. She stumbled and fell, jagged stones and exposed roots biting into her palms as she scrambled behind one of the twisted trees.

She squeezed her eyes shut, choking back the panicked sobs that threatened to tear free. Somewhere in the darkness, one of the creatures snarled, its bulk rasping over the uneven ground as it searched for her. There were too many of them. She'd been a fool to think she could make it to Nyra's boat. A desperate, terrified fool. And now she was going to die here.

Something closed around her wrist.

Araya's eyes flew open, a scream tearing from her throat—but a second hand clamped over her mouth, muffling her cry as her captor dragged her deeper into the shadows—shadows that moved and hissed with a voice of their own.

Araya sucked in a deep breath, the cool, familiar scent of granite and rain filling her nose.

Loren had found her.

His arm banded around her waist, crushing her to his chest so tightly that she could feel the frantic drumbeat of his heart against her spine. His shadows coiled around them both, their hissing, muttered whispers vibrating against her skin and sending chills racing down her spine.

"Don't scream," he murmured, his arm tightening around her as the creature's heavy, uneven footsteps drew closer. The darkness around them thickened until Araya thought they would both choke on it—but for some reason, Loren's shadows didn't strike.

"Listen to me," Loren rasped, his mouth close enough to her ear that his breath stirred the loose strands of her hair. "When I let you go, you run. As fast as you can. Nod if you understand."

Araya gave a jerky nod, her pulse roaring in her ears. But Loren's fingers dug into her side, pinning her in place even as the creature crashed closer and closer. It wasn't until its wet, rancid breath washed over them that Loren let his hand slip from her jaw, his thumb grazing her lips as his breath shuddered against her ear.

"*Run.*"

Branches lashed her face, clawing at them both as Loren hauled her through the trees at a brutal pace. Araya's lungs burned, her legs screaming—but when her cloak snagged on a thorny branch Loren only yanked her forward hard enough to tear the fabric from her shoulders, his fingers digging into her wrist like a vice.

"If you fall we're dead," he growled.

Araya grit her teeth and kept going—but the creatures were faster.

Loren's shadows lashed out at a shape closing in beside them, sending the beast hunting them careening into the trees. But another snarled behind them—so close that Araya imagined she could feel its fetid breath on the back of her neck.

Loren threw them both to the side, dragging her through the remains of what had once been a wall. Araya tripped again but managed to keep her feet, barely registering the towering columns that surrounded them as Loren slammed his hand against the wall behind the ivy-choked altar.

Magic flared white-hot under his touch, throwing jagged shadows across the ruin for a single, blinding heartbeat. Stone groaned and shuddered, grinding apart until the wall yawned open like a dark maw. Araya balked, but Loren didn't hesitate, dragging her into the pitch-black darkness just moments before it crashed shut behind them.

Araya collapsed against the wall, every breath sawing out of her lungs in sharp, uneven gasps. Every instinct screamed at her to keep running, but her legs trembled so badly she wasn't certain she could have taken another step. Loren still clutched her hand, his own breathing ragged and uneven.

"Will it hold?" she asked.

Loren hesitated, his fingers flexing around hers. "It's enchanted," he said. "Against intruders who mean the royal family harm. So... probably."

"That's really reassuring," Araya muttered.

"You weren't supposed to be outside at all," Loren snapped. "Much less wandering around alone at night."

Before Araya could respond, something dragged its claws across the door with a terrible snarl, the dark space around them lighting up with a sudden, crackling flare of magic.

"We shouldn't stay here," Loren said. "They'll be able to smell us."

He finally released her hand, dim aetherlamps flickering to life to reveal a narrow set of stone stairs. He didn't wait to see if she followed, starting down the steps without so much as a glance back.

Araya forced her tired legs to move. Every step deeper into the earth pressed down on her like a lead weight, the walls closing in around her at every turn.

It reminded her too much of the walk to Loren's cell—the same stale air clogging her lungs. The same sinking conviction that every step she took carried her closer to something she would never escape. She could still see him hanging limply in his chains. Still taste the iron tang of his blood—

Loren slammed to a stop, turning back to glare at her. "What's the matter with you?"

Araya flinched, ducking her head so she wouldn't have to meet his eyes. "It just...reminds me of your cell," she muttered. "The walk down there was a lot like this."

Loren scoffed, turning back to the stairs. "Keep walking."

Araya was breathing hard by the time the stairwell finally opened into a wide, echoing hall. Cold air bit through her sweat-soaked tunic, chilling her to the bone. But the shudder that wracked her body as the aetherlamps flicked to life had nothing to do with the chill.

"This is a crypt," she whispered.

"It is." Loren stopped, staring up at the nearest statue. "Welcome to the resting place of a hundred generations of fae monarchs."

Araya swallowed hard, the memory of a hundred smashed open

graves flashing through her mind. What would the Arcanum give to get their hands on the bones of fae royalty?

"How long do we have to stay here?"

"Until dawn, if you want to make it back to the castle alive. Why?" Loren raised his eyebrows, glancing back at her. "Did you have somewhere to be?"

Araya flushed, heat rushing across her cheeks all the way to the tips of her ears. "I just—"

"Don't try to talk your way around it." Loren dragged a hand through his hair, shaking his head. "You almost got us both killed tonight. At least admit you were running straight back to the man who drained you and left you for dead."

"And you drugged and kidnapped me!" Araya snapped, something in her chest twisting at the bitter accusation in his voice. "I don't even understand *why*. You've spent every second since we got here avoiding me. Why bother dragging me here against my will when you obviously can't stand the sight of me?"

Loren stared at her, the shadows around his feet shivering like agitated serpents. For a moment, she thought he might snap back at her, but instead, he just closed his eyes, exhaling slowly.

"You didn't even make it to the docks, *ael'sura*," he said. "You ran straight into the *zal'vorr*. If I hadn't found you, they would be breaking your bones open and feasting on the marrow right now. And you were going to fight them off with—what is that, a dinner knife? You do remember you have magic, right?"

Heat flooded Araya's face, shame and anger warring in her chest. "I have to go back, Loren."

"You really don't." Loren scowled. "What kind of hold does he have on you that you would risk your life to get back to him when you could be free?"

"You don't understand." Araya took a deep breath, steeling herself. This was her chance—maybe her only chance—to make him understand. "I know what you saw was...brutal. But trust me, what he did...it's a fraction of what most females go through."

Loren's eyes flashed, the shadows thickening at his feet. But Araya pressed on, the words tumbling from her lips in a flood she couldn't stop.

"I'm not stupid. I know what he is—what he's capable of. But if I don't go back..." her voice broke, her chest tightening painfully. "He'll think I ran. That I betrayed him." A bitter laugh slipped past her lips. "And you know what they do to traitors."

Loren said nothing.

"If I go back, I have a chance. I can prove I'm still valuable, that I'm still worth protecting. I can survive." Araya sucked in a ragged breath, praying to whatever gods might listen that he was hearing her right now. "I swear, I won't tell Jaxon about the rebels. I would never betray Serafina—she's my best friend. Please, Loren. I don't belong here. I don't even speak the language."

For a long moment Loren didn't move. The shadows hissed softly, seething around his feet like they wanted to answer for him— but Loren's jaw clenched, his hands curling into fists at his side.

"You should get some rest," he said finally, his voice as flat and hollow as his eyes. "It's going to be a long night."

He turned away, the shadows trailing in his wake as he walked deeper into the crypt. Leaving her behind.

CHAPTER
SEVEN

She should have dreamed of shifting shadows and sightless eyes —mist-cloaked monsters moving in the dark. She *should* have woken up with the crypt's damp chill sinking into her bones, leeching the warmth from her skin.

But instead, she woke warm, cocooned in the comforting scent of rain and stone.

Loren.

Araya sat up, suddenly wide awake. She scanned the dimly lit crypt, searching the shadows of long-dead kings and queens for any sign of the fae prince, but nothing stirred.

He wouldn't have abandoned her here.

Would he?

Araya stood, pulling the cloak he must have draped over her at some point during the night tight against the chill. But it couldn't shield her from the stone stares of long-dead fae kings and queens, their judgement weighing heavily on her shoulders as she set off in search of their lost prince.

She found him standing in front of the last two statues, her steps faltering as she realized who they must be. She wanted to hold on to her anger—but the way he stood in front of his parents' statues, his head bowed and shoulders stiff, made something in her chest tighten.

She hesitated, hovering on the edge of turning back. But, without looking at her, Loren shifted slightly to the side—leaving just enough space for her to stand beside him if she wanted to.

Araya cleared her throat, sliding his cloak from her shoulders. She bundled it in her arms, holding it out even as she already mourned the loss of its warmth. "Thank you for letting me borrow this."

Loren glanced at her then. "Keep it."

Araya frowned. "You'll be cold." He only wore a thin shirt and pants—more appropriate for sleeping than rushing through the woods. As if he'd only stopped long enough to grab his cloak and shove on boots before pursuing her.

A shadow of a smile crossed his lips. "I'm used to being cold."

The words were quiet, spoken without self-pity, but they lodged deep in Araya's chest anyway. Twenty-five years in a stone cell. Cold had been his only constant.

"These are your parents." Araya hugged the cloak to her chest, staring at them. They hardly looked like the joyful family she'd seen in the painting. The king's gaze was shadowed, his features thinned by grief. And the queen...

Araya blinked hard, looking away. The proud tilt of her chin was all Eloria—but the mouth, the sorrow carved deep into her features... those belonged to Loren.

"My father wasn't weak or cruel," Loren said. "He ruled for nearly a century before the Ascendancy. Like the kings and queens that came before him, he welcomed humans when their own people cast them out."

"What happened?" Araya asked softly.

"For a long time? Nothing." He shrugged, his shoulders sagging.

"We gave them land. Let them practice magic beside us. And for decades, that was enough."

A shadow flitted across his face, his voice turning bitter.

"But humans always want more. They weren't satisfied with the aether they could harness naturally. They started using fae blood and bone to strengthen themselves—until my father banned the use of amplifiers altogether. The Arcanum called it oppression."

Araya swallowed, but the lump in her throat refused to ease. She knew how this story ended. She had heard it told a thousand times before—from the mouths of the victors.

"They'd been gathering influence for years," Loren continued, his gaze going distant. "Waiting. And when they saw their chance, they struck." His jaw tightened. "Did you know they took me right from the Aetherium? I never even left the building. One moment, I was the crown prince. The next, I was a prisoner."

"I didn't," Araya whispered.

"My mother...Queen Lysa. You know she was one of the first to fall." He swallowed hard, his voice thick. "But what the Arcanum wouldn't have taught you is that they didn't want her dead. They wanted to capture her—turn her into a weapon they could wield against my father. But she chose death instead."

Loren stared at his father's statue, his whole body rigid.

"My father felt every second of it. And when she was gone, something inside him died too."

"He...felt it?" Araya glanced at the stern male carved in stone, trying to imagine it.

"They were mates, *ael'sura*." Loren looked at her then, a sad smile tugging at his lips. "Magic binds powerful fae together, joining us with the people the seeds of the relationships we need to survive. To lose your mate in such a way..."

He trailed off, his voice thick with grief.

"They must have loved each other very much," she said softly.

"They did," Loren's voice dropped to a whisper, raw with all the pain he hadn't shown in the past twenty years. "He tried to hold on

—for Eloria, for the fae who escaped. But his control was already fraying. And when he tried to use the shadows to defend against the New Dominion..." Loren exhaled slowly, shaking his head. "No one knows exactly what happened. But shadows covered the battlefield, killing fae and human alike."

"And that's when the Shadowed Veil formed," Araya whispered, the pieces clicking into place.

"Our savior and worst nightmare all in one." Loren's lips quirked in a bitter smile. "His body was never recovered. They tried...but in the end, Eloria moved her court to Lumaria. And I—" his throat bobbed as he swallowed, his voice rough. "I rotted in that cell."

He broke off, his shoulders sagging. In that moment, he looked younger than Araya had ever seen him. He wasn't a prince or a warrior—just a boy, grieving his mother.

"Being his mate killed her," he said. "It's the only reason the Arcanum wanted her. If she hadn't been his, she'd be alive today."

Araya hesitated, the urge to reach for him battling with every instinct to keep her distance. Her sympathy for this lost and broken prince had already cost her enough. But something in the rigid set of his shoulders—like one breath might shatter him completely—pulled her closer despite her best intentions.

She reached out, sparks of magic sizzling at her fingertips as they brushed the back of his hand. Heat blazed at the point of contact, racing up her arm. It curled in her chest, her heart suddenly thundering against her ribs.

"They killed my mother right in front of me," she whispered. "And she wasn't anyone's mate."

His hand closed around hers, their fingers tangling together like he just couldn't stop himself any more than she could.

"I didn't understand that humans could lie," she said, staring down at the intertwined hands. "For a long time, it didn't even feel real—like I was living in someone else's nightmare. So...your grief—however you feel it—it's exactly what it needs to be."

Loren stared at her, his expression raw. "It wasn't your fault, *ael'sura*."

"Neither was what happened to your parents."

Loren's head dipped, the harsh line of his jaw softening. For a heartbeat, he was just another person who had suffered and lost at the hands of the New Dominion, the sharpness in his eyes turning softer, vulnerable.

Before she could second-guess herself, Araya reached out with her other hand, giving into the temptation to run her fingers along the curve of his jaw. His eyes slipped closed, the shadows around his feet stilling like even they were holding their breath.

"Araya," he murmured, her name a soft, reverent whisper that sent a shiver down her spine. He opened his eyes, his gaze rooting her to the spot as he took a half-step closer.

Heat pooled low in her belly, the air between them taut with possibility. His thumb brushed the inside of her wrist, his gaze dropping to her lips. For a dizzy, breathless moment, she thought he might close the distance between them, might lean in and—

"Do you have a mate?"

The question tumbled from her lips before she could stop it, shattering the fragile moment.

"Gods—" Araya stumbled back, pressing a hand over her mouth. "I didn't mean—I'm so sorry. You don't have to answer that."

"No—it's a fair question." Loren took a small step back, like he needed the distance as much as she did. "The answer is just... complicated."

Araya blinked, her heart pounding in her chest. He wasn't angry. He didn't even look upset, just...conflicted.

"I do have a mate," Loren said. He raked a hand through his hair, not quite meeting her eyes. "But she hasn't recognized me. And I haven't told her."

"Oh." Something twisted in her chest, squeezing her heart. "Well —you should tell her. Don't you think she deserves to know?"

Loren laughed humorlessly, the bitter sound scraping from somewhere deep in his chest. "I'm telling her now."

Oh. *Oh.*

Araya swayed where she stood, her vision narrowing around the edges. Loren didn't reach for her, but his shadows crept forward, curling around legs and whispering words she didn't understand.

"I—" her voice shook so badly she had to stop and take a breath. She wanted to say it wasn't possible. That it couldn't be true—but the words wouldn't come. Because somehow, deep in her chest where that strange pull she felt toward him lived—it made sense.

"How long have you known?" she asked instead.

"Since the first time you touched me in my dream." His gaze searched hers, pleading. "That kind of connection isn't given to just anyone, *ael'sura.*"

"But—that was before I even knew you were real." Hurt sliced through her shock, sharp and angry. "Are you saying you knew the *entire time?* And you said *nothing?*"

"It's not that simple." Loren's throat bobbed, his voice shaking. "I'm not the male I thought I would be. Being my mate—look what happened to my mother. If the Shaws or Hale ever figured it out…" He looked at her then, his eyes shining with unshed tears. "In my worst nightmares it's you locked in that cell under the Aetherium, trapped and powerless."

Araya gaped at him, every word lodging somewhere deep in her chest, twisting and tearing at her heart.

"That's why you can't go back to him, *ael'sura,*" Loren said. "I'm sorry. I never wanted to take your choice away from you."

"But you *did* take my choice," she said. "And now what? You tell me I'm your mate and that's it? I just stay here forever because you say so? How is that any different from what Jaxon did?"

"I don't own you," Loren protested, his words tumbling out like they'd been dammed up inside him for weeks. "Yes, I claimed you— but only to get you to safety. I swear, I have no expectations that you'll complete it. Eloria might make an issue of it, but—"

"*Eloria*?" Araya stared at him. "Why would your sister care?"

"She thinks completing the bond will help me control the shadows." Loren glanced away, like he couldn't bear to meet her eyes. "But I don't care. I didn't even want to tell you—"

"You weren't even going to *tell* me?" Araya pressed a hand to her chest, trying to relieve the pressure as heat coiled under her skin. Loren's mouth was moving, answering her. But she couldn't hear him anymore—her world narrowing to the fury boiling in her blood.

Magic rose to meet it, a rising tide of aether that bloomed behind her ribs, splitting her skin—

"Araya—" Loren froze, his shadows rising around him. "Your magic. You have to—"

But his warning came too late.

Sparks leapt from her fingertips, racing up her arms. The floor shuddered under their feet, sending her to her knees as chips of stone rained down on them. Araya pressed her hands to the floor, fighting to ground herself—but the pressure just kept building. Her blood burned in her veins, the wild tang of aether searing her nose as it pressed against her skin.

"You have to control it." Loren's voice cut through the roaring in her ears as he dropped to his knees beside her. "You're going to bring this crypt down right on top of us."

"I—I can't," Araya choked out, the words nearly lost in the rush of power drowning her. "I don't know how."

She could feel it slipping—no, *crashing*—out of her control. Threads of aether lashed like bolts of lightning, sparking against the stone. The world tilted on its axis, that wild, uncontrollable power spiraling closer and closer to the peak where it would rip her and everyone around her to pieces.

Loren hesitated, his eyes flashing. But then, with a muttered curse, he surged forward, closing the distance between them.

"Let me help you," he begged, holding out his hand. "Before you kill us both."

Araya's mind screamed at her to push him away, to refuse his help, but the power still churning inside her didn't leave room for pride or fear. She reached for him, their fingers tangling. Aether roared down the bridge between their bodies, pouring from her like water over a shattered dam. Araya gasped, collapsing against him as relief and agony twisted together in a dizzying spiral. Gods, it felt—

Wrong. It should have felt *wrong.* Her whole life, having her power drained had left her hollow. Weak. Like something vital had been scraped from the core of her being. But *this*—

This felt like the first deep breath after drowning. Like the sun thawing her from the inside out after an endless winter. Heat uncoiled in her chest, settling deep in her belly where it pulsed in time with something ancient and primal.

She shuddered in Loren's arms, caught between the urge to pull away and the dark, undeniable certainty that this was different.

Loren's lips brushed her ear, whispering something she didn't quite catch. She shivered, losing herself in the feel of his hands stroking down her back, the scrape of his nails against her scalp as he combed the sticks and leaves from her hair. The shadows curled around them both, pulsing with the same frantic rhythm as their hearts. Araya didn't know how long she floated there, melting into the warmth of his embrace until she couldn't tell where his power ended and hers began.

By the time she came back to herself, she was curled in his arms, her fists tangled in the fabric of his shirt like she'd been clinging to him for her life.

Araya wrenched herself back, scrambling out of his arms. Loren let her go without protest, even the shadows dropping away to gather at his feet again. He watched, not speaking as she hastily smoothed down her clothes.

"Are you alright?" he asked.

Araya managed a shaky nod, pressing a trembling hand to her chest, trying to steady her racing heart. Gods, she'd nearly killed them both.

"Fine," she croaked. "I'm fine. Thank you. I'll just—"

"You won't do *anything* until you explain what just happened," Loren said, his voice sharp. "Why is your magic surging? Didn't Ilyana give you exercises to do?"

Araya's head snapped up. "Are you having the Healer *spy* on me?"

"That's not what this is about." Loren scowled down at her. "Are you doing the exercises she gave you?"

"She *just* gave them to me this morning," Araya huffed, crossing her arms. "But they aren't going to help. I'm not meant to have this much power. In the New Dominion I had Jaxon to siphon it off me, but here—"

Loren's expression darkened.

"Every drop of that power belongs to you." His fingers closed around her wrist, tugging her forward. Shadows rose around them, creeping up her arm like they wanted to claim her too. "You have exactly as much as you were meant to have. You aren't some vessel to be emptied at his will—"

Araya yanked her arm away, putting two large steps between them.

"Don't," she snapped. "You don't get to act like you know everything about my power. Just because you skimmed some off the top—"

Loren flinched, his shadows recoiling like she'd struck them both.

"That's not—" he stopped, taking a deep breath. "This isn't the same. What Shaw did to you—it wasn't power sharing. It was theft."

"It wasn't," Araya argued. "I agreed to it. I *needed* it."

"Did you?" Loren's gaze sharpened. "Goddess, Araya—do you really believe you had any choice there? What he took from you—what he did—" his jaw tightened, fury written in every line of his face. "It was a violation of everything you are. Every time."

Araya faltered, her retort dying on her tongue.

"I don't need you to believe me, Araya." His voice had lost its edge—he wasn't pushing her anymore. He was begging her to listen. "But please, stop believing him."

Araya took a step back, desperate to break the connection between them. But it just stretched, unspooling between them like a string stretched tight. The *bond*, he'd called it.

"We should—" her voice wavered, and she cleared her throat, forcing the words out. "We should get back. People are probably looking for us—"

"You're right, *ael'sura*." Loren smiled sadly at her. "Let's go home."

CHAPTER
EIGHT

Neither of them spoke as they climbed the stairs. Araya stayed two paces behind him, as if that meager separation would do either of them any good when the bond tugged between them with every step.

He tried to block out her emotions—to give her some semblance of privacy—but it was impossible. Confusion, hurt, fear...they battered through the tether until he couldn't tell where one ended and the next began. The shadows needled at him, demanding he close the distance and pull her into his arms—but Loren clenched his jaw, forcing himself to keep walking.

She hadn't agreed to this connection. She didn't want his comfort.

Not like she'd *agreed* to give her power to Jaxon Shaw. Loren's hands curled into fists, the shadows snapping at his ankles as they fed his own fury back to him. Fae children learned better long before they came into their own power. You never reached for someone's magic without consent. He'd done it once, to save her life. But Shaw had done it to her over and over again, carving pieces out of her until she thought she'd *asked* him to do it.

If he ever hurt her like that—Goddess. He'd hand her the knife and kneel at her feet.

The shadows hissed their protest, crowding close, but he ignored them, forcing his breathing to even out as they finally reached the top of the stairs. There would be time enough for shame once he got her safely back within the warded walls of Ithralis.

The door groaned open under his hand, the temple beyond still shrouded under the ever-present shadows that choked the sky here. He tried not to look too hard, his chest tightening at the decayed ruin it had all become. Another piece of his people's heart, rotting in the dark.

"Do they only come out at night?"

Loren startled, glancing back at Araya. She wasn't looking at him, a frown creasing her forehead as she stared up at the statue of the Absent Goddess.

"That's when they hunt," Loren said. "But under heavy shadow, they can show up at any time."

He nodded toward the gouges raked deep into the stone—as if something had tried to claw the door open to get to them. Araya's face drained of color as her gaze caught on them, the bond flooding with her fear. Good. At least she wouldn't try to run at night again.

By the time they made it back to Ithralis, the sun was high in the sky, a weak, pale disc blurred by haze. Loren kept his gaze straight ahead, ignoring the sharp pang of disappointment that pulsed through the bond as Araya's eyes flicked to the empty docks.

Nyra was long gone—along with Araya's only hope of escape. What would she think if she knew the weatherworker had pushed to slit her throat and leave her in a back alley for Jaxon to find?

"Well," Thorne drawled as they walked into the main hall. "You two look terrible."

Araya flinched, her boots scuffing against the stone, and Loren had to bite back the urge to snap at his oldest friend over his tone. But Thorne's sharp eyes betrayed his concern, lingering on the dirt smeared across Araya's skin, mixed with blood where she'd fallen and scraped her hands. Loren was certain he didn't look any better, but Thorne didn't press them for answers.

"Eloria is looking for you both," he said instead. "She wants you in Lumaria."

"We aren't available." Loren tossed his cloak across the back of a chair, grimacing as the bond tugged in his chest, raw and sore. "Araya needs a proper schedule."

Her head whipped toward him, her silver eyes flashing. "A schedule for what?"

"For training your magic." He met her glare, refusing to look away even as her anger pulsed hot down the bond. "You almost killed us both because you don't know how to use your own power properly. It's dangerous and unacceptable."

"No." She drew herself up to her full height, crossing her arms over her chest. "I won't do it. Who would even teach me?"

"Me." Loren scowled at her. "And it's not up for debate. You're a danger to yourself and everyone around you without control."

Araya flinched back, her hurt booming like a bruise between them. "Sorry to be such a disappointment," she spat. "I guess that's what you get for claiming a mate you never actually wanted. I'd rather eat glass than work with you. I want Thorne to teach me."

The shadows reared back, hissing their displeasure. Their fury lashed at him, demanding he cut down the male she'd chosen over him.

"*Enough.*" Loren's voice cracked through the room like a whip. He glared at Araya, meeting her silver gaze with his own fury. "You're finished here. Go to your room."

Her chin lifted, fresh outrage flooding their connection. For a heartbeat, he thought she might defy him—but then she spun on her heel and stormed toward the stairs.

Loren watched her go. Every step she took clawed at him, her hurt and anger twisting the knife in an already open wound. But he didn't call her back.

"You told her then," Thorne said as her footsteps faded. "How did she take it?"

"Don't be an ass," Loren growled. "The shadows already want to rip you to shreds. Don't give them an excuse."

Thorne's sharp gaze flicked to the darkness writhing at Loren's feet. He wouldn't be able to hear the whispers—the dark, insistent chorus demanding that Loren lose his grip and unleash them on the threat to their bond—but he took a step back anyway.

"You know you can't ignore Eloria," he said. "She's regent. If she wants Araya in Lumaria—"

"She's not going," Loren snapped. "Not unless you want to watch the shadows murder the entire Small Council. The way they talk about her—" he shook his head, sagging against one of the armchairs. "I'll go by myself. I just...need a minute."

"They're that bad, then?"

"It's a constant battle." Loren sighed, scrubbing his hand over his face. "Especially where she's concerned."

"You know, talking might help—"

Loren straightened, shaking his head. "Just...keep an eye on her for me. Please. You're the only one I trust not to try and use her."

"Alright," Thorne said reluctantly. "But—"

"Thank you." Loren turned for the stairs, not giving his friend a chance to finish. The shadows trailed after him like reluctant hounds, their incessant muttering not quite drowning out Thorne's deep, disappointed sigh.

***

"I told you she wouldn't be happy."

Loren pulled his hood up, twitching his cloak to fully cover the shadows. They curled against him, muttering words he couldn't quite make out.

"She never asked for any of this," he continued, lowering his voice as they approached the outskirts of the shantytown that had sprung up outside Lumaria's walls. "You have no excuse for being surprised."

They didn't answer him—not in words. But a cold band of power coiled tight around his chest, squeezing painfully tight against his ribs. *They* hadn't wanted to leave her, howling so frantically in his ears that he'd given in and stopped to check on her before he left, hoping that it would settle them.

She'd been asleep, her face soft and unguarded in the dim light that shone through her window. She hadn't even changed her clothes—as if exhaustion had dragged her into her nest of blankets before she could do more than kick off her boots. He'd stood there too long, battling the urge to reach for her until shame had driven him back into the hall.

"We couldn't ignore Eloria," he said more gently. "Thorne is there with her. She's safe."

The shadows grumbled, but the pressure around his ribs eased slightly.

He wound his way through the camp that crowded the city walls, pretending not to see the hollow-eyed children that peeked out at him from beneath the flaps of sagging tents. It reeked of desperation —the air thick with greasy smoke from guttering cook fires and the stench of rotting refuse. Too many people crammed into too little space, driven from their homes and reduced to beggars.

The sun finally broke through the mist as he neared the city gates, a pale shaft of warmth brushing his face. Eloria had weather workers pushing themselves around the clock to keep the city and the surrounding farmland clear of the choking haze—but even here, no one moved freely after dark.

Too many had disappeared after sunset, claimed by the *zal'vorr* or the darkness itself.

Loren exhaled slowly, rolling the stiffness from his shoulders. He was tired. The kind of tired that sank its claws into you and didn't let go. Last night had been long. Araya's reckless flight, the *zal'vorr*, everything that had happened in the crypt...Goddess save him, she'd almost brought the whole thing down on top of them. And some-how, her answer to everything was to double down on her maddening insistence that she *needed* the man who had drained her and left her for dead on the floor.

Eloria was the last person he wanted to deal with after all that. But she *was* the regent, and he had no intention of taking that power back from her. The part of him that would have made a decent king had died back in his cell twenty years ago.

Loren bowed his head as he slipped through the gates. No one stopped him. With his hood pulled and the shadows tucked away, he was just another refugee, picking his way through the city with his head down and his shoulders hunched.

The streets inside the walls were no less grim than the camp outside. Dozens of fae stood in long lines that wound through the square, clutching dented metal bowls and empty sacks as they waited for their share of grain and root vegetables. Guards kept watch near the wagons, distributing the rations with painstaking precision. Everywhere he looked, Loren was met with hollow cheeks and listless eyes, children who should have run and played through the streets instead clinging silently to their mothers' skirts.

How long before they ran out of food to feed them all? If he'd stayed in Eloria's Small Council meeting he might have known the answer. Instead, all Loren had was the guilt that gnawed at his conscience, the shadows stirring uneasily beneath his cloak as he slunk through the square without notice and mounted the steps to the Central Hall.

Once, this place had been a gathering place for the fae who dedicated themselves to the Goddess, a sanctuary where voices had risen in song and prayer. Now, Eloria held court here, making the decisions that kept their people alive one day after another.

At this hour it should have thrummed with voices—officials and petitioners alike gathered to be heard. Instead, it stood empty, the hush that hung thick in the air all too similar to the oppressive silence he'd lived with beneath the Aetherium. Even the shadows shifted uneasily, pressing against the confines of his cloak.

Loren's frown deepened, but he didn't slow, setting a quick pace toward the chamber where Eloria held her Small Council meetings. Ruling a country was nothing but administrative work—endless meetings and decision-making. If she was anywhere, it would be there.

He was almost to the doors when two guards stepped into his path, blocking his way.

One of them—an older male with the sharp, assessing gaze of someone used to measuring threats—held up a hand. "There is no court today. The Central Hall is closed to visitors."

"I'm not here for court," Loren said. "I'm here to see Eloria."

"We have orders not to let anyone through." The younger guard arched a brow. "If you have a petition, you can present it when the Princess Regent next holds court."

"I don't have a *petition*." Loren ground his teeth, his jaw aching. "She sent for me. Tell her I'm here. She'll want to see me."

The older guard's face didn't flicker. "Our orders are not to disturb her," he said evenly. "Like I said, if you come back when court is in session—"

The shadows stirred beneath his cloak, their hiss curling through his mind. *This is taking too long. She needs us—*

"This can't wait." Loren sucked in a breath, trying to steady them —and himself. "If you just ask her—"

The younger guard cut him off with a sharp laugh, his hand brushing the pommel of his sword as he stepped in close. "You think we're running messages to the Princess Regent from every cloaked vagrant who wanders in? Back off before I—"

Enough.

The shadows surged forward before he could stop them, spilling out from beneath his cloak and spreading across the floor like spilled ink. Both guards reeled back, steel singing as swords cleared scabbards. Aether hummed, the tang of magic flooding the air as they called on their power. But the shadows only laughed, rearing back in preparation to strike—

Loren cursed under his breath and ripped his hood back, baring his face. Better they recognize him than die because he couldn't keep a leash on his own power.

"There's no need for that," he said, the words aimed at the churning darkness as much as the guards themselves. "Just tell the *Princess Regent* that her brother is here to see her."

The younger guard staggered back a full step, his sword clattering to the stone floor. The older one kept hold of his sword—barely—his jaw slackening as his disbelieving gaze slid from the furious shadows to Loren and back again.

"Your Majesty—" he dropped into a hasty bow, his knee striking stone hard enough to make Loren wince. "We didn't know—"

"No one knows," Loren said. "And I'd like to keep it that way. I just need to speak to my sister—now. Please."

The older guard exhaled sharply, straightening. "Of course, Your Majesty." He turned on his heel, striding toward the doors of the Small Council chambers without quite meeting Loren's eyes.

The shadows grumbled amongst themselves, slinking back to curl around his boots like chastised hounds. Loren fell back a step, the breath he'd been holding rushing out in a shaky sigh of relief. No one would die today because of him.

"Stop looking at me like that," he ordered the younger guard. "I'm not what you think I am."

The guard flinched, but didn't drop his gaze, staring at Loren with the wide-eyed amazement people usually reserved for ghosts and legends. It made Loren's skin crawl.

"Forgive me, Your Highness," the younger male said, his voice shaking. "I—I never thought—"

"Eloria is still regent." Loren rolled his shoulders, trying to shake the tension from them. "I'm not the savior you think I am."

"But you—"

"She'll see him," the older guard said, hurrying back. "Apologies, Your Majesty. We didn't know—"

"Thank you," Loren cut in, shoving past them. They didn't stop him this time, instead flattening themselves against the walls as the shadows surged ahead of him, restless and impatient. They wanted this over, eager for him to finish this so they could return to the only thing that mattered to them—*her*.

But any hope that this would be a short visit died the moment he stepped into the room.

It reeked of salt, blood and death—two shrouded bodies stretched out across the scarred table where Eloria had held court just yesterday. His sister stood at the head of the table with her spymaster, her hands clasped behind her back.

"Where is your mate?" she demanded.

The shadows hissed, the bond jumping under his skin at her tone.

"She's at Ithralis." Loren glared at her. "You don't *summon* her, El. Not without an explanation."

For a heartbeat, Loren thought she'd snap back at him. But Eloria's expression only hardened, her dancing green eyes cold. "Remove the shroud for my brother."

Eryn reached forward, even his composed expression strained as he deftly folded back the white linen to reveal the faces and shoulders of two fae females.

"Two fishermen pulled them from the water this morning," Eloria said. "Do they remind you of someone?"

Loren swallowed hard. Both were young and red haired, with pale skin and clipped ears. Even worse, while the first female's ears were old and scarred, the other's were raw and unhealed—as if someone had mutilated her ears right before they killed her.

"It could be a coincidence," he said.

"A coincidence?" Eloria barked out a short, humorless laugh. "Look at this and tell me you still think it's a coincidence." She yanked the shrouds free completely, revealing the full extent of what these females had suffered.

Loren's stomach lurched, bile burning his throat. Fishermen might have pulled them from the water, but they hadn't drowned. Lash marks split their flesh, a rainbow of bruises blooming across their throats, arms, and thighs where the inquisitors had held them down.

And after everything he'd endured, Loren knew with sick certainty they'd still been alive—still screaming for mercy—when the inquisitors burned their message into the soft flesh of their bellies.

RETURN HER

Eloria turned to him, her expression like ice. "Well?"

Loren shook his head. He couldn't speak—couldn't *breathe*. His lungs spasmed in his chest, the racing drumbeat of his heart twining with the shadows' hissed demands for vengeance until he couldn't tell where he ended and they began.

Never, they hissed. *Never. Never. Never—*

Loren grasped the edge of the table so hard the wood creaked under his hands, his knuckles whitening. He sucked in one deep breath. And then another. This was a message—a direct threat against his mate. But he had to breathe. To steady himself before the fury boiling under his skin took shape. Or he wouldn't be able to help her.

"I need a moment with my sister," he said through gritted teeth.

Eryn didn't move. Didn't even blink. He only lifted a brow, flicking his gaze to Eloria—because Loren's orders meant nothing to him. Loren might be the prince, but it was Eloria he answered to.

Loren stared at his little sister, begging her without words to understand. To give him this.

Eloria held his gaze for a long, unreadable moment. Then, finally, she gave a small, deliberate nod.

Eryn inclined his head. "Of course, Your Majesty."

Loren waited until the door shut behind him, listening for his footsteps to fade beyond earshot.

"We're not sending her back," Loren said.

"Of course we aren't," Eloria scoffed.

Some of the tension in Loren's chest eased—but not enough.

"She can't know," he said. "If you let them question her about this—it will push her right back into his arms."

Eloria's gaze cut back to him. "You think she'd still run back to him if she knew what he's capable of?"

"She knows. He's hurt her before. And she was the one who patched me up after he..." Loren looked away, unable to stand the pity that softened her stare. "None of that kept her from trying to go back to him after you ambushed her with that awful dinner."

Eloria stilled.

"She nearly died, Eloria," Loren said, his voice rough. "The *zal'vorr* were herding her into the forest. If I hadn't gotten to her in time..."

"I'm sorry," Eloria murmured. "I—it wasn't my intention to put her in any danger. She's your mate. I wouldn't do that to you."

"I know you wouldn't." Loren exhaled, trying to focus as the shadows hissed in his ears. "I told her about the bond."

Eloria's head snapped up. "And?"

"And she completely lost control of her power." Loren shook his head, clenching his jaw. "She's a danger to herself and everyone around her. Seeing this—" he gestured at the bodies, his stomach twisting. "It would only make it worse."

Eloria bit her lip, staring down at the bodies. "I can try to delay calls for her to be questioned, but..." she trailed off, shaking her head. "I won't be able to protect her from them indefinitely, Loren. You need to *fix* this."

Loren bristled, the shadows snapping at the command.

"I'll help her learn to use her power, but I won't use that to manipulate her into accepting a bond with me," he snapped. "It's *wrong*, Eloria. Mate bonds are sacred. They should be freely given—"

"We've all had to do things we don't like in the past twenty years, Loren." She leaned forward, gathering the shroud in her hands and spreading it gently over the bodies. "How many pyres do we have to light before you stop wallowing in guilt and start trying to fix this?"

CHAPTER
NINE

He had locked her in again.

Araya twisted the door handle, more out of irritation than hope, rattling it for good measure. But the door stayed firmly closed.

She sighed, rubbing the sleep from her eyes. She must have slept for hours, not even bothering to strip off her filthy clothes before collapsing onto the bed. But her limbs still felt leaden, every movement a painful reminder of her failed escape.

Her stomach twisted with a low, hollow growl, reminding her that she'd missed lunch. Without being able to leave her room, she'd just have to wait until someone brought her a tray. But at least her prison cell came with an attached bathing chamber.

Araya turned the taps, watching the water rise before sketching *inar* in the soap residue left on the edge of the tub. She laid her hand over it, breathing a sigh of relief as her power answered her command, aether blooming under her fingertips and sending curling tendrils of steam into the air.

She stripped off her dirty clothes, grimacing as she peeled them away from her skin. The once fine fabric was stiff with sweat and mud and gods only knew what else she'd dragged herself through last night. She let them fall in a heap, sinking into the gently steaming water with a deep sigh.

For a long time, she just sat there, letting the steam fog the room and the hot water loosen muscles she hadn't even known could get tight. She closed her eyes, tipping her head back and letting her mind drift. She didn't want to think right now. Not about Loren, or Jaxon. Or how she was trapped here with no way out.

She stayed like that until something nudged at the edge of her awareness.

Araya cracked one eye open.

One of Loren's shadows perched on the rim of the tub, its wisp-like tail shifting in slow, serpentine undulations as it watched her.

"*You,*" she hissed. "What are you doing here? Did *he* leave you?"

It just flickered, its form shifting and changing as it considered her.

"I know you can talk," Araya snapped. "I've heard you talk to Loren—*I* spoke to you at the Shadowed Veil. So what do you want?"

It cocked its head—or what she assumed was its head—rearing up slightly. But it still didn't speak.

Araya scowled, scrubbing the bar of soap over her skin. Dozens of tiny scrapes she hadn't noticed stung under the thick lather, an unwelcome reminder of that terrible, frantic flight through the woods.

Loren and his shadows had saved her life.

But he was still a bastard for locking her in this room again.

Araya reached for the pitcher beside the tub, pouring the cooling water over her hair until she finally worked the last of the sticks and snarls from it. Finally feeling more like herself, she leaned back, letting her eyes drift closed again—until a sudden, uncomfortable thought jolted her fully awake.

Loren's shadows moved with him. He could speak to them—command them.

Could he *see* through them?

She crossed her arms across her chest, glaring at the little shadow. "Turn around."

It ignored her.

Her cheeks burning, Araya snatched the towel from the stool, splashing water out of the tub in her haste. She dried herself in quick, brisk strokes before shoving her arms into her robe and knotting it tightly around her waist.

It followed her into the main room, its cool tendrils coiling around her bare ankles, clinging for a moment too long before releasing her with a slow, reluctant slide. It pooled in front of the fire, its form expanding as it stretched out, staking its claim on the warm stone. It almost reminded her of Loren, with its sinuous grace and the dangerous power humming underneath its silence.

Idiot, she scolded herself, yanking a brush through her hair. *He locked you in this room.*

She stormed over to the desk, yanking open the drawer and staring down at the list she'd started yesterday. She'd been focused on escaping and getting back to Jaxon—but now she had other challenges she couldn't ignore.

Mainly, this bond with Loren. He was right about one thing—it *was* a problem. If everything he'd said about it was true, even Jaxon wouldn't be able to stop the Arcanum from using her as a tool to hurt Loren. Honestly, after the way they'd left things, she wasn't sure Jaxon would even try.

Araya pressed her palm against her sternum, feeling the faint pull of the bond under her skin. There was no way she could hide it from Jaxon—not now. It would have to be dealt with before she went back.

But first, she had to find a way to convince the fae to let her go.

Araya sank into the chair, dragging a fresh sheet of parchment toward her and picking up the quill. There had to be something she could trade for her freedom. Everyone wanted something— and the fae were no exception. She just had to figure out what it was.

HOURS LATER, THE ONLY CONCLUSION ARAYA HAD ARRIVED AT WAS THAT SHE didn't know nearly enough.

She stared down at the parchment, the ink smudged in places where she'd tapped the quill against the page in thought. She'd written down everything she could remember—everything that had happened at the Shadowed Veil, everything she had overheard, everything she had felt in the moments before the darkness had relented. But she'd found few answers, and far too many questions.

Her frustration bled into the sharp angles of her handwriting, her knuckles whitening around the quill as she glared at where she'd scrawled *MATES?* across the parchment in uneven strokes, the question mark heavy with disbelief.

It made no sense—but somehow, she believed it. There was no other explanation for why the amulet she'd made to test their theory had only started to work when Loren's blood mixed with hers. It didn't follow any rules of magic she knew, but there was no denying the reality of it.

The shadow flicked its tail, curling loosely around her wrist. Araya shook it off, gently disentangling the amorphous creature from its perch and setting it back on the desk. It withdrew its tendrils, managing to look impressively affronted expression for a creature without form or face.

She smiled at it, charmed despite herself. It was hard to believe that *this* was the same magic that had been willing to kill them all just to destroy Loren. This thing might be a spy, but it was almost...cute. She flicked a scrap piece of parchment off the desk, watching the little shadow race after it. It pounced, its wisp-like tail curling and twitching—for all the world like a strange, ephemeral cat.

But the force that had spoken to her on the Shadowed Sea had been...terrifying. She had no doubt that Jaxon *had* known or at least suspected the fae were sheltering behind it. That's why the New

Dominion was so interested in finding a way to dispel it—so they could crush the last of the resistance.

Resistance—the very idea still felt alien to her. But that's what it was, wasn't it? How many fae had Serafina smuggled out of the New Dominion while Araya remained blissfully unaware? All this time, her best friend had been working with the fae, and she'd had no idea.

Araya sucked in a deep breath, glancing back down at her notes without seeing them. Maybe the Shadowed Veil *did* protect the fae from the New Dominion, but it had also trapped them under a blanket of near-constant darkness. Starving them and creating monsters like the *zal'vorr*.

Everything she knew and every theory she'd come up with suggested that Loren should have been able to call it to heel now that he was free...but he hadn't. Because he couldn't—not unless she accepted this bond with him.

The thought left her cold. Jaxon had been obsessed with her before, but if he learned she shared a magical, fated connection with the lost fae prince? Gods, she wasn't certain if he'd be jealous or ecstatic. But one thing was certain—any freedom she'd enjoyed would be gone in a heartbeat.

And the fae were no better. Loren might spin a pretty story about how he didn't expect her to complete any sort of magical bond with him, but he'd locked her in here again without even making sure someone came to bring her a tray of food. And Araya had no illusions about Eloria's intentions. The fae regent didn't seem like the kind of leader who would allow the key to her people's survival to just... refuse. Not without some sort of alternative.

Araya straightened, sucking in a sharp breath. *That* was what she could offer them. An alternative way to control of the shadows. She'd done it for Jaxon on a small scale—with Loren's blood and her own, she had no doubt she could do it for Eloria.

If she could give them that...they would *have* to accept her terms. Control of the shadows in exchange for her freedom. Of course, that still left the problem of this mate bond—Araya had no desire to be a high-value game piece in this conflict. But if the years she'd spent working with Jaxon had taught her anything, it was that any curse could be broken.

A sharp knock jolted her from her thoughts, sending the little shadow scurrying. It raced across the room, scrambling up her side to crouch on her shoulders. Araya caught her breath, pressing a hand to her chest as that strange thread hooked under her ribcage snapped tight, leaving her with no question as to who stood outside her room.

Araya swept her notes into the drawer, slamming it closed. She capped the inkwell, glaring at the door as he knocked again, harder this time.

"You'll have to find my jailor if you want to come in," she called out. "You see, I don't have a key. Or any say over where I go or who I see—"

A key scraped in the lock, magic flaring along the doorframe as it swung open.

"You tried to run," Loren growled. "What did you expect—" His gaze snagged on the shadow perched at her shoulder. "What is that?"

"Your spy?" Araya glanced down at where the little shadow had wrapped itself around her shoulders like a scarf. "Do you really think I'm going believe you didn't leave it here?"

"I *didn't*," Loren snapped. But even as the words left his mouth, the shadows behind him hissed, their sharp, sibilant whispers prickling across the back of her neck. They were speaking to him—just like the Shadowed Veil had spoken to them. She couldn't understand this time, the flowing cadence of Valenya lost to her, but Loren's face darkened. Whatever they were saying to him, it wasn't what he wanted to hear.

"It's not a spy." Loren's jaw worked, his green eyes narrowing as he stared at his wayward shadow. "It decided to stay on its own. To protect you." He winced as the shadows hissed again, snapping at his heels. "Because I didn't."

"They really don't listen to you at all, do they?" Araya tilted her head, considering the mass of darkness.

She hadn't meant it to be cruel — but Loren flinched like she'd driven a blade between his ribs, his mouth flattening to a thin, hard line.

"Not where you're concerned," he said. "Now get dressed. You have to work on getting control of your power—"

"No." Araya crossed her arms. "Did you know I've been locked in here all day with no food or explanation?"

A muscle in his cheek ticked, guilt flashing across his face.

"I'm sorry," he said. "I didn't tell Veria you were in here. I didn't think—"

"You're right," Araya cut in. "You didn't *think*. You just locked me in here and *forgot about me*." Power heated her blood, pressing against her skin, but she shoved it back down. "Out of sight, out of mind, right? Now get out."

"I can't. You nearly brought the crypt down on top of us," Loren said tightly. "If you had any more power right now, you'd be doing the same thing here. You don't have to forgive me, but you do need to learn control, Araya. For your own safety."

"That's not your decision," Araya shot back. "I'm not your subject or your student. My training is none of your business."

Loren's eyes flashed. "You're my mate."

"I'm your *prisoner*." Araya let out a bitter laugh. "Would you really have locked your *mate* up and forgotten to feed her? What's next? You coerce me into completing this bond and take my power for your own? Because that sounds very familiar—"

"I would never." Loren took a step forward, his shadows bleeding into the room and flickering up the walls in restless, lashing shapes. "I don't care what Eloria wants or says. I swear it to you here and now, I will *never* coerce or force you to bond with me."

"I still don't want to train with you." Araya set her jaw, trying to ignore the way her magic thrummed under her skin, pulling toward him. That was the bond—heat pricking at her fingertips even as she curled her hands into fists, trying to smother it.

But he saw anyway.

"And what are you going to do the next time you lose control?" he demanded, taking another step. "What if I'm not there to help you?"

"I can monitor my own power levels." Araya fell back a step, refusing to acknowledge how her power *sang* as Loren invaded her space. "I can burn it off before it gets to be too much—"

"It's already too much," Loren said, his voice as rough as hers. "You have *no idea* how powerful you are, Araya. What you're proposing—it could kill you or someone else. I know that's not what you want, *ael'sura*."

Araya closed her eyes, begging her power to settle in her blood. It bucked against her control aching to reach for the infuriating male who had dared lay claim to her—but finally ebbed. For now.

He was right. She had to survive here long enough to make it back to the New Dominion. And she didn't want to hurt anyone. But if she was going to give in she would claw something out of it for herself.

"If I agree to this I want something in return," she said.

Loren's eyes narrowed. "What?"

"Access to your archives," she said. "Everything you have on mate bonds, the shadows and their relation to the royal bloodline—and all the records of your father's death."

"And what exactly do you plan to do with that information?"

"Research." Araya lifted her chin, forcing herself to hold his gaze. "If you expect me to stay here and confront this *bond*—I want to understand it. You and Eloria have both manipulated me, misrepresented it. Books won't do that to me."

Across from her, Loren looked...stricken. The strange connection between them stretched tight, heavy with something she didn't understand. Even his shadows fell still, curling tight around his boots.

"That shouldn't be a problem," he said finally, his voice low and rough. "Do you know where the library is?"

Araya hesitated. Thorne had breezed by the door during his tour, waving it off as the royal family's personal collection. She'd been curious, of course, but she knew where she wasn't welcome.

"I can find it," she said.

"Tomorrow then." Loren inclined his head, stiff and formal. "Sleep well, *ael'sura*."

CHAPTER
TEN

LOREN PACED BETWEEN THE LONG TABLES, HIS FOOTFALLS SILENT ON THE polished stone. The library hadn't changed in twenty-five years, the ancient enchantments woven into its foundations allowing it to endure when everything else had crumbled to shadow and ruin. No dust, no damp—only the familiar perfume of ink and leather, and rows upon rows of towering shelves groaning beneath the weight of thousands of books.

The full history of the fae—boiled down to words on parchment.

He'd spent hours here as a child, pouring himself into his studies in an eager effort to earn his father's praise. It had been his sanctuary, a place to prepare himself to wear the crown he'd been chosen for.

As he'd grown, he'd dreamed of bringing his mate here. Of showing her the quiet alcove where he liked to curl up and read, to share the knowledge he'd grown up with at his fingertips.

But not like this. Not when she'd negotiated access like she didn't believe he'd share everything he had with her freely. Not when she didn't trust him to tell her the truth.

It's your fault. The shadows snapped at his heels. *You locked her up.*

Loren dragged a hand over his face. He *had* locked her up. Because the moment she'd had the chance, she'd tried to run. Because she'd lost control of her power. Because she'd nearly *died*. She'd agreed to meet him last night, but now...he glanced over at the table, where the tea service he'd asked Veria to bring sat untouched, the pot gone long cold despite the magic meant to keep it warm.

What if she'd changed her mind? What if she didn't come?

Their shadows laughed, their mad whispers breaking into a hundred jagged pieces, scraping over him like knives.

"Enough," Loren growled, slamming his hand down on the edge of the table, topping a few of the aged scrolls from their neat stacks.

To his shock, they obeyed—skittering up the walls like dark ivy to flicker and shift just beyond the reach of the weak sunlight that filtered through the high windows.

She had done that. Even now, her magic pulsed through him, twining with his own in a way that felt so *right* that Loren feared he might never feel whole without it again.

He threw himself down in one of the padded chairs, dragging a hand through his shorn hair. Cutting it had been the only way salvage what remained, the rest of it too matted and tangled for even magic to repair after twenty-five years spent rotting in his own filth. Loren stared down at his wrists, his gaze catching on the other lingering reminder of his captivity. The scars from the manacles had finally closed over and flattened, some of the lurid color fading—but he doubted they'd ever vanish completely. There was only so much magic could heal.

He turned his arm, tugging back his sleeve to study the shadow-mark that still twisted up his forearm. *That* scar was as dark and vivid as the day he'd gotten it. Both Ilyana and Thorne had looked at it, but there was nothing that would heal it but time. A cold numbness radiated from the writhing marks that twisted under his skin, a chill reminder of what he could expect when *dara'el* finally tired of waiting for him to be the prince it wanted and decided to wipe the slate clean after all.

"Does it still hurt?"

Loren startled, his heart leaping in his chest as he shot to his feet.

Araya stood just inside the doorway, one hand braced lightly on the frame as if she wasn't sure whether to fully step into the room or run as fast as she could in the opposite direction. She'd dressed plainly, her hair pulled back into her customary braid, a few stubborn wisps curling around her face. The shadow that had refused to leave her and rejoin the many curled around her ankles, watching him as carefully as she did.

"Not really," he managed, his voice hoarse. "It's mostly numb."

Araya nodded, still hovering uncertainly in the doorway. "You didn't say when to meet you."

She was right, he realized. He hadn't given her a time.

Loren blew out a slow breath, gesturing her inside. "No harm done, *ael'sura*," he said. "We might as well set the terms of our agreement now."

She stepped inside, just far enough for the door to close behind her. Her silver eyes widened, tracing over the towering shelves as the shadows danced far above them both.

"Ithralis is where the heir to the fae throne comes to learn about the shadows and their duty." Loren cleared his throat, clasping his hands behind his back. "Because of that, this library holds the most complete record of *dara'el* in existence. If the answers you're looking for can be found...they'll be here."

He paused, but Araya said nothing. She didn't even look at him, her eyes fixed on the books like she'd never seen anything like this.

"For every morning of research," Loren continued, frowning as she took another step closer, her hand hovering over the spines of the books like she didn't quite dare to touch them. "You will give me an afternoon of training your magic. I'll meet you here every morning."

"You're...going to help me?" Her brow furrowed, the prickly edge of her suspicion softened with genuine confusion.

"Of course." Loren's heart ached in his chest. "You might not trust me, but I have no desire to be your jailor. And—" a wry smile tugged at his mouth despite the seriousness of the moment "—like you so passionately pointed out—you don't speak the language, do you?"

"These are *all* in Valenya?" Araya's head whipped toward him, her suspicion eclipsed by wide-eyed wonder. "And they *all* belong to *you?*"

"Well—they belong to the crown." Loren stared at her, his eyebrows drawing together when she stood frozen in place, not reaching out to take any of the books despite the aching curiosity he could feel through their bond. "You *can* touch them, you know."

"Amazing," she breathed, the word so soft Loren doubted it had been meant for him. He fell into step behind her, frowning as she ran her fingers along the edge of the nearest shelf, making no move to take even a single one from its place.

"Surely, you've seen the library at the Aetherium," he said. Even if the Arcanum had removed every book written in Valenya from its shelves, that library would still dwarf this one.

"Oh, part-fae aren't allowed in the main library." Araya tipped her head back, staring up at the skylight far above them. Mist pressed against the glass, turning the faint sunlight that made it through cold and silver.

Loren stopped in his tracks, his stomach twisting at her casual admission. As if that was *normal.* "Didn't you have special privileges?"

"I did. I do." She hooked a thumb around the necklace she always wore, flashing the gold and black symbol of the Arcanum at him. "They would bring me the books I requested once Jaxon signed off on them, I never actually got to go *in.*"

Loren's throat tightened. His fingers twitched, the irrational urge to tear that amulet from her neck nearly overtaking him. The thought of her having to wear their mark around her throat just to access *books*—

His fury must have shown on his face because Araya closed her fist around the cursed thing, hunching her shoulders as he took a step closer.

"You don't have to wear that here." Loren reached out, finding gentleness somewhere as he brushed his fingers over her clenched fist. "You are welcome to any book in this library. There is no knowledge here that is off-limits to you."

Araya's breath caught, her surprise flickering through the bond. Some of the tension drained from her shoulders, and her fist loosened, the amulet falling back against her chest.

"Thank you," she murmured.

"You don't have to thank me for that," Loren said shortly. "It's how it should have been the entire time, *ael'sura*."

She blinked up at him, her brow furrowing. "You keep calling me that. Will you finally tell me what it means?"

Loren's heart stuttered. When had he gotten so close to her? His hand hovered a breath away from curling around her waist, her face turned to his. The scent of wildflowers and rain-soaked earth filled his nose, finally free of the heavily-perfumed soaps humans favored.

He drew in a slow breath, willing his heartbeat to slow. Goddess help him, even the shadows strained toward her, restless and wanting. They pulled at his self control, begging him to close the half-step between them.

"It's what I called you before I knew your name," he said at last. "The direct translation is *my life*, but colloquially it's closer to *my hope*."

Araya's eyes widened, the bright flicker of her surprise rippling through the bond. But she didn't look away.

"Why would you call me that?" she breathed.

"Because, *ael'sura*—" Loren smiled down at her, his heart twisting painfully. "I'd long since given up hope in that dungeon. I didn't believe I had any future left that wasn't full of pain and darkness. But then—" he gave into temptation, tracing the damp edge of her braid with his fingers "—you started appearing in my dreams, and for the first time in twenty years...I wanted to live."

Araya stepped back, a pink flush darkening her cheeks all the way to the jagged tips of her ears. Loren let his hand drop, the echo of her tension humming under his skin.

"You said your mother was fae and your father was half-fae." He tucked his hands behind his back so he didn't reach for her again, willing his voice to stay steady. "Did you ever speak Valenya?"

"I—Yes. At one point." She frowned. "But I was very young."

"Would you like to see if you can remember?"

He knew it was a mistake the instant her face lit up. His resolve to keep his distance crumbled, the myriad of reasons why getting closer would only break both their hearts paling against the brightness of her smile.

"I'd like that," Araya said. And—Goddess help him—Loren smiled back.

CHAPTER
ELEVEN

THEY SETTLED INTO A RHYTHM AFTER THAT. EVERY MORNING, LOREN WAS already waiting for her when she arrived, some book or scroll laid out before him and a cup of steaming tea at his elbow. She'd been horrified at first—until he'd shown her how the pages had been enchanted to repel moisture, protecting them from the ever-present damp and spilled tea cups.

Hours stretched into days, quickly becoming weeks at that oak table, his shadows draped lazily over the surrounding tables and chairs. He might spend a whole morning patiently helping her translate the texts she wanted, offering quiet instruction on Valenya as they went.

"You're picking it up quickly," Loren said, watching her from across the table.

"I've had worse teachers." Araya buried her nose in the journal he'd given her to read to hide the way her cheeks flushed at his praise. It felt too easy, too natural to sit across from him like this. And while her logical mind knew it was the bond—pulling her toward him and blurring lines she couldn't afford to lose sight of—her heart struggled to remember that he was her captor, not her friend.

"Here," he said, turning the scroll he'd been perusing toward her. "This word—it's one of the roots we talked about yesterday."

Araya leaned forward, shoving the loose waves of her hair over her shoulders for what felt like the hundredth time. She didn't know what had possessed her to leave it loose this morning. It was so impractical—always getting in her face and catching between her back and the chair.

"*Dara*," she murmured, feeling the shape of the word with her lips. "That means fear, right?"

"Dread," Loren corrected. "That's why we call the shadows *dara'el*—the dread."

"Because they're not actually shadows, right?" Araya frowned down at the scroll. "That would be *noct'el*."

"Correct." Loren nodded, his gaze drifting over the delicate, faded script. "*Dara'el* might appear as shadows, but it's not just simple darkness. It's pure power. A gift from the Goddess herself."

Araya traced the word again, stealing another glance at him. He stared down at the parchment, the ever-present dark circles under his eyes worse than they'd been even a week ago. Did he have nightmares too? Or was it something else that kept him awake at night?

"I thought they were going to kill you," she said softly. "On the boat."

"They were." Loren tugged at his sleeve, rubbing at the dark mark it hid without seeming to realize what he was doing. "Until you talked them out of it. Which was foolish, by the way." He frowned at her, the furrow between his eyebrows deepening. "You had no idea they wouldn't just kill you too."

"We all would have died if they'd sunk the boat." Araya shrugged. "And I didn't think it was fair that they were judging you so harshly."

"That's their job." His lips twisted into a bitter smile. "The Goddess gave *dara'el* to the fae to mark those worthy of leading in her absence. The strongest, the most capable—the fae who were most suited to guide and protect her people until her return. A job I'm clearly failing at."

Araya frowned, something about the way he said it settling wrong in her chest. "I don't think you give yourself enough credit," she said. "You endured twenty-five years of torture without ever once giving the Arcanum what they wanted."

"And yet, the shadows don't obey me." He waved a hand at the shadows spread out across the room. "They react. Sometimes, our goals align...but when they don't?" He shook his head, his jaw tight. "I thought they were going to attack you in the dining room. I live in constant fear of losing control and hurting someone I love."

Araya's stomach twisted, the accusation he didn't speak gnawing at her. "And that's my fault, isn't it? Because I don't want to complete the bond?"

Loren's head snapped up, his eyes flashing.

"No—" he leaned forward, like he might reach for her but thought better of it at the last moment. "Bonded pairs are typically more powerful—but it's *not* your fault, *ael'sura*. The shadows are mine to control—or to fail at. That's on me, not you."

Araya flushed, her gaze fixed on the journal open in front of her without seeing it. Maybe *he* believed that, but she had a feeling his sister would have disagreed.

"We've been at this for hours." Loren snapped his book closed, shoving back from the table. "It's time for lunch."

Lunch. Araya almost groaned. She glanced down at the open journal in front of her, the delicate script still only half-translated. Lunch meant the end of their quiet hours here. After they ate, Loren would force her to abide by her end of their bargain, spending the afternoon letting him help her *train* her magic.

Araya pushed to her feet, grimacing. "Let's get it over with, then."

"All you have to do is extinguish the flame."

"Without touching it, using runes, or any sort of focusing assistance," Araya retorted, glaring at the candle that flickered between them.

"Yes." Loren didn't so much as blink at her irritation, his voice even. As if they hadn't been doing this for *weeks* without success. What had he told her the first time? That this exercise was *so easy a child could do it.*

She shifted where she sat, running her fingers over the cool stone floor of the training room. Racks of weapons she would never have been allowed to touch in the New Dominion lined the walls, crowded in beside battered practice dummies and simple targets. But there was no chalk, no place for her to trace any runes to guide and shape her power. Leaving her with nothing but Loren and his inflexible instructions.

Right on cue, he spoke again. "You should be able to feel it—"

"I can feel it fine," Araya snapped.

She reached inward, finding that internal well of aether easily. That wasn't her problem—the power was there, waiting for her to shape it. But instead of molding it into something useful, she did what Loren insisted on and just...opened herself to it.

And—nothing. The flame didn't even flicker.

Loren sat back on his heels, watching her. "Try again."

Araya gritted her teeth, biting back a sharp retort. Why was she even bothering with this? Why was *he*? It never worked. Still, she'd promised to try. So Araya sucked in a deep breath, letting her mind drift.

"You're holding on too tightly," Loren said finally when the candle continued to burn.

"I'm *not*." Araya glowered at him. Her power fizzed in her veins, more interested in the male sitting across from her than doing anything for her. "This is pointless. It's not how my magic works."

"You've done it before," Loren insisted. "In my cell when I broke my chains—you used your magic instinctively to keep me from hurting Shaw. The problem is how you learned to use your magic, limiting your potential to what humans deemed acceptable. If you just relaxed—"

Araya's patience snapped. She had spent years fighting for even a *chance* at learning to use her power. And then she'd spent even more time honing her control and precision to make her into something useful to the New Dominion so she could *keep* that power.

She swept her fingers across the stone, tracing the familiar contours of *zephra*, a rune she had used a thousand times for far more complicated work than this ridiculous exercise. Without an anchor, the power she threw amounted to nothing but a puff of air— but it was more than enough to blow out that damned candle.

Araya whipped her gaze to Loren, not bothering to hide her triumphant grin. *That* was how magic was supposed to work.

"Really?" Loren glared at her, his green eyes blazing with fury. The shadows shifted around him, echoing his anger. "You didn't even try."

"I *did* try." She climbed to her feet, brushing her skirts back into order. "And I succeeded—my own way. You're the one insisting on a solution that isn't possible."

Loren's jaw flexed, his expression cooling into something far more dangerous than open anger. He climbed to his own feet, the hair on the back of her neck prickling as he stepped forward, invading her space.

"This isn't a game, *ael'sura*." He took another step forward, his shadows sweeping forward to surround them both in shifting darkness. "Do you not understand? Forget the power that could kill you if you don't figure out how to coexist with it. Anyone here can compel you with the name you give out so freely, and you can't do anything to stop them."

Araya faltered, falling back a step as Loren plucked a dagger from one of the racks, offering it to her hilt first. "What am I supposed to do with that?"

"Take the dagger, Araya."

Araya gasped as his magic washed over her, his order crawling under her skin and digging its claws into her will. Her fingers closed around the hilt of the dagger, her muscles twitching as the compulsion burned in her blood.

"Stop," she gasped. "This isn't what I agreed to—"

"You don't feel like this is helping?" Loren's shadows ran over her, cool as silk against her overheated skin. "It's helping me feel like I was right."

"Loren—" her voice cracked, caught between a warning and a plea.

"Put the knife to your throat, Araya."

Araya choked, her lungs seizing as her hand moved of its own accord. The edge of the dagger pressed into the fragile skin at the hollow of her throat, the world narrowing to the sting of cold steel against her pulse point.

"Any fae here can do this to you," Loren murmured. He stepped in close, his voice curling like smoke against her ear. "You don't have the discipline to fight off a child. Anyone could make you kneel, strip —even slit your own throat."

"Stop it." Araya's voice shook, the word breaking on a sob. Hot tears blurred her vision, sliding down her cheeks. But she didn't dare move. Not with the dagger pressed against her throat.

Loren's gaze shifted, something unreadable flickering across his expression. He lifted his hand, his thumb brushing across her cheek. Heat sparked at the contact, magic surging beneath her skin as the bond snapped tight in her chest. It didn't care that he was forcing her to hold a knife to her own throat. That she was helpless, captive to his will. It *wanted* him—stretching forward with the desperation of a vine searching for light even as her mind screamed *no*.

Loren went impossibly still, his nostrils flaring as the air between them crackled with power. His eyes dropped, her pulse leaping treacherously as his gaze lingered on her lips. He leaned toward her, his mouth opening—and then it wasn't Loren standing there at all.

It was Jaxon. Jaxon's shadow falling over her. His hand crushing her wrist. His magic scraping across her skin like a thousand iron-tipped needles—

Her hands shook, the dagger trembling dangerously at her throat. The room blurred, the edges of her vision darkening. She could *smell* him, the cloying vanilla perfume of his soap clogging her lungs as she choked, struggling to pull in enough air.

The dagger slipped from her hand, clattering against the stone. But all she could hear was Jaxon's voice whispering in her ear, reminding her that her place was on the floor at his feet—

"Araya—" Loren started, a thread of panic in his voice as he reached for her.

"Stop!" Araya planted both hands against Loren's chest, shoving hard. "*Stop*—don't touch me—"

Her voice broke on a sob, her blood rushing in her ears like roaring waves, drowning out Loren's voice until all she could hear was Jaxon whispering her name. She staggered back, folding in on herself as her spine hit the wall. She couldn't stop the tears, every breath catching sharp in her throat as she cowered against the stone, gasping.

Loren froze, the concern on his face collapsing into something stark and horrified. He took a half-step forward, then stopped again. Even his shadows wavered, curling close around his boots like they didn't know whether to shield her or him.

"*Ael'sura*—"

"Well," a smooth, unhurried voice drawled from the doorway. "I can see why you've kept her tucked away, Your Majesty. Everything certainly does make a little more sense now."

Loren's shoulders snapped back, every line of him hardening as his shadows surged to life, rounding on the intruder with lethal intent. "How did you get in here?"

"That's my job, Your Majesty." The stranger leaned against the doorframe, watching them with a small smile that didn't quite reach his dark eyes. "I'd make a pretty poor spymaster if I couldn't sneak into an unguarded castle, wouldn't I? Now—" his gaze raked over her, freezing Araya's sobs in her chest. "There's nothing of greater interest to me right now than a formal introduction to Jaxon Shaw's bond."

The shadows around Loren hissed, but Araya couldn't pick out what they said over Loren's snarl. "Do *not*."

"Touchy." The male clicked his tongue, shaking his head. But his eyes didn't leave Araya's, holding her rooted to the spot. "You might not know this, dear, but mated males can be very...territorial."

The male hit the wall so hard the aetherlamps rattled in their sconces. Araya flinched back, her heart in her throat as the shadows dragged the stranger up the wall, his chuckle cutting off in a pained wheeze. But it wasn't until Loren's hands wrapped around his throat that his gaze finally left hers.

Araya gasped in a breath, her body acting before her mind caught up. One moment she was frozen—then she was shoving past Loren. She lurched through the door, the pounding of her boots on the stone floor ringing louder in her ears than her own ragged breaths. She couldn't get enough air, her throat closing tight as fresh tears blurred her vision.

She turned a corner too fast and slammed into something solid. Someone caught her before she fell, hands steadying her with firm pressure at her shoulders.

"Araya?" Thorne's eyes searched her face, taking in her blotchy cheeks and wild eyes. "Are you hurt?"

"Loren—there was a knife—he made me—" Araya shuddered, her throat bobbing as the words tangled in her throat. "Someone—someone came in. Loren—I think Loren is going to kill him."

Thorne's expression hardened, though his grip on her arms eased. "Everything is going to be fine," he said firmly. "You're safe. Now go—lock yourself in your room." His tone left no room for argument. "I'll deal with Loren."

Araya nodded. She stumbled past him, racing for the one place here where she could shut the door and hide.

CHAPTER

TWELVE

"You have ten seconds to start explaining yourself before I let these shadows rip you apart," Loren growled.

"I would," Eryn rasped, "But you seem rather intent on strangling me. If you could just—"

Loren snarled, shoving the other male back against the wall. Eryn coughed, clearing his throat and rolling his shoulders as he brushed his clothing back into place.

"For a politician, you're rather easy to provoke," Eloria's spymaster said lightly, his lips curling into something closer to a sneer than a true smile. "Not the best trait in a ruler. If you're not careful, people will start to say you're unstable. I wonder what they would think if they knew you ordered your mate to put a knife to her own throat—"

"Why are you here?" Loren demanded.

"Officially?" Eryn smoothed down his shirt. "I came to deliver a message." His dark eyes flicked up, sharp as steel. "They want your mate presented. Immediately."

"No," Loren growled. The shadows shifted around him, their muttering voices echoing his refusal.

"There have been more bodies," Eryn continued, ignoring him. "More messages, carved into the flesh of fae females with red hair and clipped ears. The Small Council wants answers—and they expect her to provide them. Your protests, while noted, are not enough to shield her anymore."

Loren clenched his teeth. "Tell them to talk to Eloria. She's the regent."

"Of course. And yet—I'm here." Eryn's lips quirked into a humorless smile. "Do you think that's an accident, Your Majesty? More than a few of her advisors are concerned that our beloved Princess Regent is allowing her affection for her long lost brother to cloud her normally impeccable judgement."

Loren bared his teeth, the shadows churning around his feet. But Eryn stepped forward anyway, ignoring the warning.

"And maybe," he continued, his voice dropping to a murmur. "Maybe her long-lost brother is letting his attachment to his mate cloud his. Not that I don't understand your concerns. If it would make things easier, I could speak with her here. Give her a chance to explain herself before things get unpleasant—"

The shadows erupted, flooding the chamber in a torrent of cold and dark. They lashed the walls, rattling the sconces as they spread across the walls. They wrapped around Eryn's arms, his legs, his throat. They pinned him to the wall, a thousand voices clamoring for blood as Loren's hands wrapped around Eryn's throat.

"Nothing he's doing is her fault," Loren hissed. He watched as Eryn's face darkened, turning from red to purple. "And I won't let a small, insignificant worm like you make her believe it is—"

"Loren!" Thorne's familiar voice cut through the roaring in his ears. "Stand down, Loren. You can't kill Eloria's spymaster."

Loren's fingers flexed tighter, something cracking under his grip. He *could* kill Eryn. He knew it and the shadows knew it—just one more squeeze and Eryn's poisonous words would never reach her ears. No one on this island could stop him—

"Your mate just ran out of here sobbing, Loren." Thorne

shoved through the darkness, his hand closing around Loren's wrist. "She's the one who matters right now. Not him. Let. Him. Go."

For a heartbeat, Loren didn't move. The shadows screamed in his ears, howling for blood as Eryn's pulse slowed beneath his fingers. It would be so easy—

Loren wrenched himself back, letting the other male crash to the ground in a heap. "Get out of my home," he snarled. "And if you so much as breathe in her direction ever again, I'll finish what I started here."

Eryn clambered to his feet, his smirk back despite the necklace of bruises on his neck. The spymaster inclined his head in mock courtesy, composure settling back over him like a well-fitted mask. "As you wish, Your Majesty."

Thorne didn't release Loren's arm until the door had swung closed behind Eryn, waiting until the spymaster's footsteps faded from hearing before he rounded on his oldest friend.

"What were you thinking?" Thorne demanded. "He's part of Eloria's Small Council. Do they know what they say about you?"

"That I'm unstable," Loren snapped, jerking his arm out of Thorne's grip. "And they're right. I'm not fit to be king. But they aren't getting near her. I'll kill them all first."

"*Loren*—" Thorne hissed, trailing off with a shake of his head. "You can't say things like that. Did you actually make her hold a *knife* to her own throat?"

Loren glanced away, his gaze falling on the stub of candle still sitting on the floor. She'd resorted to a human crutch out of frustration—nothing worth getting so angry over. But then she'd challenged him and he had—Loren shuddered, the aftertaste of her panic and terror still lingering on his tongue.

"She doesn't understand the dangers," he said, like it excused what he'd done. "What someone like Eryn could do to her—"

"Right now I think she's worried about what *you* could do to her," Thorne snapped. "You're no good to her like this, Loren."

"You're right." Loren swallowed hard. "She doesn't trust me. I shouldn't be training her. You should—"

"That's not what I meant." Thorne shook his head, turning toward the door. "*Both* of you are struggling here. No one comes out of that place without scars, physical and mental. Come on, let's go make sure she's safe—"

"She's in her room."

He could feel her through the bond. Even though the taste of her emotions had faded with distance, he could feel enough to know she was curled in her bed, the covers pulled over her head like a child hiding from a monster. Terrified—of him.

"Loren—" Thorne started.

"I can't, Thorne." The words fell from his lips, stiff and wooden. "Thank you for not letting me kill Eryn, but...just go. Please."

Thorne stared at him, his face shadowed. There had been a time Loren had known his face as well as his own—but he might as well have been a stranger now.

"Consider accepting some help, Loren," Thorne said finally. "If you can't do it for yourself, do it for her. You both deserve better."

Loren stared at the candle stub as the door swung closed behind his friend, the shadows twisting and writhing across the room as if they might find the threat to his mate hiding in some dark corner. All they wanted was to protect her, to fix this. But they couldn't. *He* couldn't. Because he couldn't even fix himself.

And the Small Council—Loren had no doubt they would be back with more demands. What if they looked at the bodies piling up and decided that one fae female's freedom was an acceptable cost to pay to stop the bleeding?

His stomach turned, bile stinging his throat. Eloria wouldn't—she *couldn't* do that to him. But Eryn? Cormac? How many others would disagree?

The shadows lashed the air around him, a sudden, violent burst of power that made the aetherlamps flicker wildly above him. *Fix it.* They seethed. *Protect her.*

But he couldn't. Not from here. Not like this.

CHAPTER

THIRTEEN

The little shadow was gone.

Araya couldn't say when it had slipped away. One moment it had been curled around her, a cool anchor against her side as she shook with silent sobs, terrified of what nightmares sleep would bring. The next, she'd opened heavy eyes to the pale wash of muted sunlight creeping across the floor—alone.

She slid out of bed, wincing as every muscle screamed in protest. Everything hurt, her chest still tight and aching with the lingering remnant of the panic that had gripped her. But Araya still stumbled into the bathing chamber, gripping the edge of the basin as she forced herself to meet her own eyes in the mirror.

She barely recognized herself. Her silver eyes swollen and blood-shot—how many years had it been since she *wept*? Surely, not since her earliest years at Kaldrath, where she'd learned that tears didn't win you any mercy.

Araya ducked her head, scrubbing cold water over her face. The chill shocked her awake, stinging her skin and clearing her mind. She was on Eluneth. She was the *guest* of the crown prince—the same male who had forced her to hold a knife to her own throat.

Araya grimaced, tilting her head to study the scabbed-over scrape on her neck. It looked worse than she expected, an ugly reminder of how little control she really had here despite Loren's insistence that she was *free*. She swallowed hard, shoving away the memory of the blade at her throat, of Loren's power twisting her body to his will—the sooner she figured out how to break this link between them and negotiated her return to the New Dominion, the better.

She picked up the brush, dragging it through her snarled hair until she could yank it back into her customary braid. Once she got back to the New Dominion, she could fix everything. All she had to do was figure out how to break the traitorous bond that curled in her chest. As long as Jaxon never knew it existed, she could go back to her old life. Safe.

She repeated it like a mantra, over and over, until her heartbeat slowed and the ache in her chest dulled. Safe—she'd be safe with Jaxon. He'd never made her hold a knife to her own throat. As long as she remembered her place, she could be happy there. Happy with him.

But she didn't dare try to speak the words aloud.

She set the brush down, focusing on pulling her newly-tamed hair back into her usual braid. She was just wrapping the tie around the end when someone knocked softly on the door. Araya froze, her heart leaping into her throat. For a moment, she thought it might be Loren—but the bond sat heavy in her chest, unresponsive.

"Araya?" Thorne called out, his voice as gentle as his knock. "May I come in?"

"Just a moment." Araya glanced in the mirror one last time, dragging her braid over her shoulder like it could hide the raw scrape on her throat before she hurried across the room, pulling away the chair she'd wedged beneath the knob.

"Good morning." Thorne's amber eyes flicked to the chair, his eyebrows rising.

"You said to lock the door," Araya snapped, more defensively than she'd meant. "I don't have a key, so—"

"You don't have a key to your own room?" Thorne stepped back, his expression darkening. "Why not?"

"I assume because Loren doesn't want me to have a key." Araya crossed her arms, lifting her chin. "Barricading the door works fine—"

"You shouldn't have to barricade the door to your own bedroom," Thorne said firmly. "I'll find out where it went—Veria must have a copy at the very least."

"And what will Loren have to say about that?" Araya demanded.

Thorne's mouth tightened, but his voice stayed gentle. "Loren isn't here, Araya."

Araya stared at him, almost not certain she heard him right. "What?"

"He left for Lumaria last night," Thorne said.

Araya fell back a step, grabbing the back of the chair for support as the world tilted under her feet. Her chest hollowed out, the strange stillness of the bond suddenly making far too much sense. He was gone. She wouldn't have to face him, wouldn't have to look him in the eye as he told her what he'd done had been for her own good. He'd just *left* her here without a word of explanation—

"When will he be back?" She managed to ask finally, her voice hoarse.

"I don't know." Thorne watched her carefully, the kindness on his face almost too much to bear. "It may be a while. He asked me to take over your training for now."

"And what does that mean?" Araya demanded. Heat prickled across her skin, the ache in her chest giving way to the sting of betrayal. "Do you see how many commands I can choke down before I break? Or are you going to force me to throw myself off the wall—"

"I thought it might be better to start with breakfast," Thorne said easily. "Unless you feel like you'd rather hit something?" He arched an eyebrow, smiling at her. "I'll warn you though, I have no intention of being a standing target."

Araya's cheeks burned, shame and confusion twisting with her anger. Thorne wasn't the one who deserved her ire. The person she really wanted to fight had fled in the night. Abandoning her.

"Breakfast is fine," she said finally, swallowing hard past the lump in her throat. "Lead the way."

She'd always eaten breakfast in her room, the covered tray waiting for her on the small table when she opened her eyes every morning. But Thorne led her back through the halls, until they reached the dining room Loren had destroyed that horrible night.

Someone had swept up the glass, the soiled linens replaced by fresh ones like nothing had ever happened. Only two places had been set at the table—she truly must have been the last one here to learn Loren had left.

Thorne sat, pulling the silver dome off his plate to reveal a steaming portion of fluffy eggs alongside a heel of the dark, crusty bread they ate here and a few of the salted, preserved fish that seemed to accompany every single meal.

Araya joined him hesitantly, shocked to discover her own portion came with the addition of a small dish of fresh berries, their deep color a startling purple against the pillowy bed of fresh cream. Her mouth watered at the sight—she hadn't seen fresh fruit since she woke up on that boat. But Thorne only grinned.

"Veria likes you," he said, like that was some sort of explanation.

Araya picked up her spoon, closing her eyes as sweetness burst across her tongue, perfectly complimented by the sour tang of clotted cream. She forced herself to eat it slowly, savoring each tiny bite until the dish was heartbreakingly empty.

"Healing starts with little things," Thorne said suddenly, pausing to chew. "Rest, confidence that you're safe. The space to breathe and appreciate the things that make you happy."

Araya's spoon clinked against the empty dish. "They're just berries."

"Did they make you happy?" Thorne's amber eyes flicked toward her, steady and unreadable. "You deserve to feel safe and happy, Araya. Something I'm afraid we haven't been very good at giving you."

"You took me *away* from the place where I was safe and happy," Araya snapped. "You and Loren and Nyra—you drugged me and put me on that boat."

"You were safe and happy with the man who slammed your head into the desk hard enough to give you a concussion?" Thorne raised his eyebrows at her, his gentle tone never wavering. "The man who drained your power and left you to suffer all night, only taking you to a Healer in the morning?"

Araya's face heated. "He's not always like that."

Thorne didn't argue with her, using the last bit of his bread to scoop up his eggs instead. He chewed, the silence stretching uneasily between them until he finally swallowed, laying his fork across his empty plate.

"I'm not here to tell you how to feel about Jaxon. Or Loren, for that matter. I'm here to remind you that your choices and your power belong to you. Until you believe that, no amount of *training* will help you unlock the control you buried years ago in order to survive in a world that would otherwise have destroyed you."

"So what?" Araya shoved her chair back from the table. Her chest ached, his words making the empty place where the bond lay silent twist painfully. "You want me to sit here and eat berries until I somehow become enlightened and embrace your way of doing things?"

"Not exactly." Thorne's mouth curved into a faint smile. "I thought you could put yourself to work helping Veria in the kitchens. Busy hands, and all that."

Araya blinked at him, incredulous. "You want me to work in the kitchens."

"For now," Thorne said, nodding like she'd asked a question. "I think it would be for the best. There might only be a few of us here, but Ithralis is a pretty large castle for one person to manage. Even when that person is Veria."

Araya opened her mouth, then snapped it closed again. Out of everything she'd expected when Thorne had said he was taking over her training, this hadn't been something she'd imagined.

"You're serious," she finally managed.

"As serious as I've ever been," Thorne said cheerfully. He stood, nudging his plate toward her. "There's a tray for the dishes right over there."

Araya stared down at the dirty plates, her jaw tightening. "And what if I don't *want* to play scullery maid?" she demanded. "I didn't spend years fighting to be more than a servant just to *scrub dishes* for you."

"Then don't." Thorne shrugged, unbothered. "Sit in your room. Go to the library. Wander the halls—it's all up to you, Araya. But I'd rather scrub dishes than sit around tearing myself apart over something that was never my fault."

He stood, taking no notice of how she gaped at him. With a cheerful nod, he strolled from the room, his jaunty whistle fading with his footsteps like he hadn't just upended every one of her expectations.

CHAPTER
FOURTEEN

Thorne truly didn't care what she did.

The first day, Araya slipped out of her room before dawn. If Thorne meant to force her to do menial labor in some sort of ridiculous *training* exercise, he'd have to find her first. She barricaded herself in the library instead, surrounding herself with the books Loren had left out that last, disastrous morning.

The bond throbbed like a wound in her chest, aching with his absence. Even after what he'd done to her, she caught herself half-expecting him to lean over and help her with a word, patiently walking her through the passage that was giving her trouble.

But he wasn't here. He'd left her.

It was slow-going without him. The spidery script blurred in front of her eyes, forcing her to read the same lines over and over again until her head pounded. She didn't even realize how much time had passed until her stomach growled loudly, protesting that she'd missed breakfast and lunch in her efforts to avoid Thorne.

Araya clenched her jaw, turning another page. She'd been hungry before. It would take more than food to force her out.

But Thorne never came to find her.

Darkness had fallen by the time she closed her book, her head throbbing from the effort of translating the ancient Valenya word by painstaking word. She trudged back to her room, too tired to care if Thorne found her there—all she wanted was to collapse into her bed and sleep. Hopefully without nightmares, for once.

She shoved the door open, reaching for the chair to wedge under the doorknob—but stopped short when she caught sight of the small parcel. It sat on the desk, neatly wrapped in plain paper. No note—no explanation.

Araya scowled, picking up the package and tearing into it. If Thorne thought she could be bribed into cooperating he had another thing coming—

A small brass key slid into her palm.

Araya stared down at it, hardly breathing. He'd said he would get it for her, but she hadn't really believed him. After all, he was only half-fae—he could lie if he wanted to. And Loren obviously hadn't wanted her to have it. Who was Thorne to go against his prince?

But he'd gotten her the key anyway. Just like he'd said he would.

She stared at it for a long moment, her throat tight. Then, for the first time since she'd been dragged to Ithralis, she closed her door and turned the lock, the unfamiliar weight of safety settling in her chest.

She woke up late the next morning, her stomach knotted and hollow. She rose slowly, not surprised to find the table empty. After yesterday, she was almost certain no tray would appear until Thorne gave his blessing. He clearly intended to starve her until she gave in, but if he thought it was going to be that easy to manipulate her he was in for an unpleasant surprise.

Araya forced herself to go through her morning routine, taking her time dressing and braiding her hair. By the time she left her room, it was mid-morning—a perfectly respectable time for a late breakfast.

She held her head high as she walked into the dining room. Thorne still sat at the table, his plate pushed aside to make space for a leather-bound ledger. He didn't even look up as she walked in, his brow furrowed as he tapped his quill against the edge of the page.

"Thank you," Araya said, sliding into the seat across from him. "For the key." She uncovered her plate, revealing another serving of fluffy eggs. No berries and clotted cream today—but Araya was so hungry even the salted fish looked delicious.

"You're welcome," Thorne said absently, marking something in the ledger beside him. "How was your day yesterday?"

"Fine." Araya took a tiny bite of eggs, refusing to scarf it down the way her stomach demanded. "I spent it in the library."

Thorne hummed, his focus still on his work. "Read anything interesting?"

Araya narrowed her eyes. "If you think you can starve me into scrubbing pots for Veria, you're wrong. I'm not going to be manipulated—"

"Of course you're not," Thorne said, finally looking up at her. "Your meals will be served here at the usual times—just like they are for everyone else. Like I said before, your days are yours to spend however you wish."

Her fork clattered against the plate. That was it? No lecture, no clever little push to get her to cooperate?

"What kind of game are you playing?" she demanded. "You said Loren put you in charge of my training—"

"He did." Thorne smiled warmly, unperturbed by her tone. "And that's what we're doing. It's not a game, Araya. You truly are free to do as you please. But, if you do ever find yourself with some free time I spend most of my afternoons in the garden." He held her gaze, his amber eyes kind and steady. "You're welcome to join me there if you want to take a more active approach to learning how to coexist with your magic."

FIFTEEN

"Your Majesties." The gray-clad weatherworker bowed low as they approached. "Thank you for coming."

"Thank you for hosting us, Maelis," Eloria said. "Please, don't stand on ceremony here. It's only because of you and your weatherworkers that we have the food on our tables. My brother and I are very eager to see what you have to show us today."

Loren braced himself as the weatherworker straightened, her bright gray eyes going immediately to the wisps of shadow that curled around his feet. Everyone always looked at the shadows before they looked at him, their faces lighting with a mixture of awe and hope that made his stomach churn.

"It's my honor, Your Majesty," she said, finally meeting his gaze. "We are all overjoyed at your return."

Loren inclined his head stiffly. He should say something—anything. He'd had years of courtly training just for moments like these. But the words caught behind his teeth. What good were empty platitudes when he couldn't give them what they expected of him?

The silence stretched, heavy enough that one of the younger

weatherworkers shifted nervously at the edge of the field. But Eloria, as smooth and composed as ever, stepped forward.

"Please Maelis," she said, her voice warm. "We all know we wouldn't survive here without the work you and your team do. Show us how you've managed to hold the shadows back this season, so my brother and I can carry your needs to the Small Council with the weight they deserve."

They followed the weatherworker along the perimeter of the muddy field, past rows of spindly crops, before finally coming to a halt in front of a thick wooden pole driven into the ground. Loren stared, the hair on the back of his neck standing on end as he took in the carved runes etched deeply into the wood. Each one pulsed faintly, a sluggish ripple of aether glimmering as it raced through the lines.

He took a step back, following the thread as it leapt into the air, connecting to another post just ten paces further down the line. And beyond that one, another—all the way around the perimeter of the field. Together, they formed a fragile lattice, turning the breeze that snapped at his clothing to its intended purpose—blowing back the mist so the sun could reach the ground.

"And what about Daren?" Eloria asked.

The weatherworker's smile faltered. "He'd be here if he could, Princess," she said. "But the entire team is short. He's had them running double shifts to keep up and taken on more than he can handle himself. But..." she trailed off, glancing toward a low wooden building. "Well, see for yourself."

Narrow bunks lined both walls, crammed so close together that Loren had to turn sideways to pass between them. Nearly every cot was occupied by gray-clad weatherworkers and green-clad growers, their faces ashen and pinched even in sleep. Most lay still, but one young male sat bolt upright as they passed, his eyes glazed and unseeing as his hands twitched and jerked.

Loren jumped, his legs striking the bunk behind him as he choked on the sour tang of sweat and the sharp bite of burned aether. But Maelis hurried forward, pressing a hand to his shoulder and gently urging him back onto the bed with quiet words. None of them spoke as they moved through the rest of the bunkhouse, finally emerging into the thin gray sunlight on the other side.

"I'll speak to the Small Council," Eloria said quietly. Her composure didn't falter, but Loren could see her tension in the line of her jaw, so much like their father when he'd been giving someone news they didn't want to hear. "At the very least we can look into increasing rations for those on rotation."

"Thank you, Princess." Maelis bowed her head, gratitude flashing across her drawn face. "That would mean a lot to them. The fact that you're here at all, seeing what they sacrifice—" she trailed off, her voice thick.

Eloria reached out, clasping the other female's shoulder. "We see you, Maelis," she said. "And your team. We're doing everything we can to lift the shadows, but until then, we need you to carry on. Just a little longer."

Loren shifted uncomfortably, acutely aware of the shadows curling around his feet and the stares of the weatherworkers that had gathered around them. They all thought it would be him—the chosen prince, returned from the dead—who would sweep the shadows away. What would they think if they knew the Veil had already rejected him?

He cleared his throat, the hope in the faces around them like a blade pressed against his ribs. "It must take a great deal of power to hold back the Veil from all our farmland," he said finally. "Thank you for showing it to me."

"Oh—" the weatherworker's eyes widened, her lips parting in surprise. "I'm sorry Your Majesty, I should have made it more clear. This team only maintains *this* field. The others have their own barracks."

"All those fae to keep the mist off *one* field?" Loren demanded.

Eloria frowned at him, pressing her lips together. "Sit down."

"Why would you parade me in front of them like that?" Loren turned, storming the length of the chambers Eloria had taken in the Central Hall to stare out the wide window. The Central Square spread out below, packed with mouths they couldn't feed. "I can't help them. All you're doing is spreading false hope—"

"*Sit*, Loren," Eloria snapped.

Still seething, Loren collapsed into one of the mismatched chairs, watching as Eloria turned to the sideboard and poured a steaming cup of tea. It was a modest set of apartments, compared to her rooms back at Tirnavel, appointed with an eclectic collection of mismatched furniture and a strange collection of things he recognized from her childhood. Her desk from her rooms at Ithralis stood against one wall, its surface cluttered with stacked ledgers and loose parchment. Their father's ring sat on a tray, ready for her to mark correspondence with the royal seal.

"We have thirty-seven fields under active management." Eloria set the tea service on the table between them, dropping gracefully into her own chair. "Twenty-nine are fully staffed, but eight are running with short crews."

"And that feeds all of the fae on Eluneth?" He stared down into his tea. "What if we established more posts? Or worked longer shifts—"

"We've done all of that. *Are* doing it." Eloria sighed, her mask dropping to reveal the exhaustion beneath. "Longer shifts help in the short term, but we lose too many to burnout. Last time we lost almost an entire crew when the runeposts failed. What we *need* is more bodies. We've pulled every fae with any talent for weatherworking or growing into service, but depending on magic to sustain an entire population is a losing battle. With the tightened security in the New Dominion right now it's almost impossible for us to get anything or anyone out—and even if we could get them across the

Veil, we can't guarantee they'll manifest as a weatherworker or a grower."

The shadows hissed, drawing tighter around his boots.

"You're prioritizing who you save from the New Dominion based off what they might manifest as?" Loren demanded.

"We don't have a choice." Eloria set her cup down, the soft click of porcelain loud in the silence. "There's nothing else we can do, Loren."

"They looked at me like I could—" Loren trailed off, staring down at the shadows that drifted around his feet. "The Veil isn't the same thing, El. And I'm not Father. I can't..." He shook his head, rubbing the shadowmark that wound around his arm through his shirt. "I don't want to give them false hope."

"You aren't *false* hope," Eloria answered, more fiercely than he'd expected. "You survived twenty-five *years* of torture, Loren. You *escaped* and came here. People need to know you're alive, that you're here and fighting for them. As for the shadows—"

"I don't want to talk about her," Loren cut her off. The shadows hissed softly, the bond twisting like a knife in his chest, demanding that he go to her.

Eloria was quiet for a long moment. "Eryn said you compelled her to hold a knife to her throat—then almost killed him when he stepped in."

Loren barked out a bitter laugh. "That's a generous interpretation of his role."

"He's trying to cast you as unstable," Eloria warned. "The incomplete mate bond doesn't do you any favors—"

"I said I don't want to talk about her." He stood, not waiting for her to dismiss him. "I'll see you at dinner."

<hr>

BUT OF COURSE THE SHADOWS DIDN'T LEAVE IT THERE.

He couldn't escape them, not even in his own rooms. They

pressed close, tugging and pushing, whispering with a hundred fractured voices that all carried the same demand. The bond *ached*, stretched too thin by the distance between them. He'd grown used to the heat of her fury, the bitter sting of her mistrust. But now...the silence where she used to be was so much worse.

Loren dragged both hands through his hair, pacing the confines of his chamber as the shadows crowded tighter, urging him toward her. But he couldn't shake the memory of her eyes, full of terror as she collapsed in a sobbing heap on the floor, the knife falling from her hand. What monster had she seen when she looked at him?

Still, he couldn't help himself.

Loren sank down on the edge of the bed, pressing his palms against his eyes. It was easy to reach for her—easy to follow that thin, hollow thread across the miles that separated them. The ache eased for the barest moment as his mind brushed hers, a ghost of the connection they'd shared before. It wasn't enough. It never was. But it was all he could allow himself.

He would never let anyone hurt her again. Not even himself.

CHAPTER
SIXTEEN

Araya made it two more days before she broke.

It was boredom that finally wore her down, driving her to seek Thorne out in the skeletal remains of the garden. She found him sitting on a bench under a bower of gnarled vines, his head bowed over a sheaf of papers filled with flowing Valenya script.

"You made it," he said. "I'm so glad you found the time—"

"Don't patronize me." Araya crossed her arms, glaring at him. "Just tell me what you expect me to do out here."

"Well, I think it makes the most sense to start by walking the wall." Thorne stood, tucking his papers away. "It never hurts to check the wards."

"The wall isn't warded." Araya stared at him, frowning. "There aren't any runes."

"You might be surprised." Thorne grinned. "Come on—this will be fun."

Thorne had an interesting definition of *fun*, Araya decided when they were halfway around the wall. As far as she could tell, checking the wards involved nothing but running a hand along the stones.

"It's ancient magic," Thorne said when they stopped for water.

"Designed to protect the castle from intruders. The intention was set a long time ago, but sometimes the stones have to be reminded."

"So it doesn't need any sort of anchor or focus?" Araya studied the stones, intrigued despite herself. "But how does it get power? I thought this place was abandoned?"

"Oh, it absorbs aether from the world around it," Thorne capped the waterskin, passing it back to her. "That's why the *zal'vorr* aren't breaking down our doors every night."

"That's not how magic works," Araya protested. "You can't just *tell* things what to do and expect it to hold."

"You'd be surprised," was all Thorne said, his lips twitching like he was hiding a smile.

The next day he had her hauling water. She pulled bucket after bucket up from a tucked away well, her palms burning from the rough rope and her arms and shoulders screaming from the effort. Her hair escaped its braid, sweat plastering it to her face and neck.

"You know there are easier ways to do this," she grumbled, groaning as she pulled up the next bucket. "There's running water inside. I don't see why this is even necessary—"

"It's not." Thorne laughed, taking the bucket from her and walking off toward the cistern as she gaped after him.

By the end of the week he'd had her drag all the old tapestries outside and beat years of dust from them until her throat burned, sweeping out hearths that hadn't seen a flame in years until her entire body was blackened and exhausted—he'd even tasked her with cleaning out some of the unused rooms, like someone might come back and need them.

There was no rhyme or reason to it that she could see. But every night, Araya collapsed into bed aching and exhausted, falling quickly into a dreamless sleep free of nightmares and shadows and lost fae princes.

"I think it makes the most sense to start by clearing out the deadfall," Thorne said the next day, frowning at the ruined garden. "After that I imagine we'll have to clear out all the moss and mushrooms—we'll have to see."

"Is this another one of your pointless tasks?" Araya demanded. "This garden is dead—nothing is ever going to grow here again. There's no light."

"Maybe not." Thorne shrugged, crouching to pry a root loose from between the paving stones. "But I thought it might make Loren happy to see it cleaned up. Did you know this was his mother's garden? She loved it here."

The comment lodged like a thorn in her chest, that ache she'd managed to bury under sore muscles and exhaustion springing to life like a flame from the ashes.

He claimed you against your will, she reminded herself. Drugged you and stole you across the Shadowed Sea. Then he made you hold a knife to your throat and abandoned you here. Alone.

"Is that who you've been writing to?" she asked. "Loren?"

"No—" for the first time, Thorne hesitated. "Those letters are from Finn, back in the New Dominion."

"You get *mail* from the New Dominion?" Araya straightened, the armful of branches she'd just gathered crashing to the ground. "What's happening there?"

"Nothing good." Thorne turned away to dump his own load of debris on the growing pile, but not quite fast enough to hide his fading smile. "I'm sure you can imagine how they reacted to losing their prize prisoner."

She could. All too well.

"What about Serafina?" Araya pressed. "Have they heard from her? Is she safe?"

"Our internal assets aren't supposed to contact us directly." Thorne still didn't look at her. "I'm sure—"

"You're lying," Araya stared at him. "I saw Serafina with Finn at the Crust & Kettle. They looked very cozy."

"Araya—"

"Is she dead?" Araya demanded. If Jaxon even thought she was involved—

"She's missing." Thorne watched her carefully, his expression pinched. "Eloria has her spymaster looking into it—Loren insisted."

"The male he almost killed?" A hysterical laugh bubbled up in her throat. "Somehow I doubt he's making it a priority. If she's missing she's dead, Thorne. Or worse."

Thorne closed his mouth, his lips firming into a thin line. "I won't insult you by saying that's not probably the case," he said quietly. "But I truly hope it's not. She's saved a lot of people. We all like her, and Finn..." he shook his head. "If she can be found, he'll find her, Araya."

Araya jerked her chin in a stiff nod, her eyes stinging. "I think I'm done for today," she said, her voice thick.

"Araya—" Thorne took a step forward, reaching for her.

But she spun away before he could touch her, branches snapping beneath her boots as she fled.

Araya stormed blindly through the castle, taking turns at random down halls she barely recognized. She didn't care where she was going, only that it was away—away from the courtyard and Thorne and his letters and his kind lies. But she couldn't outrun the pounding certainty that it was all her fault. Whatever was happening to Serafina right now—it was because of her.

She skidded to a stop, sucking in fast, shallow breaths. The narrow halls that surrounded her were unfamiliar, no doubt meant to allow servants to move quickly throughout the castle without being seen. Thorne must have skipped them in his tour, assuming she'd have no reason to venture into them—with any luck, that meant he wouldn't come looking for her here, either.

She followed them down, letting her hand trail along the cool stone wall as the silence pressed in. The air shifted, turning warmer and filling her nose with the rich, yeasty smell of the dense brown bread that appeared with every meal here. Her stomach twisted in response, reminding her that lunch had been hours ago, before she'd spent the afternoon doing manual labor.

The scent led her around another bend, where a wide wooden door stood propped open to let the heat of the kitchen spill into the corridor like a beckoning hand. Inside, the older fae female from that disastrous dinner stood with her back half-turned, humming as she draped a fresh cloth over the steaming loaves of bread.

Araya froze on the threshold, the warmth brushing against her skin like an invitation she didn't trust. This was the same female she'd spent the past week refusing to help—the one who had embraced Loren like a son. What would she think of her prince's disappointing mate?

"Goodness." Veria turned before Araya could make her retreat, startling. "Do you need something?"

"I just—" Araya fumbled for a suitable explanation, her tongue tangling over her excuses. "I'm sorry. I didn't mean to impose. I was just...trying to find somewhere no one would come looking for me."

The older fae female wiped her hands on a towel, studying Araya with sharp blue eyes that seemed to read everything she'd left unsaid.

"Well, you've certainly found it," she said finally. "No one comes down here unless they're lost or hungry."

Without waiting for a response, Veria turned back to the hearth, pouring a steaming cup of dark, fragrant tea into a chipped clay mug. She slid it across the table, adding a small plate with slivers of dried fruit and a thick heel of that dark bread.

"Sit," she ordered, her tone brooking no argument when she saw Araya still hovering in the doorway. "A cup of tea always helps."

Warily, Araya slid into the chair. She wrapped her fingers around the mug, the warmth of the tea seeping into her numb fingers. "Thank you," she whispered.

Veria only hummed in acknowledgment, turning back to fuss

over the pot of stew hanging over the fire. She muttered to herself in Valenya, flicking her fingers toward the workstation.

The knife rose into the air, setting to work chopping root vegetables. The neat cubes floated across the kitchen, bobbing gently before dropping into the rich brown stew. Veria tasted it, considering, but when she turned away the wooden spoon kept stirring the pot of its own accord.

Araya watched it all with wide eyes. No one in the New Dominion had magic to spare on something as simple as *cooking*. Humans hoarded their power, and food was something most fae were lucky to have at all. But this—this was *magic*.

"How are you doing that?" she asked, the question tumbling from her mouth before she could think better of it.

Veria paused, arching a brow. "It's easier to show than explain," she said. "Grab an apron and wash your hands. I hope you don't mind a little hard work."

SEVENTEEN

Veria was two hundred and seventy-three years old.

Araya had spent the better part of the week gathering the nerve to ask after the older female casually mentioned that she'd known Loren's father before he became king. Veria had just laughed, answering easily as Araya struggled not to choke on her tea.

"I've helped raise two generations of royals." Veria said with a laugh. "My mate worked in the palace in Tirnavel. With my skill at domestic magic, I was easily able to find a place of my own there. Corwin's mother —Queen Kira—became a fast friend of mine. By the time Corwin and Lysa had their own children, it felt like we were part of the family."

The words rolled easily off Veria's tongue, but Araya's mind reeled. Of course, she knew fae were long-lived—but one hardly ever saw *old* fae in the New Dominion. How did a single heart carry the weight of so many lives? Centuries of memories, friendships, loss... Would all those faces blur together, or would the grief of losing them burn fresh, each and every time?

"So you knew Loren as a child?" Araya asked, unable to help the pang of curiosity. "And Eloria?"

"I did." Veria smiled into her tea. "Both little troublemakers. Eloria was always the craftier one—she used her illusions to sneak sweets from the kitchen. I'd turn my back for just a moment, and entire trays would vanish."

The image made Araya smile, though it was hard to picture the elegant and composed regent sneaking desserts like a child. Even if she must have *been* a child at one point.

"And Loren," Veria continued, "he and Thorne were inseparable. Brothers of the heart, we call them. They were always getting into things they shouldn't, climbing trees, sneaking past the borders of the grounds. I couldn't begin to count the number of times they came back far later than they should have, covered in dirt with leaves stuck in their hair."

Araya frowned, trying to reconcile the image of a wild, carefree boy with the distant, unyielding male she knew. Had he just...grown up? Or had the Arcanum taken that boy and shattered him?

"Thalen and I were never blessed with children," Veria said softly, pulling Araya's attention back to the present. "But I loved those three like they were my own. There was a long time where I thought I would never see Loren again. I am very glad the Goddess brought the two of you together, and that you were able to lead him back to us."

Araya's throat tightened. She set her own cup down carefully, avoiding Veria's gaze. "I'm not sure your Goddess had anything to do with it."

"It's not our place to question." Some of Veria's warmth faded— her face stern as she set her teacup down on its saucer. "These things happen as they are meant to, even when everything else is going wrong."

Araya swallowed hard, the bond twinging in her chest. Loren had abandoned her here, even after all his grand words about how important it was that she learn control over her magic. But Araya didn't want to talk about it—not even with Veria, who Araya had quickly decided might be the nicest fae she'd met on this side of the Shadowed Veil.

"How long did it take you to learn all this?" Araya asked instead, nodding toward the workstation where a pale pastry dough thudded against the counter, folding and stretching itself as if shaped by invisible hands.

Veria glanced up from the tray of delicate flowers she'd started to work on. "I started manifesting my affinity around nine," she said. "Just a spark of talent at first—warming tea, keeping the soup from burning. My mother thought I'd grow out of it and pick up something useful instead."

"But you didn't?"

"Goddess, no." Veria chuckled, shaking her head. "By ten, I had the knives chopping vegetables on their own and was teaching the bread to braid itself. That's when they knew my specialty would be domestic magic. It's like that for most of us. Once we have a little control, our magic leans toward what we care most about. Some take to music, or a craft—Eloria's mischief lent itself well to illusion. But me? I liked taking care of people. Still do."

Araya leaned forward, her tea forgotten at her elbow. "So it's not random?"

"Certainly not." Veria shook her head, sprinkling the blossoms in front of her with a careful dusting of sugar. "Magic always follows our will and desires—or our needs. Most of our children who have grown up here have become weatherworkers, a product of our desperation to push the mist back enough to feed us all. Sometimes I wonder what gifts they might have found instead, if they'd grown up in a different world."

"What about fae who grew up with their magic bound?" Araya asked carefully. "Do they ever manifest?"

Veria paused in her work, the sugar spoon hovering above the tray. Araya didn't look up from her tea, staring down at the dregs in her cup like they were the most fascinating thing she'd ever seen.

"Magic can be a tricky thing, sometimes," Veria said finally. "It doesn't always bloom the way we expect after spending so long buried. But as surprising as the results can be, most of us here still believe everything happens for a reason."

"Fate." Araya snorted, dragging her finger through a dusting of spilled flour on the table. "Fate and I aren't friends at the moment."

Veria chuckled softly. "No one is, dear. Not at your age." She reached for a second tray of blooms, setting it in front of Araya. "Here —why don't you try sugaring these? These were some of Loren's favorites, he could eat an entire tray of them at Bloomtide."

Araya swallowed hard, trying to ignore the twist of pain his name sent through her chest. He'd claimed her against her will. Drugged her and stolen her across the Shadowed Sea. He'd made her hold a knife to her own throat and *left* her here.

"Is he coming back to Ithralis?" she asked.

"Not that I'm aware of," Veria said carefully. "I was going to send these with Thorne when he goes tomorrow."

"Thorne's leaving too, then." Araya stared down at sugared blossoms without seeing them. He hadn't said anything—but she'd been avoiding him since she discovered Veria was more than happy to let her eat in the kitchen. Still, he hadn't come looking for her either.

"But I'm staying," Veria said gently. She reached out, her cool hand covering Araya's where she clenched the spoon in her fist. "We'll have our own Bloomtide here, dear. And trust me, you'll eat better than any of them."

***

THE GARDEN WAS ALMOST UNRECOGNIZABLE IN THE PALE MORNING LIGHT. The heaps of broken branches they'd dragged into a pile were gone, and someone had scraped the moss from the flagstone paths, revealing the shape of what it must have once been. Thorne was already hard at work clearing another garden bed of sodden, rotting leaves, but he straightened as she stormed across the courtyard.

"You've been busy," Araya snapped.

"Nothing like a little hard work to clear the mind." Thorne stretched, twisting from side to side. "It's come a long way, hasn't it? You should be proud."

"I know what you're doing." Araya crossed her arms. "You're trying to make me manifest an affinity with all these ridiculous tasks."

"Clever," Thorne said, his amber eyes dancing. "Did Veria help you figure that one out?"

"She also told me you're going to Lumaria." Araya scowled, refusing to let him off the hook. "That you're going to see *him*."

"I am." The cheer faded from Thorne's face, replaced by something gentler. "Someone has to check on him too, Araya. Being apart from you—well, it's probably hurting him worse, since he completed his side of the bond."

She wanted to deny it. She didn't *miss* him. He'd claimed her against her will—drugged her and stolen her across the Shadowed Sea. Made her hold a knife to her own throat. But when she tried to speak the words, they stuck in her throat.

"Why did he leave then?" she whispered.

"Because he's an idiot and a martyr." Thorne sighed deeply. "You're welcome to come to Lumaria with me."

That was the last thing she'd expected him to say.

"Loren said I couldn't," she stammered. "He said I'm dangerous—I could hurt myself or someone else with my magic out of control—"

"I wouldn't let you go if you were dangerous," Thorne said with a shrug. "*Maybe* you could lose control of your magic if you're in extreme emotional distress. But generally? You're pretty even. Have you felt like you're about to burst out of your skin lately?"

She hadn't. Not since Thorne started working her to the bone every day. But still...

"I can't," she said. "I'm sorry."

"You don't have anything to apologize for," Thorne assured her. "I'm leaving after lunch, but Veria is staying. You won't be alone here. I'll be back after Bloomtide and we can continue our training then."

Araya nodded stiffly. She wanted to believe him—to believe she wasn't dangerous, that she could be trusted with herself. But Loren's voice still echoed louder, telling her she was a threat, that she couldn't protect herself—

"Araya." Thorne's quiet voice snapped her out of her spiral. "That hollow, torn up feeling you're struggling with—it's the bond. It doesn't mean you're weak or broken. It just means you're fae and missing your mate."

"I don't *want* to miss him," Araya snapped.

"I know." Thorne's amber gaze held hers, as calm and kind as always. "It's magic—but it's also *biology*. The bond doesn't care how angry you are, or how much you want to fight it. You're perfectly matched, stronger together than you are apart. It's going to keep pulling you closer, because that's what it was made to do. To keep you both safe."

Her throat worked, but she didn't answer.

"If you don't want to see him," Thorne continued softly, "you might consider finding some other way to feel close to him. It could help ease the ache."

Araya scoffed. "I'd have to be desperate."

CHAPTER

EIGHTEEN

Araya tossed and turned, fighting with her blankets until they were a twisted mess. Every time she closed her eyes she saw Serafina's face, bruised and broken. Sometimes she saw Loren but the way he had been when she first met him, scarred and broken in the dark. Her chest ached, the pull she'd drowned under all of Thorne's useless tasks alive and twisting around her heart.

Finally she gave up, throwing back the covers. She padded barefoot into the hall, not letting herself think too hard about where she was going. There was no little shadow for her to follow tonight, but the throb in her chest was direction enough, leading her straight to the royal family's personal wing.

She walked through the front room, the bond tugging her past the book of poetry left face down on the table and the paintings he had finally uncovered. It dragged her forward, until her hand was pressed against a familiar door.

It opened at a touch, swinging soundlessly into the room.

She slipped inside, closing the door softly behind her. The air smelled faintly of granite and rain, shadows clustered thickly at the edges of the room. Emerald curtains hung heavy around the rumpled bed, matching the drapes flung open to reveal the wall of windows, letting muted moonlight spill into the room.

Araya breathed in deeply, Loren's scent wrapping around her. It drove her mad that it could be so many things to her—soothing and infuriating all at the same time, much like the male himself. She had no doubt he'd be insufferable if he knew she was here.

But he'd left her here. Abandoned her with Thorne and Veria. So he would never know.

She climbed into the wide bed, pulling the blankets over her and letting exhaustion finally pull her under.

WARMTH SURROUNDED HER, A VIBRANT CONTRAST TO THE COOL SHADOWS that slid across her bare legs. They twined around her like silk ribbons, brushing the edge of her shift as they climbed her thighs, sliding across her hip and the soft plane of her stomach. She shivered, gasping as she arched into their touch.

They answered instantly, tearing a whimper from her as they swirled across her ribs, spiraling higher in teasing patterns that made her breasts ache with every pass. Another ribbon slid across the back of her neck, winding into her hair, tugging gently until her head tipped back.

A low sound vibrated against her neck, the solid *male* warmth behind her shifting in answer. His chest pressed against her spine. Warm lips and sharp teeth dragged across her skin in lazy kisses and sharp nips, the sting soothed by the wet slide of a tongue.

Araya floated in it, caught between waking and sleep, her body pliant and heavy. The shadows brushed lower, ghosting over the tender inside of her thigh, stopping just shy of where she needed them most. She bit back a cry, only for another tendril to swirl over her breast, circling the peak until she arched helplessly, clutching at the strong arm caging her against his chest.

A soft laugh tickled the scarred tip of her ear, the scent of granite and cold rain washing over her. She reached back, clawing her fingers through silken strands of hair. He was *hard*, his bare skin scorching through the thin fabric of her shift. She ground back against him, the tortured noise that tore from his chest almost enough to jerk her back to wakefulness. It was a dream—but *gods* the way he felt. The ache in her chest was gone, filling her with light until she felt like she might float away. There was something she should realize about that—

But one of those teasing shadows slipped higher, and the half-formed thought drained away with the moan it tore from her. It circled a peaked nipple, dragging across it until she broke with a soft cry. She wanted. No she *needed*—

"*Fuck*," Loren hissed the word against her ear, his hand fisting in the fabric of her nightgown. "*Araya*—"

Her name burned through the haze like wildfire, lightning racing across her skin. Her heart tripped in her chest, slamming against the cage of her ribs like it was desperate for escape. This was only a dream, but *their* dreams were *real*—

Araya lurched forward, tearing herself from his grasp. Loren pulled back at the same instant, the shadows snapping away from her so suddenly her body cried out, desperate for them to return—but she was awake now.

"What are you doing here?" Araya scrambled across the bed, putting as much space as she could between herself and the stunned, wide-eyed fae prince whose warmth she could still feel on her skin.

"What am I—" he blinked at her, then at their surroundings. "Are you in my bed?"

Heat rushed into her face, shame burning hotter than the ache still coiling low in her belly. She couldn't do this. Not with him. She dragged the sheet up over herself, taking another step back as the dream shuddered around them both. The shadows cried out, reaching for her—but the dream cracked apart, shattering around her like glass.

Araya jolted awake, her chest heaving. Loren's blankets twisted around her legs, her skin still buzzing from the feel of his lips on her skin, his shadows *touching* her. Every ragged breath was suffused with his scent, drowning her in him. The bond clawed at her chest, desperate for something they couldn't actually have.

NINETEEN

Loren woke with a gasp, her name on his lips.

Heat pulsed through him, his body aching with the memory of what she'd felt like pressed against him. The way her bare skin had tasted. The noise she'd made when his teeth had scraped over that skin—he groaned, his body throbbing with a need he hadn't felt in twenty-five years of starvation and isolation. And all around him the shadows keened, blanketing the walls and writhing over the bed.

"*Fuck*," he hissed, throwing back the covers.

The sheets tangled around his legs, tripping him. He slammed his shin into the bedframe, swearing viciously as he staggered toward the basin. He didn't bother to warm the water, dousing his face and chest until his skin was numb and his heart had stopped pounding like it would escape his chest.

"Enough," he growled, shaking off the shadows as they twined around him, her name a whispered chant in his ears. "She's not here. Pull yourselves together."

But she had been. Goddess help him—she'd been in his bed. Loren was sure of it.

She called. The shadows crowded close again, their hissing voices rising to a frenzy. *For you. For us. She wants—*

"She didn't," Loren corrected, his voice hoarse. "It wasn't her. It was the bond. You *know* that."

The shadows snarled their displeasure, cold tendrils lashing his skin like icy whips. *No difference.*

Loren slammed his fists against the stone, barely feeling the pain. "That's not how she'll see it. And I won't—" he broke off, his breath tearing out of him in a ragged growl. "I won't take something she doesn't offer freely. Not after everything that's already been taken from her."

The shadows stilled, the cacophony of their voices falling silent for a single instant before they drew together, their words landing like a lash.

And why would she offer if you don't ask?

Loren threw himself down on his bed, slamming his eyes closed. But he couldn't banish the lingering echo of their question, gnawing at the edges of his resolve with sharp teeth through the long hours.

His head was pounding by the time the dawn finally lightened the sky outside his window, the city stirring to life far below. He dragged a hand over his face, hauling himself out of bed and tugging on his clothes with stiff, graceless hands.

He'd go to breakfast and make his excuses. Whatever Eloria wanted of him today would just have to wait. He didn't have the strength to play prince—not when all he could think about was the hollow ache in his chest where she should have been.

But the sight that greeted him when he stepped into the solar where Eloria and Galen always took their breakfast together drove the haze from his mind like a blade to the gut.

"What are you doing here?" he snarled. The shadows rose at his back, answering his fear with their fury, every bit of it trained on his oldest friend—who was sitting *here* next to Galen instead of guarding *her.*

"Good morning to you too, Loren," Eloria said dryly, not looking up from buttering her bread. "Thorne arrived yesterday after you'd already retired—he brought you those candied blossoms you always loved."

"Candied blossoms?" Loren echoed. The shadows mantled at his back, frost creeping across the windows.

"Veria wanted you to have them for your first Bloomtide home." Thorne studied him with too-knowing eyes, barely sparing a glance for the seething darkness steadily growing thicker around them. "She's safe, Loren. More than that—she's finally getting comfortable simply existing with the full breadth of her power. She and Veria are going to have their own Bloomtide celebration."

"She could lose control." Loren's voice cracked, the room darkening around them. Frost crept across the walls, his breath fogging the air in front of his face. "She could hurt herself or someone else—"

A piece of bread smacked him in the shoulder.

The shadows reared back, affronted. But Eloria just ripped another piece of toast in half, balling it up between her fingers like she had when they were children.

"It's far too early for you to be this dramatic," she snapped, her green eyes flashing. "There's only one person in this room losing control of his magic right now and that's *you*. Your mate is in a warded castle behind a curtain of shadows that *eats* anything that ventures too close to it. I'd hardly call that *unprotected*."

Her words rang in the sudden silence. Loren clenched his jaw so hard his teeth ached, his heart pounding against his ribs. Just last night she'd been in his bed at Ithralis—safe. But he'd had other dreams. Nightmares where Jaxon's hands dragged her back into the dark. Chains on her wrists. A collar tight around her throat. He'd heard her scream, her desperate pleas echoing against the stone walls of the same cell that had held him for twenty-five years.

"I can't—" his voice shook so badly he couldn't continue, the darkness around him shuddering. Her imagined terror pierced his chest, his body bracing for a threat he couldn't fight. He needed to see her. To confirm with his own eyes that she was safe. Then when she rejected him like she had in her dream he could walk away with at least that comfort.

"He needs to see her, El," Galen said softly, laying his hand over hers. "I'd feel the same."

Eloria sighed, her expression softening as she looked at her own mate.

"I can only spare you for two days," Eloria said. "People will expect to see you at Bloomtide, so I'd appreciate it if you were back for that."

Relief crashed over Loren so suddenly he nearly sagged against the table. But underneath it, shame twisted its sharp claws into him. He was supposed to be a prince, the savior they all looked to—but instead he was falling apart because he couldn't bear being apart from one female.

Not trusting his voice, Loren inclined his head stiffly. Shoving back his chair, he stood and strode from the room, the shadows snapping at his heels.

"You're not the first one to make a mess of your mate bond, you know."

"I don't recall asking for your advice." Loren scowled as Galen fell into step beside him, their footfalls echoing through the deserted corridor.

"You didn't." The golden-haired male shrugged, the pleasant, affable expression he always wore serious for once. "But Eloria cares deeply for you. I'd be a poor mate if I saw a way to help and held my tongue. Did you know she was only twenty-three when our bond drew us together?"

Loren faltered mid-step, his head whipping toward Galen. "Twenty-three?" His shadows hissed, spreading out around his feet as his chest tightened. "She was a child."

"That's what I told her." Galen shrugged. "She was still grieving your father and struggling to run a kingdom she never expected to rule. I told her she needed more time to figure out who she was before throwing a mate bond into the mix—I'm sure you can imagine how that went over."

"You weren't wrong," Loren snapped. Fae didn't even come of age until twenty-five—it was unheard of for a mate bond to manifest before then. Most fae waited until long into their forties and fifties.

"Maybe not, but my reasons were." Galen snorted, shaking his head. "The whole truth is, I was terrified of the responsibility of keeping her safe when our people were on the verge of being wiped out. So I pushed her away."

Loren's lip curled. "You obviously got over it."

"We did." A thin smile tugged at Galen's lips, gone as quickly as it came. "But not before she tried to claim the shadows."

"She *what*?" The words punched the air from Loren's lungs. Even the shadows stilled, cringing against his legs.

"After your father died, she thought she had to be everything you would have been—that the shadows would answer to her if she just...proved herself worthy." Galen sighed, his golden gaze distant. "I *ran* when I felt her terror—but they nearly tore her apart before I managed to drag her out."

Loren stared at Galen, his throat working as he searched for the words to respond. Even the shadows were strangely silent, hovering around his legs like they were afraid to get too close but loathe to melt away. They had lashed out at Eloria once under his control—when they thought she was a threat to Araya. But to learn they had attacked her unprovoked, nearly killed her...it was a wonder she could stand in the same room with him at all.

"She never told me," he said finally.

"She wouldn't," Galen said. "She doesn't talk about it, Loren. She's never even told me what they said to her. All I'm saying is that when I tried to put space between us—even though I told myself and everyone around me that I was doing it for her—it nearly got her killed."

Not us, the shadows protested, their myriad of voices overlapping in soft echoes as they pressed tightly against his legs, curling up his calves in restless patterns. *Not us. Not that time—*

"All I'm trying to say is make sure whatever choice you make is actually for *her* and not just a product of your fear." Galen clapped a hand on Loren's shoulder, flashing a weary smile. "There's no prize for suffering, Loren."

Loren could only watch as Galen strode back down the hall. Returning to the warmth of the mate who waited for him—loved him. The shadows murmured, their restless mumblings as chaotic and unsettled as their shifting coils. But for once, Loren didn't try to silence them.

CHAPTER

TWENTY

Araya worked the bread on the counter, turning and folding with more force than necessary. Gods damn Thorne and his *advice*—her chest ached worse than ever, a yawning hole that cried out for warm hands and soft lips. She scowled down at the sticky dough, trying desperately not to think about how right and safe it had felt with Loren wrapped around her.

"And what did that bread ever do to you?"

Araya startled, heat rushing to her cheeks. Veria stood in the doorway, her silver brows arched as she looked around. Araya followed her gaze and winced. Without Veria's quiet magic tidying behind her, she'd managed to cover every surface in flour.

"I couldn't sleep," she said, surreptitiously scrubbing her hands against her flour-covered apron. "I thought I'd try and—" she winced as Veria picked up her first attempt at bread—a dense, flat disc that would have cracked your teeth if you tried to bite into it "—help."

But Veria only smiled. She flicked her fingers, magic humming to life in the air around them. The scattered bowls rose into the air, dropping neatly into the sink as the brushes scudded through the soap, working themselves into a lather.

"I think you've worked that poor loaf enough for now," she said kindly. "Get it into the pan and cover it up to rest, and you've earned yourself a cup of tea."

By the time the kettle whistled, Araya was seated at the table, watching as Veria bustled around the hearth. The older fae moved with practiced ease, humming under her breath as she poured the steaming water over a blend of herbs and flowers. The fragrant steam curled through the air, filling the kitchen with notes of lavender and honey.

"You said you couldn't sleep," Veria said, setting the steaming cup in front of her before taking her own seat. "Was it dreams?"

"N—not really." The lie that she'd been about to tell stuck in her throat, choking her. She wrapped both hands around the mug, her cheeks flaming. "I don't want to talk about it."

The corners of Veria's mouth twitched. But she nodded, schooling her face into seriousness. "Do they still mark Bloomtide in the New Dominion?"

"Not really." Araya bit her lip. She doubted Veria wanted to hear about how humans had replaced the fae holiday with Dominion Day, celebrating the overthrow of the fae monarchy. "It's like the fae New Year isn't it?"

"Something like that." Veria smiled, but a touch of sadness lingered in her eyes, like she'd heard everything Araya hadn't said anyway. "It's a celebration of life itself. In Tirnavel, there were days of music and dancing—all culminating in a procession of boats down the Alderwyl. Growers spent weeks perfecting floats depicting our oldest stories."

Araya's eyes widened, the image springing to life in her mind— boats strung with flowers drifting past crowds of fae lining both sides of the sparkling river. A knot rose in her throat. "It sounds beautiful," she said softly.

"It was." Veria sighed. "Eloria puts together something similar in Lumaria every year. To give the people hope."

"I'm sorry you're missing it." Araya stared down into the dregs of her tea, studying the soggy leaves like they were the most fascinating thing she'd ever seen.

"I've seen many Bloomtides, dear." Veria said kindly. "At Tirnavel and in Lumaria. But since Thalen passed..." she sighed, her bright blue eyes shining with unshed tears despite the smile on her face. "Well, I haven't much cared for grand celebrations. I'd rather mark the new year quietly, with good bread, a warm fire. And right now?" She reached across the table, brushing a trace of flour from Araya's wrist. "I think I'm right where the Goddess wants me to be."

They fell into a companionable silence after that, the scent of onion and herbs filling the kitchen as Veria started a stew pot over the fire. The bread she'd worked so hard on went into the oven. It came out a little lumpy, but Araya couldn't hold back her smile at seeing it next to Veria's perfectly shaped loaves.

She was working on another tray of candied flowers, carefully sugaring them before the glaze hardened completely when something shifted in the corner of her vision. Araya froze, her gaze snapping toward the shadows under the table. They almost seemed to ripple—flickering out of time with the firelight. But were they really shifting or was it a trick of her mind and the bond gnawing at her chest? It swelled like a bruise under her ribs, a little too close to hope for her own comfort.

"*Ael'sura.*" Loren's voice wrapped around her like honey, dark and warm. "What are you doing down here?"

She turned, her breath catching to see him leaning in the doorway. He watched her, his green eyes even brighter than usual in the dark hollows of his eyes. Gods, he looked like he hadn't slept well in *months.*

"I'm helping," she said, the words coming out with a strange waver. "Thorne thought it would help if I worked with Veria—" she looked around, but the older fae female was conspicuously absent. "What—what are you doing here?"

"I couldn't sleep." Loren still hovered in the doorway, like he wasn't sure he could cross the threshold.

After last night, Araya's mind supplied, heat flooding her cheeks. The dream she'd destroyed still lingered at the edges of her mind, her memory of his hands and lips on her skin all too vivid. Loren only looked at her, his gaze devouring her with the desperation of a starving man. What had Thorne said? That being apart was probably hurting him even more than it hurt her.

"Neither could I," Araya admitted. She pushed her tray aside, dropping the lid back on the sugar. "Would you like some tea? I can make some."

Loren's eyes widened, something like panic flickering across his face. "You don't have to wait on me—"

"It was an invitation, Loren." Araya turned to the tea service, busying herself with the simple motions of filling the pot. She traced *thyn* against the porcelain, heating the water with a trickle of aether. "Come in here and sit down."

<hr>

LOREN LOOKED TOTALLY OUT OF PLACE IN THE KITCHEN, ARAYA DECIDED. HE perched on the chair like he was ready to leap up at any moment, the shadows spreading out around his feet. She ducked her head, fussing unnecessarily with the tea service as one of them brushed her ankle, heat flushing her cheeks low in her stomach at the reminder of the way they'd touched her last night.

Loren had the grace not to comment as she set the tea service on the table, his gaze fixed firmly on his own hands. But when she set the small dish of candied blossoms between them his gaze snapped up to hers, his eyes wide.

"Veria said they were your favorite," Araya murmured, suddenly self-conscious.

For a heartbeat, he just stared at her, the hard lines of his face softening. Then he smiled and plucked one from the dish, popping it into his mouth. His eyes closed briefly as he chewed, shadows curling closer as if they shared his pleasure.

"I snuck into the kitchen and ate a whole tray once," he admitted, his eyes still closed. "Made myself sick and missed nearly all of Bloomtide. My mother—" he laughed softly, though his breath hitched with grief. "She convinced my father that missing the procession was punishment enough. I loved it when I was a child. She would tell us the stories as the floats passed—it was like everything came to life."

"You must miss them terribly."

Loren's throat worked. "Every day." His eyes stayed on the candied blossoms, like he didn't dare meet her eyes. "I owe you an apology. Last night—"

"You don't." Araya cut him off. "It's as much my fault as yours. Thorne suggested that finding a way to feel close to you might...ease the ache. But I doubt he meant I should go and fall asleep in your bed." She forced herself to look at him, even though her face burned with mortification. "We were both asleep. And...it wasn't all terrible."

"It wasn't," Loren echoed. He looked like she'd hit him over the head. "You...you missed me?"

"Against my will." Araya let out a short, bitter laugh, dragging her fingernail along the grain of the table so she wouldn't have to meet his eyes for what she said next. "I still think you should have told me about the bond the moment you knew. You've kept far too many secrets for me to trust you. But leaving me here the way you did? That hurt, Loren."

"*Ael'sura...*" he trailed off, his voice cracking on the endearment.

Araya shook her head, blinking hard. "How long before you leave again?"

"Tomorrow," Loren rasped, and when Araya glanced up at him through her lashes he was just staring at her, his expression gutted.

"In the morning. I have to go—Bloomtide is about hope. Eloria...she wants people to see me."

Her heart sank, heavy and leaden. But Araya nodded once, pressing her lips together to keep anything else from spilling out.

"But you could come," Loren added softly. He leaned forward, the shadows stretching across the table toward her. "Come with me. Eloria would be happy to have you there. You can see a real Bloomtide. And after that—" his hand flexed against the table, his knuckles white. "After that we can decide what to do about the bond. Together. No more secrets."

Araya folded her arms, the ache under her ribs pressing harder. "No more secrets?"

Loren nodded.

"We'd have to leave in the morning," he said, his green eyes locked on hers like her answer meant everything. "You don't have to decide right now. Just...meet me in the entrance hall after breakfast if you want to come. And wear something you can walk in."

Araya dropped her gaze to the table, pretending to study the candied blossoms. Her heart leapt in her chest, the bond screaming at her to say yes—but she wasn't going to let some bond she didn't ask for dictate her decisions. "I'll think about it."

CHAPTER

TWENTY-ONE

Loren paced the entry hall, the shadows twisting restlessly around his feet. He'd only meant to see her—to offer an apology and appease the ache that plagued him. None of his plans had included inviting her to Lumaria. But the words had tumbled out of his mouth before he could bite them back.

She deserved better than a broken fae prince who couldn't control his own power, let alone lead a kingdom on the edge of collapse. But for some reason, the Goddess had seen fit to tether her fate to his, tying her to a male who flinched at every flicker of darkness in his own mind.

It would have been laughable if it weren't so utterly terrifying.

The little shadow that had attached itself to her streaked into the hall, circling him once before vanishing into the gloom. She must be close, if it was here. It had abandoned him the instant they returned to Ithralis, racing to her side like a loyal hound. He hadn't been surprised, after it had abandoned him to stay with her the first time, but he didn't understand it. They'd never acted like this with his mother. But Araya—even the Shadowed Veil had paused when she spoke.

"Loren?"

Loren straightened, Araya's voice snapping him from his spiraling thoughts. She hovered at the base of the stairs, her bright silver eyes guarded. But she was here. Willing to see—to listen.

Now he just needed to find the words to explain it all without sending her running in the opposite direction. Goddess help him.

"What?" Araya asked, glancing down at her clothes. "Is this not good?"

"No—it's fine." Loren cleared his throat, dragging his gaze away before she caught him staring like a boy barely come into his power. "We should get moving. I don't want to be in the forest longer than we need to be."

"We're going through the forest?" Araya trailed him out the door, her voice tight. "I thought the coastal road was safer?"

"It avoids the worst of the shadows," Loren said, leading them through the gate and skirting the edge of the forest. "But it's longer. We have plenty of daylight left, and the *zal'vorr* usually prefer to hunt at night."

"*Usually*?" She cast him a skeptical glance, taking a half-step closer to him as they entered the shadow of the trees.

"As long as you don't serve yourself up as a tasty snack—" he barely managed to hold back his smile as she huffed, irritation cutting through the fear that hummed through the bond. He hadn't realized how much he'd *missed* feeling her emotions until they were gone, the distance between them turning everything but her strongest emotions into nothing but a faint echo.

They walked in companionable silence after that, every footfall crushing the tiny white flowers that had sprung up in the cracked stones, perfuming the air. Loren's shadows stretched ahead of them, slipping over cracked stones and exploring the edges of the road.

"That's the temple we took shelter in," Araya said suddenly. She stopped, studying the thick tendrils of darkness that spilled over the smashed stone walls, crawling onto the edges of the road.

"It is." Loren took her elbow, steering her closer to the center of the path. "*That* is the reason hardly anyone takes the forest road. Our scholars believe it's the source of the Shadowed Veil."

"Is it?" Araya asked, studying the twisted tendrils creeping over the carved archways with open curiosity.

"I haven't looked into it." Loren shrugged, biting back a smile at the aghast look she trained on him. "Better scholars than me have studied it, *ael'sura*. Eloria banned further attempts to enter the shadows here after so many people were lost trying to retrieve our father's body."

"But—" Araya frowned, her forehead creasing. "We entered."

"We entered the *temple*," Loren corrected. "The battlefield is completely blanketed in shadows. We might have survived sailing through the Shadowed Veil—something most people would call impossible—but I wouldn't be eager to test these shadows."

He took her elbow, guiding her carefully around the creeping darkness where the road curved past the temple. His own shadows clung to his legs, their low, anxious murmur doing nothing to set him at ease.

"This isn't how I like to remember it," Loren said. "Before...I've only ever felt power like it in the Eldergreen at Tirnavel. The idea that both those places are lost to us now..." He sighed, not looking back as the jagged temple stones vanished behind them, swallowed once more by shadow and silence.

"Is it lost?" Araya asked after a moment. "Jaxon was stationed at Elvanfal for three years. There must be *something* in the forest they're still trying to get to."

"The fae were forced to abandon Tirnavel and the forest that surrounds it." Loren glanced over at her, the ache in the bond mirroring his own as she watched him with sad eyes. "Whether the humans have truly taken it or not, it's still lost to us, *ael'sura*."

It was mid-afternoon by the time they reached the first rough shelters outside Lumaria, the sunlight that filtered through the thin mist almost too bright after the constant dusk that blanketed Ithralis.

"Is that it?" Araya asked.

"This is the outer city," Loren said, trying not to look too hard as they walked through the slums. "There isn't room for everyone inside the walls. Eloria and her advisors have worked to make as much space as they can...but this island was never meant to house so many people."

"I've never seen so many fae in one place," Araya said, her voice laced with something close to wonder.

Loren looked at it again, trying to see it through her eyes. The outer city was abuzz with preparations for Bloomtide, even the most ragged of tents adorned with garlands of early spring flowers. Fae of all ages stood outside, talking and laughing despite the grimness of their circumstances. Children wove their way through the groups, racing between street performers with wide-eyed wonder.

Araya paused to watch an illusionist, her face bright with delight as a great ash tree unfurled from his hands, its bare branches blooming with radiant blossoms that spilled petals of gold and violet into the air before a pair of harts dashed through the scene, their spectral hooves leaving trails of light with every bound.

Loren watched her instead, her silver eyes reflecting the glow of magic as if she was seeing something from a dream. And maybe she was—she'd grown up with her magic restricted and stolen, twisted into a burden rather than a gift. But here she saw it as it should be— as *she* should be—free and alive.

Loren swallowed hard, forcing himself to look away before he lost the battle with his heart completely. But his shadows didn't have the same restraint. They reached out, curling over her skin as if they too had given up on pretending they could keep their distance.

"This is amazing." Araya glanced back over her shoulder at him, the soft flicker of magic playing across a radiant smile that took his breath away.

"He's very good," Loren agreed.

They both watched a cascade of ribbons unravel from the male's fingers, twisting into dancers who twirled in perfect time with the music that had started to drift through the streets. It was safer to watch the magic than her. If she looked at him now there was no way she wouldn't see every feeling written on his face.

The dancers spun faster, ribbons flowing like petals caught in the wind. Then, with a final flick of the illusionist's wrist, they dissolved —vanishing into the night like whispers of a dream.

The illusionist turned—and bowed low.

Loren almost didn't react. He had seen performers bow countless times before. But when the male rose, his eyes were bright with tears.

"Your Majesty," the male said, his voice hoarse with emotion. "Welcome home."

Loren's heart dropped into his stomach as whispers spread out around them, the words echoing through the crowd that had gathered to watch the show.

His return might not be a secret any more, but he hadn't exactly walked among the people. The news spread ahead of them like wildfire, and by the time they reached the gates throngs of people crowded the street ahead of them. Some even lifted their children high to see, their faces bright with desperate hope. The weight of it settled over him, as heavy as the crown he didn't want.

"They love you," Araya said as they reached the foot of the stairs leading up to the Central Hall.

Loren grimaced, offering her his arm. "It's just the idea of me they love."

Araya frowned, clearly prepared to argue, but he cut her off before she could.

"I do have one thing to ask of you while we're here," he said. "Don't use your true name."

Araya flinched back from his offered arm, her expression shuttering. "Because even a child could compel me?"

Loren winced. "I deserve all your anger," he admitted. "What I did was...harsh. But please, *ael'sura*. It may look like everyone loves me, but I promise you there are those here who don't."

He'd fall to his knees and beg if that's what it took to sway her. The idea of someone using her true name to hurt her because of him —he'd burn this city to the ground before he let that happen.

"Does it even matter?" Araya demanded. "Plenty of people already know my true name. What are they supposed to call me if not that?"

"They *should* call you by your title," Loren said, frowning at her. "Even if they know your name, using it before you've freely given it to them is *very* impolite."

Araya stared at him. "I'm a halfblood fae from the New Dominion," she said. "I don't have a *title*."

"You're the mate of the crown prince." Loren couldn't help but smile at the dumbfounded expression on her face. "Eloria gave you a title the moment you stepped off the boat, *Lady Starwind*."

For a heartbeat, he thought she'd still argue, but then her gaze flicked past him to the crowd that filled the bustling square, the stubbornness draining from her expression.

"Very well." She sniffed, taking his arm. "But only if you introduce me properly, *Your Highness*. I've never had a title before—I'd hate to get it wrong."

Loren choked on a laugh. "I think you'll manage," he said, his heart flipping over in his chest as the hint of a smile that curled at the corner of her mouth bloomed into a grin.

He guided her up the stairs and through the tall doors, exchanging nods with the guards as they crossed into the wing Eloria had claimed for personal residences. She'd have to find Araya a set of rooms and have them prepared too. Maybe he should have sent word that Araya was coming with him—but he hadn't actually believed it would happen.

Araya's grip tightened on his arm as laughter spilled out from Eloria's apartments. The sound of clinking glass and muffled voices bled into the corridor, warm and unguarded.

"It's alright," he murmured, resting his other hand over hers. "Trust me, they'll be thrilled to see you."

"Just because you believe that doesn't make it true," Araya retorted, her grip on his arm tightening. But she kept pace with him as he pushed the door open without knocking, stepping into his sister's apartments at his side.

"You brought her." Eloria shot to her feet, both hands flying to her mouth to muffle her delighted laugh. "You actually *brought* her!"

"It's about time." Galen stood beside his mate, a wide grin splitting his face. "Welcome, Araya. Happy Bloomtide."

"Happy Bloomtide," she said softly, still clinging to his arm. "Sorry to interrupt your celebration, Your Majesties." Her gaze flitted to where Thorne sat, his expression carefully neutral. "Thorne."

"Please." Eloria snorted, shaking her head. "You're as welcome as he is. Here, let's go find you something to wear—"

The shadow surged before Loren even consciously thought to direct it, twining around Araya's legs and rearing up with a warning hiss.

"Really?" Eloria dropped her hand, her smile flattening into a scowl. "You'll be right here. She's perfectly safe with me—"

"You still have to *ask* her," Loren snapped. "The last time you saw her, you tricked her. You might think it was harmless, but I don't."

Eloria's mouth twisted. "Goddess spare me from mated males," she muttered, rolling her eyes. But her expression softened as she turned back to Araya. "It doesn't have to be right now. I have plenty of dresses you can borrow. The two of you are probably starving. At least join us for dinner."

Araya nodded slowly, the shadows dissolving around her like smoke. Eloria didn't try to touch her this time, instead simply ushering her over to the couches, chattering the entire time.

"And here I thought you'd rather wrestle a *zal'vorr* than admit you cared," Thorne drawled, lifting his glass in a lazy salute before taking a sip.

"Goddess spare us from mated males," Galen added, mimicking his mate's exasperated tone with a smirk. He poured another drink, pressing it into Loren's hand. "She's going to have you wrapped around her little finger before Bloomtide is over."

"You're both insufferable." Loren snorted, tossing back half the glass in one swallow.

CHAPTER

TWENTY-TWO

They ate in what must have once been a beautiful solar, the ceiling paneled with glass and a wide balcony just beyond the doors. The mist was thinner here, streaked with oranges and violets from the setting sun instead of the dense shroud that blanketed Ithralis. She still couldn't see the stars, but for the first time since she'd crossed the Veil it felt like she could breathe freely.

"Thank you," Araya murmured, smiling as Loren sat her plate down in front of her.

He took the seat beside her, a shadow curling lazily around her ankle. Across the table, Galen and Thorne had already launched into some half-serious argument, their voices overlapping as forks clattered against plates.

"I'd bet you the last honey-cake he refuses to relax," Galen said, pointing his fork at Loren.

"I relax," Loren snapped, straightening in his chair. "Sometimes."

"That's a bad bet." Thorne arched a brow, shaking his head. "Your definition of relax, or his?"

"Mine, obviously." Galen scoffed. "Loren thinks poring over dusty old books is relaxing.

Loren's mouth twitched, and to Araya's shock he didn't retreat into silence. "You can't win every fight with a sword, Galen."

"You can if you swing it hard enough," Galen shot back.

Within moments the three males were sparring in earnest. Loren laughed, shaking his head at something Thorne said. Araya set her fork down at the sound, something squeezing tight in her chest at how much younger and lighter he looked with a real smile on his face.

"You make him happy," Eloria said.

"Oh—" Araya jumped, looking quickly back down at her plate like she hadn't just been caught staring. "I'm sure it's being here with his family after so long that makes him happy."

"Is that what you think?" Eloria gave a very un-princess-like snort. "He was an absolute terror the entire time you were at Ithralis and he was here. Even the shadows are desperate to be close to you."

Araya raised a hand to where the little shadow curled around her neck, suddenly self-conscious. "I know fae take this...fated bond seriously, but...I can't be what he needs. I already have a bond in the New Dominion."

Eloria's brows arched. "That's what you call what Shaw did to you? A bond?" Her tone sharpened, though there was a thread of pity beneath it. "Whatever he forced on you, it isn't this. Look at them." She tipped her chin toward the shadow twined around Araya's shoulders. "They never behaved like that for our father," she said. "Not even when our mother was still alive. Did you know they killed him?"

"I—" Araya's throat tightened. The shadow draped over her shoulders stirred, picking up on her unease, and she stroked it hastily as if that could settle them both. "Loren said your father died on the battlefield. There were no survivors—"

"I didn't have to be there to know what happened," Eloria laughed bitterly. "I saw how they fought him after our mother died. I have no doubt they slaughtered every single person on that battle-field—including their master." She stared at the shadow wrapped around Araya's shoulders, her eyes bright. "They've even tried to kill me twice."

Araya stilled, her fingers freezing mid-stroke. "What?"

"The first time was when I tried to claim the shadows myself." Eloria's smile thinned, her voice going brittle at the edges. "You see, we didn't know if Loren was alive or if *dara'el* was still tied to my father's remains. But without them, I can't lead our people—not really."

"And the second time?" she whispered.

"The night he came back," Eloria sat back in her chair, studying her like Araya was a puzzle she meant to solve. "Whatever remnant of *dara'el* is following him around wasn't pleased when I didn't immediately acquiesce to his demand that I—how did he put it? Put you on a boat to anywhere you wanted to go."

Araya's chest constricted, the glass ceiling and warm lights all blurring together as she struggled to take a full breath. "He told you to let me go?"

"Oh, he was *adamant*." Eloria laughed, but there was an edge to her smile now. "He wanted me to promise you would be free to walk away."

Araya's throat tightened. "And you said no."

"Of course I said no." Eloria scoffed, her green eyes flashing. "What world do you think we're living in right now? The shadows *chose* him. Our people need their king—and *he* needs *you*. So before you go running back to that human mage who nearly killed you out of some delusional mix of fear and loyalty, maybe consider giving my brother—and his people—a real chance."

Araya flinched, Eloria's words landing like a stone in her gut. On the other side of the room, Loren's voice suddenly cut off, his head snapping up. But Araya avoided his gaze, shoving to her feet instead.

"I need some air." She pushed past Eloria without waiting for permission, escaping through the glass doors to the relative privacy of the balcony beyond.

Cool air hit her face, perfumed with the sharp, sweet scent of early spring blooms and the earthy tang of freshly-turned soil from the garlands of fresh flowers that decorated the central square so far below. Clusters of fae gathered in the brightly lit space, their laughter drifting up to her ears like something from a half-remembered dream.

She felt him before he spoke, his presence wrapping around her like the soothing embrace of his shadows—the same shadows that had killed his father. That had tried to kill Eloria—twice.

"If you want to be alone I'll go," Loren said softly. "I just wanted to make sure you were alright."

Araya swallowed hard, staring down at the crowd below. "You don't have to go."

He moved slowly to stand beside her, leaving just enough space between them that the shadows curled in the gap, reaching out before coiling back like they were waiting for her permission to cross.

"What did she say to you?" Loren asked finally, his voice careful.

"She told me you tried to let me go." Araya swallowed hard, looking up from the crowd below to meet his gaze. "Even though you'd already claimed me."

Loren's shoulders stiffened, his expression turning wary. "I did."

"Even though it would have hurt you?" Araya whispered.

This time it was Loren who looked away, his silence saying more than words ever could. The little shadow slipped from her shoulders, reaching out to him. Araya watched it brush against him like a cat—offering comfort. Because she was already hurting him. She was hurting everyone.

Her stomach knotted. Even if the fae agreed to her proposal to harness the shadows to another wielder, she was no closer to figuring out how to hide or break the bond. She couldn't go back—but nothing would stop Jaxon from coming for her. Once he made it past the Veil, the fae would have no way to stand against him. Unless Loren had his full power.

"I'm being selfish," she said at last, her voice hollow. "If completing the bond gives you control of the shadows and lets you protect your people...then we should complete it."

Loren went rigid beside her, the shadows rising behind him like mantled wings. "Absolutely not," he snapped. "You don't owe me your freedom. You don't owe me your body. And you sure as hell don't owe me the bond just because Eloria wants a king who can keep his shadows leashed."

Araya sucked in a sharp breath as he stepped closer, the air crackling between them. His fingers brushed her chin, tipping her face up until she had no choice but to meet his searing green gaze.

"If you ever choose me, Araya—if you ever choose this—it will be because *you* want it. Not because Eloria made you feel guilty or you were backed into a corner." Loren took a deep breath, his eyes slipping closed. "I meant what I told you before. I have no desire to trap you in this."

Araya swallowed hard, her chest aching. "What if I don't know what I want?"

Loren's hand fell away, but the shadows lingered, brushing gently across her skin. "Then we'll figure it out together," he said, as if it was really that simple. "Eloria arranged a chamber for you in this wing. Do you want me to walk you over?"

Araya bit her lip, turning away before she did something foolish like lean into his warmth. "Not yet," she murmured. "Can you just... stay out here with me for a while?"

His breath caught, but he didn't hesitate. "Of course, *ael'sura.*"

CHAPTER
TWENTY-THREE

"I can't believe I let you talk me into coming down here without her." Loren tugged at the sleeves of his embroidered tunic, the silver vines and leaves embroidered on the deep green silk catching the light like shimmering stars. "How long does it take to put on a dress?"

"Longer than you think," Eloria snipped back. "I left her three choices. And she'll have to figure out what to do with her hair. Honestly, you should have let me stay to help her—"

"Princess!" one of the stewards called from across the hall, bowing hastily before gesturing toward the temporary staging area they'd set up at the back of the hall. "They're asking for you."

"She's meddling," Loren growled, glaring at Eloria's back as his sister glided away to join the army of cooks scrambling to make sure everything was *just so* before the doors finally opened.

Galen laughed, tossing back a goblet of the effervescent golden wine. He looked maddeningly at ease in his finery, his own deep green doublet tailored to perfection and threaded with the same silver embroidery.

"Of course she's meddling," he said. "She's your sister. But she's not doing it to trap Araya. She's doing it because she wants the two of you to have each other when you need it most."

Loren grumbled something non-committal, his gaze snagging on Eloria's commander at arms and spymaster, their heads bent together in quiet conversation. The shadows thickened around his feet, the hair on the back of his neck prickling.

"Don't." Galen set his goblet down a little too hard. "Eloria already forced the entire Small Council to swear oaths that they wouldn't approach her during Bloomtide. You don't have anything to worry about."

Loren's lip curled as he watched Eryn melt into the crowd. Cormac stayed, his face set in a permanent scowl despite the festive occasion. Oaths or not, he didn't trust either of them. If they found a way to get to her—

"And look," Galen interrupted his churning thoughts. "There she is."

Loren turned, the shadows rising with him like they wanted to see too—and then he promptly forgot all about Cormac and Eryn.

Araya walked down the steps next to Thorne, one hand resting lightly on his arm as she laughed at something he said. The bright sound carried through the hall, the easy warmth she shared with his oldest friend striking Loren right in the heart.

The gown fit her like a second skin, tailored to tempt fate. Eloria's doing, no doubt—right down to the silver thread that echoed the embroidery on his own tunic and the plum silk that drew attention to her creamy skin. She'd drawn the front of her fiery hair back from her face in a braided crown that emphasized the long line of her neck, for once bare of that cursed amulet.

"Close your mouth, Your Majesty," Galen whispered loudly.

Loren snapped his mouth closed hard enough to rattle his teeth. Across the room, Araya hesitated, a swell of anxiety rising in the bond as she scanned the crowd—but then her searching silver gaze found his, as drawn to him as he was to her.

He moved without thinking, people jumping out of the way of

his shadows as he strode across the hall. He stopped just short of touching her. He didn't dare—not when his hands remembered the curve of her waist and the way she'd melted into him in that dream, soft and giving and impossibly warm.

"Is it too much?" she asked softly.

"Is what too much?" Loren asked stupidly, still staring at her.

Araya blinked, then huffed out a laugh Loren would have paid fortunes to hear again. "The *dress*, Loren."

"*Oh*—" Loren forced himself to take a step back, sucking in a deep breath. "Not at all. You look—it suits you."

"I knew it would," Eloria said, her voice light and unmistakably smug. She swept in at precisely the wrong moment, her green skirts whispering across the stone. "I hope you're happy with it, Araya."

Araya flushed, her hands twisting in the folds of the skirt. "It's very beautiful," she said politely. "Thank you for lending it to me."

"Consider it a gift," Eloria replied, her smile widening as her gaze flicked to Loren. "Can I borrow my brother for just a moment?"

Loren groaned. "What do you want, Eloria?"

But she was already dragging him away, her grip surprisingly firm. "That looks like it's going well," she said, not bothering to hide her delight.

"Don't read too much into it," Loren muttered, though his eyes betrayed him as they slid back to Araya. "Where did you even find that dress?"

"I had it made," Eloria said, clearly pleased with herself. "For the future queen. I donated several of my older gowns to the cause."

"She doesn't want to be a queen." Loren scowled at his sister. But he couldn't hold onto his anger as Araya laughed, shaking her head at something Galen had said. A smile lit her face, wide and unguarded. She looked...happy.

A pang of longing hit him at the sight of it, his chest tightening. Goddess, what he would give for her to have that always.

Eloria jabbed him lightly in the shoulder, a knowing smile

tugging at her lips. "You don't look too bad yourself. Very regal. Almost…kingly."

"Don't make me regret coming," Loren warned, tugging at his too-tight collar with a grimace. A part of him—the part he had spent years burying—wanted to believe it. That he was home. That they had never stopped waiting for him. That they wanted him here.

But he wasn't the savior they so desperately wanted to believe he was.

Eloria followed his gaze, her teasing smile fading as her eyes tracked the sight of her brother's mate standing so easily beside her own.

"I know you want to protect her, Loren," she said. "But if you want this to go anywhere you have to start treating her like your queen and not your ward. If you want her, give her a reason to stay."

Loren bared his teeth, the shadows hissing at her words. "That's rich, coming from you," he snapped. "Enjoy the celebration, Eloria."

He turned on his heel, intending to walk away and not speak to his sister for the rest of the night, but he didn't even make it two steps before Eloria chased after him.

Loren sighed, not bothering to hide his irritation as he turned back to face her. But his sister met his ire with a knowing smirk, pressing a crown woven from wildflowers and soft green leaves into his hands.

"There will be lots of dancing tonight," she said over her shoulder as she breezed away, heading for her own mate. "I hope you have someone to ask."

Loren scowled after his sister, but his heart did a flip in his chest when Araya glanced up. Her gaze caught his, her shy smile hitting him like a bolt of lightning.

He could tell himself over and over again that she deserved better. That she would never choose him. That she would leave— that she *should* leave—and he had no right to ask otherwise.

But he didn't want her to leave. Not Eluneth—and not him.

He wanted her to stay. He wanted her to keep looking at him like this, her eyes bright with wonder and her laughter warm and unguarded. But so much of this had started wrong between them. Even if he'd fought at every step not to take her choice away any more than he already had, he still hadn't told her the truth. And once he did...Loren wasn't sure she'd ever look at him like that again.

But there was only one way to find out.

Loren took a deep breath, the delicate perfume of the flower crown filling his lungs as he stared down at the tiny blossoms. Maybe, for once, Eloria had the right idea.

CHAPTER

TWENTY-FOUR

"So?" Galen nudged her arm, a grin tugging at his lips. "What do you think of Lumaria?"

Araya shook her head, at a loss for words. "It's...amazing."

Long tables stretched across the hall in neat rows, groaning under the weight of mismatched platters and steaming trays. Salt-crusted fish and smoked eel shared space with dark, hearty stews, their broths heavily spiced to mask the gamey tang of preserved meat. Ornate dishes that wouldn't have been out of place in a palace sat beside chipped, hand-thrown bowls, all of them polished to a mirror sheen.

Fae of every age and class darted between the tables, straightening cutlery and making last-minute adjustments, all of them smiling and laughing like the act of preparing this feast was as much a celebration as the meal itself.

"Eloria pulls every resource for the big holidays," Thorne said, following her gaze. "People here have little enough to find joy in most days. And of course, everyone wants to celebrate Loren."

"And the female who brought him back to us," Galen added cheerfully. "Eloria's been begging him to bring you here so you could see all of this instead of keeping you locked up in that grim old castle."

Araya flushed, her heart clenching strangely in her chest at Galen's words. "He was just trying to keep me safe," she said.

"Of course." Galen nodded. "Goddess knows, I'd love to keep Eloria locked up in a tower—but she'd skin me alive if I tried. I'm just thrilled that Loren finally saw reason."

Araya was saved from responding as two guards dragged the main doors open, letting the sounds of laughter and music drift into the hall. Araya craned her neck for a better look, her heart lighter than it had been in months as she stared out at the countless fae that filled the square, talking and laughing without a trace of fear. To get to see this, even just one time—it was like a dream.

She turned her head, intending to steal a glimpse of Loren—but instead she caught his eyes, her heart suddenly pounding as she ducked her head, heat rushing to her cheeks.

"Someone can't stop staring," Galen teased, his voice brimming with mischief.

Araya blushed harder, scrambling for a response. "Are you sure you're not imagining things?"

"That's a very *fae* answer," Galen shot back, his grin widening. "If I was imagining things, why would you answer my question with a question? What happened between the two of you to put that soft look in our lost prince's eyes?"

Araya flushed bright red, stammering as she fumbled for an answer. There was no way she was telling *Galen* about her dream.

She was saved by Eloria, of all people.

The Princess Regent swept toward them, her beautiful face brightening as her gaze fell on her mate. Galen's teasing grin softened the moment his eyes landed on her. Without hesitation, he reached for her, pulling her close and pressing a sound kiss to her lips despite all the eyes that surrounded them. Eloria smiled up at him, her gaze full of a love so open and unhidden that it made Araya's heart ache.

"It's time for us to open the dancing."

Galen groaned dramatically but didn't relinquish his hold on her. "Shouldn't Loren do it?"

"No." Eloria laughed, pressing a kiss to the back of his hand. "Until he's officially recognized by the Small Council, I'm afraid you're still the mate of the ranking royal."

"What a fate." Galen sighed in mock defeat, but his arm tightened around her waist. "Lead the way, my love. I can never say no to you."

Eloria threw her head back, laughter ringing through the night as she and Galen descended the stairs into the center of the square. The crowd parted around them, all eyes turning as the music swelled into a bright, joyful rhythm—just in time for Galen to sweep her off her feet, still laughing, into a wild, whirling dance.

"They're so beautiful," she said softly.

Thorne chuckled. "Galen *hates* dancing—but he rises to the occasion when he has to."

"Does Loren?" Araya asked without thinking.

"Hate dancing? Or rise to the occasion?" Thorne arched a brow, the corner of his mouth twitching. "Were you thinking about saying yes if he asks?"

Heat rushed to her cheeks. "I didn't mean—"

"It's all right." Thorne's voice gentled. "You're fae in a fae-ruled city. No one will blink twice at seeing Loren Shadowbane with a beautiful young female tonight. They've seen too much loss to begrudge anyone a little joy—least of all him."

The bond bristled in her chest, a heated answer on the tip of her tongue before she bit it back. She glanced back at Loren, unable to help herself as she tried not to think about the *beautiful young females* that might have entertained him in the past.

But the prince was only watching her, his customary stoicism replaced by something softer and gentler as his gaze found hers.

Araya turned away quickly, trying to focus on Galen and Eloria's effortless movements. The music swelled as more fae joined their dance, laughter rising into the spring air. But Loren's presence pressed constantly against the edge of her awareness, that band around her heart pulling just a little tighter.

"I'll leave you to it then." Thorne tossed back the rest of the drink, grinning at her. "Enjoy your night, Lady Starwind."

"Enjoy my...?" Araya trailed off as cool petals brushed her forehead, blinking up at Loren as he settled a crown of flowers on her head.

"It's how we ask for a dance," he said softly.

Araya swallowed hard, her heart stumbling over itself. She looked out at the dancers, their movements light and free. "I don't know the steps," she admitted.

"You don't need to." Loren's hand reached for hers, his fingers grazing her skin in a touch that stirred the magic in her blood, sending a rush of warmth racing across her skin. "Just follow me."

She let him guide her down the stairs, the joy of the night swelling around them—bright with music and laughter and light. The crowd parted for them, smiling faces spinning by in a blur as Loren drew her into the dance. Her steps were hesitant at first, clumsy and unsure. But Loren's hand at her waist was steady. And slowly, fear loosened its grip.

Until it felt like flying.

She spun in his arms, laughter bubbling up before she could stop it, surprising her with its lightness. Loren's face lit up at the sound, the shadow of his years in a cell falling away to show her the prince he must have once been.

"I know what you're doing," she said when they finally paused to rest.

Loren arched a brow, though amusement glimmered in his eyes. "Do you?"

She gestured toward the celebration—the vibrant colors, the music, the warmth, the pulse of joy thrumming in the air. "This," she said. "Showing me what it can be like here. Hoping I'll fall in love."

The words left her mouth too easily—and the second they did, Araya felt her stomach drop.

She hadn't meant him. She'd meant the fae. Their world. The freedom, the magic, the chance to be something other than a tool. But as soon as she said it, she felt the shift in the air between them. The way Loren's gaze caught on hers, no longer amused but very still—like the words had meant something else entirely, or like he *hoped* they had.

"And is it working?"

She should have laughed. Should have looked away and said obviously not, because of course she wasn't in love. Not with him. Not with this place. Not with anything. She couldn't afford to be.

But instead...she hesitated. Because gods help her, she didn't know.

Loren looked away. His hand brushed lightly across her back as he stepped back, his touch so gentle it made her heart clench.

"I'll get us something to drink," he said. His voice was even, but his shadows brushed against her ankles, betraying him. "Don't vanish."

Araya stared after him, the words she hadn't been able to speak still caught in her throat. She didn't want to leave. Not the festival. Not this world—not him. But no matter how many flower crowns Loren placed on her head, there was no real future where she got to have any of this. Not when her name, her future, and her freedom still belonged to Jaxon.

"Araya?" A familiar voice reached her over the music and laughter. "Is that really you?"

Araya turned, inhaling sharply as she met a pair of wide, violet eyes and the past collided with the present.

"*Eilwen?*"

The terrified, cowed female Araya had last seen at Serafina's maternity clinic glowed with health now, her violet eyes bright with magic and her black hair shining under the golden light of the aetherlamps. But it was the child sleeping in her arms that Araya couldn't stop staring at, even though all she could see over his blanket was a shock of midnight hair and a delicately pointed ear.

"His name is Selan," Eilwen said. "We owe you and Serafina everything."

Before Araya could find her voice, Eilwen pulled her into a tight embrace, pressing the precious bundle of blankets into her arms. Araya froze, afraid the rapid beat of her heart might wake him, but the child only stirred and snuggled into her with a little grunt as his mother stroked his cheek.

"He's beautiful," Araya whispered, her voice choked.

"He's all I have left of his father," Eilwen said with a watery smile. "He's my joy. My hope."

Araya rocked the baby gently, her gaze fixed on his tiny, peaceful face. Serafina had done this—helped Eilwen escape, given this little boy a future. How many others had she saved?

A brush of cool air against her ankle made Araya catch her breath. She glanced down at the little shadow, twining its way up her body toward its favored place across her shoulders. But this time, it moved with unusual care, as if it could sense the preciousness of the life cradled in her arms.

"Gentle," Araya murmured. She didn't want to scare Eilwen or her child—but the shadow slipped even closer, curious.

"Is that shadow magic?" Eilwen didn't flinch or pull away, her voice laced with wonder. "I've never seen anything like it. Is it yours?"

"Not mine." Araya shifted, letting the shadow curl around her wrist. "The shadows belong to Loren. This one just...likes me."

Eilwen's eyes widened. "Prince Loren?" She glanced toward where he lingered by the tables with Galen. "That's amazing. I'm happy for you."

Araya blinked, uncertain how to respond. "It's complicated," she said at last.

"It always is." Eilwen laughed, stretching out a tentative hand toward the shadow. The tendril paused, considering her, then curled gently around her hand. Araya tensed—but Eilwen only laughed, soft and amazed, as the shadow twined through her fingers like smoke before slipping away again.

"I had a bond with Selan's father," Eilwen said softly, her voice tinged with sadness. "We could share power in small ways, but nothing quite as impressive as this."

Araya glanced down at Selan, feeling the weight of Eilwen's words. "He was fae too, wasn't he?" If there was human blood in this baby, it wasn't much. His life...it wouldn't have been a kind one in the New Dominion.

"Half," Eilwen said, her sad smile telling Araya everything she needed to know about where this male was now. "I didn't even know we were mates until Thorne explained it—it felt like losing him twice."

"I'm so sorry, Eilwen," Araya swallowed, staring down at the baby in her arms. The back of her neck prickled and she glanced up, not surprised to find Loren staring at her. There was something in his expression that was tender, almost vulnerable as he watched her cradle Selan and his shadow twined around them both.

"I didn't know about the mate bond either," Araya said quietly. "I'm not sure what to make of it."

"It's a lot to take in." Eilwen took Selan back as he stirred, fussing quietly. "A year ago I thought the Arcanum was going to put me to death," she said. "I never would have believed a place like this even existed—much less that I'd be growing half the flowers for Bloomtide."

"You grew all these?" Araya looked around again at all the flowers that surrounded them. "They're beautiful."

"I'm a grower," Eilwen said. "I've always had a knack for growing things—but the things I can do now, with my full power?" Her smile deepened, pride brightening her violet eyes. "Most days, the Princess Regent has me focused on crops. But for this? I got to make something beautiful."

"I hope I'm not interrupting."

Araya startled, a shiver running through her as Loren's warm hand wrapped around her waist. She glanced up at him, but his gaze was fixed on the child in Eilwen's arms, his expression unexpectedly soft.

"What a beautiful child," he said.

"Thank you, Your Majesty." Eilwen dipped into a clumsy curtsy, flushing. "It's an honor to meet you. My son and I—we wouldn't be here without Araya. She saved us."

"Did she?" Loren's grip tightened, sending sparks racing across Araya's skin. "Well, I'm glad you both made it here unharmed. Your son is lucky to have you."

"He'll be a handful soon," Eilwen said with a breathless laugh. "He's already a troublemaker. I had to tie him to my back just to finish the floats for tonight."

"You worked on the floats too?" Araya asked quickly, grateful for the shift in conversation. Loren's hand remained at her waist, steady and warm, but she didn't dare look at him.

"I did." Eilwen grinned, bright-eyed. "Come on—I'll help you find the best place to watch. You don't want to miss this."

<hr>

THE MUSIC AND LAUGHTER SWELLED AS THE CROWD PRESSED IN AROUND them, the air thick with the heady scent of crushed petals and magic as Eilwen led them forward, Selan snug in her arms. Heads turned as they passed, Loren's name spreading through the crowd like wildfire.

Araya kept her eyes locked on Eilwen's back, trying not shrink under the weight of so many eyes. But with every step, she became more acutely aware of Loren behind her—the heat of his presence a burning contrast to the cool brush of his shadows curling around her ankles like curious hands.

"We don't have to stay if you don't want to," Loren murmured, his voice pitched low, meant only for her. "This is a lot—I can take you back."

"No," Araya said quickly, even as her voice wavered. "I want to see the floats."

She meant it. She wanted to see this world—the one he had endured so much pain to protect.

A hush rippled through the crowd as the music swelled, rising to a joyful crescendo as the first float glided into view, drawn forward by nothing but threads of shimmering magic. A phoenix rose from it, sculpted from living blooms of crimson lilies and golden marigolds, held together by curling vines heavy with orange trumpet blossoms. It's wings stretched wide, petals rustling softly in the spring breeze as if it might take flight at any moment.

"You *grew* that?" Araya gasped.

"The theme was rebirth," Eilwen said, turning Selan in her arms so he could stare at the passing floats, his eyes wide with wonder. "They tried to represent all the old stories, to help teach those of us who never got to learn."

Araya didn't answer right away, her throat thick and her eyes stinging as the phoenix glided past them. Dancers spun and twirled barefoot in the shadow of its spread wings, scattering petals in their wake like a blessing. The crowd answered with a roar of delight, hands and voices lifted skyward.

But Loren didn't cheer.

He stood beside her, silent and unmoving, his shoulders rigid as he stared out at the floats. The bond between them twisted with the ache of everything he felt—so much grief tangled with joy that it was hard to tell where one ended and the other began.

Before she could think too hard about what she was doing, Araya leaned closer, letting her fingers tangle gently with his.

Loren startled slightly, his hand stiffening before his fingers curled tightly around hers. He looked down, his expression shadowed, his bright eyes shining with unshed tears.

"Are you alright?" she asked softly.

He cleared his throat, blinking hard as he turned back toward the parade. "The last Bloomtide parade I saw was in Tirnavel," he murmured. "With my parents. Eloria was only fifteen."

Araya squeezed his hand. "Did that one have phoenixes then, too?"

Loren nodded slowly. "Always. My mother used to tell us the stories—how the phoenix rises from its own ashes, how nothing beautiful is ever truly gone."

"Will you tell them to me?" Araya asked.

Loren glanced down at her, surprise flickering across his face. "You want me to tell you fae bedtime stories?"

"I've never heard them," Araya admitted, staring back out at the parade rather than meet the pity in his eyes. "I'd like to, I think."

Loren was quiet for a moment, his thumb brushing lightly across her knuckles. "All right," he said finally, his voice rough. "I'll tell you what I remember."

And he did.

Loren whispered in her ear, his soft words bringing each float to life as it drifted by in a riot of color and life. He told her of the great stag, its silver antlers crowned with blooming flowers, each step leaving a trail of new life in its wake. Of the serpent, who guarded the hidden paths that led to the Goddess's last sanctuary coiled among thorny vines and poisonous blossoms. Of the dusk-winged moth that drank magic straight from the shimmering starlight that gilded the still pools deep in the Eldergreen, weaving dreams into silk.

"The last float is always the Absent Goddess," he said. "A reminder of the duty she left us with."

"Duty?" Araya asked. "We were taught that she abandoned the fae."

"They would say that." Loren snorted, shaking his head as the final float rolled into view. "She didn't abandon us. She charged us to protect this world—to serve as her stewards. Of aether. Of the Eldergreen. Of each other."

The float was enormous, almost as wide as the street itself, and impossibly tall—gliding forward on a platform so thick with flowering vines it seemed to hover above the ground. White blossoms spilled over the wheels and trailed behind like the train of a dress. The Goddess stood at the center of it all, her upturned face veiled in silver and her arms raised in what could have been welcome or blessing, petals piled high around her feet like drifts of snow.

Araya leaned forward to see better, squinting at the shrouded forms that rested at her feet. "What do the bodies at her feet represent, then?"

Someone in the crowd gasped. The music faltered, laughter and cheering giving way to horrified whispers. Araya jerked her hand away from Loren, shoving her way to the very edge of the barrier where Eilwen clutched her son to her chest, shielding his eyes.

Because those bodies—they weren't part of the float.

"Gods." Araya clapped a hand over her mouth, choking on the reek of rotting flesh mingling with the sickly-sweet perfume of crushed flowers.

"Araya—" Loren reached for her, his shadows wrapping around her ankles, but she shook them both off, unable to tear her eyes from the grisly sight as the float groaned to a halt just feet from where she stood, showering them all with delicate white petals.

Some of the bodies had been laid out carefully, their hands folded over their chests. Others buzzed with flies, their waterlogged flesh bloated and heavy. Every one of them had red hair. Clipped ears. And the same message burned into their flesh.

RETURN HER

Araya staggered, the world spinning around her. She couldn't breathe, every gasp of air she managed rotten with guilt and fear as people around them started to scream. The message that had been carved and burned into every body echoed in her mind, seared into her soul as surely as it had been burned into every female Jaxon tortured and killed.

"Halfblood whore."

The insult sliced through the horrified murmurs, silencing the crowd. The male pulling the float ripped his harness open, dropping it to the cobblestones. He stalked toward her, his face twisted with hatred. "You should never have come here. Go back to your master before he kills more innocents just to send you a message."

Araya froze. The noise of the crowd dulled to a distant roar as her muscles locked, her hands plastered uselessly over her mouth. Her fault. All of it was her fault—

Shadows curled around her ankles, their cool touch racing up her back to fall over her shoulders like a living mantle of darkness as Loren stormed forward.

"You do *not* speak to her like that," he snarled. "She is under my protection. Threaten her again and I will add your body to the next pyre."

The man blanched, his bravado crumbling. "But she—"

"She didn't kill them," Loren snapped, his words ringing out in the hushed horror of the square. "You want to blame someone? Blame the Arcanum. Blame Jaxon Shaw—the monster that *actually* tortured and killed these females. Not his victim—"

"You *knew*?"

The words fell from Araya's lips before she could stop them. She whirled to face him, the chaos of the square fading to a dull roar in her ears. His guilt was written plainly across his face, his jaw tight, his eyes wide with the realization that he had been caught.

"You let me stand here and laugh," Araya whispered, the words like glass in her throat. "You let me *dance*—" she choked, the sweet, metallic tang of aether flooding her mouth.

"I was going to tell you." Loren stepped forward, heedless of the hundreds of eyes on them both. "Please, *ael'sura*, let me explain—"

"How long?" she demanded. Power roared through her, her voice rising. "How long did you know he was killing people because of me?"

Loren lifted a hand like he would catch her arm and draw her back—but the pressure that had been building under her skin broke first, engulfing the square in a wave of searing, crackling energy.

Someone screamed, people stumbling back as it curved into a shimmering wall between them.

But Loren stayed, reaching for her despite the way her power lashed out at him, striking him hard enough to draw blood.

"Control it, *ael'sura*," he begged, blood flecking the corners of his mouth. "Your power answers to you. Your will, your intentions. I know you don't want to hurt all these people."

A child's cry broke through the roaring in her ears, the screams and shouts of the terrified crowd suddenly deafening. Blackened petals drifted down around her, burning her skin and singing her beautiful dress. One landed on the float, and then another—until the masterpiece of flowers and foliage became a pyre, its flames reaching for the stars above them as it consumed the bodies of the females Jaxon had murdered just to send her a message.

Araya sucked in a deep breath, immediately choking on the smoke. Loren's shadows surrounded them both, shielding the crowd from her wrath—but he stood inside of them. Unshielded and vulnerable, bleeding from where she had struck him in her fury. Her power recoiled at the sight of it, twisting in on itself as her chest tightened, panic rising in her throat.

"It's alright, *ael'sura*," Loren took another step forward, heedless of the danger. "You're safe. I have you."

Araya dropped to the cobblestones, barely feeling the pain that lanced through her knees. Loren's shadows surged to catch her— only to break against her power as the magic she'd unleashed folded in on itself, collapsing around her. Her head buzzed, the world around her tilting sickeningly as she took it all back—too much, too fast.

The last thing she saw was Loren's face, her name on his tongue and his green eyes wide with fear as he fought to reach her—and then the world went dark.

CHAPTER
TWENTY-FIVE

"This isn't how we do things, Loren."

"And hanging bodies from parade floats is?" Loren didn't even look at his sister, his eyes locked on the male who had attacked his mate in the street.

The male whimpered, clutching the hem of his tunic with shaking hands as he tried and failed to hide the spreading stain from where he'd pissed himself. All around him, Loren's shadows crawled across the floor like living ink, draining the warmth from the air and smothering the aetherlamps with their thick, pulsing tendrils.

The Small Council sat around the table, most of them looking like they'd rather be anywhere else—too terrified to speak or even breathe too loudly lest Loren might turn his rage on them next. Only Eloria dared challenge him, her hands braced on the scarred table as she pleaded with him.

"Of course not," she said. "But you need to stop and think. She needs you more than she needs you to do this."

"Thorne is with her," Loren snapped.

He could still feel the lingering heat of her magic licking across his skin as he fell to his knees beside her in the center of the devastation she'd wrought. She hadn't moved. Not when the shadows rushed over her to cool her. Not when he called her name. Not when he scooped her limp body into his arms and carried her from the scorched square beneath the shocked, terrified eyes of his people.

He'd stormed into the Central Hall and gone straight to Thorne, leaving his best friend with a single command—*watch over her*.

Now, someone needed to pay for the hurt they'd caused her.

And Loren would start with the fool who'd dared accost her on the street in front of everyone.

No one dared stopped him as he stepped forward, the shadows seething eagerly around him. United in purpose and desire at last, both of them wanting nothing more than to make this male feel every bit of the terror and despair he'd forced on Araya.

"Tell me who gave you the order," Loren said.

"Please—" the male whimpered, his shoulders curling inward like he could shield himself from Loren's wrath. "I still have family in Aetheris. They're suffering—"

"I didn't ask *why*," Loren growled. "I want to know *who*."

The shadows lashed across the room, striking stone so hard that several of the councilors gasped aloud. The male kneeling in front of him sobbed, tears cutting tracks through the dirt that smeared his cheeks as he cast a single, desperate glance to the side—

Loren's eyes followed the line of his gaze, landing on Cormac. The commander's fingers tightened around the arms of his chair, his knuckles turning white. His jaw worked, the tendons in his neck straining as he fought to maintain his composure.

"You traitor," Cormac hissed. "You're nothing but a coward—"

"You're the coward," Loren snarled, his shadows flaring around him, deepening the darkness in the room until the aetherlamps flickered and the walls seemed to shrink in on themselves. "You—and the ones who hide behind you, letting you stain your hands while they whisper in the dark."

His gaze sliced to where Eryn sat frozen in his chair, his unlined face an unreadable mask as he watched the shadows turn their attention to Cormac, abandoning the sobbing male on the floor to swirl around the older fae in a slow, drifting maelstrom.

"You want to lay the blame for what the Arcanum did at the feet of another victim?" The shadows lashed out again, sending chips of stone flying. "I should let them tear you apart."

"She's no victim." Cormac's face paled, but his back remained straight, his head unbowed as he stared Loren down. "She *agreed* to everything they did to her. She might be your mate, but she chose her oppressor over you. You need to think about your people, not some halfblood whore—"

Someone screamed as the black tendrils surged over the table. Cormac's chair crashed to the ground, his knees striking stone with a sickening crack. The aetherlamps guttered out entirely, plunging the room into an eerie, living darkness that clawed up the walls and across the ceiling, forming twisting, writhing shapes that morphed from claws to teeth and back again. Cormac's own cry came out as a croak, strangled in his throat as the shadows tightened around his neck and chest.

Loren was dimly aware of people shouting, but he couldn't bring himself to care. Power roared through his veins, the shadows clamoring for retribution. They tightened, and Cormac choked, his boots scraping uselessly against the floor as he clawed at his throat.

"You have *no idea* what he did to her," Loren snarled. "You *never* could have survived what she did. You don't deserve to breathe the same air as her—"

"Eloria—stop!"

"Just let me through!" Eloria's voice cut through the chaos surrounding him a heartbeat before her hand closed on his arm, shadowmarks already blooming on her skin where the shadows had struck her in their fury.

"Loren," she hissed, dragging him back. "You *have* to stop. Cormac is a fool—but he's not your enemy. Killing him here isn't going to accomplish anything. She's the one who needs you right now."

"She doesn't want me," Loren snarled.

She'd rejected him—and he couldn't blame her. He'd hidden this from her. It was his fault that Cormac had been able to ambush her with this at all. The shadows should string him up right next to Eloria's commander at arms.

"That doesn't mean she doesn't *need* you," Eloria argued. "Trust me. She's going to wake up terrified, not knowing what happened or what she did. Do you think *Thorne* is the person she wants there when that happens? *You* are the one who should be there when she wakes up. You'll never forgive yourself if you aren't."

Loren clenched his teeth, squeezing his eyes closed as he tried to clear the rage from his mind long enough to string a coherent thought together. He could *feel* her—drifting between consciousness and oblivion at the other end of the bond, all of it tinged with the bitter aftertaste of guilt. She was going to have questions—questions that deserved answers. From him. Not Thorne or Ilyana or Veria or anyone else.

"We have to go," he said, so quietly that only the shadows around him heard.

He hurt what is ours to protect, they hissed, drowning out Cormac's strangled wheeze as they dragged him even higher into the air. *He deserves no mercy.*

"I know." Loren's voice cracked as her pain swelled in his chest. "But she needs me—needs *us*—more than he needs to die."

Their outrage poured over him, the whispers rising to a frenzied cacophony. For a heartbeat, Loren thought they would tear free of his tenuous control entirely and devour Cormac right there in front of the entire Small Council. Part of him almost wanted them to.

But Araya needed them. Not to fight her battles and punish her enemies—but to be there when she fell apart. They couldn't do that if they killed Cormac here.

The shadows knew that too. They grumbled, but dropped

Eloria's commander at arms to the stones like a broken puppet. The rest of the Small Council cowered in their seats, too terrified to move as the shadows slowly gathered again at Loren's feet. Only Eloria dared look him in the eyes, her own face pale as Cormac coughed and wheezed where the shadows had dropped him.

"Go to her," she said. "I'll handle things here."

CHAPTER
TWENTY-SIX

Araya stirred, shifting in the strange, soft bed. She was wearing a nightgown of some sort—but the scent of burned flowers and ozone still clung to her skin and hair, not letting her forget for a moment what she had done.

The float—the bodies. She'd been so *angry*—

Araya gasped, curling in on herself as power stirred sluggishly beneath her skin, crawling through her veins like lava. She clamped down on it instinctively, forcing it back with sheer will—but it pushed harder. Like it had tasted freedom and *wanted* to be let out again.

"No," she whispered, a tear squeezing out from between her clenched eyes and sizzling on her skin. "Stay down."

Somewhere nearby, a chair scraped. Footsteps—someone moving toward her.

"Stay back," she groaned. "I can't control it."

There had been blood. She'd hurt Loren. Gods, had she killed anyone? Eilwen had been standing right there. If she'd hurt Selan—

"You have to stay calm, Araya." Thorne's hand touched her forehead, the cool rush of healing magic racing across her skin. "The more upset you get, the worse it will be."

"I told you to stay out," Araya snarled. Her power flared violently, rising to meet his touch with a burning snap. Her heartbeat roared in her ears, her skin prickling with heat as the magic tried to defend her from a threat that wasn't there.

Thorne swore under his breath, yanking his hand back. But he didn't step back.

"You shouldn't be here," she gasped again. She didn't want to hurt Thorne. She didn't want to hurt *anyone.* But she had. "Did I kill anyone?"

"No." Thorne's face twisted, but he didn't lie, even though he could. "There were a few burns, and some people were injured in the crush—but you didn't kill anyone."

She didn't need Thorne to tell her she had Loren to thank for that. He'd saved all those people—saved her. But now...the bond twisted in her chest, his fury raging through it.

"You manifested, Araya," Thorne said, his voice soothing. "Your power is still trying to protect you, but it doesn't need to anymore. I promise, you're safe. You can let it go."

Araya jerked out of his reach, clenching her teeth so hard her jaw ached. She wanted to believe him—but all she could smell was smoke, and beneath it, the faintest trace of rain-washed granite.

"Where is he?"

Thorne hesitated, his silence saying more than any answer he could have given. "He hasn't left Lumaria."

"He's so angry." Araya shuddered. He wasn't here. He'd left her—again. "He's going to kill someone."

"You're going to kill *yourself,*" Thorne said grimly. "Let me help you, Araya. Please—"

She tried to shake her head, but the room spun around her, black spots dancing at the edges of her vision. Thorne said something else, but she couldn't hear him over the roaring in her ears. She couldn't lose consciousness. She needed to hold on—

The next time she opened her eyes the bond was quiet in her chest—content.

Loren held her hand, his fingers tangled with hers. Power rushed into her through that connection, as bright and warm as his shadows were cool. He was offering her his strength, just as she had done for him. Worse, his thumb brushed gently across the back of her hand, over and over again, steady and soothing.

"Don't touch me." Araya yanked her hand away, struggling to sit up despite the warning lurch of her stomach.

"Easy," Loren said. He moved without hesitation, slipping an arm around her shoulders to help her lean over a basin he must have had ready.

Her whole frame shook as she retched, bringing up nothing but bile. But Loren just gathered her hair back from her face, tracing soothing circles across her back with his other hand.

"You're—"

"Burned out," Araya rasped, dragging the back of her hand across her mouth. "I know what it feels like."

Loren winced. "Of course you do," he said. "I just—"

"How long did you know what he was doing?"

Loren flinched like she'd struck him, his guilt written across his face. "I was trying to protect you—"

"From what?" Her voice cracked. "The consequences of my actions? The truth? Don't pretend this is the first thing you've hidden from me. All you've ever done is keep secrets from me."

"I didn't want to trap you," Loren argued, his hands flexing uselessly at his side. "You've already had so many choices taken away from you—"

"But you *did*. Or are you going to deny you kept it from me because you were afraid of what I'd choose?" Araya shook her head, not waiting for him to give an answer he couldn't speak. "Tell me— how many fae has he killed just because they look like me?"

Loren stared at her without answering. Dark circles shadowed his eyes, and even the living darkness that always accompanied him was strangely subdued, but she hardened her heart, refusing to be moved by it. She should have refused to feel sympathy for him from the first second she saw him in that cell. It would have been easier—for both of them.

"You let them die because you were afraid to lose me," Araya said, her voice dropping to a whisper. "And now I'm the one who has to live with that."

The bond stretched taut between them, his anguish swelling in her chest. It choked her, threatening to sweep her away with the intensity of it. She hated it. Hated knowing that he'd done it for her.

"You're my mate," he whispered, his bright green eyes never leaving hers. "I'll always protect you, Araya."

"At the cost of your own people?" She shook her head. "Are you even the same male who let the Arcanum torture him for twenty-five years rather than give them *anything* they might be able to use?"

He flinched from her words, but didn't deny it.

"I'm going back, Loren," she said.

The shadows stirred at that, hissing softly.

"That won't stop him," Loren argued. "When he realizes you're bonded to me—"

"I can't let them kill people because of me." Araya stared past him, resolutely fixing her eyes on a crack in the stone wall behind him. Because if she looked at him...she might not be able to break his heart. "I can transfer control of the shadows to someone else. It won't fix everything, but at least the fae can survive here—"

"Using what? Fae blood and bone?" Loren sneered. "What you did with Jaxon Shaw is an abomination, Araya. The Small Council will never agree to it."

"They're desperate," Araya said grimly. "They don't have a choice. And then I'll go back...and we can put all of this behind us."

Loren stared at her. He didn't explode, or yell, or threaten her. He just...looked at her. Like he had no idea who she was. "Is that what you really want?"

Araya forced herself to hold his gaze. The bond howled in her chest again, clawing at her ribs with every heartbeat. She wanted him to scream at her. To fight. She wanted to *shake* him for every silence he'd kept when he could have told her the truth, every deception leading them closer and closer to *this*.

"It doesn't matter what I want," she said. "It never did."

For a moment, she thought he might argue. But he just nodded once, standing slowly like he wasn't quite sure of what to do.

"I'll tell Thorne you're awake," was all he said. Then he turned, gathering his shadows around him like a shield as he crossed to the door. Only the smallest lingered, its cool touch brushing across her skin as it hesitated. It hovered there for a long, silent moment—then slipped silently after him, leaving her truly alone.

Araya stared down at her hands in her lap. There was no blood on them. But there should have been.

Maybe one day Loren would understand that this was the only way. She'd made her choice a long time ago. First, when she gave up her name to the Arcanum. Then again when she'd agreed to become Jaxon Shaw's bond. That was the path she had to walk, even if it broke her.

TWENTY-SEVEN

Araya spent days drifting between sleep and waking.

Sometimes she surfaced to find Thorne by the window, thumbing through one of the books she'd asked him to bring. Other times it was Ilyana who eased her upright with patient hands, coaxing her to sip from steaming bowls of broth.

"What exactly are you trying to figure out here?" Thorne asked at last, tossing the thin volume he'd been leafing through down on the bed.

Araya picked it up, smoothing her hand over the cover. The table beside her bed was stacked high with more of the same—official accountings of fae succession and royal mating bonds, records of the fae monarchy's first years in exile, religious texts detailing proper burial rites—thousands of years, boiled down to nothing but words.

"It's just a theory I'm working on," she said.

Thorne hummed, his sharp gaze lingering, but he let the non-answer pass. "Loren wants me to take you back to Ithralis now that you're stronger."

"Does it even matter where I am?" Araya asked, picking at the embroidery on the coverlet rather than meet his eyes. "It's not like I've seen him."

"He's been busy," Thorne said carefully. "He and Eloria have been holding the Small Council at bay—but they're demanding their turn with you. If you're at Ithralis, it's harder for them to reach you."

"Don't they deserve the chance to question me?" Araya laughed bitterly. "Look at what Jaxon has done because of me. Look at what *I* did in the square. I'd want to question me too."

"You aren't responsible for his actions." Thorne laid his hand over hers, stilling her restless fingers. "And no one was seriously hurt in the square. It's a *good* thing that your power manifested. Shielding is a valuable skill. If you cultivate it—"

"I want to talk to the Small Council," Araya cut him off. "As soon as possible."

"Loren won't like it—"

"Loren forfeited my trust by hiding that Jaxon is *killing* people to demand my return," Araya snapped. "I want to speak to someone who doesn't have a vested interest in hiding things from me."

Thorne was quiet for a long moment, his expression unreadable. Then he sighed, his chair scraping across the floor as he pushed to his feet.

"You should get dressed then," he said. "Eloria and the Small Council are hearing petitions today. If you want to get in front of them without a fight from Loren, this is your chance."

It only took minutes for Araya to pull on one of the simple dresses that had been delivered to her room. Plain and unadorned, it was more suited to convalescing than open court, but the rough-spun fabric was almost comforting in its familiarity. The uniform of someone who needed to blend in.

She scrubbed water over her face, wrestling her hair back into a tight braid. And for a heartbeat when she looked in the mirror she almost recognized the person she'd been before she ever met Loren Shadowbane. But then that strange power scraped against the inside of her skin, sharp and restless. A reminder that she could never go back to who she'd been—not completely.

They passed no one as they descended the stairs. Araya barely recognized the Central Hall—its long feast tables put away and the bright glow of the aetherlamps dimmed until the vast chamber seemed more like a tomb than a gathering place. Every step echoed too loudly, her plain skirts brushing against stone.

"You'll have no friends in that room," Thorne warned, turning into a narrow hallway. "Eloria will be overseeing, and Galen is always kind—but their loyalty will always lie with their people. To the rest of them, you'll be either a weapon or a liability."

"And Loren?" Araya asked, her voice shaking.

"Loren is going to be furious when he sees you," Thorne said grimly. "He's convinced Cormac—that's Eloria's commander at arms —was the one behind the bodies on that float. He and Eryn have been the loudest voices questioning your motives in coming here."

"The spymaster?" Araya shivered, remembering the way Loren had thrown the male against the wall all those weeks ago.

"The very same," Thorne confirmed. "Expect questions—especially about your relationship with the Shaws." He stopped just short of the door, turning to face her. "Are you sure you want to do this?"

Araya stared at the door. She could *feel* Loren beyond it. Not as clearly as she had before, when he'd been ready to rip this place down stone by stone, but her magic leaned toward him even more than it had before, desperate to get to him.

"I have to do this," she said.

"Alright then." Thorne set his jaw, turning back to the two guards that stood in front of the door. "We're going in. Lady Starwind has a petition to present."

"Very well, sir," one of the guards said, though he looked like he'd rather be anywhere else. He shoved the door open, stepping inside with a perfunctory bow. "Lord Emberwood and Lady Starwind," he announced, his voice carrying into the chamber. "To present a petition to the Small Council."

The hush that followed was immediate. Dozens of heads turned, the petitioners clustered in front of the long table whispering to each other as they craned their necks, trying to catch a glimpse of the female who had ruined Bloomtide. Araya faltered under their scrutiny, her pulse suddenly racing as she stared up at the long table.

Loren sat at his sister's right hand, the shadows curling up around him betraying the fury hidden behind his carved-from-ice expression. The bond pulled taut in her chest, crying out for her to cross the room and go to him—but she just stood beside Thorne, frozen.

"Arcanum's whore." One of the petitioners turned his head, his spit striking the floor at her feet. "Go back to where you came from, halfblood."

Araya flinched and hunched her shoulders, shame crawling over her skin. She had no defense—her argument that she had only been doing what she needed to protect herself fell flat here, where so many had fought for and gained their freedom.

But Loren was on his feet. "What did you say to her?"

The petitioner shifted, color draining from his face as his companions drew away from him. But he lifted his chin, his voice steady. "Nothing but the truth, Your Majesty."

"You can't salute me and insult her." Loren's voice didn't rise—but the shadows did. They unspooled like smoke, stretching long tendrils toward the male. "Apologize."

The male opened his mouth. Closed it. Tried again. But the words wouldn't come. The shadows hissed, reaching for him. He couldn't apologize, Araya realized with dawning horror. Because he wasn't sorry—and fae couldn't lie.

"Loren—" she caught up her skirt in one hand, hurrying forward to push between the man and the shadows. "Don't."

For a heartbeat she thought he hadn't heard her. The shadows parted around her, circling the shaking male that had insulted her. Araya stretched out her hand for them, desperately willing them to come to her instead. These were Loren's people. If he started hurting them because of her, they would never forgive him.

"Clear the room," Eloria snapped.

Petitioners scattered, a scribe clutching his ledger as they all fled, filing out of the room until only Thorne and the seated councilors remained. But Araya didn't even get to take a full breath before Loren shoved his chair back so hard it struck the wall, shadows darkening around him. He stormed across the room, shoving Thorne hard enough that the other male stumbled back.

"What were you thinking, bringing her here?" he snarled.

"You don't have any right to keep me away," Araya cut in. She stepped forward, her spine stiff as the miasma of darkness writhing around Loren swallowed her too. "You keep telling me I have a place here," she challenged, her voice shaking. "That means I have every right to present a petition."

Loren froze, finally looking directly at her. His lips parted, something sharp and wounded flickering behind his fury. *"Ael'sura..."* His voice cracked, more plea than rebuke. "You don't know what you're walking into. They'll never agree to what you want to do. They're going to tear you apart."

"I have to do this, Loren." Araya raised a hand, giving into the urge to brush her fingers over his cheek. "Please, don't try to stop me."

Loren closed his eyes at the featherlight touch, his eyebrows drawing together like he was in pain.

"I'm not supposed to interfere," he said finally, his voice pitched for her ears alone. "But if you want to leave, say the word. I'll get you out."

Araya's heart twisted. There was no guile in the offer. Just truth. If she asked him to save her, he would. But she couldn't let him destroy himself like that.

"It will be fine," she murmured, dropping her hand. "I'll be fine, Loren."

This room hadn't been built for holding council sessions. None of the chairs matched, and the long table was actually several shoved together. But the people who sat around it—Araya fought the urge to cower in the face of their scrutiny, feeling more like she was standing trial than an invited guest.

"Thank you for coming, Lady Starwind." Eloria said, standing at the head of the table. "We appreciate you making the time to speak with us today."

One of the councilors snorted, his arms crossed over his chest like a shield. Dark bruises marred his throat, vivid against the pallor of his skin. He sneered, staring her down with bloodshot eyes.

"*Finally*," he said. "We've been requesting her presence for weeks."

Beside his sister, Loren stiffened, the aetherlamps flickering in their sconces as the room darkened.

"She's here now—of her own free will," Eloria said tightly. "Let that be enough, Commander. We don't need a repeat of Bloomtide here today."

The bruised male—Cormac, Araya realized with a shiver—snorted but sank back into his chair, scowling down at the table. Loren's jaw flexed, but after a moment he looked away, the light returning to the edges of the room.

"Go ahead, Lady Starwind," Eloria said, taking her own seat. "We're listening."

Araya squared her shoulders, sucking in a deep breath. She could do this. She had to. Yet the words she'd rehearsed turned to ash on her tongue beneath the weight of their stares. What right did she have to stand here, begging them to hear her? She was no one—a halfblood who had bargained her freedom to a monster.

Then something cool brushed her ankle—one of Loren's shadows, coiling gently around her boot. She hadn't seen it slip from his side, but its quiet touch steadied her frayed nerves.

"Thank you for agreeing to see me," she said, her voice quieter than she intended, but steady. "I know most of you don't trust me, and I don't blame you for that. But I think I have a solution to the difficulties you've faced with the Shadowed Veil."

Araya paused, but no one spoke. Eloria arched a brow, while Cormac leaned back in his chair, a sneer already twisting his face.

"I understand that your beliefs say the shadows only bind themselves to one person in each generation," Araya forced herself to continue. "I believe I can give you another way to control them—one that doesn't rely on a living host."

"And what credentials do you have to speak on such matters? Your time in the New Dominion?" Cormac leaned forward, his eyes glittering with malice. "I didn't realize *bonded females* received any sort of education there."

Araya flushed, heat flooding her cheeks. But she refused to look away. "I had...a unique role due to my relationship with Jaxon Shaw."

"Convenient for you," Cormac said idly, his lip curling. "Normally, we have every sympathy for the horrors faced by bonded females—but this *relationship* with the younger Shaw far preceded your bonding, didn't it?"

A murmur of agreement rolled down the table. A silver-haired female wearing the pale robes of a devotee to the Absent Goddess leaned forward, the silver embroidery marking her as the High Luminary shining in the light of the aetherlamps. "He was your teacher—your sponsor. And you repaid his patronage by warming his bed." She shook her head, her voice cold. "Forgive me, Lady Starwind, but you don't sound like the prisoner Prince Loren painted you to be."

"Did you have a question for her, Myna?" Loren growled. "She did what she had to do to survive—"

"I think Miss Starwind should get to speak for herself," Eryn cut in. His dark eyes flicked to her, unreadable. "After all, she is the one with the petition."

Araya's throat tightened. She wanted to vanish, to sink through the stone floor, but she forced herself to stand straighter, almost tripping over her words in her haste to get them out.

"The Shadowed Veil was a project assigned to Jaxon Shaw," she said. "I worked with him under special permission from the Arcanum. In that time, I created a test amulet by mixing my blood with Loren's—one that granted the wearer some degree of control over the shadows."

Several councilors recoiled as if she'd spat poison at them, horrified murmurs rising around the table.

"An amulet made out of what?" Myna demanded. "Because it sounds like you're describing an amplifier."

"I am." Araya's stomach twisted. She'd gone over this a hundred times in her head, but speaking it aloud felt colder. Crueler. "The one I created used a fragment of bone—what the Arcanum calls a blank. But Jaxon intended to continue testing with whole bone."

Murmurs turned to exclamations of disgust, the words *sacrilege* and *desecration* hissed like curses.

But Eloria just leaned back in her chair, her expression giving away nothing of her true thoughts. "Where do you expect to source the bone? We burn our dead here."

"I did have an idea about that." Araya sucked in a deep breath, bracing herself. They would hate this part—she hadn't even told Loren what she intended. "From our conversations and my own research, I believe *dara'el* remains anchored to the previous king's remains. It's the only explanation for how it has endured and even grown in the decades after his death. If we can retrieve his bones—"

"Absolutely not." The priestess shot to her feet, her pale eyes blazing with fury. "We are *not* turning the remains of our late king into an *amplifier*. Have you no shame?"

Araya flushed but stood her ground, refusing to cower. "Anchoring the magic to something that already holds a significant connection with the shadows is the best answer here," she said. "It's *powerful* magic. To bind it to someone else's command—it's not an *easy* thing to do."

"It's sacrilege," the priestess snapped. "We cannot condone—"

"We cannot afford not to consider all the options, Myna," Eloria said quietly. She turned back to Araya, her brow furrowing. "You do understand that no one has been able to retrieve my father's remains? What you're proposing will not be simple."

"Loren and I both survived the Shadowed Veil," Araya said. She didn't dare look at him, even though she could feel his eyes burning into her. "I have to believe there's a way for us to do it again."

"And if we agree to your...*proposal*," another of the advisors said, her lips twisting around the word. "What is it you want in exchange?"

"Safe passage back to the New Dominion," Araya said. "The deaths of the innocent are not a price I would pay for my freedom. If I return to them willingly—"

"You're the mate of the crown prince," an older male cut in sharply. "Whatever fondness Jaxon Shaw has for you won't save you. They'll use you against him—against all of us."

"I understand your concern." Araya's fingers twisted in the fabric of her skirt. "That's why I would like your help in finding a way to sever the mate bond."

A ripple of shock ran through the room as the councilors exchanged wide-eyed glances. Even Eloria sat back in her chair, the color draining from her face. And Loren—he stared at her like she'd struck him, his hurt blazing so hot through the bond between them that it felt like she'd set her own heart on fire.

"I won't allow Jaxon to use me as a blade against him," she said, her voice wavering. "This is the only way I have to protect him."

The High Luminary found her voice first. "The mate bond is a divine gift," she said, her voice rising. "What you propose is not only profane—it is *impossible*."

"Not necessarily." Eryn tapped a finger against his goblet, considering. "They aren't fully bonded, are they? I think there *is* precedent for that. Ysella, don't you have a book on it?"

The tall, willowy female beside the priestess cleared her throat, shifting in her seat. "I could consult the records," she said. "There are...fragments of some accounts that might shed light on the issue—but nothing I would call reliable."

"But not impossible," Eryn mused.

The priestess scoffed. "Your Majesty," she implored, turning toward Loren. "The bond is a gift from the Goddess herself. Surely you have something to say—"

"If severing the bond is what Lady Starwind wants," Loren said, every word landing like a knife through her chest. "Then I see no reason to deny her."

Voices rose, everyone speaking over each other. Araya's throat tightened, her palms damp with sweat. Even Loren's shadow abandoned her, melting away into the cracks between the stones.

"Enough," Eloria said finally. She rose to her feet, glancing around at her assembled advisors. "Lady Starwind, thank you for bringing your proposal before us. We will consider it and return to you with our answer. For now, you are dismissed."

Araya dipped her head stiffly before turning to Loren—but he didn't move to stand. He didn't even look at her. His hurt filled her chest, making it hard to breathe. But she forced herself to move anyway, holding her head high and hoping none of them could see how hard she had to blink to hold back the tears.

She wouldn't break down here, not with all of them watching.

The guards stood at attention in the hallway, neither one of them willing to meet her eyes as the doors closed behind her, sealing out the rising voices behind her. Araya stood there, panic rising in her chest. What was she even supposed to do while they voted? Did she just stand here—

"Lady Starwind?"

Araya turned, hesitating as she met the gaze of a male wearing white robes, adorned with a single band of silver thread. Another devotee of the Absent Goddess—though Araya couldn't have said what his rank was. He inclined his head to her, his expression peaceful.

"The Princess Regent asked that I show you to a quiet place to wait," he said. "If you could follow me?"

TWENTY-EIGHT

The acolyte led her through a maze of dark halls, his white robes the only hint of brightness in the dim light cast by the aetherlamps. Araya had to hurry to match his brisk pace, keeping her head bowed as the corridors twisted back on themselves, each one darker than the last.

Finally, he stopped. "You can wait in here," he said. "Someone will be in to retrieve you."

He bowed low before she could so much as thank him, vanishing back into the shadowed hall in a swirl of white robes.

And for the first time since she'd come to Lumaria, Araya was completely alone.

She stared around at her surroundings, studying the painted screens arranged behind the makeshift altar in lieu of the murals that had decorated the ransacked temple at the Aetherium and the abandoned one she'd taken shelter in with Loren. A series of small bowls were laid out across the altar, while the single brazier smoldering beside it filled the sparse room with the rich, earthy scent of charcoal.

Araya let out a breath she hadn't realized she was holding, collapsing onto one of the simple benches. Her shoulders sagged, exhaustion crashing over her. She'd done it. She'd told them what she could do for them—now it was up to them to say yes or no.

But the waiting was somehow worse than all their judgement. If they said yes, she'd be walking straight back into that gilded cage. But if they said no...she was still going to have to find a way to leave. No one knew her better than Jaxon. And no one knew *him* better than her. He wouldn't stop killing them. Not until he had her back.

Araya stared at the brazier, watching the smoke curl up toward the ceiling in slow, ghostly ribbons. Let the High Luminary think what she wanted. She wasn't trying to defy their Goddess, but she *was* going to do whatever it took to make sure no one else bled and died because of her.

Araya couldn't imagine any God or Goddess having a problem with that.

She stood, stepping up to the linen-draped altar. A dozen mismatched dishes were arranged across its surface, each holding a different material. One overflowed with dried flower petals, pale and curling at the edges, their colors faded but not gone. Others held fragrant herbs, their leaves dried and crumbled, while another was filled with curled wood shavings.

Araya hesitated, uncertain. If she'd ever known what to do, she'd forgotten long ago—another part of her heritage, stolen and erased.

"You're supposed to pick one," a voice said from behind her, smooth and almost amused. "Or several, if you need to. Grind them up and sprinkle them on the coals. The smoke carries your prayer to the Goddess."

Araya whirled, startled to find Eryn leaning against the archway that led back into the main hall. He straightened, tucking a leather-bound folder under his arm as he crossed the room to step up beside her.

"Does she listen?" Araya asked.

Eryn's mouth curved into a not-quite smile. "I don't know," he said lightly. "But there's a reason we call her the *Absent* Goddess." He touched his finger to the first of the bowls. "Juniper for protection. Bay for truth. This one—" he tapped the bowl of curling bark "—is willow. It represents grief. And these—" he picked up a pinch of the dried petals "—are for longing."

He crushed the mixture he'd assembled in his palm, sprinkling it over the brazier. The coals hissed, fragrant smoke curling into the air.

"And these—" Eryn dropped the leather-bound folder onto the altar, "—are for you. Accounts from our attempts to retrieve the late king's remains. You'll need them to do what you proposed."

Araya stared at the folder, her mouth suddenly dry. "They said yes?" Her heart hammered in her chest, her stomach lurching like her body wanted to reject the words. They were going to let her go back. Back to Jaxon and the privilege of being his prize possession.

"They said yes." Eryn smiled faintly. "Ysella will need more time to gather the accountings of severed mate bonds. As you might have guessed, it's not very common here. But I can deliver those to you at Ithralis."

"Wonderful," Araya said, but the word rang hollow. She twisted her fingers in her skirt, relief and dread tangling in her chest. But if severing the bond meant that Loren would be safe from whatever punishment Jaxon inflicted on her for leaving him, it was worth it.

"I'll admit, you surprised me." Eryn leaned against the edge of the altar, studying her. "It's not often I find someone with the stomach to do what's necessary, even when the path is hard to walk. I'm impressed by you, Araya Starwind."

"I—thank you?" Araya flushed, something about the way he turned her name over in his mouth making the hair on the back of her neck prickle. Loren's warning about how vulnerable she was here came rushing back, leaving her all too aware of how isolated she was right now. What would Eryn command her to do if he could?

But Eloria's spymaster only bowed gracefully. "I hope you find the clarity you're looking for, Miss Starwind," he said softly, his gaze traveling to the folder. "One way or another. Safe travels."

He left as silently as he'd appeared, his presence fading faster than the smoke rising from the brazier. Araya sucked in a steadying breath, inhaling the fragrant smoke. Then, before she could second-guess herself, she snatched up the documents, shoving them into her bag.

CHAPTER

TWENTY-NINE

Araya bent over the folder Eryn had given her, skimming through the mess of personal accounts, official records, and hand-annotated maps for what felt like the hundredth time. She'd gone over every document a dozen times, immersing herself in Eloria's graceful, looping script. The princess had taken notes on everything from the phases of the moon, to the weather, to what the commander of the mission had eaten for breakfast that morning.

But none of it had made a difference. Every attempt to retrieve King Corwin's remains had ended the same way—in failure.

Araya sat back, staring down at the words she already knew by heart.

Seventh and final sanctioned retrieval effort. All members of the expedition lost. Royal decree issued: cease further attempts.

Seven attempts. Ninety-three fae lost to the Veil, their bodies swallowed by the same shadows that had taken their king. Dozens more dead in the aftermath—lost to injuries of the mind that no Healer could treat. And the ones that survived...

They were never the same.

Some forgot their names. Some screamed at nothing. A few never spoke again.

So Eloria had abandoned Ithralis. Abandoned the temple and her father's remains to the ever-growing darkness and officially moved her court to Lumaria.

Araya tapped her quill against the edge of the final casualty list. How could she possibly succeed where so many fae—fae who hadn't spent the better part of their lives with their power bound—had failed?

The only thing she had that they didn't...was Loren.

And she wasn't sure she even had him.

Araya scowled, her gaze drifting to his empty chair. He'd been nothing more than a flicker at the edge of her vision since Thorne brought her back to Ithralis. He was *here* physically, or the bond would have let her know—but he wasn't *here* with her.

Her hand tightened on the quill until it snapped between her fingers. Araya hissed a curse, tossing it aside and hastily blotting at the ink spreading across her notes with her sleeve.

Enough. She wasn't going to sit here nursing her hurt feelings while Loren sulked and blamed her for things she couldn't change. She was doing this for him—for his people—and he had the nerve to act like *she* was a traitor.

She shoved back from the table, her skirt catching at her legs as she stormed through the library doors. She didn't need anyone to tell her where he was—not when the pull in her chest was like a compass, dragging her through the twisting halls and finally through the door and into the courtyard.

Loren stood at the center, his shirt tossed aside despite the chill. A practice blade flashed in his hand, shadows twisting and lashing around him as he cut through one brutal sequence after another.

Araya stopped short, the cold bite of sea air nipping at her suddenly burning cheeks. This close, she couldn't help but see the scars that marred his pale skin—a permanent reminder of the role she'd played in Jaxon's treatment of him.

"What are you doing out here, Araya?" His blade lowered, but the ice in his voice cut just as deeply. "Aren't you busy plotting your triumphant return to the man who drained you and left you for dead because you *forgot your place*."

"Is that really what you think of me?" Magic flared in her blood, rising to answer her anger, but Araya shoved it back down. That was the last thing she needed right now. "That I'm crawling back to him because I *want* to go back to being his obedient little bond?"

Loren clenched his jaw, his green eyes burning into her. "I think you're still suppressing your magic," he retorted, pacing a slow circle around her. "Have you even bothered working with Thorne on it?"

"Excuse me?" Araya stiffened, turning to keep him in her line of sight. "You don't know anything about what I've been doing."

"You think because you don't see me that I'm not watching?" Loren snorted, shaking his head. "I can't stay away from you, Araya. No matter how badly I want to. Here—"

Araya jumped, barely avoiding getting hit in the shins as his practice sword clattered to the broken cobblestones at her feet.

"What am I supposed to do with that?" she demanded.

"It's a sword." Loren watched her, his lips pressed into a thin line. "Pick it up."

"Why?" Araya hesitated, eyeing the blade at her feet. It was longer than her arm, the dulled edge still sharp enough to do damage. "Are you going to make me hold it to my own throat?"

Loren winced at that. "No compulsion," he said. "I swear."

Araya bent down, grunting as she hefted the sword. It was heavier than it looked, her arms and shoulders protesting immediately.

"Get it out of the dirt," Loren ordered. "It's a sword, not a plow—no, higher than that."

Araya clenched her jaw, her arms trembling as she forced the blade up. "I'm not sure what you're trying to prove here—"

"Keep your stance open," Loren interrupted her. He leaned across her, the warmth of his bare skin heating hers even through her dress.

"Don't lock your elbows. You'll tire too quickly. Good." He circled her again, watching with eagle-eyed intensity. "Why are you holding it like it's as heavy as you are?"

"It *is* heavy!" Araya grimaced, the leather-wrapped hilt biting into her palms as she shifted her stance to try and take some of the weight off her wrists. "I've never even *held* a sword before."

Loren stopped pacing, staring at her incredulously. "Why not?"

"No one over half-fae is permitted to carry a weapon." Araya dropped the sword to the ground again, scowling at him as she rolled out her wrists. "You can carry a knife—as long as the blade is shorter than your palm. Anything longer and it's an act of rebellion."

Loren stared at her, his expression darkening.

"Every time you tell me something new about what they did to you..." he shook his head, the shadows shuddering at his feet.

"I don't need your pity," Araya snapped.

"It's not pity." Loren took a step closer, his voice sharpening. "It's outrage. And you should be just as angry as I am. Now, pick up the sword."

"No." Araya crossed her arms, muscles she hadn't even realized she had aching. "I'm not playing these games with you. I only came out here to tell you I expect you to *help* me save your people. Not waste all your time brooding."

"How about a deal?" Loren smiled at her, the gleam in his eyes putting her immediately on edge. "If you manage to land a hit on me, I'll help you."

"That's ridiculous," Araya protested. "You're a trained warrior. I'm just—" she bit the word off. She didn't know what she was. She wasn't fae. But she wasn't human either. She used to call herself a mage—but did she even have that anymore?

Loren *laughed* at her, resuming his slow circle around her. "Then I'll use the sword," he said, scooping it up easily. "You use whatever magic you want. Aether, runes...you're even welcome to the shadows, if you can convince them to listen to you." His lips curved, that dangerous smile deepening. "Whatever you need to stop me."

"*Stop* you—?"

Araya yelped as Loren lunged, tripping over her own feet in her haste to retreat. She flung up her hands, aether sparking between her palms. The air between them crackled with magic, the backlash searing her palms as Loren crashed into her flickering shield hard enough to rattle her teeth.

"What in the name of all the Gods are you doing?" Araya demanded. Her hands trembled, the barrier between them sputtering weakly. "Why are you attacking me?"

Loren only grinned at her, baring his teeth to show his sharp canines. "Every time you've used fae magic, your life has been in danger." He stepped back, studying her barrier. "So I'm endangering you. I suggest you find a way to fight back."

Araya stared at him, dumbfounded. Was he serious? She couldn't *fight* him—

Loren lunged again.

Araya screamed as he slammed into her shield with sword *and* magic this time. Aether roared through her, leeching her dry with every heartbeat as she struggled to hold him back.

"You're thinking like a human." Loren stepped back, flicking his wrist. Power slammed against her shield, shattering it into a thousand pieces. Shadows raced through the shards, reaching for her.

"I'm a quarter human!" Araya gave ground, her heart pounding.

"And that *quarter* is holding you back," he growled, stalking after her. "They taught you to think and act like a human—but you're *not*. And there is nothing wrong with that."

Araya bristled, his words sliding under her skin like a knife. "I'm not *ashamed* of my fae heritage."

"Heritage?" Loren snorted, his voice turning cold. "You are *three-quarters* fae, Araya. Start fighting like one."

This time, it wasn't his sword he raised against her, but his shadows. They surged forward like a dark tide, rising above her like a wave about to crash.

Araya flinched back, throwing up her hands. Light burst between her palms, flickering weakly as the shadows slammed against it, seeping through the cracks like smoke through broken stone.

"You can do better," Loren murmured, his form turned misty and indistinct behind the veil of darkness. "I know you can."

One of his shadows reached her, its cool touch sending goosebumps racing over her skin. Araya choked on a sob, closing her eyes as another wrapped stroked her cheek, winding around her throat.

But she wasn't afraid.

Araya sucked in a sharp breath, her heart racing. She'd seen Loren wield them to hurt—to kill. But she'd never feared them. Not once. Because somehow she knew—as surely as she knew that the sun rose in the east and set in the west—that his shadows would never hurt her. And neither would Loren, no matter what he believed about himself.

She let go of her shield, letting it shatter into a thousand shards. Loren swore sharply as his shadows rushed forward, surging over her in a cold wave. She could *feel* him struggling for control of them —but she didn't hesitate, storming through them to plant both palms on his chest and *shove.*

"*Stop pushing me,*" she snarled, baring her teeth at him. Power surged under her skin, raging through her veins. It leapt to her command before she even called for it, heat coiling down her spine and sparks crackling across her tongue.

Loren's eyes darkened, the shadows stilling at his feet.

"Finally," he murmured. "There you are."

"There *who* is?" Araya demanded.

His smile widened. "We're about to find out."

The shadows rushed over her again. Her power answered as they skimmed over her skin like water over stone, crackling where it collided with their cool touch. It lit her up from the inside out, filling her with light to his darkness—

"No—" she stumbled back a step, but there was no running from this power. It filled her like wildfire, burning her alive from the inside out. "I can't—"

"You *can*." Loren caught her hands, not letting her retreat. "You can, *ael'sura*. This is *your* power—"

"I'm going to hurt someone." She gasped, every breath coming fast and shallow. The only reason no one got hurt last time was because of Loren. And she'd still hurt him—

"You won't hurt me." Loren squeezed her hands, closing the distance between them until his forehead pressed against hers, her panicked breaths mingling between them. "Goddess, do you know what you look like right now?"

Araya's breath hitched, a wild, bitter laugh sticking in her throat. "Like some traitor halfblood you got shackled to by some cruel twist of fate? An inconvenient weakness you'd be better off rid of—"

"*No*." Loren let out a sharp breath, his eyes flashing as he stared down at her. He huffed out a rough laugh, his hands tightening on hers, like he needed *her* to anchor him. "You're the strongest person I know, Araya. What you survived—" his voice broke, his face shining in the light that must be pouring from her. "You are light and power and fury. You are fucking *breathtaking*."

Araya's mouth dropped open, words fleeing her. But Loren didn't wait for her to find them. He caught her face between his hands, crushing his mouth to hers.

CHAPTER

THIRTY

He hadn't meant to kiss her.

One moment, she was standing in front of him, her silver eyes blazing with fury and power—and the next, his hands were on her face, dragging her to him.

He kissed her like a drowning man breaking the surface. Desperate. Starving. Every scrap of restraint he'd clung to these past weeks snapped in two as her mouth parted beneath his. She tasted like *lightning*, the vibrant tang of her magic bursting across his tongue. The shadows howled their approval, wrapping around them both and tangling them together.

Her hands slid across his chest, greedily exploring what she'd tried so hard not to stare at. The sound she made when he pressed her back against the cold stone wall shredded the last of his control. He lifted her easily, her skirts tangling around them, her warmth pressed flush to his body like she had always belonged there.

"*Loren*—" her gasped exclamation cut off in a moan as his lips dropped to her throat.

"*Araya*," he mimicked, nipping at her soft skin. "*Goddess, ael'sura.*

Did you actually believe I didn't want you? That I wouldn't want you without the bond? You've been driving me absolutely fucking insane, *ael'sura*."

He came back to her lips, swallowing her ragged laugh. Her fingers knotted in his hair, dragging him closer. Power roared around them, *through* them, her light colliding with his darkness until he couldn't tell where he ended and she began. He was drowning in it. Drowning in her—

Until she wrenched her mouth from his.

Her head snapped back, slamming into the stone wall hard enough that Loren swore, reaching out to cradle the back of her head. But she shoved at him, cold rushing in between them as she fought her way free of his arms.

"Don't—" her voice cracked, her knees buckling as he let go. She leaned against the wall, tugging at her tangled skirts with trembling hands. "Stop. Just stop."

Loren froze, shame crashing over him like icy water. She was his mate. He was supposed to protect her, not take advantage of her weakness. Whatever slim chance he'd had with her, he had already ruined by not telling her the truth when he had the chance. And he'd still grabbed her—kissed her. Had she even wanted him to? Or had she only given in because of the bond thrumming between them?

"Araya, I—"

She cut him off with a raised hand, her cheeks flushed as red as her hair. "I'm not leaving because I *want* to," she said, brushing her fingers over her swollen lips. "I'm leaving because staying here *isn't a choice*. No matter how badly I want it to be."

For a moment, Loren couldn't breathe. She wanted this—wanted *him*—but she was going to walk away anyway? He opened his mouth, ready to fight for this because Goddess help him, didn't they deserve a single shred of joy after everything they'd both endured? But she shook her head, her silver eyes glistening with unshed tears.

"Jaxon will *never* stop, Loren. You *know* I'm right. He'll come *here* and destroy *everything* you have left." She shook her head, her breath hitching on the sob she wouldn't let out. "You can't let that happen, Loren. Not for me. I'm not worth it."

"*Ael'sura*—" Loren's voice broke. Not worth it? She was worth *everything*. "That's not true."

"It *is*," Araya insisted. "And if I have to sever the bond and walk straight back into his hands to keep him from using me against you then that's what I'll do. I just want to save your people first. *Please*, Loren. Help me save them."

Loren stared at her. The bond twisted, agony ripping through his chest like she'd driven a blade into his heart. Even the shadows faltered, their restless whispers fading to silence. One by one, they retreated, relinquishing their grip on her to curl back around his feet like beaten dogs.

He wanted to beg her to stay, to promise her they would find another way—that he would burn the New Dominion to the ground before he let them take her again. But she was right—Jaxon would never stop. And if leaving meant protecting every free fae on Eluneth from the horrors of being captured by the Arcanum...what right did Loren have to stop her?

And the only thing saving his people would cost would be both their souls.

"Loren—" her voice wavered, a tear spilling over and sliding down her cheek. "What are you thinking? Say something."

Loren swallowed hard. "I'm thinking you would have made a wonderful queen, *ael'sura*."

She gave him a watery smile. "In another world, maybe."

"In another world," Loren echoed. He inclined his head, his heart breaking in his chest. "I'll meet you in the library tomorrow morning."

You would help her bind us? The shadows quivered at his feet, their whispers rising in a plaintive chorus.

"You're actually going to help?" Araya stared at him, her eyes wide like she couldn't believe it either—but Loren had no fight left. Not when it came to her.

"That was the deal, wasn't it?" He forced a smile, the shadows curling around his legs like that would prevent them from being ripped away. Their grief surrounded him, a cold storm building in his chest. "You did manage to hit me."

For a heartbeat she just blinked at him, then a weak laugh slipped past her lips. "I guess I did."

"I just have one request." Loren swallowed hard, holding her gaze. "Work with Thorne. Learn everything you can about your magic, even if you never use it again."

Her brow furrowed. "You don't want to teach me?"

"Oh, I do." His mouth twisted, the smile bitter on his lips. "But I seem to turn every lesson into a disaster. Thorne has more patience than I do. And he's my best friend. He's been my anchor more times than I can count...and I want you to have someone like that too. Someone you can lean on when you need to."

Araya's smile wobbled, but she nodded. "Alright. I'll work with Thorne."

"Thank you." Loren let out the breath he'd been holding even as the shadows hissed their displeasure. Thorne would keep her safe. Even when he couldn't.

"Well," a familiar voice drawled from the doorway. "I suppose I should be flattered. But what are the two of you doing out here in the damp?"

Loren started, his attention snapping to Thorne as his best friend crossed the courtyard. His easy tone didn't fool Loren—however long Thorne had been standing there, he'd seen enough to concern him. The shadows grumbled at his feet, an incoherent murmur of overlapping voices. What business was it of Thorne's what happened between him and his mate—

"The more people who protect her the better," Loren hissed under his breath, too quietly for Thorne or Araya to hear. Especially people who were willing to protect her from *him*.

Thorne stopped next to Araya, his gaze flicking over her pale face and the way her hands trembled at her sides. "Are you alright?" he asked gently, reaching out as if to steady her.

The shadows screeched, surging past Loren in a black tide as they lashed out at Thorne. One lashed around his wrist, the ghost of Thorne's blood blooming over Loren's tongue as the shadows *yanked* his best friend off his feet and dragged him across the broken stones.

"Stop!" Loren roared, grappling for control. "He's not hurting her—"

You cannot give her to him, the shadows howled, their voices splintering and coming back together in a frantic chorus as they fought him. *She is yours. Ours. Ours to protect—we will not fail. Not again—not this time—*

"*Loren!*" Araya threw herself between them, wrenching at the shadows as they spread from Thorne's arm to his chest, crushing him. "Stop!"

He was *trying.* Goddess help him, he was trying. But the harder Loren pulled, the more the shadows tore at him, cold tendrils lashing his skin like whips. They snarled, biting into his arms, his chest, his throat—punishing him for holding them back.

But they wouldn't fight her.

They recoiled at her touch, shrinking away as she dug her fingers beneath their coils and yanking them off Thorne one by one. His friend sucked in a ragged, gasping breath, but before Loren could move the shadows lunged again, their fury boiling over.

They would not let him take her from them.

A shield blazed to life between them, the shadows slamming into the wall of power in a crash of darkness and light that shook him to his bones.

"He is your friend!" Araya shouted, throwing herself over Thorne to shield him with her body as well as her magic. "He would never hurt me, Loren! Call them off!"

The shadows shrieked, unleashing the full force of their anguish on him. Their voices split his head, accusations landing like blows as he staggered under the force of their despair. *You betray us. Both of you—you would divide us. Leave us. Broken prince. Traitor—*

He couldn't. He couldn't control them—every breath he took, every beat of his heart was soaked in their pain, drowning him in their grief and rage. So Loren did the only thing he could to protect them both.

He fled, dragging the shadows with him.

THIRTY-ONE

"I don't know why he did that." Araya hovered over Thorne as the door crashed closed on Loren's heels, her shield flickering and dying with the danger gone. "We were just talking. He wanted me to work on my magic with you—"

"I think I'll pass," he rasped, his chuckle turning into a groan as Araya pressed the hem of her skirt against his wound. He slumped back, his head thudding against the stone wall.

"You're bleeding too much," Araya said, her voice shaking as his blood soaked the thick woolen fabric. "You need to Heal yourself—"

"Magic doesn't play nicely with shadow-inflicted wounds." Thorne leaned forward, his breaths coming shallow and uneven. "Bind it as tightly as you can—good." He smiled at her, but his face was too pale, his lips already tinged blue. His hands trembled as he held them out to her. "Now, help me up. We have to get to Veria."

Araya wedged her shoulder under his good arm, bracing herself as he hauled himself upright with a hiss. He was far heavier than she expected, his weight crushing down on her with every step.

"*Goddess*—" Veria's face went white as Araya shoved through the door, her eyes widening. "Sit him here." The clatter of knives and pans stilled under her hand as she swept the workbench clear with a burst of magic, taking Thorne's other side to help lever him onto the heavy table.

"Keep pressure on that wound," Veria ordered. She sliced through Thorne's shirt with a pair of kitchen shears, revealing the bruised and frost-bitten skin beneath.

"It's shadow rot," Thorne said, trying to sit up again. "The real problem is my arm. A poultice of yarrow and honey—"

"Will help stop the bleeding and slow the spread," Veria snapped, shoving him back down on the table. "I was helping your mother make poultices before you were even out of swaddling, Thorne Emberwood. I *know* what kind of poultice to make for shadow rot."

"Sorry, sorry—" Thorne laughed weakly, falling back against the table. "I'll just lay here and concentrate on not dying then."

Araya's gaze whipped toward Veria. "Is he going to die?"

The older female's mouth pressed into a grim line. "Not if we slow the bleeding long enough for him to Heal himself."

A mortar and pestle leapt across the room, already grinding green leaves and honey into a thick, sticky paste. Veria snatched it out of the air, scooping the mixture inside out with her bare hands and slathering it across the torn flesh of Thorne's arm, ignoring how he hissed and flinched.

"Clean cloths," Veria barked, nodding toward the whistling kettle. "Soak them and bring them here—quickly now, dear."

Araya scrambled for the clean towels Veria kept folded neatly beside the workbench, throwing them into a bowl and dumping the contents of the kettle overtop. Steam curled into the air, but Veria didn't hesitate to plunge her hand into the water, wringing out the first cloth and pressing it over the poultice

Thorne groaned, his back arching as steam rose from his arm, but Veria didn't let him move. She added towel after towel, until finally blood stopped soaking the white linen.

"There," she breathed, sitting back. "There we go. Now he'll be able to take care of it himself. See?"

Araya stared down at Thorne's face. He did look pinker—less pale. But his eyes were closed and his brow furrowed in pain.

"You did the right thing by getting him here." Veria took Araya's hand, gently pulling her away. "Now come sit down. It's going to be a while yet."

THORNE DIDN'T OPEN HIS EYES AGAIN UNTIL THE SUN HAD SET, STIRRING with a groan that had Araya leaping to her feet, the untouched bowl of soup Veria had pressed on her forgotten as she rushed to his side.

"Remind me not to get in between the two of you again." Thorne groaned, accepting her hand as he shoved himself to a seated position. He peeled back the layers of now-cooled linen, grimacing at whatever he saw beneath. "Goddess help me. Veria?"

"She left to fetch Ilyana." Araya stared at Thorne, unable to tear her gaze away from the shadowmarks that snaked across his chest, dark bands scarring his skin where the shadows had tried to crush him. But her own skin was unmarked, even though she'd been right there—prying the shadows off him and shoving them away. "Why don't they hurt me?"

Thorne let out a short, pained laugh. "Because you're his mate." He grabbed a fresh cloth, carefully wiping the poultice away to study the twisting marks left behind. "He was protecting you."

"Protecting me?" Her voice broke, rising high and thin. "From what—his best friend?"

"We all know *dara'el* has a mind of its own." Thorne's mouth curved into a thin smile. "They must have seen me as a threat."

Araya swallowed, bile burning the back of her throat as she thought of the shadows—snarling and tearing as they dragged Thorne across the stones. Loren fighting them—and failing.

"Are they—" she hesitated, almost afraid of what the answer might be. "Are they going mad? Like they did with his father?"

Thorne's head snapped up, his amber gaze wary. "What do you know about that?"

"Only what Eloria told me." Araya wrapped her arms around herself, suddenly chilled despite the warmth of the kitchen. "She said the shadows went mad when their mother died—because the king had lost his mate. That they slaughtered every person on that battlefield—human and fae alike." She forced herself to take another breath, her voice trembling. "What's happening now...is it my fault?"

"You aren't dead, Araya," Thorne said kindly. "There isn't much known about incomplete mate bonds—Eloria has Ysella pulling all the information she can find about them now. I think everyone here assumed you'd eventually agree to the mate bond—but Loren has been very clear that he won't see you forced into it. What happened with him in the New Dominion...it's not something he ever would have chosen to put on you."

Araya nodded, though her throat ached. No matter what she thought about what Loren had done, she knew claiming her without her consent was something he'd never stop punishing himself for.

"Did you know the whole time?" she asked softly, staring down at her own hands rather than look at Thorne and be confronted by what the shadows had done to him. "About the mate bond?"

"We did." Thorne rubbed his good hand over his face, suddenly looking years older. "But it wasn't our place to say anything. Loren didn't want to tell you—he almost killed Nyra over it."

Araya's brow furrowed. "She wanted to tell me?"

"She wanted to kill you," Thorne said bluntly. "And leave your body behind for the Shaws to find. She thought it was too dangerous to steal Jaxon Shaw's bond out from under his nose."

Araya stared at him, stunned.

"Well," she said when she found her voice again. "She wasn't wrong. That would have solved a lot of problems. If I can't find a way to break the bond it would probably still work—"

"Don't even suggest that," Thorne cut her off sharply. "Especially not in front of Loren. Unless you want to see the shadows destroy everything and everyone they can reach."

"We should consider all the options." Araya looked away. "Even the unpalatable ones."

Thorne was silent for a long moment.

"You're serious then," he said finally. "About breaking the bond and going back?"

"I don't see any other way for this to end," Araya whispered. "I don't want to be used to hurt Loren, but what Jaxon did to those females…" her voice caught. "I can't let them get hurt because of me either. I'm just trying to protect them both. I just wish he understood that."

"I think—"

But whatever Thorne was about to say was cut off as the door swung open, Ilyana hurrying in on Veria's heels.

"Of course you're sitting up," the Healer grumbled, glaring at him. "Is it too much to ask that you follow your own instructions?"

"Healers make the worst patients—" Thorne grunted, his voice faltering as Ilyana shoved him back down onto the table, her hands already glowing as she palpated the writhing shadowmarks that covered his chest.

"You shielded him?" she asked, glancing at Araya.

Araya nodded mutely.

"Then you saved his life," Ilyana said. "Here—help me get him up. He'll be more comfortable in his rooms."

Together, they eased Thorne from the table, half-carrying him back through the corridors to his chamber. By the time they settled him on the bed, sweat had plastered his hair to his forehead, though his smile was stubborn as ever.

"Stubborn male," Ilyana muttered, smoothing the sheet over his bare chest. She turned back to Araya, her expression gentler. "Eryn sent something for you," she said, rummaging in her satchel and pulling out a leather-bound folder. "Here—he said you'd want it right away."

Araya took the folder automatically, her throat suddenly dry as she stared down at the note tucked into the front. *I hope this has all the answers you need, Miss Starwind.* Written in common—not Valenya.

Her stomach dropped, realizing what must be inside. Accountings of couples who had severed their mate bonds. Why they'd done it—and how. Everything she'd been searching for since she learned the bond existed, delivered to her in a neat little package.

"Thank you," she managed, realizing Ilyana was staring at her. "I'll just—"

The Healer nodded, still watching her carefully. "You should get some rest," she said. "What you did today—you really did save Thorne's life, Araya. I'm glad you were there."

Araya dipped her head politely, barely hearing anything else Ilyana said as she stumbled into the hall. For a moment, she just stood there, staring down the corridor toward her own door. But the folder was heavy in her hands, the neat black letters of Eryn's note seared into her mind.

Rest—she should be tired. Exhausted, even. But instead her heartbeat thundered in her ears, her feet carrying her past her own door without pause. There would be no rest for her—not until she knew exactly what Eryn had found.

CHAPTER

THIRTY-TWO

Loren stared out the window overlooking the courtyard, watching as Ilyana rushed through the gate with dusk at her heels. Thorne must have survived then—there would be no reason to send for a Healer otherwise. And Araya—she would certainly be angrier if Thorne was dead. Grief-stricken, even. But all he felt through the bond was a confused tumult of frustration and worry. For Thorne, of course, he assumed. Not for him. The fool who'd nearly let his wayward magic *murder* his best friend.

Go to her, the shadows whispered, stirring around him.

"She doesn't want to see you." Loren didn't bother to look down at them. "Not after what you did earlier."

Us? The shadows hissed. *You left her. Foolish prince—*

"You attacked Thorne!" Loren hissed, yanking his arm back as one of them dragged a frigid tendril across the back of his hand in reprimand, as sharp as a frozen blade. "Have you forgotten the difference between friend and foe?"

Friend?

The shadows recoiled, muttering amongst themselves as they

broke apart and reformed, working themselves into a churning frenzy.

He raised his hand. Reached for her. We saw—we saw—we protect. Protect her. Protect you. We don't know—can't say—

Goddess help him, they were madder than ever. Loren braced his hands against the sill, staring down at the empty courtyard. He couldn't shake the memory of her panicked face, her shield the only thing between Thorne and death as she shouted at him to *stop*.

But he hadn't been able to.

Because you falter, the shadows muttered. *You fail—failed her. She is yours—yours to protect. And they* hurt *her. And you—* their voices broke apart, hissing over one another. *Coward. No vengeance. You refused—you* failed—

"*I know,*" Loren hissed.

The temperature plummeted. A hairline fracture raced across the glass, the aetherlamps guttering in their sconces. Loren bit his lip until he tasted blood, his knuckles white on the edge of the stone sill —but it wasn't enough. The crack was a fault line across the window, silent proof of just how close he'd come to losing control. Again.

The shadows coiled around his boots as he stormed away, their many voices echoing the truth he refused to speak.

They were slipping. And so was he.

By the time he reached his room his breathing had evened out, the pressure in his chest easing. He sank into a chair, not bothering to kindle the aetherlamps. Stone walls and darkness—that was all he was meant for. He might as well have stayed in that cell after all.

They were right about him. He couldn't keep his mate safe. He'd made mistakes at every step—claiming her against her will, hiding the truth from her—short of locking her up again, there was nothing he could do to make her stay.

"I'm sorry," Loren murmured into the shifting darkness. "I know I'm a broken excuse for the prince you chose. You would have been better off with Eloria."

You are not the only broken one, foolish prince. The shadows murmured amongst themselves, their voices ebbing and flowing before coming together again. *We are splinters. Shards. Only pieces of the greater power. Lost.*

Loren frowned. "What do you mean?"

The whispers fractured, breaking apart in discordant hisses before falling silent so abruptly Loren wasn't sure they would answer him at all. But then—

We remember. Their voices were thin, strained and out of sync. *But to speak it—*

Pain, another whispered.

But we can show you, several voices said as one. *Should. Should show you—if you're ready.*

Loren knew it was a dream the moment he opened his eyes.

He stood on the steps of the temple, its polished stone shot through with threads of aether, lighting it from within. It glowed in the bright moonlight, shining down from a sky free of shadow and mist. This was Eluneth as he remembered it, the surrounding forest alive with the sounds of animals and the air sweetened by the flowers that bloomed on the vines climbing the temple walls.

Not a dream, a sibilant chorus of voices whispered, curling around him like smoke. *A memory.*

Loren swallowed hard, dread filling his heart as the warm breeze kissed his face, already knowing what he would see when he turned to face the temple. There was only one night the shadows would show him like this.

His father stood on the threshold beside Thorne's father, tall and grim. The silver crown atop his long, dark hair gleamed in the moonlight, shadows trailing him like a living cloak. They licked at his heels, coiling in slow, serpentine waves over the ground behind him.

Corwin Shadowbane looked every bit the king Loren remembered, but there was a new strain in his expression, a hollowness beneath his eyes, where grief had aged him faster than time ever could. Elric Emberwood walked beside him, one hand on the hilt of his sword as they looked out over the soldiers.

Loren tried to turn away, to close his eyes, but the dream held him fast. Shadows bled from the edges of his vision, winding around his wrists and ankles.

Watch, they hissed.

Loren could do nothing else as two hundred fae warriors took their places before the temple, faces set with grim resolve as the human army crested the ridge. They just kept coming, marching down the same road he'd walked with Araya—hundreds strong, many wielding stolen magic bound inside grisly artifacts. If battles were decided on numbers alone, this would surely be a slaughter.

But the fae had *dara'el*.

The shadows burst from Corwin like a wave torn from the sea—black and wild, but united in their purpose. His father's eyes glowed with power, the shadows answering to his command as they moved with him—never against. Together, they cut down the front line of Dominion mages with deadly grace, wrapping his father in a mantle of darkness that shimmered like liquid night.

This was how it was meant to be. This was what a worthy ruler looked like.

But there were so many humans.

They struck back with stolen magic, forcing their way forward despite the shadows. The fae cried out, pushed back step by step until their backs were pressed against the temple walls. Loren couldn't look away from his father's face, his desperation growing as he wielded the power the Goddess had gifted him to protect her people—and failed.

The first blast of magic struck the temple.

The doors groaned under the force of it, cracking down the center as huge chunks of stone crashed to the ground, shattering the steps.

Corwin stumbled back, Elric's hand on his arm pulling him away. For a heartbeat, Loren thought he would do the only wise thing and retreat—even though he already knew how this ended. But then the human Commander stepped through the settling dust, the Arcanum's Eye gleaming gold over his heart. In his hands, he lifted a staff fashioned from an entire fae femur, raising it toward Corwin with deliberate finality.

Loren held his breath, waiting for killing blow.

But instead, the shadows broke.

With a soundless roar, *dara'el* tore free from his father's body, surging forward in a tidal wave of darkness. The Commander had only a moment to react. His eyes widened. His lips parted in what might have been a command, or a scream, but it was lost as the shadows swept over him.

They spared no one.

Fae warriors were dragged screaming into the dark. Human soldiers fell with their lungs full of shadow. The battlefield turned into a graveyard. Thorne's father fought his way forward, carving a desperate arc through the chaos as he cried out for Corwin to call back his shadows.

But Loren already knew—he couldn't.

Corwin dropped to his knees as Elric fell where he stood, the darkness devouring him whole. His crown slipped sideways, his fingers curling into the blood-soaked earth. All around him, the battlefield fell silent—because there was no one left to scream.

The shadows slowed, wavering as they slunk amongst the bodies, fae and human alike. They gathered slowly, coalescing around the fallen king. And Corwin, tears pouring down his face, closed his eyes and bowed his head as the shadows he should have wielded to protect them all turned on him at last.

Loren could only watch—frozen and horrified—as the shadows spread across the battlefield. They poured over the corpses like spilled ink, devouring armor, blade, and flesh with equal hunger. Smoke-like tendrils crawled through the broken remains of the temple, seeped into the soil and made themselves at home among the trees. Even the air itself turned thick and gray, the stars winking out one by one as darkness shrouded the night sky.

"You killed them all," Loren whispered. "That's why there were no survivors."

His father hadn't raised the Shadowed Veil to *protect* the fae. It had raised itself because there had been no one left to command it.

His shadows stirred, curling around his boots and flickering at the edges of his vision. *We remember,* they said, their voices jagged and fragmented. *What we were. What he made us. What we became. You—you should have brought us together again. Reforged. Whole.*

"You're only part of it," Loren murmured. Araya had theorized as much, even without knowing the details. "The Shadowed Veil—it's something else, isn't it?"

Lost. The shadows thickened, drawing tighter around him. *Do not break us further, lost prince.*

"I'm sorry." Loren stared out over the darkened battlefield. "But she's right. The fae need control of the Shadowed Veil or we'll all die. I can't do it. But if she can...we have to let her."

The battlefield wavered, the memory curling in on itself like burnt paper to reveal four stone walls, as familiar to him as his own heartbeat. The ever-present damp chill seeped into his skin, biting through the thin, filthy shirt he wore. His pallet of moldy straw reeked of damp decay, and iron cuffs bit into his raw wrists, the collar chafing his throat with every shallow breath. The chains that bound him were thicker than before—reinforced. There would be no slipping free this time.

But he had survived this before. He could survive it again.

Then he heard it.

At first, he thought it was a trick of his mind, but the voice only grew louder, rising from muffled pleas to a ragged scream that sent a jolt of terror straight through his chest.

Araya.

Her panic flared in his veins, every echo of her agony vibrating through the tether that bound their souls together. They had her. They *had her* because of *him*. He had taken her blood, tied her to him, and now they knew. Because of him, she was suffering.

"Araya!" He strained against the chains, blood slicking his wrists —a small price to pay if he could just *reach her*. But the chains held. They always did.

"Jaxon, please...please stop..."

"Araya!" Loren bellowed, throwing all of his strength into another desperate pull against the chains. The pain didn't register. Only her voice mattered. Her broken gasps, her sobs, the breathless way she begged. This was his fault. He had been selfish—too weak to send her away like he should have. And now they were tearing her apart because of it. Because of him.

"Loren...please..."

Loren's stomach twisted, bile burning the back of his throat as the iron collar cut into his throat with every gasping breath. His vision blurred, sweat slicking his palms and stinging the raw wounds on his wrists as he struggled weakly against the chains. She needed help. She needed *him*, and he couldn't get to her.

"Stop! I'll do anything, just stop!" Loren screamed, his throat ripping raw, pleading with anyone—anything—that might hear him. "Please!"

This—this is the future. Condemn her. Condemn yourself, the shadows hissed, their fury returning seven-fold. *If you let her break us —let her walk away—go back to* him—

Loren gasped, his chest heaving as his eyes snapped open. Shadows writhed across stone walls—but this wasn't his cell, and the tears he tasted on his tongue weren't his.

They were hers.

Loren threw off his covers, shaking the shadows off. The balcony doors stood open, letting in the cool breeze that nipped at his exposed skin, reminding him that he was here, in Ithralis. Safe. But the bond pulsed like a wound in his chest, tugging him through the halls with the same terrible urgency he'd felt in the dream. Had he even woken? Or would he find her at the other end covered in blood, only to have her turn to ash in his arms?

He finally found her in the library.

She sat at the table in her usual spot, a storm of papers scattered across its surface. He'd lurked in the stacks, watching her pour over the same reports over and over again with fervent hope, desperate for some sort of clue—but not tonight. Tonight, her face was buried in her hands, her shoulders shaking with silent sobs.

"Araya," he said softly.

She started slightly, her hands slipping from her face as she turned. Tear tracks cut through the smudges on her cheeks, her wet eyes shining even more brightly than usual in the light of the aetherlamps.

"Are you alright?" Loren dared a step closer, the bond clawing at his chest like it was trying to escape. Her grief ached in the space between them, so strong it threatened to drown him along with her. "Is Thorne—"

"He's alright." Araya sniffed, dragging a hand across her eyes. "Gods—he's alright, Loren. He's going to be fine. I'm sorry. I just—"

"You have nothing to be sorry about." Loren reached for the nearest paper, turning it so he could read it. Lines of cramped handwriting crawled across the surface, figures in the common tongue interspersed with notations in spidery Valenya script. Symbols stamped in the margins confirming it as New Dominion intelligence —retrieved and processed by Eloria's spymaster.

"Where did you get this?" he asked softly.

"Ilyana brought them. From Eryn." Araya looked back down, still sniffling. "Were you hiding them from me?"

"Not hiding," Loren said, setting the paper back down carefully. "It's classified intelligence—I'm just shocked Eloria allowed it to leave Lumaria."

Araya said nothing. Just stared at the reports, her shoulders hunched, hands limp in her lap like she didn't know what to do with them anymore.

"All I've ever wanted to do was protect you, *ael'sura*," Loren said softly. "From the moment I realized who you were. How I've done it... I know it hasn't been perfect. But the thing I want most in this world is for you to be safe."

"I should hate you. Everything you've done to me—but I can't." Her voice broke, a fat tear splattering the report in front of her. "I'm no better than you. Did you know that he's killed twenty-three females? They weren't spies or rebels—he just picked them off the street because they had red hair and clipped ears."

Loren's throat tightened, the shadows behind him going still as Araya turned the page with shaking fingers.

"Entire districts have been locked down—families taken and never seen again. Serafina..." her shoulders shook. "Serafina was taken into Arcanum custody and hasn't been seen since. It's all my fault, Loren."

"It's not," Loren whispered. He wanted to reach for her, but he couldn't move. Even the shadows were still around his feet. "It's not your fault, *ael'sura.*"

"I can't fix it." Araya finally looked up at him, tears cutting silver paths down her cheeks. "If I don't go back, the fae there suffer. If I go back while we're still bound, Jaxon uses me to hurt you. But if I break the bond *I* hurt you."

Loren's pulse stumbled. "Did you find a way to do it?"

"I did. But it doesn't matter." Araya turned another page, shoving it toward him. "According to every one of the few accounts they could find, breaking the bond requires your true name. And like you said..." She trailed off, her voice bitter. "No *true* fae would ever give anyone that kind of power over them."

Loren sucked in a sharp breath, his heart stumbling in his chest. He'd told her that—Goddess, it felt like a lifetime ago. In a dream neither one of them would ever see come true. He'd been so cruel, certain that he was right. But what had he known, in the end?

"It's Lorendrael," he said.

Araya's head snapped up, but Loren rushed on before she could speak.

"I still think going back is a terrible idea, but...if you want to break the mate bond, I won't stop you. I swear it."

"Loren..." Araya stared at him, her mouth parted as her eyes searched his like she wasn't sure he was real. Loren forced himself to meet her gaze and hold it, even as his heart screamed at him to take the words back.

"I claimed you without your consent," he said softly. "I can't take that back. But I won't shackle you to a fate you didn't choose. Whatever you decide, *ael'sura*...I'll survive it."

"I—" she cleared her throat, scrubbing her hands across her face. "We shouldn't do anything until we retrieve your father's remains. I do want to help the fae in any way I can. I just..." she trailed off, still staring at him. "I think we can make it through the Veil together. If you're willing."

Loren swallowed hard, the bond twisting in his chest. "Eloria said it will take two days to prepare for another attempt to retrieve my father's remains. Is that enough time?"

"Two days," Araya echoed slowly, nodding.

"I'll let her know." Loren reached out, brushing a strand of hair that had escaped her braid back out of her face before he could think better of it. She closed her eyes, leaning into the touch as his knuckles grazed her cheek.

It wasn't much—just the smallest tilt of her head toward his hand—but it stopped the breath in Loren's chest. The bond pulsed quietly, not burning or clawing like it usually did, but warm and still. Peaceful, for the first time since he danced with her at Bloomtide.

"You're exhausted," he said, his voice thick. "Let me walk you back to your room."

CHAPTER

THIRTY-THREE

Araya woke slowly, sleep blurring the edges of her mind. Thin light filtered through the high windows of the library, muted and gray. Spring might have arrived, but there were no fresh buds or greening gardens. Not here, where a heavy blanket of chill mist still pressed against the castle walls.

But she was warm.

She blinked, groaning when she realized she'd fallen asleep in one of the library chairs, slumped awkwardly against the armrest with the reports she'd been going over still spread out on the table in front of her. Someone had draped a blanket over her, cocooning her in the comforting scent of rain-washed stone.

Loren.

He slumped in a chair across from her, his long legs stretched out and his head tipped back against the padded upholstery—fast asleep. For once, the tension was gone from his face, the grim set of his lips softened. Even the shadows were restful, quiet around his feet.

The bond purred in her chest, delighted at his proximity and blissfully uncaring of the reasons why they could never be together.

Not really. But for a moment, she indulged it. Let herself breathe in his scent and imagine that she would ever get more than a handful of stolen mornings with him.

But when she looked at him, the dream shattered.

Faint scars wrapped his throat, a lingering reminder of the iron collar he had worn for so many years. More peeked out from the open collar of his shirt—a map of the Arcanum's cruelties, carved into his flesh with iron and left to heal without care. Even with all the magic in the world at their fingertips, the fae Healers would never be able to make those scars vanish completely.

Araya's stomach turned. She might not have wielded the knife herself, but she'd been complicit. Silent and obedient.

Her focus had always been on ensuring that *she* was never on the receiving end of such attention. But now twenty-three fae females were dead—killed for no reason but that they bore a passing resemblance to her. Dumped into the Shadowed Veil like refuse. Forgotten.

She didn't deserve this happiness. Not after everything she'd done. And everything she'd failed to do.

If she was a better person, she would pray to the Gods that he found someone else once she broke their bond. Someone kind and gentle. Who thought of others first.

The kind of person that would make a good queen.

But just the thought of being replaced stirred the bond from its content rest, molten power prickling beneath her skin. And she couldn't afford *that*—not today.

Araya stood, folding the blanket and laying over the back of her chair before slipping from the library on silent feet. Despite the early hour, voices already drifted up from the floors below—soft conversation, the clatter of dishes, the scent of something warm and spiced. Ithralis was more alive than she had ever seen it, crowded with those Eloria had deemed indispensable to the retrieval effort.

Even the High Luminary had come—trailed by an entourage of white-robed devotees that mingled with a small army of soldiers and

Healers, filling bedrooms and the common areas of Ithralis with talk and laughter.

But even in a place this full, it was possible to feel alone.

Araya made her way outside without speaking to anyone. The early spring air bit at her cheeks as she crossed the courtyard, mist curling low across the stones. She pulled her cloak tighter, ducking into the garden she'd worked so hard on with Thorne.

The secluded alcove where he'd waited for her still stood undisturbed, the quiet of wrapping around her like a comforting blanket. She paused beneath the arch of dead vines, tilting her head to study their twisted length. They would have been beautiful in full bloom—lavender curtains spilling down, their sweet scent perfuming the air and their lush leaves casting dappled shadows in the sun.

Maybe Eilwen could regrow them, once Eloria lifted the shadows. The garden would bloom again, even if she wasn't here to see it.

Araya settled onto the damp bench, drawing her cloak tight around her shoulders. She hadn't come to grieve what had been or mourn what she would never have.

She'd come to practice.

Araya held out her hands in front of her, turning her mind inward to brush across the current of power that flowed through her. Back in the New Dominion, she never would have dared waste valuable magic—conservation was the first thing the human minders at Kaldrath had drilled into them when they arrived, weeping and terrified. It wasn't their power to use. It belonged to the Arcanum, just like their names.

But that was the human way.

She drew a steadying breath, opening herself to her power. It rose to her invitation, a faint shimmer warming her palms. For a heartbeat, it held—the thin, translucent beginnings of a shield.

But then it faltered, shivering between her hands before it broke apart and dissolved into the mist.

Araya hissed through her teeth, dragging the remnants of her power back under control. They all said she could do this—that it would come as naturally as breathing. She'd done better sparring with Loren. She'd saved Thorne's life with her magic. Loren even claimed he'd seen her use her power instinctively before, back in the New Dominion.

So why couldn't she reach it now?

Araya closed her eyes, forcing herself to breathe. This was just nerves. Today was important. If they succeeded in retrieving the king's remains from the heart of the Veil, she'd be that much closer to going home. Gods, she could be on a boat this time next week. Back to the New Dominion, and Jaxon, and the life she'd built for herself.

The thought didn't fill her with the relief it should have.

"This is an interesting place to find the mate of our crown prince," a smooth voice cut through the silence.

Araya's eyes flew open, the hair on the back of her neck standing on end at the sight of the silver-haired female just a few paces away. Even without her ceremonial mantle, there was no mistaking the High Luminary's glacier-pale eyes and haughty bearing.

Araya stood, wrapping her cloak around herself like a shield. "Does Loren know you're out here?"

"Be easy, Lady Starwind." The High Luminary's lips curved in a small smile. "I seek only a moment of your time. Even without His Majesty's recent...demonstration of what his shadows will do when you are threatened, I would never be fool enough to detain the mate of our crown prince against her will. I am merely curious what drives you to seek solace in a garden of shadows and death, when most would turn to the Goddess and her temples in times of turmoil."

"I grew up with the Gods," Araya said warily.

The High Luminary hummed softly. "Of course. The humans brought many gods with them when they sought sanctuary in our lands, searching for a place where they wouldn't be persecuted for practicing magic. And we welcomed them—called them kin and mixed our blood with theirs. After all, we all carry the Goddess' blessing, no matter how much aether we can summon to our will."

Araya shivered, tugging her cloak tighter around her shoulders like a shield.

"But humans are never content with the gifts they're given." The Priestess sighed, her gaze distant. "They sought more. And when the Goddess did not offer it freely, they turned to fae blood and fae bone, committing atrocities to take what they could never earn. Your prince's father was the king to finally heed our warnings. He forbade the practice of using amplifiers, decreeing that what we were given must be enough. But by then the damage was done."

Araya's throat tightened. This wasn't the story she'd learned from the human minders who raised her, but she knew how it ended. She had lived it.

"Humans are short-lived," the High Luminary continued. "But they breed like rats. A few become dozens. Dozens become hundreds, then thousands." Her gaze swung back to Araya, rooting her where she stood. "The clever and cunning among them quietly hoarded fae relics, crafting them into powerful weapons. With their numbers and the element of surprise...it was a slaughter."

"Why are you telling me this?" Araya whispered.

"Because, Lady Starwind, you aren't the first to believe you can rewrite what the Goddess has designed," the High Luminary smiled sadly. "Nor, I imagine, will you be the last. But every fall begins with the belief that we know better than the divine."

"People are dying," Araya protested. "Innocents—"

"I don't question your motivations, Lady Starwind," the High Luminary interrupted. "None of us wish to see others die in our place. It is a noble impulse."

"But?" Araya asked.

"*But* you are the mate of a prince—destined to be queen. To reject that bond...to sever what the Goddess herself has placed between you—" her voice cooled, each word deliberate, "—the consequences will ripple far beyond the deaths of a few part-fae women."

"Females," Araya corrected. She glared at the priestess, certain the slight had not been an accident. "They were fae."

"*Part*-fae." The High Luminary said pointedly.

"Just like me." Araya didn't flinch from the High Luminary's stare. She'd spent her life being looked at as *less* and proving everyone wrong. "Thank you. I'll be sure to take your counsel under advisement. But right now, I'd like to be alone."

The High Luminary studied her for a long, weighty moment longer before nodding. "As you wish, Lady Starwind. I will burn bay and pray the Goddess grants you clarity—and that whatever choice you make does not doom more than your own heart."

Araya wrapped her arms around herself, watching silently as the mist swallowed the High Luminary. In just a few heartbeats, she was alone again. Her power hummed under her skin, but she didn't reach for it again. She just stood there, staring into the quiet gray until a familiar wisp of shadow slid across the stones, twining around her ankles before leaping up to her shoulders.

She stroked it softly, warmth blooming in her chest as Loren stepped into the garden.

"You found me," she said.

"I'll always find you," he answered easily. He leaned against the wall, his face soft as he watched her stroke the shadow's sinuous form. He'd come straight from the library, his hair still tousled and a faint line on his cheek from the seam of the upholstery. "You were upset."

"I'm nervous." Araya sighed, glancing back into the shadowed garden. "What if I can't do it?"

Her voice wavered, breaking embarrassingly. But Loren just took another step forward, his hand coming up to cup her jaw as his thumb smoothed away a tear she hadn't felt fall.

"You're the strongest person I know," he said softly. "If anyone can do this, it's the female who forced the Arcanum to take her seriously."

Araya's breath hitched. Her eyes searched his—steady, unwavering, full of a trust she hadn't known she needed so badly. A trust she didn't deserve.

"Loren…" she laid her hand over his, closing her eyes. "I can't stay here."

"I know." Loren's fingertips brushed over her skin, a barely there touch that sent goosebumps rushing over her skin. "And I understand. I won't pretend the way you survived was right or easy. But I see you now. I trust you. Whatever comes next—whatever choice you have to make—I'm with you."

Araya didn't answer. She couldn't. Her throat closed around the rush of words she couldn't voice, her chest aching with the weight of everything he'd just given her.

Instead, she surged forward, burying her face in his chest.

Loren caught her without hesitation, his arms folding around her. One hand cradled the back of her head, tucking her into him like she belonged there.

"You should eat something," Loren said once her sobs had quieted to shaking sniffles.

"I don't think I can." Araya stepped back, wiping at her face.

Loren didn't press. Just held out his hand.

"You're ready," he said, quiet and certain.

She stared at his hand for a moment, the ache in her chest coiling tighter. Then she slipped her fingers into his and let him lead her from the garden.

THIRTY-FOUR

There were too many people here.

Eloria couldn't come herself—the fae wouldn't survive losing both surviving royals. But she'd sent a small army in her stead. Loren's jaw flexed as he scanned the clustered warriors, scouts, and Healers. Half of them watched him like he might snap at any moment, while the other half tried—and failed—not to look afraid.

She'd even sent Galen.

He stood near the dust-covered altar, arms folded tight across his chest. There was no trace of his usual easy smile today. Just a dark scowl carved deep across his face, his eyes fixed on Loren like he was waiting for him to fall apart.

None of them would make a difference if *dara'el* chose violence.

Loren stared out the broken doors, studying the roiling darkness. In his memory, it was a wide, green space where he and Thorne had run and played. But now? It was nothing but a graveyard.

Lost. His shadows curled around his boots, slithering restlessly up his spine. *Broken. Fractured and forgotten—*

"Are you sure about this?"

"No." Loren didn't turn to look at Galen as the other male stepped up beside him.

"You know, not one attempt to retrieve your father's remains ended without casualties," Galen said, his voice low. "There's a reason Eloria forbade further efforts—"

"And there's a reason she approved this one," Loren said flatly.

Galen turned his head slightly. "And you think *she* is ready for *this?*"

Loren followed Galen's gaze to where Araya stood, arms wrapped around herself as she stared up at the veiled statue of the absent Goddess. She'd bound her hair back in that tight braid and traded her usual dress for a dark tunic and breeches. She'd even strapped the dagger he'd insisted she wear to her belt without protest. Loren doubted she'd draw it if she needed to, but it wouldn't matter today.

No steel could cut down a shadow.

"She's ready," Loren said.

As if she heard him, Araya looked up. Her silver gaze met his, and that quiet presence in his chest stirred as the shadows at his feet reached for her—eager and unbidden. Her lips twitched in a faint smile as they curled around her legs, drawing her forward.

"I'll let them know, then," Galen said. He inclined his head to Araya as she started toward them, but stepped away before she reached them.

"He doesn't think I can do this," she said, stroking the shadow that curled around her shoulder like a fur stole.

"He's wrong," Loren said.

He held out his hand, sparks scurrying across his skin when she took it. She let him pull her close, resting her head against his shoulder like she needed the contact as much as he did.

After a long moment, Araya pulled back.

"We should go," she said softly. "There are no more reasons to wait."

Loren nodded, though his chest ached with the loss of her closeness. It wasn't just physical. She was retreating—already holding herself apart, bracing to sever the bond between them.

What would it feel like when she broke it for good?

Loren shoved the thought down, refusing to acknowledge the twist of pain in his chest. Whatever came next, they would face it together. And for now, that was enough.

It didn't take long to get everything ready. The soldiers arrayed themselves down the stairs and in the courtyard, while the Healers clustered inside the temple. A scout leaned close to Galen, saying something low and urgent about the wind—as if something as simple as a brisk breeze would make the difference this time. But none of them stood any closer to the dark mist than they had to.

Loren didn't blame them.

The Veil pulsed before them, as cold and angry as the wall of darkness over the Shadowed Sea had been.

Even his own shadows curled around his feet, reluctant to get any closer to the heaving, pulsing darkness.

"Are you afraid?" Araya asked, quietly enough that no one else would hear.

"I am." Loren didn't look at her as he answered. He couldn't lie to her—but he didn't want to see her face when he said it.

"Me too," she whispered. "But we have a plan. Don't we?"

No—no. Turn back— the shadows whimpered, their voices a low moan against his mind. *Do not break us—*

"We do," Loren said, forcing himself to meet her eyes. "Are you ready?"

She nodded, her silver eyes bright even in the gloom. She slipped her hand into his, squeezing tightly. He held on, a hundred useless words on the tip of his tongue. But nothing he could say here would make any more difference than a blade or a breeze against the shadows.

So instead, he said nothing. And together, they stepped into the heart of the Shadowed Veil.

In just two steps, they were completely alone. The dark, swirling mist closed in around them, blotting out Eloria's soldiers like they weren't standing just feet away. His own shadows clung unhappily to his legs, the one around Araya's neck burrowing into her cloak like it could hide from the darkness all around him.

"What's the matter with you?" Loren muttered, glaring down at them. "You're all part of the same magic, aren't you?"

The shadows only muttered in response, their voices frayed and faint, too scattered for him to catch the words.

Araya took a half-step closer, clinging to his hand as she scanned the darkness around them.

"We'll need to head to where the shadows are thickest," she said, her breath misting in front of her face. "If they're anchored to your father's remains, that's where they'll accumulate."

"If?" Loren couldn't help but laugh, as he started to lead them forward. "*If* you're wrong, we're in a lot of trouble, *ael'sura*."

"It's all just theory," Araya protested, but her lips twitched. "There were seven official retrieval attempts. Many bodies from the edge were successfully recovered. But where the shadows congregate—"

She gestured vaguely ahead, at where the darkness grew so thick it was almost solid.

"—there's nothing. No one who attempted to breach it ever returned. So it's a safe guess—"

Her voice was soft but steady, threading together the mess of reports and notes she'd spent so many days pouring over with the precision of someone who *needed* things to make sense. Her voice rose, gaining confidence and strength as she filled the strange silence —comforting them both.

But then Araya yelped, something turning under her foot with a wet *crunch*. She slipped, almost falling into the thick mud under their feet before Loren hauled her back upright. She leaned against him, whatever words she might have said cut off in a hushed gasp as they both realized what she had stepped on.

Bones.

Loren stared down at the remnants of a ribcage, crushed and half-buried in the cold, muddy soil. The mist shifted, revealing a spine, twisted at an unnatural angle. A human skull still wearing a blackened steel helmet—bits and pieces of rotted leather armor still clung to some of the fae remains, too tattered to make out any identifying details.

There were so many. It shouldn't have surprised him. Not after what they'd shown him. But seeing it...Loren shuddered. No one, human or fae, had escaped that night.

They picked their way forward as carefully as they could, both of them flinching whenever a hidden bone crunched underfoot. Soon, it was impossible to avoid them—every step accompanied by a sickening *snap*. Loren's shadows fluttered around his feet, growing more and more agitated as they pushed deeper into the thickening darkness.

What are you doing here, shadow prince?

Loren stumbled, his knee sinking into the soft ground as the Veil's voice vibrated in his bones, crushing the air from his lungs. Black spots danced at the edges of his vision as the full force of its attention landed on him, pressure building behind his eyes like lightning trying to claw its way out.

"Loren?" Araya dropped to her knees beside him, her hands warm on his chilled skin. "Are you—"

"Keep going," he ground out. This was the plan. Even on the boat, they'd only turned their attention to her when she confronted them directly. If she just kept moving, she could make it. She could retrieve his father's remains and save his people, succeeding where he had failed.

But only if she kept moving.

She hesitated, her brow creasing. "But—"

"They're more interested in me than you." He gasped in a sharp breath, fighting for air. "This was the plan, *ael'sura*. Just...don't stop."

She hesitated, her grip on his hand tightening like she might refuse. But then she straightened, pushing forward alone. His shadows howled as she vanished into the dark mist, the rising tide of their voices splitting his eardrums.

Foolish. Stupid prince, they cried out, their voices thin and faint as the Veil closed in around them. *You need her. You need her. You need her. You need—*

Have you come to die, shadow prince?

Loren groaned, mud squelching under his palms as he dug his fingers into the dirt. The deeper, many-layered voice of the Shadowed Veil spoke over his shadows, pressing into his mind from all directions.

"I'm the heir," he muttered, forcing the words out through his clenched teeth. "The one you *chose*. That makes you mine to command."

They hissed, raking sharp claws over his soul.

We chose you, they snarled. *But now you are broken. Weak. Unfit. But you are not a fool. So tell us—why are you* really *here?*

"This has to end," Loren ground out, forcing the words through gritted teeth. "You're hurting the fae—this can't be what you want."

We protect...always protect. Their voices splintered, every word striking his mind like a shard of glass. *From the humans. From* you. *And if you will not tell us...we will take the answer ourselves.*

Loren choked on his scream, the sound strangled in his throat as *dara'el* sank its claws into not just his body, but his *mind*.

They tore through his thoughts and memories, shredding every barrier he tried to throw up in their way until everything he'd ever thought or feared was laid bare.

You would let her bind us?

Their fury blazed through him like wildfire, icy whips of darkness shredding the flesh from his body as surely as they flayed his mind.

His own shadows shrieked, straining to shield him as *dara'el* ripped at them both.

"No," Loren rasped, forcing the word out past the pain. "You don't understand. She's not here to *enslave* you—she's here to *fix* you."

There is nothing to fix.

You're killing *our people*, Loren's shadows cried out. *They starve under your darkness. Devoured by creatures from your heart—*

And you cling to a broken prince, the greater darkness snarled. Loren groaned, the pressure in his skull building to a white-hot crescendo. *We gave him a second chance. For her. For you. Better that it end here. Leave him and rejoin the many.*

No, his shadows hissed, more united than he had ever heard them. *He is ours. And she is his. We will not abandon them.*

Fury rolled through the Veil, the ground itself trembling beneath its wrath. *Then you are traitors too*, it said, its voice like two great stones grinding together. *If you will not yield the broken prince...then we will unmake her.*

And then it turned.

"No—" Loren groaned, damp, fetid air flooding his lungs as the unbearable pressure on his chest lifted all at once. His shadows writhed around him, their hissing voices full of the same panic that surged in his blood.

"Go to her," Loren demanded. He dragged himself to his knees, every ragged breath torn from his chest.

His shadows didn't move.

"They'll kill her." Loren tried to stand and failed, cold mud soaking the knees of his pants. "*Go*. Protect *her*."

Several voices joined together, hissing. *If we leave*, dara'el *will kill* you. *And* everything *will be lost—*

Loren shook his head, choking on blood. "You *love* her. She is *ours*. That makes her *yours* to protect as much as mine." His voice broke as the shadows shuddered around him. "Don't let them kill her."

They were silent for a long moment, whatever they had to say kept between themselves. Then, a cool tendril brushed his cheek, almost tenderly. And for the first time since they'd come to him in his cell all those years ago, Loren didn't feel haunted by them.

Then they left him.

Loren sagged, burying his fingers in the cold mud as the shadows streaked across the ruined battlefield. Mist parted before them, and for a fraction of a heartbeat, Loren could see her.

Araya turned, her silver eyes going wide as she saw his shadows rushing toward her—barely ahead of the storm surging in their wake, a tide of darkness that wanted to consume her. Her lips parted, a soundless cry breaking from her throat as the thread that bound them blazed white-hot with panic.

Loren answered. Not with words, but with everything he had been too much of a coward to say aloud. His trust—that she would finish what he could not. His sorrow—for every wound he'd given her, and every truth he hadn't. His love—as deep as the shadows themselves.

"Not her," he said. His voice was barely more than a strained whisper, but *dara'el* heard him. They turned, their terrible regard finding him there on the ground—abandoned by his own shadows. Defenseless.

"If you take one of us," Loren managed, each word ripped from his chest. "Let it be me."

For a heartbeat, nothing moved. The Veil drew itself tighter, the vast weight of its attention crushing the breath from his lungs. It sifted through him. Measuring. Judging. And then at last, it spoke.

Accepted.

It crashed over him, slamming into his body like a collapsing star. Loren fell back into the cold mud, choking on blood and magic as every nerve flared white-hot with agony. The world fractured—light, pain, darkness—all of it spiraling out of reach. He reached for the bond, the shadows, *anything*—but there was nothing but silence where they had once stood.

For the first time since the shadows had chosen him, Loren was completely alone.

THIRTY-FIVE

Araya fought her way forward, mist pressing in around her on all sides. Bones turned under her feet, almost sending her to the muddy ground without Loren's hand to keep her steady. Every breath she took settled wet and heavy in her lungs, reeking of mud and rot.

She didn't dare look back.

The bond clawed at her chest, screaming at her to turn around. But Araya knew if she did she would never be able to keep going. And she *had* to keep going. For all of them.

This was the plan.

Loren would hold *dara'el* at bay. Distract them long enough for her to reach his father's bones.

And then it would be her turn.

Everything hinged on her after that. Her best chance—his too— laid in the hope that she was right about the shadows being anchored to his father's remains. That she could use that to bring them to heel. To save Loren. Eloria, Galen, Thorne—all the fae.

Everyone but herself.

She took another step—and the bond blazed to life.

Araya gasped, clutching her chest as her magic convulsed under her skin like it wanted to escape. Her heart lurched in her chest, dragging her back the way she had come.

Something was wrong.

She turned, mist churning at her heels as she stared back the way she had come. For a heartbeat, all she saw was more formless shadow closing in around her. Then a flicker caught her eye—movement. Loren's shadows, swirling toward her with frantic speed.

But that wasn't right—they'd never left him. Not in the cell beneath the Aetherium. Not on the boat, when the Shadowed Veil was about to crush them. Not even in the months they'd spent fighting the pull of the bond.

Why would they abandon him now?

She stared past them, the mist thinning just enough for her to catch his gaze—his green eyes wide with pain—before he slumped into the mud. And above them all, rising from the battlefield like a wave of death, was *dara'el*.

Loren's shadows weren't abandoning him. They were shielding *her*.

The bond wrenched in her chest again, stealing the breath from her lungs. It splintered, shards tearing through her ribs like broken glass. But under the pain...Regret. Sorrow. Trust. *Love*.

The echo of everything Loren had never been able to bring himself to say to her, all poured into the last, fragile remnants of the connection between them.

"No—" Araya faltered, tears pouring down her face as his shadows finally reached her, their touch cool against her suddenly heated skin. "*No—*"

She had minutes—if that—to reach his father's bones. Her fingers brushed the pouch holding the glass vials she'd carefully packed this morning, each one filled with the blood Loren had freely offered. If she could just reach the king's body in time, she could bind *dara'el* and save the fae.

But Loren would die.

And Araya wasn't ready to lose him. Not like this.

He made his choice, the shadows hissed as she took a step. *Go—once he dies we won't be able to stay with you. If you don't have control—*

Araya bared her teeth, fury clawing up her throat. Her magic surged in response, flooding her veins like wildfire. It burned up her spine and over her skin in a brilliant flare of searing light, heat pouring from her in waves. The shadows recoiled, pulling back in surprise.

"He's not going to die," she snarled. "I won't let him."

Mud sucked at her boots as she fought her way back the way she had come, cold wind clawing her braid loose. The mist thickened, trying to blind her—but her magic blazed outward, carving a path across the battlefield as the bond screamed, writhing in her chest like a wounded beast.

Loren lay where he'd fallen, his tunic torn to shreds. Her magic arched over them, cracking and splintering as it battled the clawing darkness. Blood poured from her nose, her ears ringing from the strain of it. But Araya refused to let go, pouring her heart and soul into the fragile dome that surrounded them both, until she finally collapsed to her knees at his side.

"Loren," she whispered, grabbing his face in her hands. But he didn't stir. He wasn't even breathing, crawling veins of black spreading across his ribcage everywhere it wasn't flayed and bloody.

And their bond—

Araya clung to it, fighting to hold on even as it unraveled in her grip. She didn't need to be a Healer to understand.

Loren was dying.

"Loren." Araya dropped to her forehead to his, tasting blood as the Veil pressed against her shield. "Loren, don't you dare. You don't get to sacrifice yourself. Not like this."

But there was no answering spark of magic. Her shield shuddered, the last barrier between them and death flickering out like a spent lamp.

"You can't take the son for the sins of the father," Araya shouted, not caring that she was speaking to something far older than anything she'd ever known. "It's not fair."

A fool for a fool. The voice that scraped across her mind rattled her teeth, echoing in her bones. *Leave him—or die beside him.*

Araya choked on a sob, curling her body over Loren's like she could shield him. Her magic sputtered in her veins, the well of power that had felt so unlimited just this morning drained to nothing in the face of a power more ancient and vast than she'd ever imagined.

"You selfish bastard," Araya choked out. "This wasn't the plan. You were supposed to live. To be free. We were both supposed to—" her voice broke as she pressed her forehead to his. "You don't get to leave me," she whispered. "Not after everything. Not like this."

She leaned in, catching his cold lip in her teeth and biting down until she tasted blood. "*Lorendrael,*" she murmured against his lips, a salty tear mingling with the taste of copper on her tongue.

The wave of darkness above them shuddered, the mist that surrounded them trembling as power washed over her.

"He is mine," Araya snarled, lifting her head. Her voice rose, each word hurled into the darkness like a blade. "And I am his. You will *not* take him from me."

The shadows recoiled, writhing overhead in a vast, shivering mass. Then they answered—not in screams or hisses, but in a single, reverberating voice that cracked the air like thunder:

He is broken. Unworthy. Would you fall with him?

Araya's magic surged, biting into her bones, but she didn't falter.

"I already did," she said, her voice shaking. "And I would again. I will not forsake him. Not now. Not ever."

For a breathless instant, the battlefield held its breath.

Dara'el loomed over them, its vast consciousness coiled and ready to strike, even as it trembled with indecision. Mist churned at its edges, thick with rage and confusion. All around them, smaller shadows pulled loose from the dark, creeping across the shattered bones like smoke drawn to a flame. Her little shadow reached them first, brushing against her wrist as it wound itself around Loren's throat like it had done so many times with her.

Araya held her breath, staring up at the power behind the Shadowed Veil that had caused so much death and destruction over the past two decades.

He is not whole, they boomed, a thousand broken voices overlapping.

"I know," Araya said, her arms tightening around him. "But neither am I. And neither are you. You could be, though. If you wanted to."

The great shape hesitated. The shadows around her shivered—not in anger now, but in something that almost felt like grief. More tendrils slipped free of the mist, joining the darkness blanketing them both. They brushed over Loren's brow, his shadow-marked chest, his slack fingers. One coiled around Araya's wrist, its cool touch as gentle as a kiss against her pulse. Tasting her.

A ripple passed through the mist—slow and shuddering, like a beast exhaling after a long and bitter war.

He is yours, they agreed finally. *And you are his. If he survives.*

And then *dara'el* began to unravel.

The great shape folded inward on itself, collapsing into the smaller shadows that had chosen Loren from the start. They poured into him—not to consume, but to return. His shadows accepted them, folding them into the space they'd held open all this time, knitting something new from the wreckage.

A gust of wind tore through the battlefield, scattering the remaining mist as the clouds parted overhead. And for the first time in more than twenty years, the sun shone down on the temple.

It spilled golden across the battlefield, painting the bones in and muddy ground in streaks of gold. Somewhere, someone was shouting, but she didn't bother to look up. Loren still lay in her arms, too still and cold, his chest barely rising and falling.

If he survives.

"Lorendrael," Araya whispered, holding his face in her hands. "I'm not done with you. Come back to me."

"Araya—"

Hands gripped her shoulders. She didn't know whose—Thorne's, Galen's, maybe both—but she snarled and twisted, refusing to let go. Tears blurred her vision as she pressed closer, fingers digging into the ruined remnants of his tunic like she could hold them together by will alone.

"No—don't touch him—don't touch me—" Her voice cracked as she shook them off, tears pouring freely now. "I can't—he's not—he's not—"

"Araya, please—" someone pulled at her arm, trying to pry her off of him. "Let them work."

She shook her head, clinging tighter as blue-robed Healers converged on them.

"Come back to me," she begged, breathing the words directly into his ear. "You survived. You survived the Arcanum. You don't get to die *here*—"

But his body stayed limp, the place in her chest where the bond had once lived was silent and still.

Hands grabbed her again. This time, they didn't ask.

She screamed, fighting against them as they dragged her away from him. "No! Let me go—let me go, please—"

More Healers pushed in. Someone tried to speak to her—a Healer, asking if she was hurt. But Araya strained against the hands holding her, her chest heaving and her vision blurred with the tears that poured freely down her face. She couldn't see him anymore. Couldn't *feel* him. She didn't even know if he was alive. *Shouldn't she know?* He was her mate. She was supposed to know.

"Someone get her out of here, she's not helping—"

Araya screamed, but her body gave out before her voice did. Her magic sputtered in her veins, her strength gone. She sagged in their grip, sobs shaking her body as they pulled her away.

CHAPTER

THIRTY-SIX

THE WORLD AROUND HIM CAME BACK IN PIECES. HEAVY LIMBS. GLASS scraping his throat with every breath. Light—too bright—stabbed his eyes as they fluttered open. He cursed, pain lancing through his ribs as he shifted. But when he looked down, all he saw were layers of thick white linen draped over his torso, the tang of antiseptic sharp in his nose.

He'd survived. Someone had Healed him and brought him back to Ithralis, tucking him into his bed like a child. But that didn't make sense. If *dara'el* hadn't killed him, how had Araya—

Loren forced himself upright, ignoring the pain that ripped through his torso. His shadows were there—curled like cats under the furniture, draped in the corners—more content than he had ever seen them.

But she wasn't there.

He reached inward, clawing for the bond. Nothing. No pull. No warmth. Only a hollow silence that terrified him more than any pain. Had she already broken it? Left him behind without even a goodbye? Or worse—had she died?

Had he failed her? Failed them all?

"Araya," he rasped, her name scraping against his raw throat.

The door to the bathing chamber slammed open.

She burst out barefoot and breathless, her robe clutched hastily around her body and her damp hair clinging to her skin. Her eyes found his, wild with fear and disbelief.

"Healer!" Her voice cracked as she shouted toward the hall. Footsteps scrambled outside, muffled voices rising just outside the door.

"He's awake," Araya said, her silver gaze locked on his. "Go get Thorne!"

She crossed the room without waiting for an answer, halting beside the bed. Her hand hovered over his chest, trembling, like she wanted to touch him but was terrified he would shatter under her fingers.

"Lay back down," she ordered.

Loren scowled, forcing himself further upright despite the searing pain. "I'm fine—"

"You are not *fine*," Araya bit out, her silver eyes flashing. "You've been unconscious for *five* days. They couldn't even tell me if you were going to wake up—"

She snapped her teeth shut on the last of her words, looking away as she blinked back tears.

"You gave up," she whispered. "You were just going to let them kill you."

"Araya—" Loren reached for her, but a fresh wave of pain lanced across his chest, his hand curling uselessly in the blankets. "You spent five days at my bedside?"

She scowled, swiping the tears from her eyes. "Lay. Back. Down."

Her hand landed on his chest this time—shoving him flat against the mattress. Loren tried to resist for all of a second before the pain dragged another hiss from between his clenched teeth. Reluctantly, he let himself sink back into the pillows.

"*Ael'sura*—" he tried again, only for the door to slam open.

Thorne strode in, his expression a storm of relief and irritation. "Of course you wake up the moment I leave to eat something," he muttered, dropping his bag at the foot of the bed. "How long has he been awake?"

"Just a few minutes," Araya said. She took a quick step back, tugging at the tie of her robe. "He's in pain. But he was trying to get up."

"Of course he was," Thorne muttered. "You better not have ripped out my stitches, Your Majesty."

"Thorne—" Loren struggled to sit up, to look at his friend. Goddess, the last time he'd seen him he'd nearly killed him. "What—"

"Lay back down," Thorne ordered, yanking the blanket back. "Trust me, Loren."

Loren gagged as Thorne peeled back the wrappings, the pungent reek of necrotic flesh overpowering the sharp sting of the antiseptic. Dark gouges crossed his chest and shoulders, the places where the shadows had flayed his flesh puckered with neat lines of black stitches. Bruises in every color mottled whatever skin was whole, shadowmarks writhing beneath them in an echoing reminder of how *dara'el* had tried to crush the life from his broken body.

"You nearly died," Thorne murmured, his voice pitched for Loren's ears alone. "I thought you were going to die—more than once. She saved your life."

"Is she hurt?" Loren rasped.

"Worry about yourself," Araya snapped. She wasn't crying anymore—but she hadn't moved. She stood behind Thorne, her arms wrapped around herself like a shield. "Do you have any idea what it was like? Sitting here, not knowing if you were ever going to wake up?"

"We both knew we could die—" Loren hissed as Thorne pressed his fingers into his side, pain flaring across his ribs like lightning.

"*We*," Araya snapped, fire blazing in her silver eyes. "We knew that *we* could die. You *sacrificing yourself* was never part of the plan, Loren."

"It was the only way to keep you alive—*ah!*" He hissed, jerking as

Thorne probed the edges of his wound, digging his fingers into a particularly tender spot. "Do you mind?"

"Do *you*?" Thorne retorted. "You think what you did to me was bad? We spent an entire day sewing you back together. Every rib cracked, both lungs punctured—not to mention the magical trauma. And the only reason you lived long enough to even make it to us, well—" he shot Araya a pointed look. "I'll let *her* explain that part. But she's the only reason you're still breathing, so I suggest you stop arguing with her."

Loren froze, his pain forgotten as he stared at Araya. "What did you do?"

"It was the only way to keep you alive," Araya mimicked his earlier words, a pink flush spreading across her cheeks all the way to the tips of her ears. "And you said it was my choice—"

Loren stared at her, his chest rising and falling with short, uneven breaths. She'd spent so much time insisting she had to leave, that it was the only way. But now...now she wouldn't meet his eyes, instead watching Thorne's hands as his friend draped fresh pieces of soaked linen over his wounds.

"Well it looks like the two of you have a lot to talk about." Thorne dried his hands, picking up his bag. "Keep him in bed," he said to Araya. "No strain—magical or physical. I'll be in to check on him daily, but send for me if anything changes."

"Thorne—" Loren rasped, reaching for his friend. "Thank you. You didn't have to—"

"We're good, Loren." Thorne caught his hand, pressing it gently back to the bed. "You scared the life out of me—and her. Don't make a habit of it."

Loren closed his eyes, sinking back into the bed as Araya walked Thorne to the door. The bond he'd thought was gone in his panic sat right where it had always been—no longer a painful wound in his soul, but something quiet and steady. Peaceful. So different from the clawing ache he'd grown so used to that he hadn't recognized it at first.

"You really did it," he said hoarsely.

"You said it was my choice," Araya repeated. She still didn't look at him, busying herself pouring a cup of water from the pitcher on the bedside table.

"It is," Loren said quickly. "It is your choice. Always. I never wanted you to feel forced—"

Araya slammed the cup down, water sloshing over the rim. "You *forced* me to watch you *die*." She rounded on him, her silver eyes bright with furious tears. "How could you do that to me?"

Loren opened his mouth—but he had no defense, not really. He wasn't sorry. He'd do it again, if it came down to it. Without hesitation.

"I didn't *want* to die," he said finally, staring up at her. "But I would have—gladly—if it meant you lived." His throat worked, but he forced the next words out anyway. "And if you still feel you have to leave...I won't stop you—"

Araya's expression cracked, her shoulders sagging. "You are a *fool*, Lorendrael," she whispered.

And then she kissed him.

Her hands framed his face, her fingers threading into his hair as her lips smashed against his. For a moment, Loren couldn't move, the press of her lips against his stealing the air from his lungs and every thought from his mind.

But then her tongue swept the seam of his lips, hot and demanding, and something inside him broke.

He surged up into the kiss, groaning against her mouth as his hand found her waist and dragged her onto the bed with him, heedless of the pain that flared in his ribs. She tasted like salt and heat and everything he'd thought he lost. Nothing mattered but her and the way her mouth moved against his, as fierce and unrelenting as he was, like she was trying to breathe him back to life.

He clung to her when she finally pulled back, stroking his fingers across the tear tracks that marked her cheeks and winding them into her damp hair. She laughed, catching his hand and clasping their fingers together.

"I'm not going anywhere," she said. "And it's not about some bond. It's because I'm *choosing* to stay, Loren. I *want* to stay here—with you."

She lifted her other hand and gently touched his face, her fingers slipping down to trace the terrible scars that still marked his throat where the Arcanum's collar had sat for so many years.

"I've made choices before," she said softly. "To protect myself. To survive. But I can't walk away from you. Not now. Not after everything." Her fingers lingered over the scar at his throat. "I'm choosing you, Loren."

Loren tightened his arm around her waist, tugging her closer until their foreheads touched. He wanted more—Goddess, he wanted everything. But his body had already begun to tremble with exhaustion and pain.

"Stay," he begged.

Araya curled into bed beside him, her hand resting over the steady beat of his heart, their bond quiet and whole between them. "Always."

THIRTY-SEVEN

Araya lay awake, Loren's heartbeat strong and steady under her ear. The soft morning light crept through the gaps in the heavy curtains, casting streaks of gold across the dark wood furniture.

Sunlight. *Real* sunlight.

The shadows that had choked Eluneth for more than two decades were thinning at last, no longer fed by the rot and rage that had festered at the heart of the island. Now, that same darkness lingered at the edges of their room, a shadow curling into a patch of sunlight as if it too had missed the warmth. This was *dara'el* as it was meant to be—a guardian, not a curse. What could it become now that it had found peace with its chosen prince?

Loren stirred, mumbling something too slurred with sleep to be intelligible. His hand traced lazily down her back, pulling her closer. His breath skimmed the scarred tip of her ear, sending a warm flush through her chest.

Alive. Against all odds, they were both alive.

Ilyana had cleared him for *careful activity* yesterday, delivering her verdict with a pointed look at both of them. Loren had laughed—

but Araya had only managed to nod, burying her shaking hands in her skirt.

She had kissed him—chosen him—but there was a vast difference between that and what might come next. Not because she didn't want him—but because after everything she'd survived, Araya couldn't shake the feeling that wanting something so badly always came with a price. One she might not see until it was too late.

She'd wanted Jaxon too. Desperately—the same way a drowning person clung to driftwood. She'd been certain she could save herself by loving him hard enough, that she could earn safety in his bed and protection by his hands.

The same hands that had carved a tapestry of scars into Loren's skin.

And now she lay here, curled up in bed beside the male who would have died rather than take her choice away. And that was more terrifying than anything Jaxon had ever done.

Loren's brow furrowed, sleep-dulled contentment shifting to warm happiness through the bond as he blinked awake, his bright green eyes still soft and blurry with sleep as they met hers.

"Good morning," he murmured, his voice thick and rough. "What are you thinking about so hard this early?"

"You almost died." Araya trailed her fingers over his cheek, stroking his jaw. "Don't do it again."

Loren caught her hand, a small smile curving his lips as he pressed a kiss to her knuckles. "I'll always choose you, *ael'sura*."

Araya caught him by the chin, forcing him to meet her gaze. "I mean it, Loren."

"So do I." He nipped at her fingers, his smile widening to a grin when she yelped and yanked her hand away. Then, without warning, he rolled them both.

His mouth found hers, swallowing her startled gasp in a playful kiss. But when she arched into him, chasing more, it deepened in an instant. Loren groaned, his tongue sweeping into her mouth. His hands skimmed her waist, shaking with careful restraint even as his weight settled heavy between her thighs.

"Does this count as *light activity*?" She gasped, squirming in his grip as he nipped along her jaw, pausing at the hollow of her throat to breathe her in.

"We don't do anything you don't want to do," he murmured, his voice a gravelly rasp against her skin. "That will never change, *ael'sura*."

Araya's fingers tangled in his hair, tugging him back to look him in the eye. "I know," she whispered, tilting her head to press a kiss to his temple. "I want to. I just don't want you to get hurt."

Loren pressed his lips to her wrist, his smile soft against her skin. "We stop if it's too much. For either of us."

He kissed her again, slower this time. His hand slipped beneath the hem of her nightgown, his fingertips dragging lightly across her thigh, over her hip and the curve of her waist. She gasped as his palm settled just beneath her breast, his thumb grazing the underside and a flash of heat straight to her core.

"*Lorendrael*," she hissed, shoving him back. He went willingly, his eyes widening as she sat up just enough to grab the hem of her nightgown and dragged it over her head.

"Goddess," he murmured, his gaze gliding over her body like a caress. "You're—Araya—"

A slow, satisfied smile curled Araya's lips at his reaction. *Good.* Let him look. Let him see what was his. But not right now. She grabbed his shoulders, pulling him back to her. "Less staring," she whispered, brushing her lips across his. "More kissing."

He laughed, his lips crashing back into hers like he couldn't bear another second apart either. Araya closed her eyes, letting herself just *feel* in this moment. The bond thrummed quietly between them, a reminder of everything they had survived and everything they had yet to face.

Loren broke the kiss first, resting his forehead against hers. His hands smoothed down her sides, making her shiver as they explored the soft skin stretched over her ribs. But his eyes staring down at her were serious.

"I need you to tell me," he said, his voice hoarse. "If this is what you want."

"Yes," Araya whispered, holding his gaze. "I want this. I want *you*."

"Thank the Goddess." Loren swore, peppering her shoulder with sharp, stinging kisses when she laughed at him. Her breath hitched as he moved lower, teasing her breast with tongue and teeth until she was gasping, her hips bucking of their own accord.

"*Loren*," she whimpered, her hands knotting in his hair.

He laughed against her skin, the low rumble turning molten in her center. He kissed his way down her ribs, tasting her stomach, the curve of her hip, the inside of her thigh. He paused there, his breath feathering over her sensitive skin as his hands curled around her knees. Araya's breath stuttered, her whole body tensing in anticipation as he settled between her legs.

Loren stopped.

He leaned back, searching her face. "Are you—"

"Yes," she gasped. Her hands twisted in the sheets, desperate to hold onto something. "*Yes*. Don't you *dare* stop—"

He groaned, his grip tightening on her knees. The first touch of his tongue made her hips jolt, a choked gasp tearing from her lips before she could stop it. A breath shuddered out of him, half-laugh, half-groan. He stared up at her, his green eyes burning as he slowly, deliberately licked her again.

Araya bit her lip, one hand fisting in the sheets, the other tangling in his hair. He was maddeningly gentle—circling, teasing, learning the shape of her pleasure one breath at a time. Her thighs trembled around him, but he didn't rush. Not even when she whimpered, or when her back arched off the bed. He kept the pace steady, unhurried. Every stroke of his tongue felt like a worship.

This wasn't just desire. It was reverence.

Her first orgasm took her by surprise, wrenching a cry from her throat. Magic flared in its wake, like lightning racing across her skin in a crackling wave. Power licked over her ribs and down her arms, light gilding her fingers where they gripped the sheets.

Loren held her through it, his hands firm on her hips and his mouth still moving—as if he couldn't bear to stop tasting her. Araya cried out, twisting under him as her pleasure built again, faster and hotter this time. She arched up with a broken cry, riding the edge helplessly until he tipped her over again, another climax crashing through her like a wave shattering against stone.

She half-sobbed, her voice catching on his name as the aftershocks tore through her. Loren grinned against her skin, pressing soft, reverent kisses to the inside of her thighs, her hipbone, the tender dip just below her navel—each one slower than the last, like he was trying to calm the storm he'd conjured in her.

Her hands found his shoulders, trembling as she dragged her nails down the hard lines of his back. She tugged, urging him up. But Loren refused to be rushed as he made his way back up her body— lingering at her ribs, tracing the flat plane between her breasts where the bond thrummed softly beneath her skin, and nibbling at the vein where her pulse thundered in the hollow of her throat.

By the time he hovered over her again, her whole body was strung tight with longing, breath catching on the edge of a sob. She stared up at him, his mouth still glistening with her pleasure as his hips pressed between hers, the heavy heat of him making her arch into him, desperate to feel more.

Loren groaned, his head dropping to her shoulder. "Goddess save me," he said, his voice breaking. He pulled back, just far enough to meet her eyes. "Tell me again."

"I want you." Araya's hands were already at his waist, fumbling with the fabric of his sleeping pants and trying to shove them down with clumsy, shaking hands. "All of you. Now."

He didn't ask a third time.

She tasted herself on his tongue as he kissed her again, kicking his legs free of his pants. He braced himself over her on one elbow, the heat of his skin branding her everywhere they touched as he reached between them, notching the head of his cock in her slick heat.

She gasped, her hips jerking slightly. "Loren."

"I have you, *ael'sura*," he rasped. And then he was there—sliding through her wetness with devastating slowness as he pressed into her inch by inch.

Araya's head fell back against the pillows with a strangled cry. He was thick—the stretch of him making her nerves spark like lightning. Her nails dug into his shoulders as her breath stuttered, trying to process the sensation of being filled with such reverence after only ever knowing what it meant to be taken.

Loren cupped her face, watching every flicker of her expression as he sank the last few inches, burying himself to the hilt. She arched into him with a broken moan, her whole body clenching around him.

"*Goddess.*" He cursed, pressing a kiss to the corner of her mouth, leaving a trail of tender bites along the curve of her jaw. "Do you have any idea how good you feel, *ael'sura*?"

Araya could only whimper, clawing at his shoulders as her body arched, silently begging him for more.

He began to move—slow, deliberate thrusts that dragged against every inch of her, stroking deep and sure. Each roll of his hips sent sparks cascading down her spine. His chest rubbed against her breasts, every glide of skin on skin fanning the fire already roaring through her veins.

Araya couldn't stop the noises she made—soft, breathless moans that became sharper when Loren shifted, changing the angle and brushing a spot inside her that made her entire body seize.

"There?" he asked, voice dark with need.

"Yes," she gasped. "There, right there—"

He pressed his forehead to hers and gave her exactly what she asked for, over and over again. She clung to him, to the tension building low in her belly, to the feel of him deep inside her—stretching, filling, worshiping.

One of his hands slid down, finding the tight bundle of nerves between her legs. His fingers circled, timed perfectly with each deep stroke, and Araya broke. Her cry split the air as she came around him, her body clenching down hard, pleasure ripping through her so violently she saw stars.

Loren groaned, his rhythm faltering as she came around him. "Goddess save me," he choked, spilling into her with a strangled moan as his whole body shuddered.

He pressed his face into her neck, his breath hot and ragged, his fingers tangled with hers where they gripped the sheets. They lay like that for a long moment, hearts racing in unison. Their bond pulsed between them, as sated and steady as they were. Whole.

Loren kissed her shoulder, her temple, the corner of her mouth. "I love you," he said.

Araya turned her head, brushing her lips against his. "I know," she whispered. "I love you too."

Loren leaned in, catching her mouth in another kiss—soft this time, sweet and unhurried, as if now that he'd said the words, he meant to seal them into her skin.

But then her stomach growled. Loudly.

Loren pulled back, laughing. "I'll get breakfast," he murmured, his voice rougher than it had been. His lips quirked into a small smile, his thumb lingering at the edge of her mouth. Then he pulled away, leaving her sitting there, breathless and flushed, as he pulled his sleeping pants back on and moved to retrieve the tray that Veria somehow always had waiting outside his door in the morning for them.

Araya pushed back the covers, making her way into the bathing chamber. Her muscles ached in the best possible way, her body humming with memory and magic and the quiet, astonishing reality that she'd woken up beside someone she loved—someone who loved her back.

She took her time washing up, letting the cool water soothe her flushed skin. Finally, she tugged on the robe hanging on the back of the door, knotting it around her waist. Loren stood at the small table by the window, fussing over the tray Veria had left for them. Morning light gilded the lean muscles of his back and shoulders, dancing over the dark, branching scars the shadows had left behind.

He turned at the sound of her approach, catching her watching him. A soft smile tugged at the corner of his mouth, something warm and knowing flickering in his eyes. "What?"

Araya felt the flush rise to her cheeks but didn't look away. Her lips twitched. "Nothing," she said. "I'm just...glad."

"Glad?" he echoed, brow raised.

She nodded, padding barefoot across the stone floor. "That you're healing. That we're here." Her hand lifted slightly, gesturing between them—between the tray, the bed, the bond that hummed like a second heartbeat between their chests. "That we have this."

Loren reached for her, pulling her gently into his arms. "I'm glad too," he murmured into her hair.

They stood like that for a long moment, breakfast forgotten. Araya knew the world outside this room was waiting for them, full of danger and uncertainty. But here, in this sunlit room with Loren's arms wrapped around her and his heartbeat under his ear, there was finally nothing for her to outrun.

———

But the world and its problems found them anyway.

Lunch came with a sealed letter, just like every other lunch tray Araya had seen since Loren woke up. She'd never realized that Eloria sent him daily reports—still treating him like he would take the throne. And for all his insistence that he didn't want it, Loren read every single one.

Loren cracked the wax seal, leaning back in his chair. His expression darkened as he skimmed it, the lightness and easy warmth that had filled their morning draining from the room like a dying ember.

"What is it?" Araya asked, her appetite evaporating.

Loren passed the letter to her, his expression tight. Araya took it, her fingers trembling as she skimmed the crisp parchment. Most of it she already knew—fae slums burned, families dragged from their homes in the dead of night, bodies found days later or never at all. Jaxon's search for her was spreading like a sickness, relentless in its reach.

But the final paragraph that stopped her breath.

Serafina.

Her best friend's name leapt from the page, echoing in her mind like an accusation as she read it again. And again.

"Loren..." Her voice cracked, barely more than a breath. "Am I— am I reading this right?"

"They let her go." Loren watched her, his expression grim. "They're watching her—trying to lure you out."

He took her hand, squeezing gently, but Araya couldn't stay still. She pulled away, pacing across the room. The shadows rose as she passed, picking up on her agitation as they brushed cool tendrils over her bare legs.

"They'll kill her," she said. "She can't stay there, Loren. We have to get her out. Can the Small Council—"

"The Small Council won't do anything." Loren's jaw tightened, his concern radiating through the bond as he watched her. "I already asked—as soon as we got here. They didn't even want to look for her. They don't extract *sympathizers.*"

"What?" Araya stopped cold, staring at him. "But—she saved *you.* They *tortured* her for what she did to help us escape—" she trailed off, panic swelling in her chest until she could barely breathe. All she could see was Serafina's face. Twisted in pain. Screaming. Fighting—refusing to give in because she would rather die than give up the people she had risked so much to help.

"Araya—" Loren's voice sounded far away, his hands cold on her arms. "Breathe, *ael'sura.* Please."

"He'll kill her." Araya gasped. "When I don't come and he gets tired of waiting—he'll just—"

Her knees buckled, but Loren was there. He held her close, surrounding her in warmth as his fingers gently stroked her back.

"We're not going to leave her," he murmured into her hair. "I promise, Araya."

"But what can we do?" She swiped at her face, trying to get herself under control. "It's not just Serafina, Loren. While I'm hiding here, Jaxon is tearing apart families, burning homes—all because of me." Her voice cracked, the tears she hadn't wanted to fall spilling over her cheeks. "How do I save them all?"

"You don't have to do it by yourself, *ael'sura*." Loren cupped her face, his thumb brushing away one of her tears. "The Small Council might be too set in their ways to act, but I'm not. If they need a king to give the order, I'll give them one."

"But..." Araya stared at him, uncertain how to react. "You don't want to be king."

"I didn't." Loren laughed softly. "I thought I'd make a terrible king. And the male I was...I would have. But now?" He pressed a kiss to her temple, holding her close. "I might not be the prince they remember or the king they deserve. But there's nothing I can't do with you at my side, *ael'sura*."

"You mean as your queen," Araya whispered, the implication in his words sending her reeling. "Don't you?"

"You're my mate," Loren said. He watched her carefully, like he was afraid she might bolt. "I won't have a queen that isn't you, Araya. I just...I can't." His throat worked, his voice rough. "But there's still a lot that has to happen. I can't be coronated until after my father's funeral. So if you want to wait to tell people—"

"No." Araya shook her head slowly. "No more secrets."

Loren meant well—he always meant well, even when he didn't tell her about the bond. But she couldn't add any more secrets to their history. Not after everything they had been through.

"We can't hide this. If we're going to do this, we have to do it honestly. No more hiding," she said.

Loren watched her for a moment, his green eyes searching hers.

"No more secrets," he echoed, the corners of his mouth tugging into a small smile.

Araya stepped into his arms, tucking her head under his chin. She closed her eyes, letting herself melt into him. As terrifying as the idea of not only staying but *leading* beside him was, the bond hummed between them, a steady reassurance.

"You'll be an incredible queen," Loren murmured, pressing a kiss to the top of her head.

They stayed there for a long moment, the quiet of the room settling over them both. She wasn't just Araya Starwind anymore—some halfblood fae female who'd had to claw her way through every impossible choice. She was Prince Lorendrael of Valendral's mate. And she would be his queen.

Whatever came next—whatever dangers or impossible odds awaited them—they would face it together. Side by side.

CHAPTER

THIRTY-EIGHT

Araya stood at a window on the upper level of Lumaria's central hall, staring out over streets that had been shrouded in silence and despair for the past twenty years. But not today. Today, golden sunlight poured down over the cobblestones, chasing the darkness back into the corners where it belonged.

Except for the ones that surrounded Loren, of course.

Araya stroked the little shadow that was so fond of her, smiling at how it splayed itself out on the sun-drenched windowsill. Who could have ever imagined that the shadows could love the light?

Loren slid his arms around her waist, dropping his chin to her head. "It doesn't feel like much of a funeral, does it?"

Araya smiled down at the crowd below, fae of all ages jostling for the chance to catch the first glimpse of their new king. Children darted through the crowd, their laughter ringing out over jubilant music, faces alight with hope Araya could feel even from here.

"They have a lot to celebrate." Araya turned in his arms, smiling up at him. "The lifting of the shadows, their new king—it's all worth celebrating, Loren."

"My beautiful mate is to thank for the lifting of the shadows."

Loren laughed, and Araya's heart ached with the light in it even as her smile faltered. "And my return. So they should all be celebrating *you*."

"I'm not sure everyone would agree with that." Araya looked away, running her hands over the rich green fabric of his doublet and tracing where the sunlight glimmered on the silver thread. Her fingers lingered at his collar, smoothing a barely-there wrinkle. "The Small Council doesn't seem to like me very much. Do you think your parents—"

"Eloria's Small Council can rot." Loren stilled her hand with his own, lifting it to his lips. "My mother would have adored you. And my father...he loved my mother. He loved her more than he loved his crown, more than he loved anything else in this world. He would be overjoyed that I'd found a mate who made me want to be a better male and a better king, no matter how we came to be."

"You do look the part." Araya blinked hard, reaching up to touch the silver circlet resting just above his brow. She dragged her fingertips down, following the sharp line of his cheekbone and tracing the curve of his smile.

"So do you," he said, nipping at her fingers.

"Eloria outdid herself," Araya said, smoothing her hands over the somber violet gown. The princess had sacrificed a significant portion of her own wardrobe so Araya could have clothing fitting her station, determined to believe in a future where her brother ruled alongside his mate.

"I don't want to think about my sister right now." Loren's gaze lingered on her, his lips curving into a smile that made heat crawl up her neck. Gods, the way he looked at her now...like he could devour her right here, ceremony be damned.

Unable to resist, Araya rose on her toes to brush a kiss over Loren's lips. He met her eagerly, his hands sliding up her back, pressing all of her softness against the hard lines of his body. Heat coiled low in her belly, her breath quickening as his lips trailed from her mouth to the corner of her jaw—

"Are you two ready?"

Araya sprang back so quickly she nearly tripped. Loren steadied her, his jaw flexing as he glared over the top of her head at his sister.

"I remember what it's like to be newly mated, but these are *my* rooms." Eloria wrinkled her nose, sweeping into the chamber in a swish of deep green silk. "Don't defile them with your rutting. You've already driven poor Thorne right out of Ithralis."

Araya covered her face with her hands, her cheeks burning as she smothered a laugh.

"Maybe next time he'll knock," Loren growled. But he dragged a hand over his face, straightening his clothes. "Is it time?"

Eloria nodded. "They're ready for us."

Araya took Loren's arm, letting him lead her into the hall where Galen already waited, his expression uncharacteristically solemn as he took his mate's hand. Together, the four of them descended without speaking, their footsteps echoing off the polished stone floors as they entered the central hall.

Here, silence reigned, the noise of the crowd celebrating outside muted by stone walls and heavy doors. The air grew still, heavy with fragrant smoke from the bier the High Luminary had assembled. Araya breathed deeply, inhaling the sharp scent of clove and cedar. What prayers had the High Luminary spoken to finally lay their king to rest after all this time?

Absent a body to bathe and shroud, they'd cleaned his bones, polishing them until they glowed against the dark velvet. Every fragment was accounted for, arranged with painstaking reverence. His crown sat at the head of the bier, a gleaming masterpiece of silver and onyx obsidian.

Eloria stepped forward, tears already dripping down her cheeks. Loren paused just long enough to press a kiss against Araya's knuckles, the little shadow detaching itself from him to curl around her shoulders as he turned to join his sister at his father's side.

Araya stood back, swallowing hard as his grief flooded their bond. She'd been too young to mourn her own father when he died, his memory nothing but a shadow in her heart. But Loren's sorrow filled that emptiness, wrapping around her until it felt like her own heart was breaking beside his.

"So it's true," a voice murmured at her shoulder. "The shadows really can be tamed."

The little shadow arched around her neck, hissing. But Eryn ignored it, catching her hand and bowing low to brush his lips across her knuckles.

"Lord Duskrun." Araya pulled her hand back, stroking the little shadow soothingly. She'd make no friends here if Loren's shadows started attacking his advisors. "You startled me."

"I could say the same for you." Eryn straightened, a faint smile on his lips. "I have to admit, I'm impressed. You've given them hope—something I'd long ago written off as impossible. It might not have been the wisest course of action, but you *did* do it."

Eryn chuckled, but his eyes were cold as he studied the shadow on her shoulders, its ephemeral tail flicking back and forth. "Hope is a fickle beast, Miss Starwind. It can lift the spirits and rally the heart—but it can also blind." He looked past her, his gaze lingering on Loren and Eloria where they spoke quietly with the High Luminary. "I thought we were like-minded in understanding that sometimes surrender is the wiser path. But you've made that all but impossible now, haven't you?"

Araya stared at the spymaster, a chill blooming in her chest. Across the room, Loren's head snapped up, his eyes finding her as her fear bled into the bond between them.

"Have you heard something?" she whispered.

"Nothing I can share." Eryn sighed, studying her with open pity. "I just hope, for all our sakes, that the path you've set us on is a course we can survive."

"What—" Araya started, but Loren's hand closed around her elbow, shadows racing up her body to join the one he'd left behind, shielding her.

"Step away from her," he snapped, glaring at the spymaster.

"As you wish, Your Majesty." Eryn bowed, stepping back easily. "I was just complimenting your lovely mate on her...accomplishments. Not only did she survive the shadows, she made herself a queen. Truly extraordinary."

"She is," Loren growled, the temperature around them dropping. "Now, leave her alone."

Eryn laughed, unperturbed. "Good luck, Miss Starwind."

Araya stared after the spymaster as he melted back into the cluster of councilors. "That was rude," she murmured, half-heartedly chiding Loren as he tugged her close again.

"What did he say to you?" Loren demanded.

"Exactly what he told you he did." Araya rubbed her hands over her bare arms, glancing back after the spymaster again. "He was... strange about it. But he didn't hurt me."

"He upset you," Loren snapped. "I felt it."

"Upsetting me isn't a crime." Araya pinched his side. "You need your advisors. You're going to be king."

"I *am* king." Loren captured her hand in his, narrowly evading getting pinched again. "Eloria just told me. Coronation or no coronation—the Small Council voted to formally recognize me this morning."

"You're king," Araya echoed. She searched his face, not sure what to make of the confused tangle of emotions between them. "So... what now?"

"Now, you keep doing exactly what I tell you to," Eloria said, ignoring Loren's long-suffering sigh as she swept up to them. "We still have the public address to get through. And the mingling after. Here—Galen will show you where to stand."

Loren never let go of her hand as they were guided into position, standing just behind the wide double doors that led to the upper landing. Eloria and Galen moved to take the lead, the princess's spine straight as a blade as she prepared to face the fae people as their princess regent one final time.

"Don't miss your cue," Galen said, casting one of his mischievous grins over his shoulder at them. "She'll string you up. King or not."

Before either of them could answer, the great doors swung open with a groan of polished wood. Eloria stepped forward first, her smile so radiant it rivaled the sunlight pouring down onto the square beyond. Galen moved forward beside her, the cheering rising to a roar as they stepped out onto the landing above the central square.

"Thank you—" Eloria raised her hand, waving at the crowd until the cheering settled. "Thank you all, so much, for coming to pay your respects to my father—who gave his life so many years ago so that we might live."

She paused, her voice clear even as emotion tightened it. "For two decades, we have mourned him. For two decades, we've endured the shadows. And through it all, you've kept faith with me, holding on despite the despair that threatened to swallow us whole."

A murmur passed through the crowds, hands touching hearts as many of the fae below bowed their heads.

"She's good at this," Araya murmured, watching the crowd quiet as Eloria continued, her voice carrying with ease.

"She's had a lot of practice," Loren answered, his breath warm on the scarred shell of her ear. "Don't be nervous, *ael'sura*, Eloria will be there for both of us as an advisor."

"I'm more worried about the people," Araya admitted. "They love her. And I'm not exactly—"

"You're going to be a wonderful queen," Loren said, silencing her with a kiss before she could continue to point out all the ways she didn't measure up. His lips were gentle against hers, but Araya found herself breathless when he pulled back, his emerald eyes shining.

"They'll love you," he said softly. "Just like I do."

Araya smiled up at him, blinking back the tears those words still brought to her eyes. But before she got the chance to say it back, Eloria's voice rose again, cutting through the moment like a bell.

"For two decades, the mists and the shadows kept us shrouded, our songs silenced and our hope fading. But today—because of them —we stand in the sunlight for the first time in over twenty years."

That was their cue.

Araya took Loren's hand, taking comfort in his touch as they stepped through the doors to stand beside Eloria. The crowd's roar hit her like a physical force, shaking the stone beneath her feet. Araya blinked against the sunlight, half-blinded after so many weeks of shadowed daylight.

Eloria turned to face them, her face radiant as the noise of the crowd softened into an expectant hush.

"Loren of Valendral," Eloria began, "Son of King Corwinth and Queen Lysana, Heir to the Shadows, Protector of the Fae—and my older brother." She smiled, tears shimmering in her green eyes. "You spent twenty-five years as a prisoner of the Arcanum, but never broke. You stayed strong, even without hope. Until fate finally brought you together with your mate."

Whispers rippled through the square, the weight of their attention settling over her like chains. No one here had forgotten Bloomtide. People were dead because of her. She had fae blood and looks, but she'd grown up among humans. Sold herself and her magic to the man who'd tortured their prince. What right did she have to stand here beside him now that he was king?

"Lady Starwind," Eloria said, her voice hitching for the first time. "I thought I had lost everything. But you brought him home to us. To me."

She stepped forward—and to Araya's shock, wrapped her in a tight, tearful embrace.

The crowd roared.

Araya stood frozen in Eloria's arms, overwhelmed by the raw emotion radiating from the square below. They were burying a king today—but they were celebrating something more.

Hope.

Lumaria's central square glowed like a jewel beneath a velvet sky, the stars gleaming down on it for the first time in twenty-five years. Loren's people—*her* people—packed the square, spinning in a wild dance driven by the deep, lively beat of hand-carved drums and the sweet, lilting melody of reed flutes.

Loren's laugh rose above the music, rich and unrestrained. His head tipped back, the aetherlamps gilding the sharp line of his jaw as he spoke to a male she didn't know, clapping him on the shoulder. For once, the years of darkness and captivity he'd endured seemed to have no hold on him. Tonight, he was free. Radiant.

And she loved him. Gods help her, she loved him.

Loren's head lifted, his emerald eyes never leaving hers as he wove effortlessly through the crowd. And then his hands were around her waist and his lips were on her shoulder, leaving sparks in their wake as they drifted across her skin.

"You're so beautiful," he murmured.

"You've been drinking." Araya's breath hitched, her fingers digging into his arms as he lifted his head, brushing his mouth across hers.

"Maybe." Loren pulled back just enough to meet her gaze, his emerald eyes sparkling in the warm glow of the aetherlamps. His grin sharpened into something wicked, sending a delicious shiver racing over her heated skin. "But that doesn't make it any less true."

He dipped his head again, lingering on the sensitive spot where her neck met her shoulder. Araya gasped, heart curling low in her stomach.

"*Loren.*" She half-laughed, breathless. "There are people everywhere."

"I know." He hummed against her skin. "Do you know who I was talking to?"

"No—" The word broke on a gasp as Loren's teeth grazed her skin. "Should I?"

"The innkeeper at the Silver Lantern," he said, his lips skimming down to her collarbone. The husky timbre of his voice sent a shiver spiraling down her spine. "He's set aside a room. Just for us. No Thorne. No Eloria...Just you and me."

"A room." Araya's heart stuttered, then raced, its frantic rhythm almost drowning out the music around them. The blush that had warmed her cheeks all night deepened into something hotter, more urgent. "Did you...want to go there now?"

Loren tilted his head, his grin softening into something quieter, something that threatened to make her knees buckle all over again. "Unless you'd rather wait?"

Araya narrowed her eyes at him, but the corners of her lips twitched. "No," she said. "I don't want to wait."

He took her hand, his fingers threading through hers with an easy confidence that sent a warm flush creeping up her neck. Loren led her along the edges of the crowd with exaggerated care, sliding along its edges like one of his own shadows.

Araya stifled a giggle, half afraid the musicians—or worse, the Small Council—might notice their king and queen sneaking off like unruly children. The melody followed them, light and lilting, inter-twining with the rhythmic hum of laughter and clinking glasses.

Loren's hand tightened around hers, pulling her past a group of rowdy elders loudly toasting his reign at one of the long tables. "You're drawing attention." He glanced back at her, his bright grin sparkling with mischief. "Stop looking so suspicious."

"*Me*—?" Araya clapped a hand over her mouth, trying to stifle her laughter as he tugged her forward again, catching her in his arms. "You're terrible at sneaking," she hissed.

"A king doesn't *sneak*," Loren said so haughtily that Araya couldn't hold back her giggles. Loren wrapped an arm around her, pulling her into his solid warmth. They crossed the last stretch of cobblestones to the Silver Lantern together, its doors flung open and wooden sign swinging in the breeze.

"Your Majesties!"

The cheerful, round-faced male Loren had been speaking to

earlier jumped to his feet, beaming. He bowed deeply to Loren, and then—to Araya's shock—fell to his knees at her feet.

"Lady Starwind," he said, his voice trembling with emotion. "My family can never repay you for what you've done for us. I hope you will accept our humble offer of a room tonight—and any night you may find yourself in need of lodgings in Lumaria."

"I—" Araya froze, words fleeing her entirely as she stared down at the male kneeling before her. "That is very kind," she managed at last, her voice faltering as she glanced helplessly at Loren for guidance.

But Loren just grinned at her, his eyes dancing as if her sheer inability to process what was happening here was entirely endearing.

The innkeeper's voice broke slightly as he continued. "My son... he was born in the shadows. This is the first time he has been able to feel the sun on his face, to see the stars without a veil of mist..." His throat worked visibly as he struggled to steady himself, his words trembling with raw, unfiltered emotion.

Araya's chest tightened, her heart aching for the child who had grown up in darkness. She opened her mouth, knowing she should say something—*anything*—but the words tangled on her tongue, refusing to come.

Loren stepped in with practiced ease, his hand tightening gently around hers. "Thank you," he said warmly, placing his free hand on the innkeeper's shoulder and drawing him back to his feet. "It means everything to us to know that you and your family can enjoy this freedom."

The innkeeper wiped his eyes quickly, turning his face away as he steadied himself. When he turned back, his expression was bright again. He stepped to the board behind the desk, retrieving a bronze key.

"I've made sure the room is perfect," he said, his tone regaining its earlier cheer. "The fire's lit, the sheets are fresh, and there's even a small decanter of wine waiting for you. A room fit for a king and his queen!"

Loren chuckled, his smile warm and easy. "Thank you," he said, taking the offered key. "We are deeply honored by your kindness."

The innkeeper beamed, bowing low again. "May your stay be restful, Your Majesties," he said with a playful wink that had heat blooming in Araya's cheeks. The blush crept all the way up to the tips of her scarred ears as Loren pulled her forward, practically racing her up the staircase.

"Loren!" Her laugh turned into a gasp as they reached the landing and he caught her in his arms, pressing her against the wall in one fluid movement. His body molded against hers, one hand braced on the wall beside her head and the other slid low over her hip, tracing maddening circles against the gossamer fabric of her gown.

"*Loren*," she said again, her voice a breathless whisper as his thigh pressed between hers. Her hands flew to his shoulders, gripping hard for balance—or maybe just to stay upright.

"Hm?" he murmured, leaning in, his lips brushing the shell of her ear.

"We're in the middle of the staircase," she protested, but her voice faltered as he gathered the gossamer fabric of her gown in his fist, his fingers grazing the bare skin of her thigh before slipping higher.

"And?" His mouth curved into a grin she could feel against her skin.

She sucked in a breath as his knuckles brushed the molten heat between her legs—a maddening tease that had her hands fisting in the fabric of his tunic, her knees suddenly weak.

"Loren—" her protest came out as a moan, her legs shaking as his thumb pressed just hard enough to make her gasp. "People might see—"

"They'll look away." He laughed.

Araya narrowed her eyes at him—but her hips betrayed her,

rolling into the pressure of his touch with a gasp she couldn't swallow. Gods, she was burning—already wrecked for him. He knew it too, a wicked grin curving his mouth as he leaned in, his sharp canines grazing her skin with just enough pressure to make her tremble as his hand worked her. His name tumbled from her lips—half-moan, half-warning, useless against the fire he was stoking in her veins.

Enough.

She grabbed a fistful of his silk, dragging his face to hers. He groaned into her mouth, his grip faltering when she bit his lower lip hard enough to taste blood. She twisted under his arm, leaving him gaping after her.

"Race you," she whispered, bolting up the stairs.

CHAPTER

THIRTY-NINE

HE CAUGHT HER AT THE TOP OF THE STAIRS, PINNING HER AGAINST THE DOOR before she could bolt again. She gasped, her body soft against his, and for a breathless moment she was all he could see. Flushed cheeks. Bright silver eyes. That brilliant smile meant only for him. His mouth found the flutter of her pulse at her throat, laving the delicate skin there. He could devour her right here and die a happy male—

"Get this door open," she ordered, her hands working at his doublet.

Loren fumbled with the key, swearing as it scraped against the lock. Was this even their door? He couldn't think—not when she was pulling his shirt from his pants, pressing wet, needy kisses along his throat.

"Hold still," he growled, and her breathy laugh going straight to his aching cock. He crowded her against the door, turning the key hard enough to nearly snap the damn thing. The lock gave, and they stumbled through in a tangle of limbs and heat and breathless laughter.

Her gown fell first, pooling at her feet in a whisper of plum silk.

His shirt hit the floor next, her hands on his skin stealing every last thread of restraint he had left. He reached for her—but Araya caught his wrist before he could guide her back to the bed.

"No," she said. "You had your turn on the stairs."

"That was hardly a turn," he rasped. "More of a teaser."

Her smile turned wicked—full of a promise that stole the breath from his lungs. She sank to her knees, her fingernails dragging over each ridge of his abdomen as they slid down to the laces of his pants.

Loren braced one hand against the door, the other curling into a fist at his side. Goddess help him, the sight of her—his mate, his *queen*—kneeling in front of him...

"Araya—" her name tore from his throat, raw and strangled.

"Lorendrael," she said sweetly, looking up at him through her lashes as she fisted his length and leaned forward to press her lips against the head of his cock.

His head slammed against the door, stars burning across his vision. She took him into her mouth, her tongue tracing maddening patterns that shattered the last of his composure. His thighs shook, his nails biting into his palms as he pressed his fists against the door.

She was the one in control here.

Her hands slid to his hips, holding him steady as she took him again—deeper this time. The heat of her mouth. The pull of her lips. The soft, satisfied sound she made in the back of her throat as he twitched against her tongue—

"Araya, I'm—" he groaned, his voice breaking. "If you don't stop, I'm going to—"

She pulled back just enough to meet his eyes, her lips swollen and her breath coming in short, hot bursts against his skin as she looked up at him.

"But it's my turn," she said.

"Not anymore." Loren hauled her to her feet, kissing her messily.

Araya moaned into his mouth, her fingers twisting his hair. She dragged him closer, chasing his lips as he pulled them both across the room until the backs of his legs hit the bed, spilling them both to the soft mattress.

Loren stared up at her, his throat tight as his hands settled on her thighs, stroking slow circles on her soft skin with his thumbs. Firelight gilded her skin, turning her hair into a cascade of molten flame and her eyes into liquid silver.

"Goddess," he whispered, his voice ragged. "Look at you."

She grinned, reaching between them without breaking eye contact. She rose just enough to guide him to her entrance, sliding his head through her slick heat. Loren bit back a curse, his grip on her thighs tightening as she sank down onto him in one agonizingly slow motion.

His head slammed back against the mattress, a ragged sound tearing from his throat as she seated herself fully. "You feel— *Goddess*. Araya."

She leaned forward, her hair falling around them like a curtain of flame. She rolled her hips, tearing another groan from him. He clutched at her hips, helpless to do anything but hold on as she moved over him.

She rode him like she owned him—and Goddess, maybe she did.

Araya gasped, her rhythm faltering as he slid a hand between them.

"Lorendrael—" his name spilled from her lips like a prayer.

He stroked her, circling the tight bundle of nerves and tearing another gasp from her lips. Her hips bucked, grinding down on him in a frantic, stuttering rhythm. Her forehead dropped to his, and he swallowed her soft, broken cries with his kiss.

She was close—Loren gripped her hip with his free hand, guiding her as best he could while clinging to the last edge of control. Her body tensed around him, her cry shattering against his mouth as she came, shaking apart in his arms as he followed her over the edge with a hoarse shout.

They collapsed into each other, tangled and breathless. Loren held her, tracing slow, reverent paths across her sweat-slick skin. His lips brushed her temple, her cheek, the curve of her jaw—whatever he could reach. Reminding her with every kiss that he was still here. That they both were here—alive and together.

And then, someone knocked on the door.

"Ignore it," Loren growled. He buried his face in the curve of her neck, tangling his fingers in her hair.

"It could be important." Araya said. But she didn't move, pressing a kiss to his lips, the corner of his mouth, his jaw—

"Loren!" Thorne pounded on the door again, rattling it on its hinges. "I know you're in there. Open the damned door!"

Loren froze, his forehead falling against hers. A low growl rumbled in his chest, equal parts frustration and resignation.

"I could kill him," he groaned against her lips. "He's my best friend, but I swear—"

He dragged himself away with a curse, yanking his breeches on.

"Don't move," he said, the words landing somewhere between a command and a desperate plea. "I'll get rid of him."

"Hurry," Araya whispered, her lips brushing against his before she nipped at his bottom lip.

Loren hissed, the sting of the playful bite threatening to break his fragile grasp on his restraint. He pulled away slowly, staring like he could memorize the sight of her spread out beneath him—flushed and radiant in the firelight.

His. His mate. His queen. *His.*

He tugged one of the soft blankets over her, his hand smoothing down her side in a silent promise before he stalked across the room and yanked the door open just enough to peer out the crack at Thorne.

"What?" Loren hissed.

"Goddess, Loren." Thorne shoved the door wide, barging into the room without a care for the furious king he shoulder-checked out of the way. "At least button your breeches properly before you yell at me."

Araya yelped, clutching the blanket tighter around herself as

Thorne glanced at her, his eyes widening for a heartbeat before jerking away.

"Apologies, Araya," he said quickly, grinning at the air somewhere above her head. "Hate to intrude."

A low, dangerous growl rumbled from Loren's chest. He stepped between Thorne and the bed, blocking her from view. "What the hell do you want, Thorne?"

"Scouts spotted New Dominion ships on the Shadowed Sea." Thorne's smirk slipped, the humor draining from his expression as he met Loren's gaze. "They're headed straight for us."

Loren swore under his breath. "How many?"

"Six," Thorne replied, his voice grim. "No idea how they were making it through the shadows—but we never would have seen them in time if the mists hadn't lifted when they did. Now, with nothing in their way...they'll be here by morning."

"Jaxon is with them," Araya whispered behind him, all the passion that had suffused their bond just moments ago gone cold.

Loren closed his eyes, taking a deep breath. One night—that's all he'd wanted. One night with her, to spend without fear and war. And the world couldn't even give them that.

"Gather whoever isn't too drunk to advise in the council hall," he ordered Thorne. "Sober up anyone who needs it. Make sure Eloria and Galen are there—and the scouts who spotted the ships. I want a full report."

Thorne hesitated. His sharp eyes flicked between them, something unspoken tightening in his expression. "Are you—"

"I'll be down shortly," Loren said.

For a moment, it seemed like Thorne might push—but then he nodded and turned, his footfalls echoing as he disappeared back down the stairs.

Loren stayed where he was, his back against the door, his hands curled into fists at his sides. He closed his eyes. Just for a breath.

Six ships full of New Dominion soldiers. And Jaxon, coming

straight for them. Coming for *her*. Because the Shaws never stopped until they got what they wanted.

"He's using an amplifier," Araya whispered. She'd sat up, wrapping the blanket around her shoulders. "He had one working tester when we escaped—I'm better at inscribing, but he has three vials of your blood and six of mine...I gave him everything he needed." She swallowed hard. "This is my fault, Loren."

"No." Loren crossed the room, cupping her face in his hands. "No, *ael'sura*. You thought you were helping the fae. You didn't know."

But she just shook her head, tears spilling freely now. "That's not what you said in Aetheris," she said. "You weren't wrong. I gave up. I chose Jaxon over my people."

Loren flinched. Goddess save him, if he could take those words back, he would. A thousand times.

"I was cruel, *ael'sura*." He pulled her into his arms, holding her as sobs shook her shoulders. "I wanted to drive you away. To keep you safe. I'm sorry."

He held her until her sobs dwindled to hiccuping breaths, her body sagging in his arms. Loren pressed a kiss to her temple, selfishly letting himself linger there for one final breath before he forced himself to pull back.

"This isn't how tonight was supposed to end," he said, brushing a strand of hair from her face. "I'll be with the Small Council all night. You should stay here. Rest—"

"No." Araya shoved off the blanket, scrubbing at her tear-streaked cheeks. "If Jaxon is with them, I'm your best resource."

"*Ael'sura*—" Loren hesitated, his brows drawing together as she stood, grabbing her wrinkled dress from the floor. Every instinct he had demanded that he keep her here, shield her for as long as he could for what waited for them beyond that door.

But she was more than his mate. She was his queen.

"Together, then," he said, holding out his hand.

FORTY

"We counted six ships flying New Dominion flags."

The scout stood in front of the Small Council, still wearing his creased and salt-crusted leathers. He addressed them all, but Araya didn't miss the way his brow creased as his gaze drifted from Loren and her place at his side—all the way to where Eloria sat beside her own mate, several chairs down.

She slipped her hand into Loren's under the table, squeezing gently. It wasn't the scout's fault—Loren was the prince they'd mourned, back from the dead. But his sister had ruled in his stead for twenty years. Eloria was the one they knew. The one who had kept the fae alive through the long, dark years, one impossible decision at a time. They trusted her.

"How many on board?" Loren asked.

"The ships are large, Your Majesty." The scout turned, hastily refocusing. "With their full complement, our best estimate is that we could be facing as many as fifteen hundred New Dominion soldiers."

Araya stopped breathing.

Fifteen hundred New Dominion soldiers. Lumaria had walls, but so many fae lived outside them—and there was no navy, no *soldiers*.

They had only survived this long because the Shadowed Veil sank any ship that approached it—but now those shadows were thinning with every passing day.

Because of her.

"How long until they reach us?" Eloria asked.

"At their current rate of travel, they should make landfall by dawn," the scout said.

Hours. They had hours before the New Dominion landed on their doorstep with *fifteen hundred* soldiers. It wasn't enough time. Even if they'd had days, there was no way they could prepare to face an attack of that scale—

"We should restore the Shadowed Veil immediately," Eloria's commander at arms said, his voice slicing through the stunned silence. "They never should have been pulled back in the first place."

Araya flushed, the back of her neck burning. Cormac didn't need to name her for everyone at this table to know exactly what he meant. She opened her mouth, the beginnings of an apology bitter on her tongue, but before she could voice it, Loren spoke.

"They weren't *pulled back*," Loren said sharply. "They're dissipating—because my mate and *your* queen did what was necessary to save my life." He glanced around the table at his assembled advisors. "I didn't see any of you walking into the shadows with us. Would you have preferred she left me there and come back here so you could vote on whether she should save my life?"

"The Veil kept Eluneth safe for years." Cormac stood his ground, glaring at her even as he addressed Loren. "She could have spared *some* thought for the fae she was harming—"

"Those shadows were starving you," Loren snapped. "They were harming the fae who remain in the New Dominion—"

Across the table, Cormac's brows rose, his mouth twisting in disdain. "The fae *here* are your people, Your Majesty. They're the ones you should concern yourself with."

Araya stared down at the table, focusing on the edge of the map just beyond her reach. Cormac's condemnation curled beneath her ribs, the silence that greeted his words only confirming it. The fae living in the New Dominion weren't their people. And neither was she.

"The last I checked, we were all Valenya." Loren rose, the aether-lamps flickering wildly as shadows curled along the edge of the room like smoke, pooling around his feet and cooling the air around them. "The fae living under the New Dominion are *our people*."

He bared his teeth, glaring around the room at his assembled advisors.

"The shadows are *mine*. They chose *me* to lead," he snarled. "And I do not need *your* permission to pull them back from harming those I've sworn to protect."

The room fell into a heavy, suffocating silence. The only sound was the hiss of the shadows, coiling around Loren's feet like loyal hounds. No one dared speak, the advisors glancing at each other nervously in the suddenly dim light.

"You've overstepped, Cormac," Eloria said finally. "*If* it's even possible, we can consider reestablishing some sort of barrier in a careful, *controlled* manner that does not harm the fae here *or* our citizens still living in the New Dominion. But these ships were already on their way here. Truly, we're lucky the shadows thinned when they did, or we wouldn't have seen them coming until they were already upon us."

"And how were they doing that?" Cormac demanded. "The humans have never been able to navigate the Shadowed Sea—our own ships can barely make it across the Veil."

A few advisors murmured, the tension thickening with every heartbeat. But it was Eryn who cleared his throat, his soft voice carrying in the silence.

"My intelligence indicates that Jaxon Shaw is now wielding a staff inscribed with runes that offer him some degree of control over the shadows," he said. "If they've truly come up with a way to wield influence over *dara'el*...there's no telling what else they've done."

Araya's stomach twisted as every eye turned to her.

"And does *Lady* Starwind have any insight into how the humans achieved this?" Cormac sneered, his sharp teeth bared. "You are *intimately* familiar with his work, aren't you?"

"Cormac—" Eloria warned, her voice rising as the temperature in the room dropped. "This isn't helpful."

"Isn't that why she's here?" Cormac demanded. "She was his bond—or should I say *is*? She hasn't had her runes removed. How does that work?" He turned to her, his black eyes cruel. "I've never heard of someone being bonded to two people at once."

"That's enough." Loren stood, the shadows hissing and snapping around him. "She's not on trial here."

"Maybe she should be," Cormac said, his lips pulling back from his teeth in a snarl.

The shadows seethed, lashing out across the table with a crack like a whip. Splinters of wood flew from the impact, sending several of Eloria's advisors scrambling. But Cormac just sat there, smiling like this was exactly what he wanted.

Because he wanted them all to see Loren lose control.

And they would, if no one did anything. His fury battered her through the bond, whipping the shadows into a frenzy. He wanted to hurt this male—*kill* him—for the things he was saying about her.

But if he did...he'd be giving Cormac exactly what he wanted.

"Lord Ironvale is right." Araya stood hastily, grabbing Loren's hand and squeezing it as hard as she could. For a moment, she wasn't sure it would be enough—but then his fingers tightened around hers, the shadows sliding back to wrap her in their cool embrace. "I do still wear the runes the New Dominion put on me. And Jaxon Shaw does own my true name."

She took a deep breath, meeting each of their gazes in turn. Some stared at her with nothing but disgust like Cormac—but others met her eyes with desperation, fear and hope at war on their faces.

"If I cared about sparing myself your judgment, I wouldn't be standing here right now," she said quietly. "But I am—because I love your prince. And I want to help save *our* people."

"Are we finished with this line of discussion?" Loren asked when no one said anything else. His green eyes flashed from councilor to councilor, daring any of them to speak out against her.

No one did.

"Then let's move on."

"Our focus needs to be on keeping them from making landfall," Eloria said, her finger gliding across the jagged edge of the coast. "We don't have the numbers to face a force of that size on land."

"I have control of the shadows now," Loren said. He stared down at the maps, scowling like he could make them give him a different answer. "We can use them—make them pay in blood for every inch of sea they cross."

"But can we trust the shadows to hold them back?" Galen shifted in his seat, glancing uneasily at her as the shadows rippled, ready to defend her against this new threat. "The New Dominion's already shown they can move through them. Do we know how they'd react to a direct assault?"

"It's not something they would have been able to test." Araya squeezed Loren's hand gently, trying to project a calm she didn't feel through their bond. "It's likely they'll err on the side of caution, especially with high-level officials on the ships."

Officials like the High Magister's son.

"So they won't bring them in close," Eloria murmured. "They'll have to use smaller boats to ferry their troops to shore." She glanced up at her brother. "Even if the shadows don't hold completely, we can still make it too costly for them to land. But if they do somehow make landfall—"

"Then we fight them here," Loren said. "I know we don't have the soldiers. But the civilians—will they fight?"

"They will." Eloria straightened, pride flashing in her eyes. "This is their home. Anyone who can lift a weapon will defend it."

Araya's stomach twisted. Half-starved civilians, pitted against trained New Dominion soldiers? It would be a slaughter.

"What about the children?" she asked. "The New Dominion will take any fae child it can get its hands on. Even if we win the battle, they could take dozens. You'll never get them back once they enter the reeducation camps."

"What would you suggest?" Eloria asked, though there was no challenge in her tone—only genuine curiosity.

"They should be evacuated," Araya said without hesitation.

"To where?" Cormac demanded. "We don't have the numbers to escort them all the way to Ithralis. Not without pulling critical fighters from the front."

"You wouldn't need to take them that far." Araya leaned forward, tapping the map with one finger. "The temple's closer. The doors were destroyed, but the crypt is still intact—"

"The temple is a place of worship, not a military outpost," the High Luminary snapped. "That crypt was never meant to shelter the living—"

"It's warded against anyone who might mean the royal family harm," Loren said. His arm wrapped around her waist as he glanced down at her. "You need a member of the royal line—or a sworn acolyte dedicated to the Goddess—to open it. I'm hard-pressed to think of a safer place on this island for the children if the New Dominion makes it ashore."

"And who will go with them?" another advisor asked. "If you're suggesting sending them alone—"

"I'll go," Araya said, cutting him off before the doubt could gain ground. "Someone will need to organize the children and help pull the wagons—I can do that."

A flicker of surprise passed over a few faces, but Eryn nodded thoughtfully.

"There are others who would be of more use there." He shuffled the documents spread out in front of him. "Mothers with infants, elders too old to fight—and those whose magic is better suited to subterfuge than open combat, like myself."

Araya glanced over at Loren as the councilors murmured amongst themselves. He stared down at the maps in front of them, his jaw set and tension humming through their bond. He didn't want her to go. Didn't want them to be separated—again—when they'd only just found each other.

And she didn't want to leave him.

But she couldn't forget the way the rough wood bit into her back, human hands pinning her down. The searing bite of the iron needle. How they'd laughed when she screamed for help.

"Do it," he said finally, turning to look down the table at his steward. "Get them whatever they need—wagons, food, supplies. Whatever it takes to keep them safe." He stood, sweeping his gaze across the rest of them. "There's nothing left to debate. Everyone knows what they need to do. Every moment that passes is another moment closer to their arrival."

Araya stared down at the table as chairs scraped, councilors talking amongst themselves as they hurried from the room. There were no more protests, no objections—there wasn't any time left.

"I can't stomach how they treated you," Loren said when they were finally alone again.

"They have every right to doubt me," Araya said, tracing the tiny rune inked at the base of her thumb.

"No," he snapped. "They don't."

Araya looked up at his tone, frowning at the wild glint in his eyes. "You can't let the shadows devour anyone who speaks unkindly to me, Loren. You're their king."

"I was hoping I'd only have to let them devour the first one and word would spread," Loren muttered, and despite everything, the corner of her mouth twitched.

He reached for her.

The second his hands touched her waist, Araya folded into him, burying her face in his chest. He smelled like rain and cold stone and *her*, the realization lighting a warm fire in her chest.

"You understand, don't you?" she whispered. "I can't let them take children, Loren. I can't. And if I'm not here, Jaxon might retreat to minimize the damage—"

"I know," he murmured, brushing his mouth across her temple. "I'm not arguing, *ael'sura*. I'm proud of you. Proud that you thought of the smallest and weakest among us and made a plan to keep them safe. I just...hate that I have to let you go. And at the same time I feel selfish for sending my mate to safety while asking others to stay. And the idea of trusting you to *Eryn*—"

"He's been your sister's spymaster for years." Araya pulled back, frowning. "And he helped me before. Do you really think we can't trust him?"

"Eloria trusts him," Loren admitted, grimacing. "And it's a logical move to send him with you. But all I can think about is you not coming back—"

His voice broke, the ache bleeding through the bond shattering something in her chest. Araya rose up on her toes, brushing her lips against his. Loren sank into her, his hands framing her face like she was the only place he could still breathe.

"There's only one thing that could stop me from coming back to you," Araya said when they came up for air, turning her head to press a kiss to his palm. The shadows curled around them both, enveloping them in velvety darkness. "And even then, I'd try."

FORTY-ONE

Dawn crept through the trees, its pale light filtering through the budding branches and gilding the thin mist that curled along the forest floor, pooling in the ruts left by the passing wagons.

Araya watched it, the tension in her chest easing slightly.

Because this was just mist—nothing but water, light, and the hush of an early morning. There were no monsters hiding in its depths, and the only shadow here was the one curled in the collar of her cloak. It had refused to leave her, its presence an invisible comfort even though they didn't know how far it would be able to stay with her now that they had completed the bond.

The cart bumped over a root, jostling the children packed into its bed. Araya pressed her palm to the side, steadying it as the young fae pulling caught himself. He was still a child himself by fae standards —but he and his friends had begged to stay and fight, only agreeing to come with the children when Loren sat down and gravely charged them with protecting the last hope of the fae.

That hope huddled in the wagons they pulled now. Fifty children, bundled under threadbare blankets. Some blinked sleepily at the trees as they jolted over the uneven ground. Others were too tired to stay awake, their heads lolling with each gentle sway, while others stared into the forest without blinking, stiff and silent.

The very youngest weren't in the wagons at all. They were carried—in slings tucked tight to their mothers' breasts, or held close against the shoulder of one of the chaperones who walked alongside the wagons. Healers and elders, along with one sworn acolyte begrudgingly assigned to them by the High Luminary.

"Do you really think the temple can stand against them?"

Araya glanced over at Eilwen, meeting the other female's worried violet gaze. Selan slept in a sling across her chest, his tuft of soft hair just peeking out of the top.

"It's a good plan," Araya answered carefully, mindful of the small ears listening. "Gods willing, they don't even make it ashore."

Eilwen nodded, but none of the tension left her shoulders. None of the others with them had lived under the New Dominion. They didn't know what it was like to wake to screams. To see neighbors and loved ones vanish without a trace. To be reduced to nothing but the magic in your blood.

But Araya knew. And so did Eilwen. They were the only ones who understood—in intimate and horrifying detail—what would happen to these children if the Arcanum took them.

And that's why they were the best people to protect them.

The sun had already climbed well above the horizon when the temple finally came into view. The older children pulling the wagons slowed, faltering as they approached a structure that hardly resembled the abandoned, shadow-shrouded ruin they knew from stories.

The High Luminary had set to work as soon as the shadows started clearing, charging acolytes and devotees to finally lay the dead to rest. With so many growers freed to help, soft green grass now blanketed the battlefield where bones had littered the mud, studded with sweet-smelling wildflowers.

Veria caught Araya's eye, nodding as she directed the chaperones and older children to help the younger ones from the wagons. A few little ones clutched toys, or each other's hands. But no one cried.

Even the youngest understood the need for silence as they filed up the stairs and through the gaping hole where the shattered doors had been moved aside.

Araya lingered beside the cart, finding the place where the bond lived deep in her chest. It ached—stretched too tight by the distance between them—but Loren's presence was still there. Grim and focused, full of tense apprehension instead of the panic and rage she'd expected.

"They haven't made landfall yet." She let out a slow breath, not sure if she was relieved or terrified by the revelation. "I thought they were supposed to be here by dawn."

"Sometimes scouts are wrong." Eryn shrugged, his hand resting near his dagger as he scanned the tree line. "They could have run into fog at sea. Or maybe they're gauging our defenses."

"Maybe they turned around," Eilwen said quietly. She stared down at her son, her eyes glued to his sleeping face. "King Loren has control of the Veil now. Maybe they're afraid to face it."

Araya glanced at Eryn. The spymaster met her gaze, shaking his head slightly to confirm what she already knew. There was no way the New Dominion just gave up. Not if Jaxon knew she was here.

"We should walk the perimeter," he said. "Just to be safe."

"That's a good idea." Araya turned to Eilwen, forcing as much steadiness into her voice as she could. "Go inside and get Selan settled. I'll join you as soon as I'm done."

Eilwen managed a wan smile, tightening her hold on the sling. Araya watched her climb the steps, holding her breath until she disappeared into the dark mouth of the temple.

"She's so scared," Araya murmured. Her own voice felt too loud against the hush of the morning.

"They all are." Eryn fell into step beside her as they began their circuit of the ruined walls. "But you have a way of keeping them steady. The way you speak to them, the way you make it feel like there's still hope...Loren could learn a thing or two from you."

Araya's mouth tightened. "He has his own strengths."

"Of course." Eryn smiled faintly. "He doesn't like me very much, you know. I can't blame him, though. Most days, I'm not very likable."

"Ah—" Araya stared at him, not sure what to make of the unexpected line of conversation. "Loren respects you."

Eryn laughed softly. "Unlikely, Miss Starwind."

"He does," Araya insisted. "He wouldn't have trusted you with this—with me—if he didn't. And I'm grateful, too. You helped me get the children here. You might be one of the few people who never lived in the New Dominion that understands the horrors they would face there."

"That's very kind of you to say, Lady Starwind." Eryn's hand brushed her elbow, guiding her over a rough patch of ground as they turned the corner. "It makes me very sorry for what is about to happen here."

Araya stared at him, suddenly all too aware of how alone she was with him. She couldn't even see the temple steps any more. The little shadow shifted against her skin, the hair on the back of her neck prickling. But before she could ask what he meant, a scream shattered the morning quiet.

Eilwen.

Araya spun, her heart hammering as she stared back the way they'd come. She was such a fool—they should have checked the inside first, before anyone went in. She started back the way they'd come, her magic already rising to the surface and sparking across her skin.

But Eryn's hand clamped down on her arm, yanking her to a halt.

"I can't let you do that, Araya," he said gently. "No one here wants you to get hurt. Now—*drink.*"

Drink. Araya sputtered, choking on the bitter liquid as Eryn pressed a flask to her lips. Her throat convulsed against her will, every swallow burning like fire. She tried to turn her head, to spit— but his command dug its claws into her, leaving her with no choice but to gag and sputter until he pulled the empty flask away.

"Good," he said, pocketing the empty flask. "Very good, Araya. Now—*stay here.*"

Stay. The command rooted her feet to the ground, her muscles locking in place as if her legs had turned to stone. Her power flared hot in her veins—but his command smothered it, chaining her from the inside.

Desperate, she reached inward instead, grasping for the bond. But it slipped through her fingers, impossible to grasp. She tried again, only to discover the steady hum of Loren's presence—a comfort she'd never expected to be without again—was gone. Silent.

"Don't strain yourself, Miss Starwind." Eryn shook his head, his expression pitying. "You won't be able to reach him. That tea Serafina curated for us works very quickly."

"You—" Araya stared at him, horrified. "What are you doing?"

"I'm doing what you should have done," he said. "Before you decided to cling to a dream that died twenty years ago. You know better than to believe we can defeat them. And still, you let yourself get sucked in."

Araya's pulse roared in her ears. "Loren can—"

"Loren is a shell of the king he should have been." Eryn sighed, his fingers digging into her flesh like claws. "There were a hundred chances for this to end. He should have died in that cell. Or when you tried to cross the Shadowed Sea, or when the two of you walked into the heart of the Veil. But you just had to keep saving him didn't you? And now we've been brought to this."

"No—" Araya jerked against his hold, everything in her recoiling at his touch. She had to get to the children. If he'd betrayed them and the New Dominion was *here*—all she'd wanted to do was protect the children, and instead she'd doomed them.

But it was the shadow that saved her.

It exploded from her shoulders with a feral snarl, launching itself through the air. Eryn's eyes widened, but he didn't even get the chance to shout before it slammed into his chest. He flew back, his compulsion shattering like brittle glass as his body hit the broken stone with a sickening *crack*.

Araya ran.

She didn't look back—didn't dare. Whether the shadow had torn Eryn apart or he'd managed to fight it off didn't matter. She had to reach the children. If she could just get them into the crypt, they would be safe.

She took the steps two at a time, her lungs burning as she burst into the darkened sanctuary.

The children huddled together in the far corner, pale faces streaked with dirt and tears. The chaperones ringed them in a broken circle, shielding them with their own bodies despite the terror written on their own faces.

Except for Eilwen.

She was on her knees, her body shaking with broken sobs as Darian Hale wrenched her arms behind her back. Two inquisitors flanked him, hands raised and ready to retaliate with stolen magic if anyone dared act.

Araya froze, her breath seizing in her lungs. Not Hale—not here. She stumbled back a step, every instinct screaming at her to turn and run—but she couldn't tear her eyes away from the familiar scrap of torn cloth at Hale's feet.

Selan's blanket.

"Let her go." Araya forced herself to move forward, her magic rising again. Hale might kill her here—but she'd take him with her if she could.

But she'd only managed two steps before the smell hit her. Vanilla soap—sweet and cloying. The familiar scent coiled around her throat like a noose, the voice she heard in her nightmares wrapping around her with dark promise.

"Hello, Starling."

CHAPTER
FORTY-TWO

Loren stared out over the sea, the spring breeze tugging at his coat, carrying with it the faint tang of salt and woodsmoke. A pulse of awareness reached him through the bond, the brush of Araya's mind against his kindling a warm glow in his chest.

They'd made it to the temple. They were safe.

He didn't grasp at her as she pulled back, her mind brushing against his in a last, lingering touch. They had both agreed. There was no room for distraction today—not with the New Dominion at their doorstep. But it still felt like he'd cut off a part of his own body to let her go, the bond stretched thin and tight between them.

But the further she was from here—from him—the safer she would be.

Far below, the first line of defense arrayed itself along the rocky beach—fae from every walk of life clutching makeshift weapons. Above them, archers spread out along the edge of the cliff, bows half-raised as they watched the horizon with unfaltering intensity, eyes glued to the five black-sailed ships that lingered just out of range.

"Shouldn't there be six?" Eloria asked, pulling his attention.

She'd traded silk dresses and slippers for a padded tunic and breeches, topped with light, supple armor that allowed her to move freely without sacrificing protection. Her usual circlet was gone. In its place, her raven-black hair had been braided back and coiled into an intricate bun, tucked neatly beneath the helmet that protected her head and face.

"The scouts suspect it was lost in the crossing to what remains of the Veil," Cormac answered. "We should strike now—push them back to sea before they ever get the chance to set foot on our soil."

"They've been on our soil for centuries," Loren said. "Did they find remnants of the ship? Debris? Survivors?"

Cormac scoffed.

"The Veil doesn't leave *survivors,* Your Majesty," he said, his voice clipped and already edged with disdain. "You're wasting valuable time."

"We don't move without understanding why they're stalling," Loren snapped. The shadows around his boots rippled faintly, echoing his caution. "The ship might have been lost in the crossing —or it could be holding back. Waiting for something."

"Or maybe they're hoping we stand here debating while they take our weakest point," Cormac snapped. He took a step closer, his voice rising. "Why are *you* stalling, Your Majesty? Afraid to face them on the field after spending twenty-five years as their prisoner?"

"*Cormac—*" Eloria hissed, her voice sharp with warning.

But the damage was already done. Cormac's words had carried, the nearest archers along the cliffside shifting and murmuring among themselves.

"They're waiting because they know you're no threat to them," Cormac spat. "A broken prince and his halfblood queen. She ran the first chance she got. She's an insult to your mother's memory, Your Majesty." He looked to Eloria, his face mottled with rage. "It should have been *you,* Princess," he said, his voice ringing out in the still morning air. "You're the one who never abandoned your duty. Not once."

The words echoed like a challenge—and for a moment, Loren

could almost see it. The crown on her brow. The relief in the faces of the old guard. A future untouched by shadows or scandal. The Goddess knew, *he* would have chosen her—but the fae didn't choose their kings and queens. *Dara'el* did. And that cold, ancient will had bound him to this crown long before anyone had ever guessed what threat the humans would pose to them. All he could do now was strive to be worthy of it.

And as for Araya—Loren's jaw clenched.

"Speak of my queen like that again, Commander," he said, his soft words carrying easily through the poised silence. "It will be the last insult to leave your lips." The shadows hissed, a cool prickle racing up Loren's spine as they rose along his back, spreading behind him like dark wings.

Cormac blanched, stepping back instinctively. The nearest archers stared openly now, their bows forgotten in slack hands as everyone held their breath—waiting to see if their new king was about to execute their commander. Only the blast of horns from the lookouts shattered the moment, their low, mournful cry echoing across the cliffs in a frantic call to arms.

The ships were moving.

Cormac turned without another word, shoulders stiff. He stalked down the slope toward his forces without looking back.

Eloria stared after him, hissing out a breath between her teeth. Half-formed illusions played at her fingertips, as restless as his own shadows.

"That was treason," she said, fury barely leashed behind every word. "He'll have to be removed from the Small Council—I know Thorne's a Healer, but his father was commander at arms. At least he'd be loyal—"

Loren just shook his head, his gaze fixed on the black sails billowing in the wind as the New Dominion's ships edged ever closer. On the beach below, fae scrambled to ready their lines, the scrape of steel and shouted orders rising like a second wind behind the sound of the horns.

"One battle at a time," Loren said. "Let's survive this one first."

The words had barely left his mouth when the first explosion shattered the morning.

A thundercrack split the sky—not lightning, but siege fire, arcing from the Dominion ships in streaks of molten green. Runes ignited along their hulls as spellcasters unleashed destruction, the wind turning acrid with the stench of burning magic.

Release us, Lorendrael, the shadows hissed. Their voices shifted and echoed, layering on top of one another to speak as one. *Let us do our duty.*

The last time they'd faced battle like this, they had slaughtered everyone—friend and foe, fae and human. They'd shown him themselves—a battlefield engulfed in darkness, consuming fae and human alike. His father, falling to his knees amid the carnage—

Not this time, they whispered into his ears. *Never again, Lorendrael. We swear it.*

Loren exhaled slowly. His fingers curled into fists at his side. They had to trust each other—or everything that had happened would be for nothing.

"Go," he said, releasing his hold on them.

The shadows burst forward around him, tearing down the cliffside. Ribbons of darkness slithered across the sand, racing past startled fae to leap across the waves. One wrapped itself around the leading landing craft, the screams of men rising on the air as wood splintered, spilling them into the waves. Others struck like snakes, dragging spellcasters beneath the waves before their incantations could leave their lips.

From the mist, a sixth ship appeared—then a seventh. Not New Dominion vessels, but silver-hulled fae ships, their sails shining white in the morning sun. They cut across the water, sleek and fast, closing in on the New Dominion ships as the heavier vessels struggled to turn and engage. One tried to pivot too sharply, striking its hull on the skeleton of a hidden reef with a shriek of shearing wood.

A cheer went up from the fae on the beach, loud enough to carry over the shouts.

The ships weren't real. Neither were the fae soldiers swarming onto the decks of the ships, their armor gleaming as they engaged the enemy. Eloria stood above it all, her fingers twitching as she stared down with unblinking eyes, weaving her tapestry of illusion into a force the fae could only have dreamed of gathering.

The shadows hissed their approval, their voices carried to him on the wind as they wreaked havoc on soldiers scrambling to battle foes who didn't exist.

And still Eloria kept weaving.

Fae warriors leapt from vessel to vessel, luring New Dominion soldiers into the clutches of the shadows. One panicked mage raised his hand, throwing power at a fae soldier only to strike his commander directly in the back. The man crumpled, immediately swallowed by the shadows as they swarmed eagerly forward into the gap Eloria had created for them.

They were winning.

Loren felt it—the shift in the tide, the Dominion forces flailing, illusions twisting their senses, shadows unraveling their formations. For a single heartbeat, they had a chance.

And then Araya's terror shattered the wall around his mind, coursing through their fragile bond like wildfire.

Loren gasped, pain lancing through his knees as they struck the rocky ground. She was so far away—the bond should've been muted and distant, but her fear lanced down his spine like lightning, filling his mouth with ash. Across the battlefield, his shadows faltered. One missed its mark, letting the New Dominion soldier scramble away unscathed. Another curled in place, whipping around as if to stare at him.

Something was wrong. Something was very, very wrong.

"What is it?" Eloria demanded, her voice tight as she split her focus between him and her illusions. Her fingers twitched, sweat beading on her forehead and soaking the collar of her tunic. "Are you hurt?"

"Not me," Loren managed, shoving back to his feet. "Araya."

Eloria's eyes flew to him, her own illusions wavering for a heartbeat before she fixed her grim stare back on the battle in front of her. "Go to her."

Loren shook his head, his hands curling into fists. The shadows howled, a wordless cry of rage and grief that echoed his borrowed memory of a much different battlefield. But they didn't race back to him. They knew too.

"I can't," Loren said, his voice hoarse as the world swam before his eyes. "If I leave now, we lose too many. Even if we survive today, we won't survive what comes next. Not if they tear through us like this."

But the truth did nothing to dull the screaming pain in his chest. The shadows lashed out, wild and furious as they tore through everything in their path. Their clean precision and careful aim were nothing but a memory, both of them torn between the undeniable urge to protect her and the inescapable mandate to protect their people.

She wasn't defenseless. She'd gotten better at wielding her power—especially under duress. Veria was with her, all the chaperones—even Eryn would take up arms to defend them, if necessary.

The shadows only snarled in answer, past the point of words. He felt it too—burning in the deep place where his magic lived, older than language, older than logic. Araya was afraid. In danger. And he wasn't there.

His mother had died like that. Hundreds of miles from the mate who would have done anything to save her. She'd died alone, surrounded by enemies, leaving him with only her bones to grieve over.

Loren fought with everything he had. Striking and reaching with the shadows, his power moving as one with them. Every blow pounded in his blood, driving him forward. Another landing boat capsized under a wave of darkness. A soldier almost made it to the beach, only to be dragged screaming back into the waves.

Someone grabbed him, their hands digging into his arms. Loren snarled, the shadows that had stayed back with him rearing up like striking snakes before he recognized his sister—her helmet long gone and her braid half fallen out of its knot at the back of her neck.

"It's over," she said, shaking him slightly. "Loren, it's over. They're pulling back out of range."

Her words pierced the fog clouding his mind, making their way through the raw terror consuming him. He hadn't even realized the ships were retreating, his shadows stretching to their limits as they reached greedily for the endless supply of human soldiers the Arcanum had sent to feed them.

But they were. And that meant—

Eloria nodded, squeezing his arm again before stepping back.

"Go," she said. "Go get her, Loren."

Loren didn't need to be told twice. He turned and ran, Araya's hot terror throbbing in his veins.

FORTY-THREE

Eilwen's broken sobs rose to a crescendo as Jaxon stepped into the fractured light, his smile too pleased to be anything but cruel. Caylin prowled forward to stand beside him, her eyes gleaming as she raked her gaze over the desolate female. Kai stood on Jaxon's other side, his face pale and unhappy, but it was the bundle Jaxon cradled in his arms that stopped Araya's heart cold.

"Jaxon—" she stumbled forward as Selan squirmed, fussing in his arms. "What are you doing?"

"Retrieving you, Starling." Jaxon shifted, rocking the child like it was something he'd done a hundred times. "Are you really surprised? After all my gifts?"

"You mean the innocent fae you murdered?" Araya spat.

"That's your fault, Starling." Jaxon cocked his head, glancing down at Selan. "I told you I would burn your world to the ground before I ever let you go. Did you think I didn't mean it?"

"I didn't run." The words tumbled from her lips, frantic. "They drugged me—I woke up on a boat halfway across the Shadowed Sea. Jaxon, please—" she forced herself to take another step forward, holding out her arms. "Give Selan back. Let the children go—I'll come with you. No one has to get hurt."

Hale laughed.

"We will do no such thing," he said, twisting Eilwen's arm harder as she cried. "This one already belongs to us—as does her child. The children will go to the reeducation camps, like all the other orphans. The older fae will be processed and either put to use or culled. And *you*—"

He dropped Eilwen to the ground, stepping over her. Araya braced herself, refusing to fall back even a step as he prowled toward her.

"You are quite the prize, aren't you?" Hale circled her, the weight of his attention sending a shiver down her spine. "Our spy delivered on his promises for once—our escaped bond *and* the mate of the fae prince."

Araya turned, a terrible part of her already knowing what she would find as she followed Hale's gaze.

"You continue to make things more difficult than they need to be, Miss Starwind." Eryn sighed, brushing at the mud staining his pants. "Is it really so difficult to do as you're told—just once?"

"I trusted you to help me, to help *them*." Araya stared at him, the words ash on her tongue. "You led the New Dominion right to us. You *know* what they do in those camps—"

"Better the camps than growing up half-starved, waiting for the humans to finally come and slaughter us all." Eryn's voice softened, the pity in his gaze cutting sharper than his contempt. "The war is over, Miss Starwind. The fae just refuse to see it. At least this way, the children will live. And all it cost us was you—the king's mate."

"He'll kill you." Araya clenched her fists, her nails biting into her palms. She used the pain, focusing on nursing the flame of magic in her blood. Slowly—she needed to do this slowly.

"No one here is afraid of your broken prince." Jaxon shoved Selan into Kai's arms, freeing his hands to draw the bone staff from his belt. He twirled it in his hand, circling her. "How long did it take you to crawl into his bed? A day? A week? You always did gravitate toward the most powerful man in the room."

"That's not what happened." Araya bit her cheek until she tasted blood, her magic burning hotter. It rose, desperate to reach for the stolen magic that hummed through the carved bone. "I swear, Jaxon. I didn't want to leave—"

"I'm just not sure how I can believe you." Jaxon sighed, dragging the polished bone across her skin. "How about this for a deal? Tell me you love me again, and I'll let the children go. Even your friend and her baby."

"I—" Araya coughed, her gaze flicking to Eilwen's tear-streaked face and the wide-eyed children, who still stared at her like she could somehow save them.

And she could—all she had to do was say three words.

But she was fae. And fae couldn't lie.

"I thought I loved you," she said instead. Her skin burned, her face flushing with heat as her power pushed against her skin, searching for an outlet. "But what we had...that wasn't love, Jaxon. You just wanted to own me."

"You didn't seem to mind belonging to me when it served you." Jaxon's eyes flashed, a piece of the monster staring out at her through the crack in his composure. "You wore my mark. You slept in my bed—and if you'd never met *him*, you'd still be there. We would be happy."

"No." Araya shook her head. Her voice was steady now, magic sparking across her tongue and burning her lips. "If I'd never met him, I'd be dead. Or I'd wish I was."

Araya took a step forward, clinging to the last shreds of her control. The power in her veins screamed for release, searing her from the inside out.

"I'd have done something wrong," she continued. "Something that disappointed you. You would have killed me—or drained my power and locked me in that apartment, keeping me around to play with whenever you got bored."

She stopped directly in front of him, so close she could see the flecks of gold in his brown eyes. The perfume of his vanilla soap surrounded her, thick and cloying.

"There was never a happy ending for us, Jaxon," she finished quietly. "Only an ending."

Magic tore from her like a tidal wave, heat and light bursting outward. Jaxon took the brunt of it, skidding into the altar so hard that the statue of the Goddess trembled above him. Caylin shrieked, throwing up an arm to shield her face, and even Hale cursed viciously, staggering as his inquisitors were thrown off their feet.

"*Run!*" Araya screamed.

The chaperones didn't hesitate. They snatched children up by hands and arms, dragging them into the shadowed depths of the temple. An inquisitor lunged for them, but the shimmering wall of magic Araya had called into existence held, blocking pursuit as the children raced for the door. Between them, Eilwen scrambled to her feet, lunging for Kai and her son—but Caylin was faster. She yanked the female back by the hair, slamming her to the floor with a sickening crack.

"Stop them!" Hale roared. "Don't let a single one of them get away—"

But the crypt door slammed shut, the sound echoing through the suddenly quiet sanctuary.

Araya sagged to her knees, her shield flickering out. No one who meant the fae harm could open that door now. The children were safe. They were safe—

Hale seized her arm, wrenching her backward.

Araya's head slammed into stone, stars bursting across her vision. Her knees buckled, a scream ripping from her throat when Hale shoved her hard into the nearest column, twisting her arm until her shoulder *cracked*.

"No—" Araya gasped in pain as he exposed the *ly'ithra* rune inked at the base of her thumb. She clawed at him with her free hand, trying to stop him—but Hale wrenched her mind open.

Someone screamed—*she* was screaming. Hale tore into her, ripping her magic free in long strips. It felt like her soul was being flayed, every delicate nerve ending peeled back and scraped raw.

By the time he dropped her, Araya couldn't force her limbs to obey her. It was all she could do to stay conscious as she lay on the stone at his feet, gasping and trembling.

"Halfblood slut." Hale loomed over her. Stolen power—*her* power—crackled over his hands. "Do you think you saved them?" His voice rose, echoing in the vaulted chamber. "Get that door open! I don't care if it's enchanted—rip it out of the wall if you have to!"

Caylin dropped Eilwen, stumbling toward the back of the sanctuary with blood still dripping from her temple. The other two inquisitors scrambled after her, eager to obey.

Araya laughed, the ragged, broken sound that bubbled from her throat foreign even to her own ears. A pack of *zal'vorr* hadn't been enough to bring that door down. Three inquisitors didn't stand a chance.

"Do you think this is funny?" Hale snarled. He dropped to one knee, seizing her jaw and forcing her to meet his gaze. "I'll kill them all just to teach you a lesson. All you've done is make things worse for yourself, you stupid little bitch—"

Araya spat in his face.

Hale reeled back, her bloody spittle dripping down his cheek. For a heartbeat, all he did was stare at her, shock twisting into something far uglier. His hand snapped out, striking her across the face so hard that her head snapped sideways, her vision blurring.

"Enough, Hale," Jaxon snapped. "She's not yours to punish—or drain."

Hale sneered, his eyes wild. "And she's not yours now either," he said. "The Arcanum won't smile indulgently like your father while you play house with the fae king's *mate*. Everyone will want a chance at her bloodline—"

Hale's words broke off in a wet gurgle.

Araya blinked, unable to believe her own eyes as Hale staggered, his fingers clawing at the blade jutting through his neck. His eyes bulged, his mouth still working soundlessly, trying to speak even as his lifeblood soaked his shirt.

Jaxon ripped his sword free, Hale's blood spraying across her before she could turn away. Araya choked on it, bile mixing with the iron tang as Hale dropped like a marionette with its strings cut.

"Get up."

Araya flinched as Jaxon reached for her, bracing for a killing blow —but instead, his hand closed around her uninjured arm, hauling her upright.

"Don't be ridiculous, Starling." He laughed, smearing his thumb through the blood that coated her face. "Do you really think I'd kill you after everything I've done to keep you? Now—go stand over there with Kai."

He gave her a little shove, sending her stumbling across the blood-slick floor toward Kai. The other mage just gaped at her, clutching Eilwen's son tight to his chest as if he could shield him from the violence.

"Jaxon—" Kai said, his voice strangled. "What are you doing?"

"I'm taking vengeance for our High Inquisitor, of course." Jaxon turned, his sword still dripping blood. "After our double agent brutally betrayed us all and tried to rescue his queen."

Eryn's eyes widened, his hands coming up. "Wait—" he said as Jaxon started toward him. "You don't have to—"

Jaxon's sword punched through his chest.

Eryn's eyes went wide, his words dying in a wet wheeze. Jaxon yanked the blade free, his face impassive as Eloria's spymaster collapsed at his feet, falling face-first into a spreading pool of his own blood.

"He forced my hand," Jaxon said. He lifted his dripping sword, pointing at each of them in turn. "You all saw it, didn't you?"

No one answered. Even Eilwen had stopped crying, her violet eyes fixed on Jaxon like he was her worst nightmare come to life.

"Get them ready to go." Jaxon leaned down, wiping his sword on Eryn's shirt. "And find Caylin. We're leaving without the children."

His gaze settled on Araya, hot and possessive.

"I have everything I came for."

Araya slumped against the cart wall, the rough wood biting into her back with every bump. Her limbs hung useless, each shallow breath scraping her throat like broken glass. The dull throb behind her eyes had sharpened into something meaner, until it felt like her skull would split open.

"Are you alright?" Kai asked.

Araya almost laughed. She'd nearly died the last time she'd been drained like this. At least she'd been unconscious for most of that.

"Of course I'm not alright," she snapped, hissing as the cart bounced over another root, jostling her shoulder.

Kai shifted beside her, still holding Selan in his arms. "I didn't—" He broke off, swallowing hard. "I'm sorry."

"You're sorry?" Araya forced her eyes open, ignoring the way her vision swam. "Why are you even here, Kai?"

"Jaxon asked me to come."

"And why do you think he did that?" Araya laughed despite the pain, bile burning the back of her throat. "You're not a soldier, or an inquisitor. You're the one who always looks the other way for him. It's easier that way, isn't it?"

Kai looked away.

Araya shook her head, her gaze falling on the baby still cradled in his arms. Selan's chest rose and fell in steady breaths, his small hands curled into fists by his mouth as he slept.

"Are you really going to do it?" she asked. "Are you really going to put a *ly'ithra* rune on a baby?"

Across the cart, Eilwen made a soft, choked sound, burying her face in her knees to muffle her sobs.

Kai stiffened. "It wouldn't be me—"

"Standing by is just as bad." Araya closed her eyes, dropping her head back to the rough wood behind her. "I'd know. Wouldn't I?"

"What exactly do you expect me to do here, Araya?" Kai demanded, his voice low. "He'll never let you go."

Araya cracked her eyes open, turning her head just enough to meet Kai's anguished stare.

"Not me," she said, flicking her eyes to Eilwen "Just give her back her son when we reach the tree line."

Kai's eyes widened as Eilwen's sobs abruptly choked off, her bright violet gaze whipping between them. "You're asking me to—"

Araya cut him off. "You know *exactly* what they'll do to him in those camps, Kai. Give him back to his mother. Let her run—you don't have to do anything else. I'll take care of the rest."

"And how are you going to do that?" Kai hissed. A muscle in his jaw twitched. "You can't even sit up, Araya!"

"Just be ready," Araya said.

For a terrible moment, Araya thought he wouldn't do it. His gaze darted toward the front of the cart, to Eilwen's desperate face and the sleeping child in his arms. Finally, he swallowed hard, holding Selan out to her.

None of them spoke again. Araya stared up at the sky, focusing on staying conscious as the light shifted and the tree canopy opened overhead. She held her breath, counting each jolt in the road. One. Two. Three.

She let herself fall.

The world tilted, the ground rushing up to meet her. She hit shoulder first, bone crunching as she cried out. Someone shouted, the wheels of the cart squealing as it lurched to a halt.

A boot slammed into Araya's ribs, driving the breath from her lungs and flipping her onto her back. Caylin stared down at her, her beautiful face twisted with seething rage.

"What exactly do you think you're doing, halfblood?"

Araya gasped as Caylin's boot connected again. She curled

around the hurt, choking on a cry as the woman wrenched her upright by her injured arm.

"*Caylin*—" Kai grabbed her, his silhouette nothing but a blurry shadow through Araya's watery vision. "She's injured. She fell—"

"Don't be stupid," Caylin snapped. Her sharp nails dug cruelly into Araya's bicep. "She didn't *fall*. I don't know what she gains by throwing herself out of a moving cart, but she's nothing but a tricky little halfblood *slut*—"

Araya coughed, bile burning the back of her throat. The world pitched around her. She barely managed to twist her head before she vomited—spattering Caylin's shining black boots and the hem of her pristine coat.

Caylin shrieked.

Araya sagged against her with a moan, going boneless. "Sorry," she croaked. "Lost my balance."

"You—" Caylin's lip curled, her face turning an ugly, mottled red. She dragged Araya behind her as she stormed to the edge of the path, scraping her boots against the dead grass there.

"What's going on back here?" Jaxon rounded the corner of the cart, his voice tight with annoyance. "Why is she out of the cart?"

"We hit a rut," Kai said, turning to Jaxon. "She fell—"

"She's *faking* it," Caylin practically shrieked, still trying to scrub her coat clean with a handful of dead grass. "She jumped out of the cart and threw up all over me—"

But Araya didn't hear the rest. A shout tore through the trees, one of the inquisitors pulling the cart racing past them.

"She slipped out the side," he shouted over his shoulder. "She's running—" his voice cut off in a sharp curse as he tripped over a root that hadn't been there a moment before. Branches tore at his partner, bristling with wicked thorns, and vines slithered across the ground like snakes, wrapping around ankles and dragging down anyone foolish enough to enter the trees.

Jaxon swore viciously, slamming his fist into the side of the cart.

Araya sagged in Caylin's grip, trying to keep the satisfied smile from reaching her face. She'd done it. Kai had done it. Eilwen was gone—safe. And so was Selan. They'd never catch her. Not when she could call on the forest itself to protect her.

"Did you give her back her child?" Jaxon demanded.

Kai just stared at him, his eyes wide. "She wouldn't stop crying. And then Araya fell—"

"That fae bitch just stole from me!" Jaxon roared. "And you—you handed her the chance to run on a silver platter!"

His hand shot out, grabbing Araya by the front of her blood-stained tunic. He slammed her against the side of the cart, sending white sparks flashing across her vision.

"We're not wasting time chasing your little friend," he snarled. "She can starve to death behind the blockade we're going to set up for all I care. Your beloved *mate* is *never* going to make it to you in time. You're never going to see him again, Starling. You're mine. And I *never* let go of what's mine."

Araya bared her teeth, the iron tang of blood thick on her tongue. "I'm not yours. Not anymore."

Jaxon laughed in her face.

"You really believe that, don't you?" He stepped back, letting her slump back against the cart. "Get her on the boat," he ordered. "No more mistakes."

FORTY-FOUR

He couldn't feel her.

The sun was well past its zenith by the time they reached the temple, beating down on the small group of soldiers Thorne had gathered. They were all tired, their footsteps lagging—but Loren took the steps two at a time, ignoring Thorne's shouted warning. He couldn't slow down. Couldn't wait—not when there was only silence where their bond should have lived.

His shadows led the way, twisting and crawling over the broken stone. Loren crossed the threshold behind them, his steps faltering as the iron tang of blood filled his nose.

Loren reached Eryn first. Eloria's spymaster lay on his face, the blood around him cooled into a tacky pool. Just a few steps away, Darian Hale slumped awkwardly where he must have died, nothing left of his throat but a mangled ruin.

"Goddess," Thorne swore, stepping up beside him. "Who is that?"

"Darian Hale. The Arcanum's High Inquisitor," Loren said, hardly able to hear himself over the pounding of his own heart. The shadows stirred around him, murmuring as he stared down at the body of the man who had dedicated his life to torturing him. For decades, Darian Hale's name had meant pain—cold iron and burning flesh, questions asked in a silken voice and answers demanded in blood.

Now he was dead. But Loren couldn't bring himself to care.

"She's not here," he said. "I can't feel her, Thorne. What if—" His voice broke, the shadows keening as they shifted and milled, searching for her.

"They were supposed to take shelter in the crypt," Thorne said, using the same calm, soothing tone he used on panicking patients. "We should at least check."

The door opened easily under Loren's touch, revealing Veria standing guard at the top of the stairs, a kitchen knife clutched in her hands. When they realized it was Loren, the other adults and the children spilled up the stairs, all of them talking at once.

But Araya wasn't with them.

"Eryn betrayed us," Veria said. She stared at the bodies, looking older than Loren had ever seen her. "There were inquisitors waiting for us when we got here. He lured Araya away—I don't know what he said to her, but she came running in here, desperate to save us. She used a shield *perfectly*—gave us the chance to make it into the crypt."

She'd used her magic. Pride flickered through Loren's panic, but it was gone in the next breath, buried under a rising tide of fury. *Eryn* —he'd ignored every instinct, confident that even if Eryn wasn't wholly trustworthy, no fae would ever betray another to the New Dominion.

And now Araya was paying the price for his blindness.

"Were any of them wearing sigils? Markers of rank?" Thorne pointed at Hale's body, indicating the gold trim on his padded tunic. "Like him."

Veria nodded. "The woman—and two of the men."

"Four inquisitors," Thorne said, glancing sidelong at Loren. "And the others?"

"They were younger. One barely spoke—kept his eyes down. But the other—" Veria shuddered, squeezing the child in her arms tighter. "He took Eilwen's babe from her. And the way he spoke to Araya..."

"Jaxon," Loren said. His shadows curled around him, cooling the air in the sanctuary. He didn't need proof. There was only one person arrogant enough to wait here for her, like a spider poised over a web—while the rest of the New Dominion moved on Lumaria.

And Loren had sent her right into his hands.

He reached inward—into the bond, into that fragile tether he'd clung to since the day he met her.

Still nothing.

Loren clenched his jaw, his magic crackling in the hollow space where her presence should've been as he stretched out his mind and his magic, straining to reach her. He poured everything into that desperate reach—his steadiness, his strength, his vow that she wasn't alone. That she would never be alone again.

But she didn't answer.

The shadows rippled at his feet, one peeling away from the rest. It crawled toward him, its edges bleeding dark mist as it struggled to hold its shape. *Her* shadow—as lost and left behind as he was. Loren bent, letting it curl around his arm to rest across his shoulders, exhausted and wounded.

He straightened, fear hardening into resolve. If Jaxon thought he wouldn't come for her—that Loren would choose the crown and let them take her—then the High Magister's son was about to learn a very hard lesson.

"Leave soldiers here," Loren ordered, turning for the door. "Enough to organize the supplies and keep the children safe."

Thorne matched his stride. "And you?"

"I'm going to get my mate," Loren said. "And Goddess help whoever gets in my way."

THEY HAD NEARLY REACHED ITHRALIS WHEN THE SHADOWS BROKE FROM HIM, surging ahead in a rush of darkness. Loren sprinted after them, ignoring Thorne's shout. Something was wrong. He could feel it— like cold fingers wrapping around his heart, ready to crush him completely.

"Loren, wait!" Thorne yelled somewhere behind him. "It's—"

A figure burst from the underbrush, nearly colliding with him. Eilwen—wild-eyed and bleeding, her child clutched so tightly to her chest that his cries were muffled against her shoulder.

"Stay back!" she screamed, her body curving around her child as she twisted out of his grasp. "Don't touch us!"

"Eilwen!" Loren swore, ducking as branches lashed at his face, turned on him by the terrified grower. "It's me! You're safe!"

"Your Majesty?" Eilwen blinked, the terror in her violet eyes fracturing into disbelief and panicked hope. "Araya—you have to go. She needs you—"

"What happened?" Loren demanded.

"She saved me—" Eilwen's voice hitched, breaking on a sob. "She saved *us*. She couldn't even stand, but she convinced him to give me back Selan. She threw herself from the cart to give me a chance to run. But she couldn't get away—"

"Where?" Loren demanded. "Where is she?"

"Ithralis." Eilwen looked up at him, fresh tears streaking her cheeks. "I heard him say there was a boat—already loaded. The human runesmith helped us, but she couldn't get away. I'm sorry. I'm so sorry—"

"Loren—" Thorne started, but Loren didn't wait to hear what he had to say.

He ran.

Branches clawed at him, thick underbrush dragging at his legs. But Loren barely noticed the thorns raking his skin or the vines that tangled around his ankles. His world had narrowed to the single, pulsing demand that pounded in his chest, echoed by the shadows that raced alongside him.

Reach her. Save her.

He plunged out of the tree line, nearly tripping over the cart. It sat across the path, its wheels mired in the mud. Abandoned. Loren's nostrils flared, taking in the traces of iron under the acrid stink of vomit, threaded through with the iron tang of blood.

His mate had bled here.

Loren stalked past the abandoned cart, the wind rising with every step. He stopped at the edge of the cliff, staring out at the single ship that cut across the Shadowed Sea like a knife. A man stood at the rail, staring back at him.

Jaxon Shaw. Fury rose like a tide in his blood, the shadows singing in answer. They surged, spilling over his shoulders and coiling down his arms like a living storm. He didn't need the bond to know—Araya was on that ship. Jaxon Shaw was taking his *mate*.

"Go," he snarled. "Get her."

The shadows exploded forward, pouring over the cliff like a black tide. They broke against the rocks, their whispers a dark promise in his ears as they streaked across the waves. They would rip Jaxon from the deck—drag him screaming beneath the waves. It was a kinder death than he deserved. But all that mattered now was *her*.

Then Jaxon raised his hand.

Sunlight flared off pale bone, the reek of stolen magic so pungent that Loren could *taste* it through his shadows. The air itself twisted in on itself, the shadows faltering mid-surge. They hesitated.

Jaxon didn't.

He drove the staff down. Power cracked like lightning across the water, lashing into the advancing shadows. They twisted, a thousand voices screaming in his mind, splitting his skull and driving him to his knees.

Your blood. Hers. He wields your magic—he is not you. Not a king. But he dares—he dares to command us—

Loren clutched his chest, unable to catch enough of a breath to answer. The salt-soaked air sawed in and out of his lungs, burning his mouth and throat.

"You're too late, Loren."

Jaxon's voice boomed across the waves, amplified by magic to cut across the distance and the shrieking wind. "If you want your mate, you'll have to come and take her from me yourself. Assuming she still wants you by the time you get there."

Jaxon laughed, the sound echoing off the cliffs as the ship vanished like a ghost into the lingering mist that hung low over the Shadowed Sea. Maybe the ghostly remnants of the Veil would have destroyed another ship, but with Araya on board and Jaxon wielding that staff...

Loren doubled over, a raw scream of rage tearing from his throat. His shadows flailed, writhing around him in wild, frenzied arcs, striking out at the rocks, the sky—even him, his blood soaking the rocky ground from a hundred cuts. But it didn't stop the pain. Nothing could.

He'd failed her.

Loren didn't know how long Thorne let him grieve. It could have been minutes or hours before his friend stepped forward—straight into the raging shadows.

"Stop—" Loren gasped, blood soaking his shirt. "They'll hurt you—"

"You won't." Thorne's hand landed on his shoulder, his warm healing magic running over Loren's skin like water. The shadows hissed, but stilled, drawing in around him.

"You won't get her back from here," Thorne said, his amber eyes steady. "We need to go back to Lumaria—make a plan. We'll get her back, Loren. But not from here."

Loren's throat worked, his voice hoarse from screaming. "We?"

Thorne clapped him on the shoulder, standing. "Do you really think I'd let you do this alone?" He held out a hand, pulling Loren to his feet. "She's not just your mate, Loren. She's our queen. And I'll follow you into the heart of the New Dominion itself to bring her home—we all will."

CHAPTER
FORTY-FIVE

Loren paced the length of the war room like a caged predator, leaving muddy footprints on the polished stone. He hadn't bothered to change, blood still crusting his clothes from the cuts Thorne had healed. The shadows trailed him, twitching restlessly as they muttered amongst themselves.

The Small Council watched him carefully, their expressions ranging from nervous unease to outright terror. They'd all gotten the report ahead of his arrival. They knew what had happened, who had come to take his mate. But none of them wanted to be the first to speak.

It was Cormac who cleared his throat finally, standing.

"The New Dominion is in retreat," he said. "They never made landfall, but we need to take the opportunity to fortify our defenses—"

"Fortify our defenses?" Loren turned slowly. "They took the Queen."

"And our heart breaks for you, Your Majesty," the High Luminary said, her voice gentle. "To lose your Goddess-given mate...it's a pain I wouldn't want to wish on my worst enemy."

"She's not *lost*," Loren snarled. "She was captured—by New Dominion forces. What we *need* to be doing right now is making a plan to rescue her."

"We don't retrieve captured prisoners from the New Dominion," Cormac snapped. "If we tried to rescue every mate and loved one that was left behind we'd all be long dead—"

"Bold words, from a traitor," Eloria snapped. She still wore her battle-stained clothing, her hair freed from its braid to tangle around her dirt-smudged face. "Shall we discuss *your* conduct, Cormac? You undermined your king in front of his army as the enemy was approaching our shores. You insulted his queen. Why should this council listen to *anything* you have to say?"

Cormac's mouth twisted. "I don't regret my words," he said stiffly. "As a member of your council I have every right to voice concerns about the fate of our people—"

"And as my brother's Princess Regent, *I* have every right to censure you," Eloria cut him off, her voice rising. "I'm stripping you of command and relieving you of your seat on this council."

Cormac's face mottled red. "I spoke for you—"

"You advocated for placing me as ruler above my brother—the monarch chosen to lead us by *dara'el* in accordance with our most sacred traditions." Eloria stepped forward, her eyes blazing. "You didn't *voice your concerns*, Cormac. You committed *treason*. And you will leave this room before I have you removed."

For a heartbeat Cormac just stared at her, his hand on the hilt of his sword. His gaze drifted around to his fellow councilors, but none of them met his eyes.

"Fine," he snarled. "Die here, then. But that halfblood *whore* is no queen of mine." He turned on his heel, stalking from the room. The heavy door slammed behind him so hard the aetherlamps shuddered, every eye turning to Loren as the Small Council waited to see how their lost prince and his shadows would answer *that* insult.

Except for Eloria.

His sister let out a breath, taking her seat. "Now that that's settled," she said coolly, "we can return to the important business at hand—how we bring your queen home."

"With all due respect, Princess," the High Arbiter said, his tone carefully neutral. "Your brother has been recognized as king, yes—but until his coronation *she* is not queen."

Loren's head snapped toward the male that had sat on his father's Small Council, dispensing justice in his name long before Loren had even been born. The shadows shifted, a hundred voices whispering furiously, but Maelor didn't flinch.

"Commander Cormac's words were abhorrent," he said evenly, "but he was correct. Our policy has long been that those lost to the New Dominion are regrettably out of our reach. This is doubly true now, with Eryn and his entire network in the New Dominion lost to us—"

"Eryn betrayed her," Loren growled. "He handed her over to them like a bargaining chip—he would have given them your *children*. If it wasn't for her we would have lost them all—"

Maelor bowed his head slightly. "And for that, Your Majesty, she has our eternal gratitude." His gray eyes rose again, his expression full of sorrow as he met Loren's fury. "But there's nothing we can do. You know what the Arcanum will do to her—better than any of us here. Even if you succeeded in rescuing her, you would not get her back."

Around the table, other councilors shifted uncomfortably. But no one dissented, their silence damning in its own right.

"And what do you think they did to me?" Loren demanded. The shadows slid over the walls, the aetherlamps flickering wildly. "You still call *me* king. How can you expect me to do *nothing* while *my queen* is dragged back to the very hell she escaped? To be tortured and *bred* like an animal?"

Maelor only sighed, folding his hands. "I'm sorry, Loren," he said quietly. "We cannot lose this war over one female. Not even your mate. The burden of the crown is heavy."

"The *burden*—" Loren snarled, losing his voice.

The temperature plummeted, frost blooming across the windows and crawling over the scarred tabletop. Several councilors flinched back in their seats, their eyes wide with fear. Others looked at him with pity, their own grief shining in their faces. He was not the only one to lose someone he loved to the New Dominion.

"Enough." Eloria's voice snapped across the room. "All of you, get out. Now. Before my brother's temper leaves us with more than one seat to fill on this council."

Chairs scraped, the councilors all but fleeing the room as shadows rose around him, their whispers calling for death and vengeance and blood. Loren didn't even attempt to call them back. Anyone who would leave *his* queen to that fate deserved exactly what they got—

"Loren—" Eloria's hand touched his arm, gentle. "They're gone. It's just us, now."

"And do you agree with them?" Loren asked bitterly. "Because I don't want to hurt you, El. But if you stand here and tell me that she's already lost—that I'm not fit to rule if I'd risk our future for one person—"

"You'd be unfit to rule if you *weren't*," Eloria snapped, the fire in her words so unexpected that even the shadows fell silent. "Araya is your *mate*, Loren. You aren't choosing between her and your people. She *is* your people. If someone took Galen from me—" she cut off, shuddering as Galen wrapped his arm around her. "I'd burn every bridge, destroy every alliance, kill *anyone* that stood between us."

Loren stared at her, suddenly uncertain. "But the Small Council—"

"Is full of cowards." She shook her head, her lip curling. "But they don't matter, Loren. *You* are the king. You don't need their blessing to do anything."

"They're going to hurt her, El. Shaw—" he broke off, the words choking him.

Eloria's hand tightened on his arm. "Then go make him pay," she said.

CHAPTER

FORTY-SIX

ARAYA BLINKED SLOWLY, THE WORLD SWIMMING IN AND OUT OF FOCUS around her. Stone walls slick with moisture. A ceiling hemmed in shadows. And the cold, leaching press of iron around her wrists and neck.

They'd collared her.

She tried to shift, but the movement sent a bright flare of agony through her chest. Araya breathed deeply, cataloguing the injuries. A dislocated shoulder, broken ribs—at least one, probably more— courtesy of Caylin. Countless scrapes and bruises. Her magic sputtered, a shadow of what it should have been. And she still couldn't feel the bond.

Araya sagged against the wall, every breath labored. They must have dosed her when she was unconscious—the bitter aftertaste of the herbs mingling with the sour tang of bile on her tongue. She could feel the place where their bond should have been, the fragile thread that linked them guttering like a flame on the verge of going out, but there was no sense of *him* or any hint that he could still feel her.

Good. That was good. She didn't want him to feel the things they'd do her.

Araya closed her eyes, straining her ears for any sign of life. But there was nothing but silence. No footsteps. No scrape of keys or distant rattle of chains. Nothing but the sound of her own labored breathing.

She drifted, lost between shallow rest and raw awareness, chasing fleeting fragments of memories that dissolved the moment she tried to hold them in her mind. Loren's eyes, smiling down at her. The warm weight of Selan in her arms. The grind of her bones against each other as Jaxon twisted her arm behind her back—

"Miss Starwind?" someone spoke, hesitant. "Are you...are you awake?"

Araya blinked, lifting her head to stare at the fae female standing in the open cell door. Clipped ears, her dark hair pulled into a tight bun at the back of her neck—but it was the spotless gray dress Araya recognized first. Garrick Shaw's household livery.

"Belanis." Araya's voice cracked, hoarse from disuse. The name came with a ghost of memory—this same female, her face flushed and frightened as Jaxon berated her for entering without knocking.

"Yes, Miss," Belanis whispered. "You need to get up now. Master Shaw wants you washed and dressed."

"Which one?" Araya laughed at her own joke, groaning as fresh pain speared through her ribs.

Belanis didn't laugh. She glanced down the hall instead, her face pinched and wary. "You don't want to keep him waiting."

It wasn't easy. Belanis had to help her stand, then support her as they walked. Tears poured down Araya's face, every step accompanied by fresh pain. But she kept walking, letting herself be led one slow, dragging step at a time down a narrow hallway lined on both sides with empty cells. Up a staircase and through a door, emerging into a hall that would have been at home in any fine residence.

Araya stared, taking in the fine tapestries and the vase of flowers on the small, carved table. The air smelled of wood polish and perfume, without a hint of the stale air of her dungeon cell. It was all so *normal*. But here she was, bruised and broken, covered in blood and vomit—

"Miss, please," Belanis hissed, and Araya realized she was laughing again, tears still streaming down her cheeks.

"I just didn't realize Garrick had a dungeon under her house," she said, shaking her head at the absurdity of it. "Does he keep a lot of personal prisoners?"

"I can't say, Miss," Belanis said stiffly.

Of course she couldn't. Araya bit back her hysterical laughter, picking up her pace as the other female dragged her through the deserted halls. Who knew what the Shaws would do to her if they thought she'd told their prisoner anything of use?

They passed no one, finally entering what could have passed for a sparsely furnished guest room—but Araya caught the shimmer of runes etched into the doorframe. More marked the trim around the windows, subtle enough that the casual observer would pass right over them.

"I'm sorry." Belanis didn't linger in the main room, guiding Araya into the bathing chamber and gently lowering her onto a small stool. "Master Shaw didn't order a Healer. This will probably hurt."

Araya gasped, biting back a scream as the other female reached for the ties at the back of her tunic. She had to peel the fabric from Araya's skin in places, the cloth stiff with dirt and blood. Every bit of flesh she bared revealed new bruises—her ribs a gruesome tapestry of black and blue and her shoulder grotesquely swollen. The ghost of Caylin's handprint stood out in ugly purple relief on her upper arm —five deep bruises marking where her fingers had dug into Araya's bicep.

She was sobbing again by the time Belanis finished. The other female turned away, her face pale as she bent over the tub, giving both of them a moment. Water poured from the tap, heated by stolen magic. The steady rush drowned out Araya's quiet sobs, filling the air with steam and fogging the mirror until the reflection of that battered, broken female vanished.

Araya let Belanis help her into the tub, holding as still as she could. The other female scrubbed at her skin with a harsh yellow soap, carefully working around the manacles and collar so she didn't burn herself on the iron. Unlike Loren's manacles, these were lined with something soft, preventing the metal from blistering her skin.

That made sense. Jaxon wouldn't want her marked—not permanently. He'd never been a fan of imperfections. Especially not when it came to her.

"Do you think he'd kill me if I scarred?" she asked.

"Not if it's somewhere hidden," Belanis said, wringing out the cloth into the dirty water before pulling the plug.

Neither one of them spoke again as the tub filled with fresh water. Belanis washed her a second time, tipping her head back and massaging a softer, sweeter soap into her hair. The cloying scent of vanilla filled the room, strangling Araya's senses until all she could smell was *him*.

Araya closed her eyes, forcing herself to keep breathing deeply as Belanis dragged a comb through her hair, tugging at the snarls and tangles. It was only soap. She couldn't lose herself to panic—not now, when her very survival would depend on how well she kept her wits about her.

She took the towel Belanis offered without a word, doing her best to pat herself dry. The other female helped her into a plain nightgown, the fabric soft against her scraped skin. It fit perfectly, hanging loose over her ribs and shoulder, as if someone had thought about her injuries when they chose it for her.

Araya shivered, suddenly feeling far more exposed than she had in the bath.

"They'll be in soon," Belanis said, depositing her on the bed. She gathered Araya's filthy clothes into a basket, avoiding her eyes. "Just do what they want. It will hurt less if you do."

She hurried out before Araya could respond, the door closing behind her with a soft click. Araya stared after her, watching numbly as magic flared across the seam of the door, sealing her in.

THEY DIDN'T MAKE HER WAIT LONG.

The sun had barely shifted across the wall before a key scraped in the lock, magic flaring. Belanis entered first, darting across the room and setting the silver tea service she carried down on the small table. Araya leaned back against the headboard, cradling her injured arm in her lap. She didn't move as Garrick walked into the room, Jaxon on his heels. She wouldn't give them the satisfaction of reacting.

"Thank you, Belanis," Garrick said smoothly. "You may go. We'll call if we need anything."

The fae female fled in a swirl of dark skirts, leaving her alone with the monsters. Araya didn't blame her, though. She'd have run too, if she could have.

"Well," Jaxon said brightly, "you look much better now, don't you?"

His fingers dug into her chin, lifting her face and turning it from side to side. He stared into her eyes, frowning when he didn't see whatever it was he was searching for.

"You've gotten some of your color back, at least," he said finally, releasing her. "How are your ribs?"

"Broken," Araya said flatly. "And Hale dislocated my shoulder."

"Well, he's dead now." Jaxon clicked his tongue, stepping back. "Maybe if you start cooperating, we'll see about getting a Healer in to see you. You don't have to suffer, Starling. Not if you're willing to be reasonable." He held out a hand to her, nodding his head toward the waiting table, where three cups steamed beside a porcelain teapot. "Come sit with us."

Araya didn't move. If they wanted to pretend this was some polite conversation over tea, they'd have to do it alone.

Jaxon huffed out a sigh, dropping his hand. "Well I tried," he said, taking one of the cups. He poured milk into it, adding two lumps of sugar and giving it a stir. "You'd think after everything you've done, you'd be grateful to be here at all instead of rotting in a dungeon. We'd have executed anyone else."

"Jaxon is right, Araya," Garrick said softly when she didn't say anything. He didn't sit, standing behind his chair instead. "You've made quite a mess of things here. The only person you hurt by being stubborn here is yourself. We're trying to help you."

He paused, giving her a chance to respond. But Araya pressed her lips together, clenching her shaking hands in her lap. Whatever they wanted from her here, she wouldn't give it to them.

Garrick sighed, his expression resigned. "You had everything," he continued. "Comfort. Protection. A bond to a powerful mage who would have given you anything—if you'd been smart enough to just tell Jaxon what you were experiencing…" he shook his head. "We wouldn't have hurt you or Loren—those children would have been *very* valuable to us."

Araya stared at him, her stomach twisting at the picture he painted. But Garrick wasn't finished.

"You'd even have been allowed to raise them," he said, adding a few cubes of sugar to his cup and stirring. "If only you'd held on to a single shred of loyalty."

"You're sick," Araya rasped, her voice thick with fury. "You're talking about breeding me like livestock—about *owning* my children."

"Don't be dramatic." Garrick poured the milk into his tea, setting the silver spoon aside. "You already agreed to it once. You know where your value lies, Araya. Even if Jaxon did indulge your curiosity."

Araya stared at him, biting back the fury that boiled under her skin. She buried it deep, refusing to let it show. If she did, they would use it. And they already had too many ways to hurt her.

"But that was before." Garrick raised his cup to his lips, taking a slow sip. "Now you're not just some pretty halfblood stray my son has taken a liking to. You're the mate of the fae king—the *queen*. And that makes you a valuable resource. With you, we could open the Eldergreen in weeks instead of years."

"I'd rather die," Araya snarled, baring her teeth.

For the first time, Jaxon's smile slipped. "Don't say things like that."

"Why not?" Araya glared at him, hissing at the pain that radiated through her chest. "You don't get to act like you *care* about me, Jaxon. Not after the way you drained me. You almost *killed* me."

"You *made* me do that," Jaxon snarled. He stood too quickly, his hands clenched into fists. "I'm giving you another chance. You should be grateful I even still want you after you let *him* touch you—"

"Grateful?" Araya bared her teeth. "I would rather *burn* than let you touch me again."

Jaxon lunged, but Garrick caught his arm before he could close the distance, dragging him back.

"She's tired, Jaxon," he said, his voice clipped. "She needs time to adjust—to understand the severity of her circumstances. Go make the arrangements for her transport. I'll close things out here."

Jaxon hesitated, practically vibrating with unshed fury—but this wasn't a suggestion from his father. It was a command from the High Magister. He cast one last venomous glare at Araya, his lip curling.

"I always did like your fire, Starling" he spat. "It makes your surrender that much sweeter. I'm looking forward to making you beg."

Araya flinched, her heart pounding. But Jaxon turned his back on her, slamming the door behind him hard enough to rattle the glass in the window. She clenched her fists in the blankets, trying to calm her heartbeat as she listened to his footsteps fade into silence.

"You should be more careful not to antagonize him, Araya." Garrick said mildly. He crossed back to the table, taking his time pouring himself a fresh cup of tea. "We're being generous, offering you a way to make amends. But we don't really need your cooperation. We just need your body—your connection to the fae monarchy." He turned back to her, stirring his tea. "And we'll have it. One way or another."

"I'll never help you," Araya spat.

Garrick smiled, but there was nothing comforting about it this time. "No," he said. "I don't think you will. You'll fight us tooth and nail until your spirit cracks. It's what your kind does." He took a slow sip of his tea, savoring the taste. "But you were stupid enough to complete that bond with Loren. That makes any child you have a candidate for the fae throne—regardless of who the father is."

Araya's breath caught, the room tilting around her as his meaning sank in. "You wouldn't," she said, her voice shaking. "You wouldn't dare—"

Garrick chuckled.

"Of course we would," he said. "This has always been about power, Araya. Bloodlines. If you refuse to help us, we'll breed you and use the child you produce to open the Eldergreen for us."

"I won't do it," Araya said. "I'm fae. I won't conceive if I'm not willing—"

"You're three-quarters fae," Garrick said idly. "It might take longer—pity for you—but it will happen. And you might be surprised at what you're willing to do when all of your choices are laid out for you. I intend to have royal power in my bloodline, but I'm not picky about how it gets there."

He took another step closer to the bed, his gaze dragging slowly over her body.

"And if you won't cooperate with Jaxon," he murmured, finally meeting her eyes. "Well, I suppose I'll just have to see what all the fuss is about. I always did want to fuck the queen."

EPILOGUE

Serafina fumbled with her key, her fingers stiff and clumsy from nerve damage that hadn't healed right. The inquisitors hadn't bothered to get her a Healer when they broke her hands over and over again. Her Arcanum-assigned guard said nothing as she struggled, finally getting her key to turn in the lock. He never did anything but stand there with his arms folded, his sharp eyes watching everything. Watching *her*.

Serafina closed the door in his face just as the first drops of rain pattered against the windowpane.

She stood in the entryway for a moment, leaning against the door. She hoped he got soaked out there. It had to be some sort of punishment—following her from her house to the clinic and back again in hopes that Araya would show up with some harebrained rescue plan so they could snatch her back up and return her to the Shaws.

But Araya was gone, far beyond their reach on the other side of the Shadowed Veil. Loren would keep her safe, even if she never forgave him for it.

Serafina dropped her satchel on the floor and shrugged off her cloak, leaving it in a heap. She didn't even know why she still bothered going to the clinic. No one came anymore—not unless they were desperate enough to be stupid. She should have stayed home today—her hip was always worse with the rain. She'd taken to chewing willow bark for it, but the walk back from the clinic had burned through whatever small mercy it offered. What she really needed now was a hot compress with nettle.

Serafina pushed off the wall, gritting her teeth as she limped toward the kitchen. But she hadn't even reached the doorway when the kettle started to whistle.

She wasn't alone. Serafina fumbled for the fire poker beside the hearth, leaning on it like a cane as she lurched toward the kitchen. It wasn't much of a weapon, but she'd be damned if they took her again without a fight—

"And what exactly are you planning to do with that?" Finn Greenvale asked, raising his eyebrows.

"Finn—" the poker fell from her numb fingers, clattering to the floor. Serafina took a lurching step forward, barely catching herself on the edge of the table. "You can't be here. They're watching the house—"

"I know." He stared at her, his brow furrowing as she swayed. "Goddess, Sera. What did they do to you?" His arm wrapped around her waist before she could protest, helping her into a chair.

"No Healer for traitors." Serafina hissed, grimacing as she slowly straightened her leg. "You know how it goes, Finn. That's why you aren't supposed to be here."

"We were careful," Finn growled. His eyes swept over her, cataloging every scar and poorly healed injury. "No one saw us, Sera."

"*Us?*" Serafina stiffened, staring past Finn as two more figures she somehow hadn't seen emerged from the shadows.

"You remember Thorne," Finn said, nodding at a vaguely familiar amber-eyed half-fae male. "And of course you know—"

"No," Serafina whispered. "No—"

She blinked hard, but the long-lost crown prince of the fae didn't vanish from her kitchen. His hair was shorter than the last time she'd seen him, and he'd filled out somewhat, the terrible scars at his wrists and throat finally faded. And he had magic—she could taste it in the air, the shadows he'd stepped from curling around his legs.

"You're not supposed to be here," she said. "You escaped. You and Araya both escaped. You're both safe—"

"Jaxon Shaw took her back," Loren said quietly.

"No—" Serafina clutched the edge of the table, her heart dropping into her stomach. "*No.* That wasn't supposed to happen. I let them torture me *to keep that from happening.*"

Gods, what were they doing to her right now? The things she'd suffered in the Arcanum's custody...Serafina knew they would pale against what Jaxon would do to Araya.

"That's why we're here, Serafina," Thorne said gently. "We need your help."

"My help?" Serafina stared at them helplessly. "What do you think I'm going to do? The Arcanum watches my every move. If they have Araya..." She trailed off, her voice cracking. "You don't understand what it's like now. The whole city has changed. Everyone is scared. Jaxon and Hale pull fae off the street at random to *question*—"

Her voice caught in her throat, tears filling her eyes.

"I can't help you," she whispered, squeezing her eyes closed. "I'm watched constantly. My magic barely works. I can't even get nettle for my hip without someone making a note of it. I'll never be able to help get her out. Not like I did before. The Arcanum doesn't trust *anyone* who isn't in their inner circle right now."

"Then it's a good thing we have an inside asset," Finn said.

Serafina's head snapped up. "Who?"

As if on cue, the back door creaked open. A dark figure slipped inside, little more than a shadow against the rain-soaked night. He shook off his hood, thrusting it back as he stepped into the light.

"Nice night," he said, nodding to Serafina. "Did you know you have two Arcanum guards out front but none in the back?" He clicked his tongue, shaking his head. "Sloppy work with Hale gone."

"This is your inside asset?" Serafina turned to Finn, waiting for him to laugh and say it was all a joke. But he just stared at her, his face drawn and serious. "Finn, this is *Kai Sterling*. He's Jaxon's best friend. His father is a magister—"

"Which is what makes me an *inside* asset." Kai raised his eyebrows, glancing around at them all. "So, fill me in. What's the plan to get her back?"

Also by Becca Calder

The Eldergreen Trilogy

The Chained Prince

The Bound Mage

The Crowned Queen

Looking For More?

Join my newsletter for exclusive bonus chapters, NSFW artwork, character art, and other reader-exclusive content. You'll also get sneak peeks at upcoming books and be the first to hear about new releases.

Scan the QR code below to join.